THE BESTSELLING NOVELS OF
TOM CLANCY

EXECUTIVE ORDERS

The most devastating terrorist act in history leaves Jack Ryan as President of the United States . . .

"UNDOUBTEDLY CLANCY'S BEST YET."
—*Atlanta Journal & Constitution*

DEBT OF HONOR

It begins with the murder of an American woman in the back streets of Tokyo. It ends in war . . .

"A SHOCKER CLIMAX SO PLAUSIBLE YOU'LL WONDER WHY IT HASN'T YET HAPPENED!"
—*Entertainment Weekly*

THE HUNT FOR RED OCTOBER

The smash bestseller that launched Clancy's career—the incredible search for a Soviet defector and the nuclear submarine he commands . . .

"BREATHLESSLY EXCITING!"   —*Washington Post*

D0036752

continued . . .

RED STORM RISING

The ultimate scenario for World War III—the final battle for global control . . .

"THE ULTIMATE WAR GAME . . . BRILLIANT!"
—*Newsweek*

PATRIOT GAMES

CIA analyst Jack Ryan stops an assassination—and incurs the wrath of Irish terrorists . . .

"A HIGH PITCH OF EXCITEMENT!"—*Wall Street Journal*

THE CARDINAL OF THE KREMLIN

The superpowers race for the ultimate Star Wars missile defense system . . .

"*CARDINAL* EXCITES, ILLUMINATES . . . A REAL PAGE-TURNER!"
—*Los Angeles Daily News*

CLEAR AND PRESENT DANGER

The killing of three U.S. officials in Colombia ignites the American government's explosive, and top secret, response . . .

"A CRACKLING GOOD YARN!"   *—Washington Post*

THE SUM OF ALL FEARS

The disappearance of an Israeli nuclear weapon threatens the balance of power in the Middle East—and around the world . . .

"CLANCY AT HIS BEST . . . NOT TO BE MISSED!"
        —Dallas Morning News

WITHOUT REMORSE

The Clancy epic fans have been waiting for. His code name is Mr. Clark. And his work for the CIA is brilliant, cold-blooded, and efficient . . . but who is he really?

"HIGHLY ENTERTAINING!"   *—Wall Street Journal*

AND DON'T MISS
TOM CLANCY'S
FASCINATING NONFICTION WORKS...

SUBMARINE:
A GUIDED TOUR INSIDE
A NUCLEAR WARSHIP

"Takes readers deeper than they've ever gone inside a nuclear submarine."
—*Kirkus Reviews*

ARMORED CAV:
A GUIDED TOUR OF
AN ARMORED CAVALRY REGIMENT

"Tom Clancy is the best there is." —*San Francisco Chronicle*

FIGHTER WING:
A GUIDED TOUR OF
AN AIR FORCE COMBAT WING

"Clancy's writing is so strong that readers feel they are there."
—*Boston Sunday Herald*

MARINE:
A GUIDED TOUR OF
A MARINE EXPEDITIONARY UNIT

"No one can equal his talent." —*Houston Chronicle*

AIRBORNE:
A GUIDED TOUR OF
AN AIRBORNE TASK FORCE

AT BOOKSTORES EVERYWHERE!

Tom Clancy's
POWER PLAYS

POLITIKA

CREATED BY
TOM CLANCY
AND
MARTIN GREENBERG

BERKLEY BOOKS, NEW YORK
http://politika.power-plays.com

If you purchased this book without a cover, you should be aware that this book is stolen property. It was reported as "unsold and destroyed" to the publisher, and neither the author nor the publisher has received any payment for this "stripped book."

TOM CLANCY'S POWER PLAYS: POLITIKA

A Berkley Book / published by arrangement with
RSE Holdings, Inc.

PRINTING HISTORY
Berkley edition / December 1997

All rights reserved.
Copyright © 1997 by RSE Holdings, Inc.
Book design by Erin L. Lush.
This book may not be reproduced in whole or in part,
by mimeograph or any other means, without permission.
For information address: The Berkley Publishing Group,
a member of Penguin Putnam Inc.,
200 Madison Avenue, New York, New York 10016.

The Putnam Berkley World Wide Web site address is
http://www.berkley.com

ISBN: 0-425-16278-8

BERKLEY®
Berkley Books are published by The Berkley Publishing Group,
a member of Penguin Putnam Inc.,
200 Madison Avenue, New York, New York 10016.
BERKLEY and the "B" design
are trademarks belonging to Berkley Publishing Corporation.

PRINTED IN THE UNITED STATES OF AMERICA

10 9 8 7 6 5 4 3 2 1

Acknowledgments

I would like to thank Jerome Preisler for his valuable contribution to the preparation of the manuscript. I would also like to acknowledge the assistance of Larry Segriff, Denise Little, John Helfers, Robert Youdelman, Esq., Tom Mallon, Esq., the wonderful people at The Putnam Berkley Group, including Phyllis Grann, David Shanks, and Tom Colgan, and Doug Littlejohns, Frank Boosman, Jim Van Verth, Doug Oglesby, the rest of the *Politika* team, and the other fine folks at Red Storm Entertainment. As always, I would like to thank Robert Gottlieb of the William Morris Agency, my agent and friend. But most important, it is for you, my readers, to determine how successful our collective endeavor has been.

—Tom Clancy

ONE

HEADACHES, VODKA, AND ASPIRIN; ASPIRIN, VODKA, and headaches.

The combination was enough to make anyone reel, President Boris Yeltsin thought, massaging his temple with one hand as he popped three tablets into his mouth with the other.

He reached for the glass on his desk and took a long drink, then silently began counting to thirty, swishing the vodka in his mouth to dissolve the aspirins.

Twenty-eight, twenty-nine, swallow. He put down the glass, lowered his head, and pressed his palms into his eyes. And then waited.

After a little while the pain in his head eased. Not as much as on previous days, however. Not nearly. And he still felt some dizziness. Soon he would have to add another tablet to his home remedy. Four to a swallow. Or perhaps he would experiment. Increase the amount of vodka, chase down the medicine with a good, clean shot. Certainly that would make things more palatable. Still, one had to wonder about certain things. Was it possible to overdose on aspirin and alcohol? And where would it lead? Actually, he already knew that. Perhaps, before it was all over, he would again turn on the television news and see himself dancing foolishly to rock and roll music at a campaign stop, behaving for all the world like some drunken teenager.

Yeltsin sat there at his desk with his eyes closed, the curtains drawn over his windows to block out the sunlight pouring in over the high east wall of Red Square. He wondered what the headaches, dizziness and early morning drinking said about the general state of his health. Certainly nothing good. And why not be expansive and think about its meaning vis-à-vis the state of the body politic? If, as he believed, the power of an elected president was largely symbolic in the modern world, how might the declining condition of a man who held that position be interpreted? A man who had scarcely had so much as a cold—and *never* had a drink during the day— in his entire life before taking office was now a man who had lost his appetite for sex but arose from bed each morning with an irresistible lust for his vodka. A man who had already spent too much time under the surgeon's knife, he thought, absently rubbing the scar left by his last bypass surgery.

Yeltsin straightened, opened his eyes. The bookcase opposite his desk doubled and trebled in his vision. He took a deep breath, blinking twice, but the room remained unfocused. Dear heaven, he felt ugly. Much of it, he knew, was due to the pressures of dealing with Korsikov and Pedachenko. Especially the latter. He had been infecting the nation with his rhetoric for some time . . . and the infection had been spreading more rapidly than ever since he'd acquired a televised platform from which to promote his extremist views. What would happen if the situation in the southern agricultural areas worsened? It was one thing for Pedachenko to rail about the corrupting influence of Western dollars, and the threat that he believed

NATO—and especially the Founding Act—represented to Russian interests. These were abstractions to his audience. But hunger was another matter. Everyone was capable of understanding it. And it would not be assuaged by calming words from political rivals. Pedachenko was clever and opportunistic. He knew which buttons to push. And there was no escaping his charisma. If the dreadful projections being made about the crop failure were even close to accurate . . .

Yeltsin jettisoned the thought before it could complete itself. He capped off the vodka, put it into his bottom drawer. At any minute the lights on his phone would begin to flash. His aides would arrive with their file folders and summary briefings. He would be presented with a multitude of problems, many requiring his immediate attention. Be given documents to read and sign.

He needed to pull himself together.

He stretched his legs, pushed back his chair, and stood. The bookshelf swelled in his eyes again. He put his hand on the edge of the desk to steady himself and waited. This time the blurriness didn't subside. He waited some more, perspiring now, queasy and light-headed. He could hear his heart beating in his ears. The collar of his shirt suddenly seemed much too tight. It was as if all the air pressure had been let out of the room.

What was *wrong* with him?

He reached out for his phone console, thinking he would have to cancel his appointments for the next several hours. He needed to rest.

But before Yeltsin could push the intercom button, the pain tore through his head in a blinding, jaggedly excruciating white bolt that made him stagger back from the desk, his eyes wide and bulging, his hands flying to his temples as if to keep them from blowing apart. Groaning and terrified, he propelled himself toward the phone, literally dove across the desk for it.

His fingers were still fumbling for it when the seizures came on. He began helplessly thrashing around on the desktop, then rolled to the floor, his arms flapping with uncontrollable spasms, his hands hooked into claws.

Yeltsin was already falling into a coma when he was discovered by his secretary ten minutes later.

Two hours after that, agitated doctors at Michurinsky Hospital pronounced the President of the Russian Federation dead.

TWO

FOR THE LONGEST TIME, ROGER GORDIAN HAD BEEN uncomfortable hearing the word "visionary" precede his name when people talked about him in the media, or introduced him at lectures and business functions. But he'd gradually acknowledged that everybody got labeled and that some labels were more useful than others. Heavy-hitters in Congress didn't make certified visionaries languish in their waiting rooms. Military procurement officials paid closer attention to their ideas than those of someone with a reputation as an ordinary fellow with a little intelligence, a strong work ethic and some old-fashioned, Wisconsin-bred entrepreneurial zeal. There was the way he saw himself, and the way other people saw him, and both had their own sort of validity. He ran with what best served his goals.

None of which meant Gordian was inclined toward false modesty. He was proud of his success. It had taken him just five years to turn Tech-Electric, a failing electronics firm that he'd bought for a song in 1979, into a leading manufacturer of business and personal computer products. By the early eighties his company, rechristened UpLink International, had become a major government contractor specializing in satellite reconnaissance technology. Toward the end of that decade his heavy investment in research and development, and his commitment to designing a complete intelligence system for the expanding military of that era, had resulted in GAPSFREE, the fastest and most accurate recon tech on the worldwide market, and the most advanced guidance system for missiles and precision guided munitions ever devised. And all that was before he'd diversified his holdings . . .

Still, you had to keep things in perspective, Gordian thought. Despite twenty years of professional accomplishments, he apparently still didn't know how to make a marriage work. Or maybe that was something he'd forgotten along the way, as his wife Ashley believed.

He expelled a long sigh, glancing at the oversized manila envelope that had arrived on his desk along with his usual stack of news dailies. The envelope had been overnighted from the ad firm that was designing his newest prospectus, and doubtless contained preproduction mechanicals for him to review. He would get to that in a while. First, however, there were his black coffee, a blueberry muffin, and the morning paper to go through.

Gordian took his copy of the *New York Times* off the pile, separated the International Report from the other sections and scanned the table of contents. Alexander Nordstrum's guest editorial was on page A36. He chewed a bite of the muffin, took a sip of coffee, set down the cup, carefully wiped his fingers on a napkin, and began flipping through the paper.

In an interview he'd given to a televised news magazine the previous week, Gordian was asked if he spent his days in some vast electronic control center, surrounded by walls of flickering computer screens, monitoring global events on CNN and the on-line services like a technocratic Big Brother. He'd admitted to being a compulsive newsprint junkie first and foremost, despite his own contribution to—and frequent reliance on—state-of-the-art means of information access and communications. The interviewer shot the camera a skeptical and mildly accusing look, as if to let his audience know Gordian was putting them on. Gordian had known better than to try convincing him otherwise.

As he turned to Alex's piece, two pages spilled from the middle of the section onto his lap, lingering there briefly before fluttering to the carpet. Gordian leaned forward to gather them off the floor, almost knocking over his coffee in the process. Then he slipped them back in place. And then he realized he'd inadvertently put them in upside down, and turned them right side up.

Okaaay, he thought. *Talk about seeing oneself in perspective. We can add an utter and abysmal failure to master the subway fold to my list of personal shortcomings.*

It took Gordian another minute or so to finally wrestle the paper into submission. He found Nordstrum's column midway down the Editorial/Op-Ed page. It read:

Russia's Ruling Troika:

Can the Three-Headed Watchdog Survive Its Own Bite?

BY ALEX R. NORDSTRUM, JR.

In the weeks following the sudden death of Russian President Boris Yeltsin, Western observers believed a showdown between opposing political forces to be a near certainty, with many fearing a coup similar to the takeover by old-guard Communist party animals which ended the Gorbachev era in 1991. The crisis, however, was averted—some would say postponed—with the formation of the provisional government currently in place. But does a war within the Kremlin seem any less inevitable now Vladimir Starinov is acting president, and Arkady Pedachenko and Andrei Korsikov have agreed to share power with him until such unspecified time as the state of national emergency is lifted, and a democratic election can be held? Again, there are those in the West who think not—and who see a popular uprising being born in the deep rifts among the three leaders.

Indeed, the signs are impossible to ignore. While having proven himself a deft political operator, former Vice-President Starinov remains weakened by his close association with Yeltsin, whose popularity had been on the wane among the Russian people. Besieged with problems ranging from critical grain shortages to rampant AIDS and drug epidemics, Starinov has become the focus of growing discontent throughout his nation. Meanwhile, official statements to the contrary, sources in Moscow report that his archrival Pedachenko, who heads the nationalist Honor and Soil Party, has been refusing to meet with Starinov for weeks, citing conflicts in their schedules.

Pedachenko has, in fact, been busy. He has made unusual use of the media to steal the political limelight and urge acceptance of his extremist views, which are unguardedly anti-American and hearken back to the ''good old days'' of Communist rule. As tensions between Pedachenko and Starinov seem to be leading toward a face-off, Korsikov, an old-style apparatchik, with strong support from Russia's military, seems content to remain on the sidelines, waiting to see which of them is left standing when the dust settles.

We can only wonder how this collection of political bedfellows, which has been unable to get beyond bickering over when to sit down together in the same room, can be expected to arrive at a consensus about major issues of national and international policy that will affect Russia's future relationship with America and other world powers. Amid this tangle of doubt, one thing is clear: the President of the United States must reach out promptly to Starinov, whose Reformist philosophies, dedication to economic reform and strong ties to the West represent the clearest line of continuity with the previous government. Without the credibility he would gain from such support, he is almost sure to become a sacrificial lamb on the altar of Russian politics. Yet the White House has been characteristically indecisive . . .

Gordian frowned and put down the paper. Trust his foreign affairs consultant not to pull any punches. An expert in the fields of history, politics, and current affairs,

Nordstrum had an uncanny talent for predicting political events through an analysis of the nation's past, and the past of the personalities involved.

Not to mention a knack for ruining my mornings, Gordian thought.

Well, that wasn't quite fair. The truth was that he'd already gotten Nordstrum's assessment of the Russian situation straight from his lips . . . that was, after all, what he paid him for. But it distressed him that Alex had expressed his lack of optimism in such a public forum, given that construction of the new ground station was about to begin in Kaliningrad next month . . . and especially in light of Starinov's upcoming trip to Washington.

Now Gordian raised his coffee to his lips again, realized it had gone cold, and put it down. No great loss; there'd be plenty of fresh cups to drink before the day was over.

Shaking off his gloom, Gordian reached for his phone file, thinking he'd call Dan Parker for the skinny on how the House was reacting to Starinov's appeal for agricultural aid. After that he'd confer with Scull and Nimec, get their take on things.

He snatched the receiver off its cradle.

It was 9 A.M.; time to get to work.

THREE

CAUCASUS REGION
NEAR THE CASPIAN SEA,
RUSSIA, OCTOBER 10, 1999

THE FLOUR MILL WAS SILENT.

In his half century of life, Veli Gazon had grown all too familiar with the monstrous things nature could do when it turned hostile. He had lost two sons in the cholera epidemic just six years ago, his wife in an earthquake two decades earlier, part of his farm in the floods that had swept across the grasslands when the river overflowed its banks. The lines and wrinkles on his face were a record of the hard times he had weathered. The somber depths of his eyes spoke of survival despite bitter loss.

He was not a man who had a great need for physical comfort, or believed it was anyone's due. That way of thinking was alien to him; he could not understand it. An Alan tribesman whose people had been cultivating the soil for centuries, he had an inborn belief that it was enough to work and persevere with dignity. To complain, or wish for more, might only bring a curse upon oneself, and provoke the world into another cruel demonstration of its power.

And yet today, standing here amid the empty storage bins that had once been filled with wheat; amid the huge, still framework of elevators and conveyors and scouring machines and rollers and sifters . . .

Today he felt angry. And scared.

Very scared.

He took a long pull on his hand-rolled cigarette, held the smoke in his lungs a moment, and let it gust out his nose. His family had managed the flour mill since the days of Soviet controls and collectives, and assumed full ownership when state factories were sold back to the territories. Combining their resources, Veli, his brother, and their cousins had paid corrupt officials many times the value of the old machinery to purchase it—and somehow, even during the worst of the previous shortages, had kept that machinery running.

But now . . . now the mill was silent, shut down, its shipping floor deserted. The rail cars that normally transported the raw wheat from the farms to the mill, and sackfuls of processed flour from the mill to warehouses in the northern regions, sat clustered at the receiving station, their engines cold and dead beneath the gray October sky.

There was no grain to process.

Nothing.

The *chyornozyom*, the fertile black earth that had nourished the crop through the most devastating of catastrophes, had failed to produce even a meager harvest. In August, when the wheat had come up stunted, some men from the Ministry of Agriculture had arrived from the capital and tested the soil and explained that it was fouled. It had been overfarmed, they said. The rain had poisons in it, they said. But what the bureaucrats had not said was that the overfarming had been ordered by their own ministry back when it would set compulsory production quotas and regulate the distribution of food. What they had not said was that the water had been contaminated by wastes from government chemical and munitions facilities.

What they had not said before they finally left was

whether there was any way to repair the damage in time for the next planting season, or even the one after that.

Perhaps it was too late, Veli Gazon thought.

The mill was silent, now.

Silent as a tomb.

There was no grain.

Veli moistened the tips of his thumb and forefinger with a little saliva, pinched out his cigarette, and dropped the stub into his shirt pocket. Later, he would add the tobacco inside it to that of other stubs and reroll them, wasting nothing.

There was no grain.

Not in his village, or the neighboring one. Not in any of the fields between the Black Sea and the Caspian.

And what that meant was that soon . . .

Frighteningly soon . . .

The only things that would be plentiful in Russia were the cries of the hungry and the dying.

FOUR

"... IN RUSSIA, BREAD IS EVERYTHING," VLADIMIR Starinov was saying in fluent but heavily accented English. "Do you understand?"

President Ballard considered Starinov's words.

"I think so, Vladimir," he said. "As best I can from where I sit, anyway."

Both were silent a moment.

The Rose Garden photo ops behind them, the two men had retreated to the large, wood-paneled conference room down the hall from the Oval Office, eager to rough out an emergency aid agreement before their luncheon with congressional leaders. On Starinov's side of the table were his minister of the interior Yeni Bashkir, known to be a strong supporter of the Communists, and Pavel Moser, a high-ranking member of the Federation Council. With the President were Vice President Stephen Humes, Secretary of Agriculture Carol Carlson, and Secretary of State Orvel Bowman. A White House interpreter named Hagen sat at the far end of the table, looking and feeling superfluous.

Now Starinov gazed across at the President, his broad, round face sober, his gray eyes steady behind a pair of wire glasses.

"I want to make it clear that I am speaking literally," he said. "What matters to American voters is the availability of choices. If costs and incomes are stable, choices expand and politicians win reelection. If the economy falters, choices narrow and leaders are replaced. But the concerns of the Russian people are more basic. They do not worry about what they will eat, but whether they will eat at all.'' He paused, took a deep breath. ''Perhaps the best way to illustrate my point is with the exception. Have you ever seen the McDonald's restaurant in Moscow? Men and women save for months before bringing their families there for a meal . . . those with jobs, that is. They stand in line for hours to get through the door, as if it opens to some strange and unimaginably wondrous place. And in a sense it does. It is an extravagance for them. A rare indulgence. And for those outside the capital, who are often without work, it is a place no one even dreams of visiting. Do you see? Bread is all they can afford. Without it millions will have nothing on their tables. Absolutely nothing. Their children will die of hunger. And fairly or not, their anger will turn toward their leaders.''

The President leaned forward, his elbows on the table, fingers tented under his chin. ''Most of all, I'd think, on a leader who appeals to the United States for assistance and comes back empty-handed.''

Their eyes met.

''Yes,'' Starinov said. ''He might indeed appear ineffectual. And, regrettably, there are elements within the government, some of whom still harbor cold war resentments toward your country, who would be pleased to use such a failure to incite the Russian electorate and gain greater standing for themselves.''

Touché, the President thought. *You scream, I scream, we all scream for ice cream.*

He turned to Secretary Carlson. ''Carol, how much aid can we provide, and how fast could we get it moving?''

An elegant woman of fifty-five with the inexhaustible energy and slender good looks of someone ten years younger, she pursed her lips in thought, pretending to make some hurried mental calculations. In fact, she and the President had run through this whole scenario in advance. Ballard liked, respected, and, most importantly, needed Starinov as an ally. He was prepared to do whatever it took to bolster his popularity and keep him in office. And, not to be too cynical, he liked the idea of getting food into the mouths of starving babes. Still, it was hardly beneath him to also use food as leverage—or even as a weighty club—in certain ongoing arms reduction and trade negotiations.

"We have sufficient reserves to provide at least a hundred thousand tons of wheat, oats, and barley, with a somewhat lesser quantity of cornmeal," she said after what seemed a reasonable pause for thought. "As far as a time frame, my best guess is we could get our first shipments out within a month. Of course, that's assuming we can persuade Congress to go along with us."

The President nodded, shifting his attention to the Veep. "Steve, what about financial aid?"

"I've been recommending three hundred million dollars in loans as part of an overall package. Realistically, we might be able to secure half that amount, with strict conditions attached to its use and repayment."

"In my opinion, it's the distribution end of this effort that's going to be the hardest sell," Secretary Bowman said. "Even with the participation of U.S. troops kept to a minimum, everybody's concerned about another Somalia-type situation."

Which, everyone in the room knew, was a moderately delicate way of saying a situation in which American soldiers were forced to repel violent mobs of looters trying to raid cargo from trucks and grain storehouses.

Bashkir gave Bowman a sharp look. A dour man of middle age whose dark complexion and thick, flat features bore the somatotype of his Far Eastern ancestry, he was known in diplomatic circles for being as personally loyal to Starinov as he was outspokenly critical of his pro-Western policies.

"With all due respect, Mr. Secretary, my government is fully capable of dispensing the food to its own citizens once it arrives," he said. "I see no reason for direct involvement by your military."

"Actually, I was thinking in terms of a larger World Food Program mission." Bowman cleared his throat. "If the U.N. contributes as expected, it's likely to ask that my country send forces as a component of a multinational disaster relief team. We'd have great difficulty denying such a request."

Bashkir shifted in his chair but made no further comment.

Noting his ramrod-straight posture, the President decided it would be a good time to cut in and break the tension.

"Why don't we cross that bridge when we come to it?" he said, and produced a version of the folksy smile that had served him so well on the stump. He checked his watch, then looked over at the vice president again. "Our parley with Congress starts in less than a half hour. Who can we count on for support?"

"Senator Sommers from Montana looks strong," Humes said. "He's a key man on the Foreign Relations Committee, and has tremendous admiration for Minister

Starinov's efforts to preserve and advance vital economic reforms.''

Not to mention the fact that his state's had a bumper grain harvest for the past three years, the President thought.

''What about on the other side?''

''Senator Delacroix is sure to oppose. But his own party will be divided on this issue, and I doubt he'll do much more than grumble.''

President Ballard nodded.

''Okay, I think we're all ready for lunch,'' he said in an enthusiastic tone. ''I hope I'm not alone here in feeling very good about our prospects.''

Starinov smiled. ''Thank you, my friend. I, too, have confidence—both in your leadership, and the generosity and compassion of your people.''

He reached across the table, gripped the President's hand, and shook it vigorously.

His face expressionless, Bashkir watched them in brittle silence.

FIVE

GREGOR SADOV MOVED THROUGH THE DARKNESS LIKE
a thief in the night. But Gregor wasn't a thief. Not on this
mission. He and his team had a larger goal in mind.

Their target loomed out of the darkness. A low, squat
building, it stood less than three stories tall yet took up
most of this city block. It was a warehouse, with service
entrances on all sides and a loading dock that ran along
most of the back. In better, more prosperous times, there
had been two shifts of workers, bringing foodstuffs into
the warehouse and loading it onto the trucks that passed
through in a steady stream.

But these weren't prosperous times. These days, the
warehouse was less than half-full, and had only a single
shift working—a shift that wasn't due to arrive for another three hours.

Gregor held up a hand. Around him, his team merged
with the shadows surrounding them and froze, waiting for
his next command.

Sadov smiled to himself. This was a new team, but they
were improving. After months of intense training, the four
who had survived to this point were beginning to show
real promise.

Still smiling, he reached down and unclipped the night
vision goggles from his belt. Gregor had spent the last
seven nights watching this warehouse, timing the guards,

counting the assets arrayed against them, and laying his plans.

There were fourteen guards, ten on irregular foot patrol within and around the building, the rest up on the rooftop. None of them were hidden. The owners of this warehouse didn't want their guards to catch anyone; they wanted the guards to scare away thieves and looters, and so kept their presence highly visible.

The guards were all armed alike, small-bore handguns strapped to their sides and AK-47s in their hands. Gregor was sure that they had riot guns locked in a cabinet somewhere inside as well, but he wasn't concerned about their weapons. If he and his team found themselves in a position where the guards were likely to fire at them, they had failed in their mission.

No, it wasn't the weapons he was most concerned about. It was the K-9 units: one guard with a German Shepherd in each unit. The patrols appeared to be random, but Gregor had noticed that the two dog units managed to always stay on opposite sides of the building.

That would help. It gave his team a window of approximately two and a half minutes to get in, do their work, and get out. It might be longer than that before one of the guard units passed near their exit, but that was the minimum time they would have.

It would have to be enough.

Slipping the goggles into place, he motioned for his team to do the same. Within moments they were set. Now all they had to do was wait.

It didn't take long. Gregor was watching intently, tracking the dog unit patrolling the two sides he could see. From its position, he could make a good guess as to where the other unit was.

Less than three minutes after they'd gotten set, Gregor saw the K-9 unit come into position near the far corner of the building. Reaching down, he hit the squawk button on the small radio attached to his belt, twice. He didn't say anything. He didn't need to. The double signal was enough.

On the far side of the building, Nikita, the fifth and last member of his team, silently unlatched the doors on the covered cages she had brought with her. Opening the doors, she pressed a button on a control she had laid on the ground before her, discharging a small battery and sending a mild electrical shock through the floor of the cages. The reaction was immediate as two rabbits darted forward, fleeing the cages and the unexpected pain of the shock.

They would veer away shortly, she knew, as soon as their pain faded and they became aware of the dogs, but by then it wouldn't matter. All they had to do was to attract a little attention.

They did. Just as Gregor had planned. The nearest dog started barking and, moments later, the second one joined in. Nikita smiled softly to herself. Picking up the cages, she melted back into the night to await Gregor's return.

Gregor Sadov heard the dogs start barking, but he did not give the command to move forward. Instead, he waited, watching for the moment when, as they had done every night this past week, the guards all turned their heads to see what had gotten the guard dogs so worked up.

His hand went up, holding his team in check, and then, when the last guard turned away, he formed his hand into a fist and let it drop. Instantly, his team moved forward, keeping to the shadows as much as possible and moving quickly into the warehouse.

Sadov went with them, leading from the front as he always did.

Security was light within the warehouse itself. Some of the guards patrolled inside as part of their irregular rounds, but mostly they stayed outside, on display, warning away any who might try and steal the foodstuffs stored within. In times like these, food was worth more than gold—and Gregor was there to drive its value even higher.

Taking up a position with a good vantage point, he gave the signal for his team to disperse. Outside, the dogs grew silent, but that didn't matter anymore. Inside the darkened warehouse, Gregor's team had the advantage over the guards. And soon they would be making their own distraction.

Through his goggles, Gregor watched as his team scattered through the darkness, dropping their little devices at all the preplanned points. These devices—each a block of paraffin with grain and sawdust mixed in, along with a tiny piezoelectric mechanism that would create a single spark on command—were all Gregor needed to help bring down a regime. At his signal, these devices would ignite. Strategically placed, they would bring a touch of fire to the grain stored here and, within a very short time, the entire place would go up in flames.

The best part was that no one would ever be able to prove arson. The paraffin was similar enough to the wax sealing many of the crates and cartons, and the sawdust and grain would be indistinguishable from the crates and their contents. Only the piezoelectric devices would stand out, but they were small enough that they would most likely be utterly destroyed when the warehouse burned.

As his team placed their paraffin blocks, Gregor disabled the sprinkler system. It was old, and hadn't been tested in years, and probably wouldn't have worked anyway, but Gregor never took unnecessary chances.

Gregor was turning away from the sprinkler system, about to head to his next task, when some unexpected movement caught his eye. One of the guards had come in through the far door, and was making his way deeper into the warehouse, toward Gregor's team.

That was a problem. One guard would not be able to stop them, but he might be able to get off a shot—and that would bring more guards than Gregor and his team could handle.

And there was another, bigger problem. Even as Gregor began moving forward, toward the guard, he saw Andrei, the youngest and most impetuous member of his team, also moving toward the guard. And Andrei was drawing his gun.

Gregor could not allow that. Any shot—whether it came from the guard or from one of Gregor's men— would draw more guards. For that reason, Gregor would have liked to have had his young team tackle this assignment unarmed . . . but that would have been tempting fate. Even the best laid plans could go wrong, and his team deserved every chance to survive a screw-up.

Gregor started to reach for his radio, but it was already too late. He could see Andrei bringing up his pistol.

Gregor had no choice. He didn't hesitate. Drawing his gravity knife, he flipped it once in his hand and then threw it.

He could have gone for the guard, but he didn't dare. He knew Andrei. Seeing the guard fall, Andrei would have simply assumed that he was ducking, and would have fired anyway. So Gregor did the only thing he could do. He threw the knife at Andrei.

The heavy blade went into Andrei's throat, but Gregor wasn't watching. As soon as he threw the knife, he started moving once more, heading toward the guard.

Andrei grunted, already strangling on his own blood. The guard, hearing the faint noise, started to turn, and Gregor's hands closed around his neck. A squeeze, a twist, and the guard was dead, moments before Andrei, too, died.

"Shit," Gregor said, softly. He lifted a crate from a nearby pile and leaned it against the guard's neck. It wasn't perfect, but it was the best he could do on such short notice. Besides, it wasn't necessary to convince the authorities that this was an accident.

His job was to set this fire without making it obvious that it was arson. With luck and the usual Russian incompetence, the fire would still look like an accident. But if not, it wouldn't matter. The people were starving and terrified. Even if the government pieced the puzzle together, they wouldn't dare announce that these fires were deliberate. Not unless they wanted to start the very panic they were working so hard to avoid.

Turning to Andrei, Gregor retrieved his blade, cleaned it and sheathed it, and then hoisted Andrei's body onto his shoulder. The rest of the team had finished placing their blocks, and it was time to leave.

Gregor settled Andrei's body more comfortably on his shoulder and gave the signal to withdraw. His team met him at the door farthest from where the fire would begin. None of them said a word, but from the way they looked at the body he was carrying, Gregor knew they had all learned a valuable lesson tonight. None of them offered to carry the body.

Standing in the darkness beside the door, looking out into the night for signs of any guards, Gregor reached into his pocket and pressed the ignition switch. Moments later, he caught the first faint whiff of smoke.

The guards reacted quickly—more quickly than he'd expected—but that was good. The fire was already too well set for them to stop, and their quick response only let Gregor's team slip out that much sooner, and increased their slim safety margin. Gregor knew grain, and how it burned, and he wanted to be well away from this area before the fire really got going.

Once more, he gave the signal to move out. Their job here was done, and Gregor had a report to call in. His masters would be very pleased with this night's work, and with the work Gregor and his team would do over the next few days.

Slipping out into the night, Gregor tried not to think too much about the mistakes they had made as, behind them, the first orange flames leaped toward the night sky, and the first stores of grain exploded.

SIX

DOTTING THE BANKS OF A WATERWAY THE RUSSIANS call the Amur, and the Chinese refer to as Heilongjiang, or the Black Dragon River, the handful of dwellings that compose the village of Sikachi-Alyan housed a population of indigenous Nanai tribesmen too small to be measured on any census, and more than glad to remain overlooked. Without a single hotel or restaurant, the settlement lay well off the major shipping routes, and drew few outsiders besides the scholars who occasionally arrived to inspect the thousand-year-old petroglyphs carved into the boulders scattered along its muddy shoreline.

This very isolation—and its proximity to the border— had made it an ideal place for the group to meet in secrecy.

Their rented wooden fishing trawler had left Khabarovsk at sunset and cruised some forty kilometers downriver through the gathering dusk, its half-century-old Kermath engines clanking and wheezing, the running lights at its bow gleaming like tiny red eyes in the mist and drizzle. It had been stripped to the handrails of all gear. There was no crew aboard. Its cubbyhole cockpit had room enough for just a single occupant, a Nanai wheelman who spoke little Russian and had been told to remain on deck as a strict condition of his payment.

Now, moored in the black offshore waters flowing past

the village landings, the stout little vessel's engine was silent. Behind the clamped door of the hold, its passengers sat on transom seats that had been set down along the bulkhead, bracing uncomfortably against the heave and sway of the boat.

All but one of them were men. The Russians, Romual Possad and Yuri Vostov, had arrived on separate commercial flights from Moscow earlier that day. Teng Chou had traveled a slower, more exhausting route, flying from Beijing to the airfield in Harbin, then riding through the night in the backseat of a military jeep. Having reached Fuyuan at 7 A.M., he'd gone directly to the river station and taken the hydrofoil to Khabarovsk on the Russian side of the Amur, where he had been met by members of the Chinese consulate three hours later. The little sleep he'd gotten in their guest quarters had hardly refreshed him.

Seated opposite him, Gilea Nastik, the only woman in the group, silently cursed the chill and dampness. In this part of the world, she thought with disgust, there were no seasonal transitions—it was summer one day, and winter the next. Her wiry, desert-tanned body had not been bred for such a miserable climate.

"Well, it's up to you," she said in Russian, tiring of Possad's indecisiveness. He hadn't uttered a word in almost ten minutes. "Will you obtain the approval of your superiors in the ministry, or are we wasting our time?"

He gnawed on his bottom lip.

"It depends," he said. "Make no mistake, I see how it could work, providing we have the money. And a reliable network of contacts."

She stared at him, the skin tightening over her cheekbones, giving her face a sharp, almost predatory appearance. Then she looked down at her hands, shaking her head.

"I have already guaranteed unlimited funding. And the necessary materials," Teng Chou said in a clipped tone. "You should know I am as good as my word."

Possad swung his gaze over his shoulder to Vostov.

"Your people in the United States . . . you're certain they can be trusted?"

Vostov struggled to conceal his irritation; Possad's thinly veiled superiority filled him with a dislike bordering on hatred. From the lowliest bureaucrats to the most highly ranked officials, government men were all hypocritical bastards, never looking in the mirror, as if they knew nothing of self-interest, greed, and betrayal.

"If everyone sticks to the bargain, there won't be any problems," he said. "Pure and simple."

Possad worried his lip some more, tasting his own blood. The moment he'd met these three, he had felt as if he'd gone plunging off a bridge into a bottomless chasm. But he'd been given his instructions. What choice did he have except to follow them?

Communiqués from the delegation in Washington indicated that Starinov had struck a quick agreement with the President, and that a majority of congressmen seemed inclined to give it their support. A hunger relief effort spearheaded by America would be under way before too long. And the Moscow press was already hailing Starinov as a political savior. He had used precious food aid to enhance his image and shuffle his critics into the background. And soon he would use it to sell the Russian people on more of his never-ending concessions to the West.

Only a drastic action would change the course that

events had taken, Possad thought. And if his allies in plotting that action were to be a thug who had made his fortune through narcotics, theft, and vice; an Indonesian arms dealer fronting for Beijing; and a soulless woman who dealt in blood and carnage . . . well, having been driven into hell by necessity, what choice was there, indeed, but to consort with demons?

"All right," he said at last. "The plan has teeth, and I'm prepared to advise the minister to go ahead with it. But there's one other thing—"

"I know the game we are playing, as my team's action in Kaliningrad last night should prove," Gilea said. She stared at him, her eyes dark and bright as chips of polished onyx. "Rest assured, blame will be assigned to the right party. Mr. Chou and I have already exchanged some thoughts as to how that might be done."

Chou bowed his head slightly in acknowledgment, but said nothing.

They were silent awhile in the cramped, unheated hold. The boat rocked, water sloshing rhythmically against the bottom of the hull. Rusty fastenings creaked and squealed.

"Too bad this rattletrap is without creature comforts," Vostov said. "Right now, we should be opening a bottle of champagne, and drinking a toast to our shared fortunes."

"And the coming of the new year," Gilea said.

A grin crept across Vostov's fleshy lips.

"Yes," he said. "That would be most appropriate."

Possad glanced at them and felt his stomach tense. There was, he supposed, still very much for him to learn about human cruelty.

After a moment he shifted his eyes to the smeared circle of glass that was the compartment's single porthole, needing to look away, to remind himself that the world he had always known was still out there, that he had not entirely left it behind . . .

But he saw nothing outside the window except blackness.

SEVEN

**KALININGRAD, RUSSIA
NOVEMBER 2, 1999**

"LISTEN, VINCE, NOT TO BUST BALLS, BUT YOU WANT to explain again why we had to come all the way into the city?"

"My job title's risk assessment manager, isn't it?"

"Well, obviously . . ."

"There's the first part of your answer. I'm here assessing risks. That's my bailiwick. It's what Roger Gordian pays me the big bucks to do. Now, you want the second part of the answer?"

"Well, I suppose I *did* ask for it . . ."

"That's right, you did, and I'm happy to give it to you." Keeping both hands on the steering wheel, Vince Scull glanced over at the man sitting beside him in the Range Rover. "The second part is that *you* also work for Gordian. And that your job as a member of our crackerjack Sword team is to provide security. Which you are doing by making sure nothing happens to me."

"Right." Neil Perry gestured out his window. "I think I see a parking space . . ."

"Forget it, there's plenty to choose from, we'll find a better one up ahead," Scull said. "Now, to finish answering y—"

Cutting himself off midsentence, he stomped his foot down on the brake, jolting the Rover to a halt behind a battered Volga taxi that had stopped in the middle of the road to discharge its passengers.

Scull counted to ten under his breath, staring balefully at the idling cab as a soot-black cloud of exhaust fumes chuffed from its tailpipe and came rolling over his windshield. Then he opened his power window and leaned his head outside.

"C'mon, *tovarishch,* you wanna get that stinking pile of shit out of my way, or what?" he shouted, grinding his palm down on the horn. *"Skahryeh!"*

"Vince, you really ought to try and stay cool when you're driving. This *is* a foreign country."

"Don't remind me. I'm still jet-lagged after flying twelve hours from the States to St. Petersburg, and then another three to this godforsaken *oblast*," Scull said. "And being jet-lagged makes me cranky."

"Sure, I understand. But your wallet's already lost enough weight thanks to those GAI robber barons on the highway—"

"Don't remind me about that, either," Scull said without easing off the horn. Scowling, he thought back a while to when they'd been stopped near the city line by a squad of the *Gosavtoinspektsia*, or State Automobile Inspectorate, for allegedly doing 100 kilometers per hour in a 60 km/h zone. The bastards had come shooting up from behind in a Ford Escort patrol car, the blue gumball light on its roof whirling, its siren whooping like crazy as they signaled him to pull over. He had done so immediately, passing his driver's license, corporate registration, U.S. passport, and triple-entry visa to an officer who'd demanded in broken English to see them. Then he had sat there fuming while the one cop scrutinized his documents, and two others pointed Kalashnikovs at his head, which was pretty much SOP at Russian traffic stops. After twenty minutes, Scull was informed of the offense he was supposed to have committed, made to pay an exorbitant cash fine on the spot—also typical—and sent on his way with a warning that he could have his driving privileges revoked, or even be hauled into the station on criminal charges, if he disregarded the speed limit again.

Now, the taxi in front of him finally having rejoined the sluggish flow of traffic, he gave the horn a rest . . . much to Perry's relief.

"Anyway, Neil, getting back to my answer," he said, and shifted his foot to the gas pedal, "the third and next-to-last reason we came into town is so I can buy some smoked herring, which the stores here mainly stock for our neighbors from Krautland, and is one of the few things I find appetizing in this country, and is also impossible to find out in the boonies, where our ground-station-in-the-making happens to be located."

Perry grunted vaguely, figuring he might as well get it all over with. "And the last reason?"

"Two, three blocks up, there's a nice little watering hole where some Americans who work for Xerox hang out," Scull replied. "And I thought maybe we could get soused."

Perry grinned and settled back in his seat.

Now *that* had been an answer worth waiting for.

As Scull viewed it, the specs that accompanied his fancy job title were simple and straightforward: he'd been hired to help his employer plan for the future by making plausible guesses about what that future would be. What wasn't so simple was actually isolating the factors that were key to an analysis. Say Gordian wanted his predictions about how an agricultural crisis in Russia would turn out, what effect that outcome would have on the nation's sociopolitical climate, and what bearing it all would have on completion of UpLink's European low earth orbit satellite communications gateway. The usual way to do that was to rely on news summaries, historical precedents, and dry statistical reviews, which Scull believed was a lazy man's cop-out. There were limits to how much trouble-shooting could be done from behind a desk; inevitably, forces that couldn't be quantified on paper would come into play and drive events along one course or another. To detect them you had to use your personal radar, read subtle wind changes, keep your eyes and ears open for anything that might be important. The more you got around, the better.

Which was what he'd meant when he told Perry he was in Kaliningrad "assessing risks." It had been twelve weeks since he'd flown back to the States, and all the information he'd gotten while he was there suggested the Russian food shortage was rapidly worsening. Alarmed by the reports, and wanting to see for himself how serious it was, he had decided to make a trip to the nearest population center his immediate priority upon returning to the region. And from where he stood right now, the situation looked a lot like the divorce settlement a judge had handed down to him a couple of weeks ago, formally dissolving his third marriage and sticking him with whopping alimony payments: pretty damned grim.

The grocery in front of him was locked up tight, its window displays bare of merchandise. The plate glass was pocked with starry fractures of the sort that would have been made by rocks or blunt-ended sticks. A cardboard sign in the doorway read "NYETU PISCHA"—"NO

FOOD''—in handscrawled Cyrillic characters. It was similar to the sign he'd seen in the bakery down the block, which had said, "NO BREAD.'' Or the one above the empty market stand that said, "NO FRUITS OR VEG-ETABLES."

Scull thought it significant that none of the signs merely had "CLOSED" written on them. Obviously, the absent storekeepers had wanted to discourage property damage from break-ins, making it clear nothing had been left behind for potential looters.

He moved up to the storefront, shaded his eyes with his hand, and peered in at the vacant shelves.

"Shit," he said in a rueful tone. "So much for my smoked-fucking-herring."

"Hope it's easier to get drunk than fed around here," Perry said.

He stood with his back to Scull, his gaze wandering up and down the street. It seemed somehow appropriate to him that Kaliningrad had taken its name from one of Vladimir Lenin's less distinguished cronies; on its best days, it was a drab and cheerless place. The cars looked old. The people looked shabby. The streets were a blockish grid of factories, commercial warehouses, and precast concrete apartment buildings. Shoehorned between Poland, Lithuania, and the Baltic States, the region—which had been part of Germany until after World War I—was separated from the rest of Russia by several borders, and valuable primarily for its strategic position as a territorial buffer and port city. Even its attraction to German tourists was unromantic, based not on sightseeing or other leisure activities, but its status as a duty-free import-export zone.

"Might as well head for the bar," Scull said, turning from the window.

"Hold on, I think we might be in luck." Perry nodded his head toward the corner, where a street vender had begun unloading crates from the rear hatch of his van. There were fifteen or twenty people clotting the sidewalk around him, most of them women in shapeless gray clothing with big canvas grocery sacks on their arms.

Scull frowned and smoothed down a wisp of his thinning hair. It instantly sprang back out of place. His frown deepened.

"Forget it, I'm not waiting in any goddamn line," he said, becoming surly. "Let's go."

Perry continued to hesitate. A pair of young men in ugly leather jackets—he guessed they were in their twenties—had sidled up to an old woman as she left the entrance to the shop. One of them was very tall, the other about average height. The shorter one was drinking out of a brown paper bag and walking slightly off balance.

Wrapped in a dark, well-worn winter shawl, her grocery bag weighted with goods, the woman tried to brush past them, but they quickly flanked her on both sides, keeping pace with her.

Perry felt a little jolt in the pit of his stomach. It was a sensation he'd experienced often in his days as a New York City detective.

His pale blue eyes locked on the three of them, he tapped Scull on the shoulder and motioned in their direction.

"Tell me, Vince, what's wrong with that picture?" he said.

Scull stood beside him and looked blank. He was thinking exclusively about getting a drink now.

"Looks to me like a couple black marketeers making

a pitch, is all.'' He grunted. ''Maybe they've got herring.''

Perry was shaking his head. ''Black marketeers go after
tourist cash. You ever see any of them stick to a babushka
like that?''

Scull was silent. The old woman had stopped in the
middle of the sidewalk and pulled her satchel closer
against her body. The two guys in cheap leather were still
crowding her. The taller of them had slipped his right
hand into his jacket pocket and was pointing at the satchel
with the other.

''Those punks are gonna boost her,'' Perry said.

''It's none of our business. Let the locals handle it.''

''You see anybody about to do that?'' Perry made a
sweeping gesture with his hand that encompassed both
sides of the street. The pedestrians moving past the old
lady didn't seem to understand what was happening. Or
maybe they did and just weren't getting involved.

What the hell am I waiting for? he thought, and hustled
down the block.

''Goddamn it, Neil,'' Scull said, trotting along at his
heels, ''this is a *foreign country*!''

Ignoring him, Perry reached the two men and put his
hand on the taller one's left shoulder.

''All right, that's enough, leave her alone,'' he said,
waving him on.

The tall guy stiffened a little but remained where he
was. The shorter guy glared at Perry and took a slug of
whatever was in the brown paper bag. Scull moved up
next to him and waited. In the center of the group, the
old woman had raised her hand to her mouth and was
looking around uncertainly, her face nervous and fearful.

''I said to take a hike,'' Perry said, conscious that the

guy still had his right hand in his pocket. *"Pahkah!"*

The guy glanced at him sideways and jerked his shoulder, trying to shake him off. He had small, close-set eyes and needed a shave. Perry tightened his grip.

The guy looked at him another moment, then suddenly rounded on him and spat in his face, his hand coming out of his pocket, something metallic flashing in his fist. A knife.

As the blade slashed up at him, Perry shifted his body to avoid the attack, clamping his left hand around the guy's wrist in mid-thrust and then pushing it downward. The punk struggled to bring the knife back up, but Perry slammed the back of his right hand with the outer edge of his palm in a crisp chopping motion. He felt the snap of bone, and then the guy groaned in pain as his hand went limp, hanging from his arm at an unnatural angle, his weapon clattering to the pavement.

Still holding the guy by his wrist, Perry moved in on him and jammed his knee into his crotch. The guy doubled over, clutching himself. Then he sank to the ground.

Perry was bending to snatch up the knife up when he heard the loud crash of breaking glass.

He glanced quickly over at the shorter man. Holding the bottle by its neck, he had smashed it against the side of a building, shaken off the paper bag, and was waving its jagged stump at Scull. Beer and suds were running down the wall where he'd shattered it.

Scull grinned slightly. The guy swiped the bottle stump at him, shaking droplets of liquid from the pointy spurs of glass. Scull felt a rush of air against his face and slipped backward an instant before it would have torn into his cheek. Then he reached into his jacket pocket, brought out a thin metal OC canister, and thumbed down its spray-head. A conical mist discharged from its nozzle into his attacker's face. The guy gagged, dropped the broken bottle, and began to stagger around blindly, clutching at his face as the pepper spray dilated the capillaries of his eyes and swelled the soft membranes in his nose and throat. Scull shoved the canister back into his pocket, spun him around by the shoulder, and drove an uppercut into his middle. The guy sagged to his knees beside his friend, gasping for breath, thick ropes of mucus glistening on his chin.

Scull looked down at him without moving. Disoriented, his eyes red and teary, the guy still hadn't quit. He struggled to pull himself upright and somehow managed to get his knees under him. Scull swung his leg out and kicked him full in the face. He dropped back to the ground, his hands covering his nose, blood spurting through his fingers.

"Should've stayed down," Scull muttered.

Perry realized that he still had the taller guy's gravity knife in his hand. He folded the blade into the handle and slipped it into the back pocket of his trousers.

Then he felt a tug on his sleeve. The old woman. She had stepped forward, a smile on her plump, upturned face.

"*Spasibo,*" she said, thanking him in Russian. She pulled two oranges from her canvas bag and held them out for him to take. "*Bolshoya spasibo.*"

Perry put his hand on her arm.

"Thanks for offering, Grandmother, but you should keep them for yourself," he said, motioning for her to return the fruit to her sack. "Go home now. *Bishir yetso.*"

"We'd better get out of here ourselves," Scull said.

Perry glanced both ways. A crowd had begun to gather around them. The cars and buses had continued their

slow progress along the street, though many rubberneck-
ers were pausing at the curb to get a look at the commotion.

"Yeah," he said. "Still want that drink?"

"I'm thirstier than ever," Scull said.

"Then lead the way," Perry said.

They hurried off down the street.

EIGHT

IT SEEMED TO GORDIAN THAT DAN PARKER HAD BEEN watching his back for as long as they'd known each other . . . which was now something like thirty-five years. In Nam, when both served with the 355th Tactical Fighter Wing, he had been wingman to Gordian's lead in the countless bombing runs they had made over enemy territory. Going low against VC strongpoints in their F-4 Phantoms, they had learned the difficulty of hitting camouflaged, dug-in targets with their payloads at speeds approaching Mach 2—and come to understand the importance of developing guided weapons systems that would allow pilots to drop their ordnance in tight spots without having to fly multiple passes over their objectives, while practically holding their fingers up into the wind to decide which way it was blowing.

Gordian's final day in a warplane—and in the war, for that matter—had been January 20, 1968, when he was downed during a close-support mission about four miles east of Khe Sanh. Ditching out of his fiery cockpit over an enemy-held ridge, he had scarcely shucked his parachute before he found himself surrounded by a bristling ring of North Vietnamese machine guns. As a pilot, he had been a prized catch, able to provide information about Air Force tactics and technology . . . and valuable enough for his captors to put him in a specimen cage rather than mount his head on a trophy wall. But throughout his five-year imprisonment in the Hanoi Hilton he had kept what he knew to himself, resisting carrot-and-stick coercions that had ranged from promises of early release to solitary confinement and torture.

Meanwhile, Dan had completed his second tour of duty in '70 and returned to the States with a chest full of military decorations. The son of a prominent California congressman, he'd successfully pressured his social and political contacts to get a Red Cross pipeline through to Gordian. The humanitarian teams had provided basic medical treatment, delivered letters and care packages, and reported back to Gordian's family about his condition, all despite an uncooperative North Vietnamese government that had done little more than pay lip service to the Geneva Convention.

Dan's efforts on his friend's behalf hardly stopped there. As the Paris peace talks staggered toward a cease-fire agreement, he had twisted arms to ensure that Gordian was among the first prisoners of war to be released. And although Gordian emerged from captivity weakened and underweight, he was in vastly better shape than he would have been without Dan's unfailing support.

In the following decades, that support would reach across to the professional arena even as their friendship and mutual respect took on increasingly greater dimension. Their experiences in Vietnam had left both men convinced of the need for technology that would combine advanced navigation and reconnaissance capabilities with a precision missile delivery system. Together they had been forced to rely on guesswork time and again when making their strikes, placing their lives in jeopardy and causing unnecessary collateral damage to civilian locations. And Gordian had never forgotten that he owed his incarceration in a POW camp to a Russian surface-to-air missile that he hadn't seen coming. While things had changed dramatically since the advent of smart weapons, there was still a lack of integration—a gap, so to speak— between infrared-targeting and radar surveillance systems.

By the late eighties, Gordian had begun to see how it was at least theoretically possible to fill that gap using modern satellite communications . . . and Dan was in a position to help him obtain the funding he needed to make those ideas a reality. Having followed in his father's footsteps, he had pursued a career in politics, and in his third term as a congressman from California occupied seats on several House allocations committees. His confidence in Gordian had been instrumental in shaking loose underwriting grants which, added to Gordian's own huge investment of corporate profits into R&D, opened the way for the development of GAPSFREE, the most impressive jewel in UpLink's wire-and-silicon crown.

In terms of its adaptability to existing avionics and communications hardware, GAPSFREE was almost too good a package to be believed. Interfacing with orbital Global Positioning System satellites, it allowed the pilot or weapons officer of a fighter plane to know exactly where he was in relation to his target, or what was targeting him, providing real-time data relayed directly from the satellites to onboard navigational computers, and using synthetic-aperture radar to peer through fog and battle smoke. The system was also light and compact enough to be enclosed in a weapons pod that could be affixed to hardpoints on even low-tech aircraft like the A-10, transforming them—in combination with some cockpit modifications—into lethal fighter-bombers able to launch the smartest of smart weapons. This versatility made GAPS-FREE the cheapest and most effective guidance system for missiles and precision guided munitions ever designed.

Not surprisingly, it also made Gordian's firm the world-wide leader in recon tech.

And made Gordian a very, very rich man.

Having reached this sort of professional milestone, many entrepreneurs would have retired, or at least rested on their laurels. But Gordian had already begun pushing his ideas toward their next logical phase. Parlaying his tremendous success, he expanded his corporation in numerous ways, moving into dozens of countries, opening up new markets, and absorbing local chemical, communications, telephone, and industrial holdings on all four continents. His ultimate goal was to create a single, world spanning, satellite-based communications network that would allow phone transmissions to be made inexpensively from a mobile phone—or fax, or modem—to a destination anywhere on the globe.

What drove him was neither ego nor a desire for greater wealth, but a belief that this system could truly make a difference in the lives of millions, perhaps *billions* of people, bringing communications services and technology to every spot on earth. In his eyes, rapid access to information was a weapon. He had returned from Vietnam with a firm commitment to do what he could to stand up to totalitarian governments and oppressive regimes. And he had seen firsthand how no such government could stand in the face of freedom of communication.

To achieve his goal, however, he needed the support of the governments of a dozen or more key countries. He needed them to assign radio frequencies to his company; he needed them to give him access to their space programs to provide for the scores of low-earth-orbit satellite launches that NASA simply couldn't handle; and he needed them to allow him to build ground stations in countries scattered all across the planet, to link into his satellite network and feed signals into existing land lines.

He also needed Dan Parker. Again. Of course. Since 1997, Dan had been guiding him through the regulatory tangle that had accompanied the evolution of handheld satellite communications. More recently, he'd been keeping tabs on events in Congress that could affect Gordian's plans to have his Russian ground station operational by the end of the year.

Now, sitting across from Dan at the Washington Palm on Nineteenth Street, Gordian took a drink of his beer and glanced up at the sports and political cartoons covering the walls. Stirring his martini to melt the ice cubes, Dan looked impatient for their food to arrive. Gordian couldn't remember him ever *not* being impatient when he was expecting his food.

They were at their regular corner table beneath an affectionate caricature of Tiger Woods. A decade ago, when they'd started having their monthly lunches here, the drawing in that spot had been of O.J. Simpson. Then that had come down and one of Marv Albert had taken its place. Then Albert was removed and Woods had gone up.

"Tiger," Gordian mused aloud. "An all-American legend."

"Let's keep our fingers crossed he stays up there," Parker said.

"He goes, who'll be left?"

Dan shook his head. "Secretariat, maybe."

"Maybe," Gordian said.

They waited some more. The people around them were

mostly political staffers, reporters, and lobbyists, with a sprinkling of tourists hoping to catch a glimpse of someone important. So far Gordian hadn't noticed any stargazers looking in his direction. He wondered idly if he was having a bad hair day.

"So," he said, "how about you tell me about Delacroix's latest isolationist rants."

Dan eyed someone eating a corned beef sandwich at the next table.

"I want my food," he said.

"I know," Gordian said. "I was hoping to take your mind off it."

Dan shrugged.

"From what I hear from my colleagues in the Senate, Delacroix's been pressing the themes you'd expect. Talking about the cost of an aid commitment to Russia, pointing out—correctly, I should mention—that the bill for our peacekeeping mission in Bosnia has wound up being five times higher than the early projections. And that the Russian parliament and banking system are largely controlled by organized crime, which means a percentage of any loans we extend will probably be skimmed by corrupt officials."

Gordian took another drink of beer. "What else?"

"He's claiming the President's offer amounts to appeasement . . . the argument being that he's trying to buy concessions in the next round of START and nuclear test-ban talks with candy, rather than score points through hardball negotiations."

Gordian spotted a waiter moving toward them with a serving tray balanced on his arm.

"Our sirloins are here," he said.

"Thank God," Dan said, and snapped open his napkin. "How long we been waiting?"

Gordian checked his watch. "A whopping ten minutes."

They sat in silence as their plates were set in front of them and the waiter zipped off.

Dan reached for his silverware and attacked his steak.

"*Gooood*," he growled, mimicking Boris Karloff in *Bride of Frankenstein*.

Gordian started on his own lunch, giving Dan a chance to come up for air before resuming their conversation.

"You've given me Delacroix's publicly stated objections to the proposal," he said. "What about his underlying, politically opportunistic ones?"

Dan looked at him and chewed a slice of meat.

"Nice to know you think so lowly of your elected officials."

"Present company excepted," Gordian said.

"You remember when Delacroix led the push for social services reductions a few years ago?" Dan asked.

"Hard to forget," Gordian said. "Didn't he spear a giant stuffed pig on the Senate floor or something?"

"Actually, that happened during a more recent session. And it was a *piñata*." Dan worked at the steak with his knife and fork. "His prop for the cutback debate was a giant mechanical mouth."

"At least he consistently thinks big."

Dan grinned. "The point is, *nobody's* forgotten his stance, which was considered bullish and hard-hearted even by conservatives. And now he's afraid it'll look bad if he keeps quiet about millions of dollars' worth of food and financial aid going to foreigners . . . Russians, no less."

Gordian shook his head. "The two issues aren't related. Even if we want to ignore the critical nature of the emergency—"

"Which is being questioned . . ."

"It still boils down to a matter of strategic importance for our country," Gordian said.

Dan drained his martini and signaled for another one. "Look, I don't like having to defend the Louisiana pit bull. But try to imagine what Delacroix's political opponents will make of his going along with the aid program. The very same people who are in *favor* of it will accuse him of hypocrisy, and remind the public that he's the guy who wanted school lunches taken away from American kids."

Gordian was silent again. He looked down at his plate. Ever since Ashley had instructed their personal chef to omit the red meat from their meals—he couldn't quite recall if it was the saturated fat content, carcinogenic antibiotics, or steroidal growth additives that bothered her— his steak lunches at the Palm had taken on a rebellious air, become a respite, even an escape, from the healthful monotony of tossed greens and seafood and grilled chicken breast. And to enhance this forbidden pleasure, to experience it in all its cholesterol-soaked fullness, he had gone from having his steaks served medium-rare to a bare, dripping step from raw. Once a month, he broke free of all dietary shackles to become a wolf, a carnivorous alpha male, sinking his fangs into bloody flesh after a successful hunt.

Today, however, he hadn't been able to muster much of an appetite. His steak looked so neglected he almost wanted to give it an apology.

"A couple of people from my Russian team were in

Kaliningrad the other day,'' he said. "You remember Vince Scull? I introduced him to you a while back.''

Parker nodded.

"The scenario-planning expert,'' he said. "Sharp guy. Kind of struck me as the, uh, moody type, though.''

"I don't pay him to be adorable. There's nobody better than Vince at anticipating big bang problems, and he left that city convinced there'll be food riots throughout Russia within a month.'' Gordian paused a moment, caught the waiter's eye, and motioned at his empty beer mug. "Twenty years ago, when he was working for a Canadian investment firm in Iran, he advised his employers to get their staff out of the country. The company honchos thought his appraisal of the political climate was overly bleak. Six days later, the Ayatollah assumed power and the U.S. embassy staff was taken hostage. Scull stuck around to smuggle out some of the company's American workers. When the danger to them was past, he resigned, and I snapped him up.''

"What makes him so certain of disaster this time?''

"A lot of things. I can fax you a copy of his report, if you'd like. But his contention's that Kaliningrad is less reliant on domestic food supplies than other cities, I think because a lot of imported stuff comes through its free trade port. Yet the markets there were dry. If the people in that city are hurting, it's going to be rougher in places like St. Petersburg, or even the capital.'' Gordian's fresh beer arrived and he took a drink. "I know it's anecdotal, but Vince even got into a confrontation with some punks who tried running off with an old lady's grocery bag. This is a half hour after he drove into town.''

"As goes Kaliningrad, so goes the Federation,'' Parker said. "That what you're telling me?''

"Pretty much, yeah."

Dan sighed. "Maybe the incident you mentioned clouded up Scull's crystal ball. Or could be he's just plain wrong. It happens to the best."

"So Starinov came here begging for a handout for nothing? Is that what you're trying to tell me?"

"You ask Bob Delacroix, he'd say the minister's been exaggerating the severity of the crisis. That he needs a hot-button issue that'll grab attention away from that Pedachenko character. Make him look like a statesman who can stand among other world leaders."

Gordian looked at him, his gray eyes firm.

"I'm not talking to Delacroix," he said. "Dan, I've got over a hundred employees in western Russia at this moment. Another eighty or ninety contract workers who've been hired to build the ground terminal. Let's forget my investment a minute. Forget the broader national interest, too. Those people are in vulnerable positions and my main concern is their safety. If the relief agreement is on its way to being scuttled, I'm pulling them out. So tell me how you think it's going to go."

Dan listened in silence as Gordian spoke, rotating his martini between his hands, his fingertips leaving faint prints on the chilled surface of the glass. Finally he lifted it to his mouth and drank.

"The President will probably be able to cut a deal, get at least some of the assistance under way," he said. "With any luck, it'll be enough."

"That's three qualifiers in two sentences," Gordian said.

Dan looked at him and shrugged. "The toughest thing I learned during my freshman year in Congress was to curb my expectations. It's also the thing that's kept me hanging in there.''

"So you're telling me to sit tight and hope for the best.''

"Yeah.''

Gordian sat back in his chair and sighed, lost in thought.

Dan ogled his plate.

"You gonna finish that steak?'' he asked.

Gordian shook his head.

"Then how about sliding it over,'' Dan said.

NINE

GREGOR SADOV STOOD IN THE SHADOWS AND watched the fires burn. Over the last four days, he and his team had torched seven different warehouses. The good news was that he hadn't lost anyone since Andrei. The bad news was that it wasn't enough.

But then, it never was.

His left hand was pressed to his side, holding a cloth tightly against the minor wound he'd received. He wasn't sure if he'd caught a piece of shrapnel from when the grain in that last warehouse blew, or if one of the guards had gotten off a lucky shot and creased his side. Either way, it didn't matter. The wound was painful, but not deep, and Gregor wouldn't let a little pain slow him down.

No, it wasn't the wound that was bothering him. It was the message he'd gotten that morning. Short and to the point, as always, the message had said simply, "Warehouse fires effective, but more needed. Prepare your team to target U.S. assets in area."

That was it. No information on *which* U.S. assets to target, or when to strike. Gregor knew he'd be given that information when the people he worked for decided to tell him. Which was fine with him. They knew how he worked, and that he wouldn't attack until he and his team were ready.

Standing there in the shadows, his hand pressed against

his side, Gregor looked out on the destruction he had caused, and he smiled.

Elaine Steiner closed up the toolbox at her feet, dusted her hands, and stood up slowly, arching her back to relieve the strain of kneeling for so long. A wisp of her graying hair had come loose from the kerchief she wore when she worked, and she absently reached up to tuck it back in place. Beside her, Arthur, her husband, closed the door of the service panel and rolled his head left and right, trying to get a knot out of his neck.

They were in one of the smaller buildings on the perimeter of the compound Roger Gordian was having put up here in a sparsely populated area of the Kaliningrad region. The nearest town was over ninety kilometers away, so the compound they were building had to be pretty much self-sustaining, with an apartment complex for the various personnel and various forms of entertainment as well. And security. Lots of security. But that was true wherever they went.

Elaine and Arthur had been with Gordian for the better part of twenty years. He picked the sites for his ground stations, and the Steiners went in and got them up and running. It was a good partnership, and a good life, especially when, as now, they were getting close to bringing a ground station on-line for the first time.

"That wasn't so bad," he said, looking over at Elaine.

She smiled softly. Arthur was always looking on the bright side. It was one of the things she admired most about him, perhaps because she was always so pessimistic.

"Not like Turkey," she said, turning Arthur around and massaging his neck for him. "Remember when we couldn't get the system to stay on-line for more than ten minutes at a time?''

"Yeah," he said, letting his head roll forward to make her massage more effective. "Those damn outdated transistors the Afghanis sold us kept overheating. Took us forever to figure out what was going on.''

"And this was just a bad stretch of cable. I told that Russian service crew that they couldn't run a cable that long without a support, but when have the locals ever listened to us?''

"They will," Arthur said. "They'll learn.''

Elaine sighed and shook her head, but there was a tolerant smile on her face as she continued to rub his neck. It was good to know that some things in life would never change.

"Come on," she said. "There's one bottle of wine left over from the last shipment. I think we should have it with dinner tonight.''

Arthur turned and put his arms around her. Reaching up and wiping away a smudge of grease from her cheek, he kissed her softly and said, "See? Things are looking up already.''

TEN

THE FLOOR-TO-CEILING MIRROR OCCUPYING AN EN-tire wall of Nick Roma's office was without a speck of dust, without a smudge, nearly without a flaw of any kind on its gleaming silvery surface. Nick would have one of the boys—he liked using that phrase, "the boys"—clean the mirror with Windex two, maybe three, times a day, occasionally more often if he noticed even the slightest blemish marring his reflection. Once there had been a small scratch in the glass and he'd had the panel replaced that same morning.

Nick didn't think this was being compulsive. He paid close attention to his appearance and the mirror was ex-tremely important to him. Certainly it was the most im-portant thing in his office here at the Platinum Club, more important than his multimedia center, his telephone, or his scratch pad. At least as important as his MP5K.

Now Nicky stood at his mirror making minute adjust-ments to his clothing—pulling up the collar of his black turtleneck shirt, smoothing the shirt over his chest, being careful that it was tucked into his black designer jeans just right. Every detail had to be perfect.

Outside his window, a truck was backing into the load-ing area, rumbling out there by the freight door two stories down on Fifteenth Avenue.

He glanced at his Rolex.

11 A.M.

The delivery had arrived exactly on time. He was sure the pickup would, too. The people he was dealing with paid close attention to that sort of thing.

He looked down at his boots and checked that their shine was as flawless as the mirror's. The boots were black Justins, some kind of lizard skin, and they required special care—much more than leather, anyway. One of the boys would clean and shine them every day, same as they did the mirror. But you had to keep an eye on them, make sure they used neutral wax on the boots instead of black polish. The polish would ruin the skin, and he'd wind up looking like some newly arrived immigrant from Little Odessa. And the mere prospect of that was something that filled him with anger and disgust.

Six months ago, he had been tried for gasoline bootlegging in a federal district court, the specific charge being that he had defrauded the IRS out of three million dollars in income taxes through the use of complicated paper transactions. When they made their closing arguments, prosecutors had told the jury he was *vory v. zakone*, a godfather in the Eastern European underworld. They had used words like *bochya*—"big man," in Russian—to describe him. He had been accused of managing the American arm of a criminal syndicate they had alternately called *organizatsiya* and *mafiya*. At one point they had claimed its influence was on the way to becoming as powerful as that of the Cosa Nostra families and Asian gangs.

On the way, he thought with annoyance, pulling his comb from the back pocket of his jeans and sweeping it through his shock of wavy hair.

The trial had lasted two months but he had beaten the indictment, been acquitted of all counts. It had proven somewhat tricky, because the identities of the jurors had been closely guarded. They had been shuttled to and from the courthouse in unmarked vans, escorted by a swarm of cops from the Organized Crime Task Force, and addressed only by number in the courtroom. The blonde with the good legs whom Nick had smiled and winked at throughout the trial was Juror Number One. The fat man who sat with his arms crossed over his belly was Juror Number Nine. Everything top secret. But Nick had sneered at the government's secrets. Nick had been persistent. His people knew clerks in the U.S. Attorney's Office with access to what were laughably called "high-security" databases, and had gotten the information they needed to reach two members of the panel.

Fifty thousand dollars—along with guarantees that the jurors' families would be protected from sudden accidents and disappearances—had bought Nick Roma an acquittal. He had thought that a fair deal. In fact, he considered himself primarily a deal*maker*. At thirty-five years old, he had already forged reciprocal arrangements with the Italians, the Chinese triads, the Colombian cartels, even the Yakuza. He'd built steadily and creatively upon street-level enterprises such as prostitution and narcotics trafficking, gaining footholds in the banking system, launching elaborate financial schemes, cracking open new markets wherever he'd seen a dollar. He had made contacts in the legitimate corporate and political communities, and set up clearinghouses for his activities in over a dozen states . . . which was why he'd taken personal affront at the government attorneys' characterization of him as a greenhorn thug, the leader of a ring of ethnic wannabes.

In his mind, nothing could have been further from the truth.

He had immigrated from Russia with his parents when he was six years old and since then had never been out of the country, never even been away from New York City. When he was twelve, his mother had successfully gone through naturalization proceedings, gaining citizenship for him as well. He had worked on his pronunciation until he spoke without any trace of an accent. At twenty-one he had altered the spelling of his first name and dropped the last syllable from his surname. Thus, Nikita Romanov had become Nick Roma.

He was as solidly American as anyone in that courtroom. And every time he thought of the prosecutors he promised himself that their insult would be repaid with interest. He was nobody's joke. He—

Nicky heard a knock on his door, put the finishing touch to his hair, and returned the comb to his back pocket.

"What is it?" He turned to look out the window. The truck downstairs was empty now, its small load wheeled into the nightclub on a handcart. He watched the driver lower the rear panel, hop back into his cab, and then start pulling out into the street.

The door inched open and one of Nick's crew, a muscular kid named Bakach, leaned his head inside.

"The Arab woman is here," he said in thickly accented English. "With her friend."

Nicky shifted his attention back to the mirror and gave himself a final inspection. She was even earlier than he'd expected. Whatever her ultimate plans for the merchandise, she obviously wasn't wasting a minute.

"Send them in," he said, satisfied with his appearance. "And tell Janos and Kos I want the packages."

Bakach nodded, disappeared, and returned a minute later with Nick's two visitors.

Nick turned toward the woman as she entered.

"Hello, Gilea," he said, looking at her. She was beautiful, really very sexy, her shoulder-length black hair cut at a neat angle, her large slanting eyes reminding him of an exotic cat. Her tweed coat was open and revealed fine long legs below a short leather skirt.

He wondered fleetingly whether she might be interested in something more than a professional relationship.

"Nick," she said, her high-heeled boots clicking on the floor as she came farther into the room. The tall man who had arrived with her had a thin scar curling down his cheek under a scruffy growth of beard. He followed a step behind her and stopped moving when she stopped. Nick saw the slight bulge of a pistol beneath his car jacket.

"I saw the truck outside," she said. "Can I assume my delivery has arrived?"

"My men are bringing it up right now," he said, and motioned to a chair by his desk. "Why don't you relax while you wait?"

She stared coldly into his face.

"I'll stand," she said.

Minutes later there was another knock on the door. Nick opened it and a couple of his men came in carrying a medium-sized wooden shipping crate between them. There were two more crates in the outer corridor. The men carefully set the first crate on the floor and brought the others in one at a time, putting them down beside it. The third box had a crowbar resting on its lid.

Gilea stood there in silence, her dark brown eyes trained on the crates.

"I want to have a look," she said.

Nick gave Kos a nod.

Kos lifted the crowbar, slid its flat edge between the lid and the upper corner of the box, and began prying it open. While he waited, Nick glanced over at Gilea. Her eyes had narrowed, and the tip of her tongue was gliding back and forth across her bottom lip.

The lid finally came loose. Gilea bent over the crate and reached inside, her hand burrowing through a layer of Styrofoam packing material.

The crate was filled with mirrored globes of the sort that would throw off whirling spangles of light in theaters and dance halls. Each was about the size of a grapefruit. Nick had a much larger one suspended from the ceiling in his own club and usually referred to it as a "disco ball."

"Give me the crowbar." Gilea extended her hand toward Kos, still looking raptly down into the wooden box.

He passed her the tool without a word.

She studied the reflective globes a moment, then lifted one of them out of the crate and brought the edge of the crowbar sharply down against it. A crack spread across its circumference. She hit it again, splitting it into several pieces, letting them drop to the floor in a small avalanche of glitter dust.

Leaving only the smuggled contents of the globe in her hand.

The flat, rectangular packet had Chinese markings on one side. Its transparent wrapping contained a white, waxy substance that resembled a stick of modeling clay.

"The plastique," Gilea said. She closed her eyes and stood with her head cocked back, her lips trembling a little, her fingers tightly gripping the packet.

Watching her, Nick thought she almost looked like a woman in ecstasy.

"You do nice work," she said, turning to him after a long moment. Her eyes gleamed.

He smiled and met her gaze with his own.

"Always," he said.

Nick Roma watched through the window in his office and waited. Finally Kos stuck his head inside the door and confirmed what Nick already knew. Gilea and her henchman had gone. He nodded to Kos. Kos left, shutting the door behind him.

It was time to check his insurance.

Nick walked across to his mirror, pulled his comb from his back pocket, and straightened his hair. He'd mussed it bowing over the beautiful hand of a dangerous lady.

Then he put his comb up and pressed a small button on the lower left panel of his mirror—a button so completely unobtrusive you had to know it was there to see it.

The giant mirrored panel slowly opened before his eyes. Behind that panel were banks of VCRs, each recording its assigned sector of the building. The tapes in the machines were endless loops, recording for twenty-four hours, then overtaping onto the previous material. That way, he only had to pull them if something worth saving was likely to be on them.

Like insurance.

He reached into the cavity behind the mirror and pulled the tape that recorded events in his office. That tape—of Gilea opening the disco ball and rubbing the C-4 inside like it was a sex toy she couldn't wait to take home and try out—was a keeper. Not that he'd ever be caught. But if he was, he was betting that that tape, and a library of tapes much like it that he'd stashed in a very secret location, would buy him a really nice "get out of jail free" card.

After he reloaded the tape machine with a new blank tape, he pushed a button inset in the mirror's inner frame. He watched a giant ultra-thin TV screen pop out of the ceiling at the back of his office, along with eight Bose speakers placed at strategic points throughout the room. Nothing but the best for Nick Roma. As he waited, he couldn't help thinking of the other uses his mirror could be put to with such a beautiful lady. It made for a very pleasant picture.

Unlikely as such a scene was, a man needed his fantasies.

They kept him young.

He popped the tape into the VCR/DVD reader inset behind a hidden panel in his office wall, then settled back in his desk chair to watch the show.

Halfway across the city, in an abandoned warehouse whose ownership was shrouded by so many shell companies that even the most motivated searcher would never sniff it out, a remote feed of the very same footage that Nick was watching loaded itself in digital format into a powerful computer. Stamped electronically with the date the footage was taken and the location it was taped from, the information existed quietly, secretly, almost invisibly. Nick's system performed its job perfectly.

In its own way, the scene just recorded, and all the others like it stored on the hard drive, were as explosive as the C-4 Nick had just sold Gilea.

Information, like plastique, could kill.

And, soon, it would.

ELEVEN

POLICE COMMISSIONER BILL HARRISON COULD HARD-
ly wait for the *Titanic* to sink so he could hurry home to
his report.

In general, he hated musicals. Just didn't get them. And
the one he was watching right now had to be the most
confusing one he'd ever sat through. The worst maritime
disaster in history, maybe fifteen hundred people
drowned, eaten by sea creatures, God only knew, and
somebody'd gotten the idea to turn it into a Broadway
spectacle. He really didn't see the entertainment value in
such horrendous human tragedy. What was everybody
singing and kicking up their heels about? They were all
going down with the ship!

He glanced over at his wife, who was in the seat beside
him gazing intently at the stage. She seemed to be enjoying herself. No, not *seemed to be*. Was. He could tell from
the tilt of her chin, the faint dimples at the corners of her
mouth. When two people were married as long as they'd
been, it got so you could read each other at a glance.
Later, over coffee and cake, she would speak apprecia-
tively of the sets, the score, the choreography, the staging.
And he would study her with something akin to the love-
struck awe he'd felt thirty years ago on their first high
school date, admiring her lively, intelligent features, her
smooth coffee-brown skin, the way she put together her

clothes, and the graceful movements of her hands as she commented on the various aspects of the show, marveling at *everything* about her for that matter, and wondering what he had ever done to deserve the constant support she had given him throughout their marriage, a faith and perseverance that helped lift him from the tough streets of Harlem to the highest post in the New York Police Department.

But later was later, and now was still Act One of a maddeningly incomprehensible songfest about a magnificent wreck whose passengers had suffered a cold, airless death. Harrison glanced at his watch, wondering how much longer his own torment would last. Nine P.M. An hour to go. Maybe more. Didn't some plays run until ten-thirty or eleven?

Harrison felt a sudden twinge of embarrassment. That was something the city's top cop really should know, wasn't it? He damn well hoped he wasn't losing touch. You could dress Times Square up all you wanted, you could even push the sex shops off the strip to make room for the wonderful world of Disney, but the hands under those bright white Mickey Mouse gloves would always have grimy fingernails, and it would always be a place where vice and violence could reach out of the shadows and drag you down like those dancing fools onstage. So much fuss had been made about the neighborhood's renaissance in recent years, one could sometimes forget that a decrease in crime did not necessarily mean the criminals had packed their bags and gone south. In fact, it was only an intensified and very visible police presence in the area that held the bump-and-run muggers, junkies, hookers and other lowlife at bay. There were still pockets of darkness amid the lights of the Great White Way, and people needed to be aware of them. Especially the PC.

Harrison tried to concentrate on the show, wanting to keep track of the storyline so he would have something to say about it to Rosetta. Who was the character with the beard? The captain? A mad scientist? Jesus, it was no good, he was lost. A lushly melodramatic chord swelled from the orchestra pit, and one of the actors broke into song. The lyrics mentioned something about a ship of dreams. Harrison listened for a minute, but then faded back into his reverie, as if he were a radio moving beyond the broadcast range of a particular station.

His eyes staring at the stage without seeing anything on it, he thought again of the plan he wanted to look over before going to bed. He'd been calling it Operation 2000, which had the sort of nice, official-sounding ring that would inspire confidence in City Hall.

Over the past month, he had been conferring on an almost daily basis with his chief deputies, as well as commanders from the Transit Police, the Emergency Services Unit, and the NYPD-FBI Counter-Terrorism Task Force, about the problems they would face trying to safeguard the multitude of celebrants who would be crowding Times Square on New Year's Eve. Even in an ordinary year, the job was a major pain in the ass—and this year was far from ordinary. This time around they were looking at December 31, 1999. The turn of the century. A once-in-a-lifetime Event, capital *E*, ladies and germs.

And while Harrison and his team of planners had been laboring to draw out a sound logistical blueprint for a situation that unquestionably *defied* logistics, what had the mayor been doing? Why, hitting the media in pursuit of visitor dollars, of course! He had been on every local news program frothing about the city's plans for the big countdown. He had been plugging away on *Letterman* and *Conan O'Brien*. He had even been on radio shows like *Imus in the Morning* and *Howard Stern*, billing the triangle formed by the intersection of Seventh Avenue, Broadway, and Forty-second Street as the "center of the world," all but popping open a champagne bottle over the airwaves as he invited listeners to join the millennial bash.

Harrison's mind filled with an odd blend of worry and resignation. From every indication, people were responding to the mayor's pitch in droves. Based on the massive volume of tourist inquiries, polling data, and the record number of hotel and restaurant reservations in the midtown area, it had been estimated that two million revelers would be thronging Times Square to watch the ball drop. Add to that three or four million *more* spectators scattered throughout Battery Park, the South Street Seaport, and the entire Brooklyn shoreline to watch the fireworks over New York Harbor, and the police force would be stretched far beyond its capacity to maintain anything close to an adequate presence. And for what? There were some who believed an age of miracles was approaching, and others who were expecting the end of existence. Harrison just kind of figured that, come January 1, the world would be the same orbiting lunatic asylum it had always been—minus a somewhat higher than usual number of holiday fatalities.

He sighed without being aware of it. In his more nervous moments, he had fantasized about giving up, taking a hike, escaping the whole damn chocolate mess so it could fall where it belonged, which was right on the mayor's lap. Maybe he'd get a job working security in Stonehenge, or Mount Fuji, where the crowds of millennialists were bound to be thinner. Or how about Egypt?

He'd heard that ten grand would buy admission to a gala some tour organizer was throwing at the Great Pyramid of Giza. Surely a seasoned big city police commissioner could be of help keeping things orderly over there. If Hizzoner wanted to be an impresario, ringmaster of the greatest show on earth, fine, more power to him. But what right did he have to drive anybody else crazy with it?

Harrison heard a crash of applause and studied the stage. The curtain had gone down. The houselights slowly brightened. What was going on? A glance at his watch revealed that it was only nine-thirty, too early for the show to have ended. Besides, he hadn't seen the *Titanic* sink yet.

Intermission, then. It had to be intermission.

Rosetta was nudging him with her elbow.

"So, what do you think of the show?" she asked. Sounding, well, buoyant.

It's hackneyed and tiresome and I can't wait to go home, he thought.

"Love it," he said. "Especially that song about the ship of dreams."

Rosetta nodded in agreement and smiled. "Can't wait to see how things work out for Ida and Isidor. Should we go to the bar and have a drink?"

He took hold of her hand.

As they rose, brushed past the couple sitting at the end of their row, and began moving up the aisle toward the lobby, Harrison mused that Ida and Isidor, whoever they were, really didn't have too many options. Either they'd squeeze into one of the lifeboats and be rescued by the *Carpathia*, or they'd sink with captain and crew. But he didn't comment on that to Rosetta.

Whatever lay ahead, he sure as hell didn't want to be the one to spoil things for her.

TWELVE

MINUTES BEFORE HIS DEATH, JULIUS AGOSTEN WAS
rolling his vender's stand out of the parking lot on
Twenty-third Street and trying to imagine what he would
do if he hit the lottery.

The first thing on his list, he thought, would be to turn
his stand over to his brother-in-law, vender's license, garage space, and all. Stefan was still young enough to tol-
erate the long hours out on the street, leaving the house
at four o'clock in the morning, getting home after eight
at night, sometimes after midnight on weekends, summer
and winter, rain or shine. What with Rene and Stefan
having had the baby recently, the stand would give them
a chance to make some decent money, maybe even put
away a few dollars for the little girl's future.

There were only a limited number of vender licenses
available in the city, and even fewer locations as busy as
the one Julius had staked out for himself, Forty-second
Street and Broadway, the heart of midtown. During the
week you had the professional people, men with brief-
cases, women in stylish outfits, thousands of them jam-
ming the sidewalks, pouring from the subways, rushing
this way and that out there on Times Square, stopping for
coffee and something to eat—a Danish, roll, whatever—
as they hurried to their jobs. And then you had the cab-

bies, the cops, the shop clerks—everybody, really. Who had time for breakfast at home nowadays?

Julius pushed the stand down the block toward his waiting van, its metal casters rattling on the pavement, the noise very loud in the predawn hush. In three hours the city would awaken, but now the insurance gates were still drawn over the storefronts, and no one was pushing through the revolving doors of the office buildings, and the only traffic was an occasional newspaper truck or taxi swishing by under the dim throw of the street lamps. *Thankfully.* Because if the street got crowded, the traffic cops would come out in force, and he'd be fined for illegally parking the van while he got his stand out of the lot. But what else was he supposed to do? Wheel it all the way uptown on foot, twenty blocks, which was a long walk even in decent weather, and seemed a lot longer in December?

Forty million bucks, he thought, remembering the Lotto ticket in his pocket again. If he won, he would retire and head someplace warm. Buy a big house, a mansion, one with acres of lawn and a curving gravel driveway behind high iron gates. Maybe it would have an ocean view on one side—Gerty, God rest her soul, had always loved the ocean. There would be no more leaving the wagon overnight in the parking garage, no more paying two hundred a month for the privilege of keeping it safe from vandals and thieves. No more dragging himself out of bed at three A.M. so he could drive to the wholesaler in Queens for his rolls and pastries, then get the wagon out of the lot, and be set up on his corner by the start of the rush hour.

This had been his routine for over a decade, week after week, year after year. And while Julius wasn't a man to forget his blessings, he couldn't deny that it had taken a toll on him. Waking up early was getting more difficult every day. His work hours left him with no time to spend with his grandchildren. The circulation in his right leg had been giving him trouble, and his left shoulder very often ached.

Most of all, though, he was getting sick and tired of the brutal winters.

Today he was wearing a quilted parka and had the hood drawn up over his head, but the sharp wind coming off the Hudson stung his exposed cheeks, and his bones felt brittle from the glacial cold. These days, Julius was always adding layers of insulation to his clothing, but somehow there were never enough to keep him comfortable.

It was, he supposed, all part of becoming middle-aged . . . but why hadn't he noticed his youth slipping away until it was too late to prepare for it?

Reaching the van now, he pulled the stand around back and knelt to connect it to the trailer hitch. *Forty million, forty million, forty million.* Given the size of the jackpot, maybe he should have bought more than a single ticket this week, he thought. He'd heard it made no difference in the odds if you had one or a hundred, going strictly by the math. But still . . .

Julius had nearly finished hitching up the stand when he heard hurried footsteps behind him. He jerked his head around, startled. They seemed to be coming from around the corner, on Fifth Avenue.

A moment later the woman turned onto the block.

At first Julius thought she was probably a hooker. What respectable woman would be out on the street at this hour, let alone on such a frigid morning? Anyway, despite the citywide cleanup campaign, there was still a thriving skin trade in the neighborhood—like the drive-through line, as it was called, right over on Twenty-eighth and Lex, where you'd see the cars double- and-triple parked on busy Friday nights, heads bobbing under the dashboards.

As she came walking in his direction, though, Julius found himself thinking that she really didn't look like a streetwalker, at least not like any of the girls he'd seen in this part of town, most of whom plastered on their makeup an inch thick and dressed to advertise their goods even if it meant freezing their behinds off. In fact, she seemed more like one of the businesswomen who'd be stopping to buy a croissant from him in a few hours.

Wearing a tweed overcoat, dark slacks, and a beret that was pulled down almost to her ears, she was a striking beauty, with an exotic, high-cheekboned face, and a wedge of straight black hair blowing back over her shoulders in the wind.

She walked right up to him now, stepping quickly through the darkness, vapor puffing from her mouth.

"Help me," she said, sounding very upset. "Please."

Julius stared at her in confusion.

"What?" he said awkwardly. "What—what's the matter?"

She stopped maybe an inch away from him, her large black eyes meeting his own.

"I need a ride," she said.

He frowned. "I don't understand . . ."

"Here, let me show you," she said, and fumbled in her shoulder bag.

Julius watched her with growing confusion. Why would she walk up to a perfect stranger and ask . . . ?

Before he could complete the thought, he heard a rustling sound behind him, then suddenly felt something hard and cold push against the back of his head.

The woman nodded slightly.

Not to him, he realized, but to whoever had stolen up on him from the shadows.

His heart knocked in his chest. He'd been tricked, *distracted*—

Julius never heard the silenced Glock go off, never felt anything except the jolt of the muzzle against his head as the trigger was pulled and the bullet went ripping through his skull, blowing out his right eye and a large chunk of his forehead.

As his body dropped faceup to the ground, its remaining eye still wide with shock, the pistol angled downward, spitting three more muffled rounds into his face.

Gilea looked both ways, saw that the street was empty, and then crouched over the body, avoiding the puddle of blood that was already spreading over the sidewalk around it. She unpinned the vender's license from the front of the parka and slipped it into her purse. She hastily searched through the coat and pants pockets, found a wallet and key ring, then glanced up at the bearded man with the gun.

"Let's get out of here, Akhad," she said, tossing him the keys.

He slipped the Glock under his jacket, opened the side of the van, then returned to the corpse and dragged it in behind the front seat.

Out on the street, Gilea finished hitching the vender's stand to the back of the van, went around the side nearest the curb, and leaned her head in through the panel door. She noticed a blanket on the floor of the rear compartment and tossed it over the body. Then she climbed into the passenger seat.

Sitting beside her, the bearded man found the ignition

key amid the cluster in his hand and started up the engine.

They pulled away from the curb, driving west along Twenty-eighth Street, the vender's stand bumping along in tow.

The van rolled into the auto repair lot at Eleventh Avenue and Fifty-second Street at ten minutes past five. Although the shop would not open for business until 8:30, the garage door was elevated and Akhad drove right in. Three men in gray mechanics' coveralls were waiting inside near the door to the office.

Gilea pushed out of her door and jumped down off the running board.

"Where's Nick?" she asked.

"On his way," one of the men said in Russian.

She gave him a look of displeasure. "He should have been here."

The man didn't answer. Gilea let the silence expand.

"The body's in the van," she said finally. "You'll have to dispose of it."

"Right."

She reached into her purse for the laminated vender's license, and handed it to him.

"That should be altered immediately," she said. "And I want the stand ready by tonight."

"It'll be done."

"It had better," she said. "We have less than three days."

"Don't worry, there won't be any problems."

She shivered and wrapped her arms around herself.

"It's miserably cold in here," she said. "How can you take it?"

He nodded toward the van and grinned.

"It helps to keep busy," he said.

THIRTEEN

WITH JUST MOMENTS TO GO UNTIL AIRTIME, ARKADY Pedachenko was having trouble deciding how to begin his weekly television program. Of course this had nothing to do with any format change or lack of preparation. Each broadcast invariably opened with a ten-to-fifteen-minute spot in which he sat alone on camera and editorialized about a variety of issues. This was followed by a phone-in segment that gave Pedachenko a chance to address his viewers in a conversational, interactive mode, supposedly taking their calls at random—although the questions and comments were, in fact, mostly scripted, and fed to him by plants in the network audience. The second half hour of the show featured interviews or panel discussions with politicians and other public figures.

No, his problem wasn't the format. Pedachenko valued structure above all else and was averse to deviations from the tried and true. Nor was the show's content in doubt, since his opening remarks were already cued-up on the teleprompter, and his guest, General Pavel Illych Broden of the Russian Air Force, had arrived at the studio on schedule and was presently in the "green room," as the producers called it, getting ready for his appearance.

It was, rather, a question of style, of tone, that was occupying Pedachenko's mind right now. Should he deliver his commentary with his usual strident flair, or take a softer, cooler stance? His media consultants had advised the latter, suggesting he avoid anything that might be interpreted as pessimism at a time when viewers were emotionally geared for a celebration, longed to forget their hardships, and were in desperate need of inspiration from their leaders. On the other hand, what better occasion than the eve of the new millennium to stir their emotions? To remind them of the evils of internationalism, and the failure of governmental policies which had been passed down directly from Yeltsin to Starinov? To present himself as the only man to lead the country forward at a critical juncture in history?

Pedachenko thought about it. He was not someone to let an opportunity go to waste. But a little surface restraint might be a good idea. He would make it clear to his audience that there was room for hope and optimism as they stepped into the twenty-first century . . . *If* they followed along the path he was charting out for them.

"Sixty seconds!" the stage manager announced.

Pedachenko glanced at his image in the monitor. A handsome man of fifty with brush-cut blond hair, a carefully trimmed mustache above a mouth full of white teeth, and a build conditioned by frequent and rigorous exercise, he viewed his good looks chiefly as a tool, important for whatever competitive advantage they gave him rather than reasons of vanity. He had learned as a boy that a loose and easy smile could gain the indulgence of his parents and teachers, and later in life had found that same charming manner useful in attracting women to his bed, and ingratiating him with people of influence. He knew his acceptance as a media personality owed as much to his telegenic features as his political opinions, and it didn't bother him at all. What mattered was summoning up popular support any way he could. What mattered was getting what he wanted.

He motioned to a hot spot on his forehead and a makeup woman scurried from behind the camera, brushed some powder on it, then dashed off the set again.

The stage manager raised his hand and counted down the seconds to airtime, ticking them off with his fingers. "Four, three, two, one . . ."

Pedachenko looked at the camera.

"Friends and fellow citizens of the Russian land, good evening," he said. "As we join in preparing for a new century, I believe we would do well to look back a moment and stand in remembrance of history. And as we strive toward a greater future, let us allow ourselves to feel a noble rage at the slackness of authority that has damaged our national will, and caused so many of the problems that we—every one of us—must face. Two centuries ago, in the first Patriotic War, our soldiers fought against Napoleon's Grand Army and drove them from our capital in defeat. Earlier in our present century, we again mustered our courage, our determination as a people, to defend our soil from German fascists, overcoming them in what came to be known as the Great Patriotic War. Tonight, then, let us all commit to the final Patriotic War. It is a sacred war that will be fought not on the Field of Mars but a moral battleground; a war in which we are threatened not by guns and bombs, but by cultural stagnation and decadence. A war, my dear countrymen, that demands we examine our souls, stand by our cherished traditions, and fight temptation with iron discipline . . ."

". . . war that cannot be won by scampering after American dollars, or standing with our hands out for American bread crumbs like hopeless beggars, or letting our younger generation be corrupted by American fashion and music,'' Pedachenko was saying, his voice earnest and persuasive. ''I do not deny that things are bad, but we must take responsibility for ourselves . . .''

Watching him on the television screen in his office, Starinov had to give him credit. Grinding away at the same old themes, yet finding sensitive points in the national psyche that no one else in recent times had struck as effectively. His use of the phrases ''sacred war'' and ''noble rage,'' both allusions to the most famous military anthem of World War Two, was nothing less than brilliant. And repackaging his familiar political agenda as a new Patriotic War was an inspired, even sublime manipulation of simmering passions, evoking Russian pride at its deepest roots, likening his country's current problems to the hardships of the past, and placing the struggle to overcome them within the same context as legendary battles against foreign invaders . . . battles won, in each instance, only after the motherland fell back on its own resources, and its citizens and soldiers mobilized in an explosive uprising of solidarity.

Starinov inhaled, exhaled. He would never forget the May Day celebration of 1985, the fortieth anniversary of the victory against the Nazis—huge crowds gathered for the memorial ceremony at the Tomb of the Unknown Soldier in Alexander Park, the thunderous procession of soldiers and tanks and marching bands, the fireworks splashed across the sky over Red Square, the inspirational songs and waving Soviet banners, the groups of aged World War Two veterans passing in military lockstep, straight and dignified and somehow glorious despite their frailty . . .

Starinov had stood with General Secretary Mikhail
Gorbachev and other high-ranking Party officials that day
on a balcony of the Lenin Museum, observing the endless
parade, his eyes swelling with tears of pride, convinced
that in spite of the failings of Communism, in spite of its
social and economic problems, the Soviet Union would
stand strong and vital and unified as it advanced toward
the future.

He understood the appeal of Pedachenko's fervent rhetoric all too well, was even moved by it at a heartfelt level
he could not control, which was what made it so acutely
dangerous. Now, at the cusp of the new millennium, he
feared he was witnessing a Nationalistic revival that
would irretrievably set his country toward isolationism
and conflict with the West . . . and that was why his nights
had become such restless ordeals, his brief intervals of
sleep enmeshed in spidery nightmares from which he
would awaken in a cold sweat, his mouth filled with the
taste of dust and ashes.

On the television, Pedachenko had wrapped up his
commentary at last. He folded his hands on his desk and
leaned forward, smiling, his piercing blue eyes seeming
to look directly at the viewer. "Now, friends, I invite you
to phone the studio with your questions . . ."

"No thank you, *friend*," Starinov said. He thumbed the
off button on his remote control and Pedachenko abruptly
blinked into the void, his intrusive presence rejected—but
that wasn't quite true, now was it?

Unfortunately, Starinov thought, things were never that
easy. For outside the walls of his office, from one end of
the Federation to the next, Pedachenko was everywhere.

· · ·

"You're on the air."

"Good evening, Minister Pedachenko. I would like your opinion of Minister Bashkir's recent visit to China and his pledges of increased cooperation between our countries."

"Thank you, caller. I think we must look at the minister's intentions and specific agreements with China separately. In light of NATO enlargement and other recent efforts by the United States to monopolize world affairs, I would agree with him that we share many common interests with our Asian neighbor. American power is a menace that must be shackled, and to do it we have no choice but to turn eastward. But I believe Minister Bashkir was in foolish dereliction of duty when he announced plans to import Chinese technology and military products. Our own munitions plants, the best in the world, are suffering from decreased production orders. Furthermore, China has always been one of their largest customers. Why, then, should we reverse the arrangement now? It seems idiotic and misguided . . ."

In his *dacha* northeast of Moscow, Leonid Todshivalin had been dozing off to the sound of the television when the crash of breaking glass startled him into full awareness. He jerked around in his reclining chair and saw that one of the back windows had been shattered. Cold wind swept into the living room through the jagged remnants of the pane. Spears of glass were sprayed across the rug beneath the sill. In a corner of the floor, he noticed a large rock lying amid the shards. A folded piece of paper had been bound to it with a rubber band.

Pulling his bathrobe closed around him, Todshivalin sprang off the chair and hurried over to the window. He knelt to pick up the stone, careful not to step in the glass, cocking an eye out the window at his snow-covered yard. He didn't see anybody. But he thought he knew why the rock had been thrown.

He pulled off the rubber band and unfolded the slip of paper. Written on it in a large hand were two words:

BLOODSUCKING ASSHOLE

He felt a flash of anger. For two months his railroad had been relaying American grain deliveries bound from central warehouses in Moscow to the nearby western provinces. The amount shipped to each region was calculated according to population, and if not for his skimming off a portion of the reserves, his town's allotment would have been negligible. He had assumed the risk. Why then did he not deserve to make a small profit by adding a surcharge to the grain he distributed?

"Ingrates!" he shouted, lobbing the rock back out at his unseen harassers. "You've had too much to drink! Go away!"

There was no answer. He rose, cursing under his breath, thinking he had better clean up the mess. Somebody would pay for this. All he had wanted was to spend New Year's Eve relaxing in peace and quiet. Somebody would pay.

Todshivalin was starting toward the closet to get his broom when he heard a loud bang at the door. He halted suddenly, then turned and looked out across the backyard again. There were several sets of overlapping footprints in the snow. Had they been there before? He wasn't sure, and he supposed it really wasn't important. What mattered was that they swung around to the front of the house.

There was another bang on the door. Another. He shot his gaze at it, saw the hinges quivering.

"Get out of here!" he shouted. "Get out before I call the *polizei*!"

The door thudded and shook. Its bolt lock racketed in its socket. A spear of wood splintered off the jamb.

Todshivalin heard the dry rasp of his own breath. Beads of sweat had formed on his nose and forehead. He felt the hair on his scalp bristle at the nubs.

More drumming crashes at the door.

He stood in the entry hall for several breathless seconds and then decided to get his rifle from his bedroom closet. He had to do it fast, before the door buckled.

He lunged toward the bedroom and reached the entrance just as the door burst open, shaves of wood flying from its frame. His eyes cut back to the front of the house. Three men in stocking masks came surging in. Two were holding metal pipes. The third had a jerry can in his hand.

"You're all out of your minds!" Todshivalin screamed. "You can't do this! You—"

One of the men thrust himself at Todshivalin and swung a pipe across his middle. He collapsed like a ruptured accordion, the air whooshing out of his lungs. Now both of the men with pipes were standing over him, pounding him with blows. He raised his hands to protect his face and one of the pipes smashed his fingers. He grunted in pain and curled up on his side, whimpering, tucking his hands between his thighs.

The men continued beating him relentlessly, their pipes slamming his neck and face. They hit him in the mouth, knocking his front teeth down his throat. Blood gushed from his nose and an open gash on his cheek.

Tears spurting from his eyes, he saw the third man tilt

the jerry can forward. Something poured from its spout and the room filled with the stink of gasoline. The man moved quickly around the room with the can, dousing the curtains and furniture. Then he came over to where Todshivalin was lying and splashed some gasoline on his bathrobe

"Please, don't," he moaned weakly. His head spun and his mouth was swamped with blood. "I can . . . give . . . you . . . money . . . food . . ."

"*Shut up!*"

A pipe slammed Todshivalin just below the jawline and he emitted a high, choked whimper. Then the men stepped back from him. He caught a blurred glimpse of one of them pulling a lighter and a hank of cloth from his pocket, holding the lighter to the cloth, setting the cloth on fire.

"*Shliúkha,*" the man said through his mask.

And tossed the fiery swatch of cloth onto Todshivalin's gasoline-soaked robe.

He shrieked and writhed on the floor, flames leaping up his back, flashing hungrily as they enveloped his body.

Todshivalin heard footsteps pounding away from him, and then he was alone in the house, fire roaring in his ears, black smoke churning around the room. He was burning, burning! He heard a voice, started to cry out for help, but then realized it was only the television, Pedachenko still droning away in the background as the fire ate him alive. He tried to pull himself to his knees, rose about an inch off the floor, then sank back down under a ragged fringe of flame, his flesh searing with agony, thinking that they'd killed him, the bastards, the *bastards,* they'd—

• • •

"You're on the air."

"What I would like to ask, Minister Pedachenko, is your opinion of why the American grain has been so slow in becoming available. Some towns in the east have received a single truckload for hundreds of families to share. And where I live outside of Stary Oskol, we have seen none of it."

"A good question, my friend. As you know, there are members of our government who insist that political squabbles in the United States have been responsible for the irregular deliveries. But we might at least consider another explanation. Could it be the Americans have engaged in economic sabotage by deliberately having assistance reach us at a trickle? That their goal is to dominate us through long-term dependency? Sooner or later we must ask ourselves . . ."

Vince Scull glanced at the clock on the wall above him, and turned off the television. Enough was enough. He'd had about all he could take of Pedachenko's contrived outrage for one night. Even in Russia, a man was entitled to enjoy himself on New Year's Eve. Or at least keep the unwanted shit outside where it belonged.

He looked at the bland round face of the clock again. It was eight P.M. Meaning it was not yet noon in California, where his wife Anna—no, strike that—where his *ex*-wife Anna and their two daughters would be getting ready to celebrate the big event. If his memory was accurate, they were all going to Anna's mom's place in Mill Valley. He wondered if he should phone the kids there; probably they would be staying up till midnight to ring in the new year, century, millennium, and maybe another cosmic turning point or two Scull wasn't aware of.

Midnight in California, he thought. That was, what,

seven A.M. tomorrow his own time? Which would make it three A.M. in New York, where Scull's mother still lived, eighty-two years old and going strong. He guessed she'd be celebrating in her own fashion, watching the ball descend from the roof of One Times Square on television, a glass of wine on one side of her armchair, and a tray of cocktail weenies on the other.

Scull rose to get his coat. His private quarters here at the Kaliningrad installation—three rooms in a modular living and recreational building that housed over a hundred people—were boxy and claustrophobic, like something that had been made with a giant Erector set. He needed, really needed, some fresh air.

Zipping into his parka, Scull went to the door, hesitated with his hand on the knob, then turned back inside and entered the kitchenette. He stepped on the foot pedal that opened his tiny refrigerator, knelt in front of it, and eyed the bottle of Cristal on the upper shelf. He'd been planning to pop it at midnight, but what the hell, why wait? Surely midnight had already arrived somewhere in the world.

He pulled out the bottle, then reached into the shoe-box-sized freezer for a tulip glass he'd left in there to chill. It was funny when you got to thinking about time. Look up at some distant star in the sky, and what you were really seeing was the way it looked a few million years back. Turn that perspective on its head and it got even weirder—some alien skywatcher in a far-off system looking at Earth through a futuristic megatelescope would actually see dinosaurs walking through prehistoric jungles. All the human effort that had gone toward reconstructing a part of the past, the fossil digs, the scientific debate over how the monsters lived, whether T Rex was fast or slow, smart or dumb, whatever, and meanwhile Mork the Astronomer out in space would know the truth at a glance. For him, tonight was New Year's Eve 2000 going on a million years ago.

And it gets even weirder, doesn't it? Scull thought. *A million years from now, when there's nothing left of me except dust—if that much—an egghead on that same planet might see me leaving the building with my bottle of champagne, taking the walk I'm about to take. A million minus ten, and he'd see me and Anna on our first vacation together, a romantic cruise to the Caymans, most of which we spent in our cabin cooking up baby number one. A million minus one, though, and Mork would be witness to the sorry episode of Anna catching me with another woman, stupid, irresponsible fucking fool that I was.*

Scull sighed. The whole thing not only got his brain in a twist, but made him feel about as deep a shade of blue as there was on the color spectrum.

He uncorked the Cristal. Then he turned his champagne glass upside down over the neck of the bottle, and carried them back to the door.

His quarters were on the ground level of the building, and when he stepped through his doorway, he was gazing out across a large, flat field toward the complex's three spherical satellite receivers. Perched atop concrete platforms some three hundred yards distant, their angular metallic tiles gave them the appearance of huge, multifaceted gems.

For no particular reason, he started walking in their direction. The air was dry and bitterly cold, the ground frozen solid beneath a thin crust of hardpacked snow. Dense, unbroken woodland hemmed the field on three sides, with a single paved road giving egress through the forest on the eastern perimeter. The bare, ice-sheathed branches of the trees shone like delicately blown crystal in the clear winter night.

Scull stopped midway between the dwelling facility and the array of antennas, listening to the silence. Lights were on in most of the windows behind him, smudging the whitened ground with their reflections. Most of the crew would be at a party that a couple of the techies, Arthur and Elaine Steiner, were throwing in one of the rec rooms. The rest would be at smaller get-togethers in their rooms. And Anna and the kids were thousands of miles away.

He took his glass off the bottle, poured it half full of champagne, and then set the bottle down on the ground. That done, he stood there some more with the wind slashing at his cheeks, trying to think of a toast.

It was a while before anything appropriate came to him.

"May my vices die before I do," he said at last, and raised the glass to his lips.

FOURTEEN

GORDIAN LIFTED HIS FOOT OFF THE BRAKE ALMOST long enough for the tires of his Mercedes SL to make a complete rotation, then halted again and frowned impatiently. To say he was doing ten miles an hour in the bumper-to-bumper traffic would have been far too optimistic. Flanked by two huge semis in the center lane of I-280, he felt like a minnow caught between two stalled whales.

He checked his dash clock. Almost eight P.M.

Shit!

He reached into his sport coat for his flip phone and pressed in his home number.

"Yes?" his wife answered on the first ring.

"Hi, Ashley, it's me."

"Roger? Where are you? What's all that racket in the background?"

"I'm on my way home," he said. "And the noise is highway traffic."

There was silence on the phone. As Gordian had expected. He didn't try talking into it.

"Nice to see you're not cutting things too close," she said finally, her voice edged with sarcasm.

Gordian figured he'd deserved that. He looked out his windshield at the back of a Jeep Cherokee, saw a little white dog with a black bandit stripe across its eyes staring back at him through the window of the hatch.

"Listen, Ashley, I take this road all the time. If I'd known it would be this jammed tonight—"

"If not on New Year's Eve, then when else?" she said. "And do I have to remind you we have dinner reservations for nine o'clock?"

"I'll call the restaurant, see if they can switch our reservation to ten," he said, knowing how stupid his offer sounded even before it left his mouth. As his wife had just pointed out, it was New Year's Eve. Trader Vic's would be booked solid.

Gordian waited for her answer. Nothing moved on the congested road. The dog in the Cherokee nuzzled the window and continued watching him.

"Don't bother," she said. Her sarcasm had curdled into anger. "I'm standing here in my good dress, ready to leave the house. Damn it, you gave me your word you'd be on time."

Gordian felt his stomach sink. He was thinking that he had not only given her his word, but he'd also very much intended to keep it. With most of his staff having left early for the holiday, however, he'd decided to play catch-up with his paperwork in the rare absence of distractions, figuring he could leave for home at six-thirty and be there within an hour. Why hadn't he allowed for the possibility that he'd get stuck in traffic?

"Honey, I'm sorry. I wanted to get some odds and ends done—"

"Sure. As always. To the exclusion of anything remotely connected to a personal life," she said, and took an audible breath. "I'm not going to argue this over the phone, Roger. I won't be reduced to the role of a nagging wife. And we've been through it all before, anyway."

Gordian couldn't think of anything to say. The silence in his earpiece had a barren, hollow sound. Ashley had been talking about a separation for the past several months. He never knew what to say to that, either. Other than to tell her he loved her, didn't want her to leave, and was surprised she felt things were so bad between them that she would even *consider* leaving.

There was a mild surge in traffic. It started in the left lane, where one of the flanking trucks hissed and rumbled forward as its driver released its air brakes. Then the Jeep began to move and Gordian toed the accelerator.

He figured he'd gained about a car length of blacktop before the taillights of the Jeep flickered on and he had to brake behind it.

"I don't think I'd better be home when you get here," Ashley said.

"Honey . . ."

"No, Roger," she said. "Don't. Not now."

Gordian's stomach dropped some more. He knew from the flatness of her tone that there wouldn't be any further discussion. She had closed up tight.

"I need some room," she said. "It can only make things worse if we see each other tonight."

"Where are you going to be?"

"I'm not sure yet. I'll call you later and let you know," she said.

And hung up.

Click.

Gordian held the phone to his ear for almost a full minute after the line went dead, then finally slipped it back into his pocket.

He leaned back against the seat rest and rubbed his forehead, expelling a tired, resigned sigh.

No reason I need to hurry home now, he thought.

In front of him, the little dog with its face in the window had started barking and wagging its tail. Or looked like it was barking, anyway, since he couldn't actually hear it through two panes of glass and the drone of several hundred idling motors.

Gordian held his hand up and waved and the dog swished its tail back and forth more rapidly.

"Happy New Year," he said to the interior of his car.

FIFTEEN

NEW YORK CITY
DECEMBER 31, 1999

11:40 P.M.

ON AN UPPER STORY OF A SLEEK STEEL-AND-GLASS OF-
fice tower at Forty-fourth Street and Broadway, a group
of German executives from the international magazine
empire Fuchs Inc. had gathered behind floor-to-ceiling
windows to watch the proceedings below. Well in advance of their holiday visit, office space used by their
American editorial staff had been converted into an ob-
servatory/banquet area that included plush lounge chairs,
high-magnification telescopes, a wet bar, and gourmet
hors d'oeuvres served by a white-glove waiter staff. Also
prior to their arrival, a memo instructing employees to
leave the building early on New Year's Eve had circulated
down through the corporate hierarchy. It was their express
wish that the observation deck be inaccessible to Americans, regardless of their positions in the company. The
spectacle taking place in Times Square, so oddly crass and
colorful, was one the foreign management wanted to
view—and comment upon—in secure, uninterrupted pri-
vacy.

While the hectic New Year's Eve gathering might be
an American tradition, the German businessmen, who had
poured millions of dollars into glossing up the district,
felt it was theirs alone to enjoy from on high.

11:43 P.M.

A large outdoor parade stand had been erected on the concrete island occupying the middle of the square from Forty-second Street to roughly Forty-third Street, the military recruiting office and benches that normally stood in that area having been uprooted prior to the festivities by the mayor's New Year's 2000 Organizing Committee. It was here that the mayor and other public officials stood with their families, friends, political patrons, and a smattering of entertainers, making speeches, waving to the crowd, leading cheers of "I love New York!," smiling to camera lenses, and urging people to have a good time while please, please, *please* remaining considerate of the guy with his elbow in your ribs and his hand on your girlfriend's fanny. Overlooking the street on the uptown side of One Times Square, the Panasonic Astrovision Giant Display Screen, which had replaced the Sony Jumbotron Screen in 1996, and been leased to the NBC television network shortly thereafter, flashed enormous images of everyone on the stand across 890 square feet of pixels, so that all in the crowd could bask in their charismatic nearness.

Seated beside his wife and daughter on the platform—where a famous, born-on-the-lower-east-side comedian had just begun snapping off one-liners at the mike—Police Commissioner Bill Harrison felt like a cold piece of meat on a makeshift smorgasbord. Any minute now somebody was going to flip the damn thing over on its side, and the starving rabble would feast.

He looked around skeptically, wishing he could be more confident of the precautions that had been taken for the safety of the big shots on exhibit, not to mention the safety of his wife and daughter, who had cheerfully (and against his protestations) insisted on accompanying him to this fiasco. Half the City Hall establishment, and enough stars to fill a week's worth of *Entertainment Tonight* programs, were in attendance. Despite the transparent bulletproof shields protecting the speakers, despite the constellation of uniformed officers, plainclothes detectives, and private bodyguards surrounding the stand, despite the mounted cops, bomb-sniffing dogs, and rooftop surveillance teams sweeping the scene, despite the endless hashing over of Operation 2000's details by its planners, there was still room for something nasty to slip through the net. With over a dozen crosstown streets and every major subway line in the city feeding into the neighborhood, how could it be otherwise?

As his eyes continued making their circuit of the immediate area, they fell briefly on the Emergency Services Unit's One-Truck, parked in close proximity to the VIP stand on Forty-second Street. Besides being chock full of rescue and tactical equipment, the big, bulky vehicle was loaded with firepower ranging from Ruger Mini-14s to 12-gauge Ithaca shotguns to belt fed Squad Automatic Weapons to M16s equipped with grenade tubes and multipurpose ammunition. Behind it on standby were two smaller Radio Emergency Patrol trucks, a surveillance van, a temporary headquarters vehicle, and a bomb truck.

Harrison took more than a little comfort in knowing that the elite ESU personnel were trained to respond to virtually any crisis; if something bad went down, they would be able to meet the challenge of coping with it head-on. But response wasn't the same as prevention, and Oklahoma City loomed darkly over his thoughts tonight, reminding him that it only took a second for hundreds of innocent lives to be lost.

"Is that Dick Clark?" Rosetta said, pointing toward a sudden swirl of activity near the stand. "By those TV cameras over there?"

He sat forward, craning his head.

"Don't think so," he said. "That guy looks too old."

"You never know, Bill. He'd have to be around seventy by now."

"Dick Clark stopped aging at thirty," he said. "Unlike your poor bedraggled husband, whose energies are on the wane as we speak, and who will be sleeping like a rock the moment his head hits the pillow tonight."

"Is that so?"

"My days as a late-night party animal are behind me, sweetheart," he said.

She put her hand on his thigh and let it rest there, a slanted little smile on her lips, her eyes glinting in the way that never failed to make his throat tighten and his heart skip a beat.

Tonight was no exception.

He looked at her with surprise, catching his breath.

"Like I said, old man, you never know," she said.

11:45 P.M.

"Yo, cuz, you got jelly donuts?"

The bearded vender lifted his eyes from his wristwatch and shook his head.

"How 'bout custard?"

"No more."

Des Sanford looked over at his friend, Jamal. Jamal looked back at him and shrugged. Both teenagers were wearing hooded sweatshirts with knit caps underneath. Both also happened to be very confused by this white guy who you'd think would be interested in making a buck here tonight, but didn't seem to have shit to sell. A minute ago they'd smoked a little ganja, caught themselves a buzz, and then zipped straight over to his stand, figuring something sweet would go down fine. Maybe a couple coffees to get the chill out of their bones.

Des rubbed his hands together for warmth. Why the fuck couldn't New Year's be in July?

"Don't be tellin' us there ain't no chocolate sprinkle," he said. "I mean, you *gotta* have chocolate sprinkle."

"Sold out," the vender told the teenagers, glancing at his watch.

Des poked a finger under his cap and scratched his forehead. He swore to God, if he lived to be a hundred, he'd never get these white dudes, didn't matter if they came from the Bronx or had some kind of foreign accent like this one. Man has himself some prime turf, southeast corner of Forty-second Street, right under the building with the big screen, right where the ball gonna come droppin' from the roof any minute now, and what's he do but stand there concentrating on his watch like he had someplace better to be, telling people he's out of this, that and the other thing.

Des leaned forward and read the name on his vender's license.

"Julius, m'man, maybe you oughtta try tellin' us what you *do* have."

The vender nodded vaguely toward the sparse row of plain and powdered donuts on the upper shelf of his cart.

Des blew air through his compressed lips, making a small sound of disgust. Not only did the donuts look stale, but he was positive they had come out of a box.

"Eats like that, you know, we coulda bought at the deli," he said. "Sign on your stand be sayin' *fresh* donuts.

I mean, how you be cleaned out when it ain't even midnight yet?''

The vender looked at Des, his blue eyes holding on him, seeming to stare right through him. Then he reached under the counter.

Des looked at Jamal again, puzzled, wondering if he'd gone too far razzing the guy, if this was some kind of crazy mutha had a problem with black people, maybe kept a piece tucked away under his apron just in case somebody mouthed off to him. Jamal was asking himself the same thing, and was about to suggest that they move on when the vender's hand reappeared holding a brown paper bag.

"Here," he said, stuffing the handful of donuts on display into the bag, then crunching the bag shut and holding it out to Des. "No charge."

Des looked at him tentatively.

"You sure, man?"

The vender nodded and stretched his hand farther out over the counter, shoving the bag against Des's chest.

"Take them," he said. "Last chance."

Des grabbed the donuts. He had a feeling that if he hadn't, the dude would have just opened his hand and let the bag drop to the sidewalk.

"Uh, thanks," he said, and glanced up at the Astrovision Screen. It showed a closeup of the mayor, who was giving his rap from that stand in the middle of the street, working up to his countdown, talking all kinds of shit about New York City being an example to the world, millions of people in Times Square, everybody having a good time, everybody getting along, peace, brotherhood, togetherness, and please don't drink and drive. Not a word in his speech about donut guys that didn't have any donuts, but what the hell, this was a party. Below his face, the time was being displayed in bright red numbers, 11:50 now, ten minutes and counting to the Big 21.

Des had to admit, he felt *pumped.*

"C'mon, let's move back come. I wanna get a good look at the ball when it come down," he said, turning to Jamal.

Jamal nodded. He looked at the vender, acknowledged the freebie he'd given them with a halfhearted little dip of his chin, then started walking off with his friend.

The vender watched them brush against a woman in a black leather coat and beret who was approaching the stand, pause to apologize while eyeing her up and down, then vanish into the crowd.

"Enjoy yourselves," he muttered.

11:47 P.M.

Shouldering past the two black kids, Gilea moved up to the donut stand and looked across the counter at Akhad.

"Are you sold out?" she asked.

He nodded. "I was just closing."

"Too bad," she said.

"There should be other venders," he said. "They also sell donuts."

"I've seen them around."

"Good," he said. "Then you shouldn't have any problems."

"No, I shouldn't."

She stuffed her hands into her coat. In her right pocket was a radio transmitter roughly the size and shape of a lipstick tube—and identical to one Akhad was carrying as a fail-safe. One clockwise twist would send a coded-frequency signal to a receiver/initiator inside the donut stand, detonating the sheets of C-4 explosive sandwiched between thin aluminum panels along its front, back, and sides. Separate blocks of plastique totaling over a hundred pounds in weight had been packed behind the doors of its storage compartments. In addition to the C-4, the compartments contained thousands of tiny nails and ball bearings. Dispersed in every direction by the blast, the shrapnel would buffet the area for hundreds of yards, exponentially compounding the destructive force of the explosion, chewing through human flesh like buckshot through tissue paper. While an independent electronic blasting cap had been wired to each compartment, all of the wires threaded into the same firing system, so that the ignition of the charges—and the release of their deadly projectiles—would be simultaneous.

And that would only be the beginning.

Gilea checked the watch on her right hand, her opposite hand still in her pocket, the transmitter still nestled within it.

"Almost midnight, I'd better be on my way, " she said, her eyes meeting Akhad's. "Thank you for your help."

"Sure," he said. "Good night."

She smiled, turned, and strode toward the south side of the block.

Akhad took a deep breath and checked his own watch. He himself would be leaving the booth in exactly two minutes—and that was none too soon.

He wanted to be as far away as possible when the area turned into a shrieking, flaming pit out of deepest hell.

11:48 P.M.

". . . take our viewers live to Times Square, where Fox TV's own Taylor Sands has been in the thick of things all night. Taylor, what's it like out there?"

"Jessica, the temperature might be dropping fast, but that hasn't kept the number of people in the square from going up—and to quote the Buster Poindexter song, they are feeling hot, hot, *hot*. A few moments ago, a representative from the NYPD told me the crowd has exceeded all predictions, and may well top three million in the final count . . . and let me tell you, from where I stand, it is virtually impossible to see an inch of pavement that isn't occupied. Yet everybody seems to be having fun, and so far there have been only a few minor incidents requiring police attention."

"Taylor, the mayor really seems to be—"

"I'm sorry, Jessica, could you repeat that? As you can probably hear, people already have their noisemakers out, and it's getting a little hard to hear you . . ."

"I was just saying that the mayor appears to be playing the part of master of ceremonies to the hilt."

"That's right. He's been saying a few words to the crowd before leading them in the final New Year's countdown of the century, and just moments ago put on a red-and-gold foil top hat with crepe paper streamers. The word is, incidentally, that he's going to be joined onstage by the legendary musician and songwriter Rob Zyman, whose song 'The World's A' Gonna Change' became the anthem of an entire generation, and who, as you may know, rose to stardom in the streets of New York's own Greenwich Village. Also expected is a reunion between Zyman and his occasional collaborator Joleen Reese. This promises to be amazing!"

"It sure does, Taylor. Thanks for your report. We're going to cut away for a brief commercial break, but will be back to resume our live coverage of New Year's 2000 in just sixty seconds . . ."

11:50 P.M.

Sadov reached the end of the tiled corridor in the IND station at Fiftieth Street and Rockefeller Center, then climbed the stairs leading up to the sidewalk, taking his time, in no rush to arrive at his destination. He had gotten off an uptown B train fifteen minutes earlier and lingered on a bench on the subway platform, pretending to wait for a connecting train until he felt it was time to move. If he had chosen to, he could have come by one of the lines that ran closer to Times Square—but Gilea had pointed out that security would be tighter in and around those stations, and there was no sense taking unnecessary chances.

He saw a strip of night sky between the crenellated rooftops beyond the stairwell exit, and then cold air came sweeping over him and he was out on the street.

Even here, two long avenues west of the square, he could hear shouts of excitement and whoops of laughter bubbling up above muddier layers of sound, a dense torrent of human voices rushing between the high office towers on either side of him.

He turned north on Sixth Avenue, then continued at an unhurried pace, his leather jacket creaking a little as he adjusted the shoulder strap of his athletic bag. The bag was dark blue nylon, very inconspicuous. Still, the police had set up sawhorses at the intersections, and it was likely they would conduct spot inspections of carry bags and packages. The plan, therefore, was for Sadov to wait outside the checkpoint at the northeast corner of Seventh Avenue and Fifty-third Street until the primary explosion drew their attention elsewhere. Only then would he briefly join the surging press of bodies and drop his bag. At the same time, Gilea's man Korut, along with two of Nick

Roma's soldiers, would do the same at the other three corners of the square. Each of their satchel charges was on a ten-minute time-delay fuse and would detonate at the height of the crowd's confusion.

Those within the kill zones would be ripped to shreds. Hundreds, possibly thousands, more would be injured during the pandemonium, trampled by the stampeding herd of humanity. And the screams of the dead and the dying would echo over streets awash in blood.

Sadov swung west on Fifty-third and looked up ahead, where a blue-and-white police barricade stood crosswise in the middle of the street, a huddle of uniformed officers around it, laughing, talking, standing with their arms crossed over their chests and very little to do but collect their overtime pay.

Slowing in the long shadow of an office building, Sadov checked his watch. In mere minutes, he thought, the policemen would have their hands *full* of things to do. Whatever the final number of casualties in the bombings, this night would be remembered ten centuries later, as the world turned toward yet another new millennium, and common minds filled with dread of things to come, and the leaders of nations yet unborn wondered what sins might have inspired such awesome rage.

11:51 P.M.

On loan from the FAA at the police commissioner's personal request, the bomb detection team had brought two of their best dogs to the scene. Fay, whose name was an obvious homage to her organizational keepers, was a five-year-old black Labrador that had sniffed out suitcase bombs at Kennedy International Airport four times in the past two years. Hershey, a Doberman retriever, had used his phenomenally sensitive nose to set off a red light at the Republican Convention the previous summer, preventing a catastrophic explosion by alerting security personnel to a chunk of A-3 plastic that had been concealed in a vase of flowers on the speaker's platform. Though generally regarded as the smartest dog on the team, Hershey's greatest weakness was a tendency to be sidetracked by the smell of chocolate . . . hence, the origin of *his* name.

Agent Mark Gilmore had been with the FAA's civil security branch for a dozen years, and had been a canine handler almost half that long. He loved the dogs and knew their outstanding capabilities, but was also highly sensitive to their limitations. And from the outset, he had been concerned that his current assignment just wasn't doable.

The bomb dogs were most effective at searching relatively closed-in areas, or at least areas in which distractions could be kept to a minimum, such as jetliner cabins, airport baggage holds, hotel rooms, and, as in the case of the Republican convention, empty auditoriums. The more sensory input they were hit with, the greater the chance they would be fooled or simply wander off track. Large spaces with open access and lots of hubbub diminished their ability to fix on the minute olfactory traces of explosive chemicals. Times Square on a normal night would be tricky; tonight, when it seemed like a cross between a mosh pit and the Mardi gras, it would be overwhelming— a hectic, blaring jumble of sights, sounds, and odors.

Basic movement was another difficulty. Earlier in the night, when the crowd was much thinner, the dogs still had had some roving room. Now, however, the crush was all but impenetrable and they were getting stressed. Which meant keeping them on a short leash, and narrowing their range to cordoned-off peripheries, like the restricted zone around the VIP stand.

A further problem for Gilmore was making sure the excited animals didn't become dehydrated, a condition that could throw their systems into shock, even kill them, within minutes if it were severe enough. At 150 pounds each, they needed plenty to drink to prevent their revved-up canine metabolisms from overheating. Mindful of this, Gilmore had brought several gallon jugs of water in the bomb-detection van parked outside One Times Square, and the panting dogs had led him in that direction twice in the last hour.

He had been standing to one side of the stage, watching Rob Zyman and Joleen Reese take their places beside the mayor, when he noticed Fay tugging at the leash again. This had gotten him kind of disappointed. In these last few moments before the countdown, he had wanted to stick close to the worn but not worn-out folkies for a reason that was, he had to admit, not entirely professional. Gilmore had been a Zyman fan since his older brother had come home with his first album, *Big City Ramble*, back in the late sixties and, Zyman's public appearances being few and far between nowadays, he'd figured this might be his last chance to see him perform before he slung his battered Gibson guitar over his shoulder and rambled off down the lonesome highway. Even if all he did was sing a verse or two of "Auld Lang Syne" in his famed and often-parodied sandpaper rasp, Gilmore had figured it would be an event worth catching.

But then Fay had started panting and tugging, signaling him in no uncertain terms that she needed her radiator filled.

Now he was making for the van with the dogs out

ahead of him on about six inches of leash, staying inside the area that had been cleared below the stage, Fay's tongue hanging halfway to the pavement. Hershey, in this instance, had stayed on the job, his head slouched low, sniffing this way and that, acting as if he'd gone along with his partner just out of canine chivalry.

Suddenly, thirty feet or so from where the van was parked, Hershey stopped dead in his tracks and turned to the left—toward the crowd—whining and barking, his triangular ears angling back against his head. Gilmore looked down at him, puzzled. The dog was frantic. Odder still, Fay was also barking like crazy, facing in the same direction as Hershey, her thirst seemingly forgotten.

Unease creeping up on him, Gilmore added more slack to the leash. The dogs began pulling to the left, hunting further, almost leading him into a collision with the horizontal plank of a police barricade. He made them heel with a sharp command, then steered them to a gap between two sawhorses, his eyes scanning the crowd.

All he could see was people. Thousands and thousands of them, crammed so close together they seemed to form a single amorphous organism. Most were looking at the stage or the Panasonic screen in anticipation of the countdown, now less than ten minutes away.

Then Gilmore spotted the vender's booth about ten feet up ahead at the corner of Forty-second Street, the words "FRESH DONUTS" emblazoned across its front in big block letters. His gaze might have passed over it except for a couple of curious things: the glass display cases were empty, and the vender was exiting it through a side door in what appeared to be something of a hurry.

He glanced back down at Fay and Hershey, both of

whom had raised their hackles and were staring straight at the donut booth.

Warning bells went off in Gilmore's head. Not loud ones, at first—he still thought it very possible that Hershey had picked up the smell of nothing more deadly than a leftover chocolate donut, and that Fay was simply getting swept up in his food fervor—but the ringing was insistent enough to make him want to go investigate.

He let Fay and Hershey lead him forward again. They went for the booth like homing missiles, growling, the whites of their eyes showing large. Intimidated by their size and agitated behavior, the sea of revelers parted to let them through.

As they came within a yard of him, the vender halted between the snarling dogs and the booth, his eyes dropping to look at them, then leaping up to Gilmore.

"Excuse me, sir," Gilmore said, looking steadily at him. The dogs were yanking at the leash so hard he thought they would wrench his shoulder from its socket. "Would you mind stepping aside a moment? I'd like to have a peek at your booth."

The vender stared at him.

"Why?"

"Just routine," Gilmore said.

The guy stood there, his eyes flicking between Gilmore and the dogs. Gilmore observed that a sheen of perspiration had formed on his cheeks above his beard.

"I'm busy packing up," the vender said. Licking his lips. "I don't understand what you want from me."

"Sir," Gilmore said, his internal bells of alarm clanging stridently now, "I'm afraid you're going to have to move out of my way."

The guy stood there.

Swallowed twice.

Then he shoved his left hand into his coat pocket.

"Go fuck yourself, American," he said.

And pulled a small cylindrical object from his pocket and gave one end of it a twist with his left hand.

Gilmore started to reach for his sidearm, but never got the chance to draw it from its holster.

Insofar as what happened next, however, that really made no difference at all.

11:55 P.M.

The cop in the ESU radio surveillance van had enough time to notice a blip in his monitoring equipment, some kind of low-frequency transmission in the thirty-to-fifty-megahertz range—less than you might pick up from a pager or cellular phone, but much more than you'd get out of an electronic car-door opener of the sort drivers carried as key-chain fobs.

He turned to his partner on the stool beside him, figuring it was sufficiently unusual to be worth mentioning.

"Gene," he said, "what do you ma—?"

The roar of the blast sucked the words out of his mouth as the van, its crew, and everything else in it were vaporized by a sweeping wave of fire.

11:55 P.M.

On the corner of Sixth Avenue and Forty-second Street, Gilea had been waiting for midnight, her detonator tucked in her palm, when the explosion filled the sky with unimaginable brilliance. The sound of it came next, rolling over her with physical force, hammering her eardrums, sending tremors through her bones, shaking the ground under her feet. Car and burglar alarms began howling everywhere around her. Windows shattered in office buildings up and down the avenue.

Akhad, she thought, her heart racing, the metallic taste of adrenaline flooding her mouth.

Breathless with exhilaration, Gilea reached out to steady herself against a wall, facing west toward Times Square, her eyes reflecting jags of light from the red-orange mountain of flame rising above it.

"Magnificent," she muttered. "My God, it is magnificent."

SIXTEEN

IT WAS FIVE MINUTES PAST MIDNIGHT IN NEW YORK.

Where the television cameras had been quick-cutting between scenes of raucous celebration in Times Square, they now showed a mass of orange flame, shot with glare, bulging upward within a spray of smaller blazes that, viewed from above, resembled glowing matches scattered across a dark tabletop.

Matches, Roger Gordian thought. *If that were only the case.*

His face ashen, horror and disbelief slapping through his brain, he gripped the armrest of his sofa with a hand that would not stop trembling. The glass of Courvoisier that had slipped from his fingers lay overturned on the floor, a wet purple splotch soaking into the carpet around it. He was oblivious to the spreading stain, oblivious to the fact that he had dropped the glass, oblivious to everything but the unfolding tragedy on the screen.

Five past midnight.

Ten minutes ago, the people of the world had been about to greet the new century as if they were gathered at the railroad station to watch the circus roll into town—but instead something that looked much more like the Apocalypse had come thundering down the track. And strangely, in those first numbing instants after the blast, Gordian had tried to resist the truth of what had happened, pushing back against its intrusion, trying to make himself believe it was all a mistake, that some technician at the television station had hit the wrong switch, run some god-awful disaster film instead of the Times Square broadcast.

But he'd never been one to duck reality for very long, especially when it was coming on broadside.

Now, a pulverized expression on his features, he stood motionless, holding onto the couch for support, holding on as though the floor had tilted sharply underneath him. Yet as he stared at the television, largely overcome with shock, a small part of his mind continued to function on an analytical level, automatically interpreting the images in front of him, adjusting for scale, calculating the extent of the destruction. It was an ability—some might have called it a curse—he had brought home from Vietnam and, like a black-box flight recorder aboard an aircraft, that embedded observational mechanism would keep working even if the rest of him were emotionally totaled.

The fire at the bottom left looks like it could be a building. A large one. And above it, the bright teardrop-shaped spot there, that's an extremely hot flame, reflecting a lot of light. Probably ignited gasoline and metal . . . a burning vehicle of some kind, then. Not a car, but more likely a truck or a van. Maybe even a bus.

Gordian drew in a long, shaky breath, but still didn't think he could move without tripping over his own feet. Standing there with the television flashing its nightmarish overhead view of Times Square, and the news anchor stammering off disconnected snippets of information about what had happened, he remembered Vietnam, remembered the bombing runs, remembered the flames dotting the jungle like angry red boils. Whether playing tag with a Russian surface-to-air missile or looking down at a VC bunker that had just become the recipient of a five-hundred-pound bomb, he had known how to read the fiery dots and dashes of aerial warfare as signs of success, failure, or danger. He supposed he'd never expected that skill would be of use to him in civilian life, and right now would have given anything not to have found out he was wrong.

The strew of tiny dots, they're bits and pieces of mixed debris. And that mottled black-and-red area where smoke is roiling up the thickest, that's got to be ground zero.

Gordian forced himself to concentrate on the CNN report. The anchorwoman's voice seemed dim and distant, although he knew the volume on his set was turned up high enough to be audible several rooms over. Lonely, missing Ashley, he'd been listening to the New Year's 2000 coverage from the den, where he'd gone to pour himself a brandy, and had heard what he had heard loud and clear.

Ashley, he thought. She had phoned at ten to say she was staying with her sister in San Francisco, and he briefly considered calling her there now. But what would he say? That he didn't want to be alone at a time like this? That he ached for the comforting warmth of someone he loved? Given how he'd been ignoring her almost all the time lately, his need seemed a selfish, unfair thing.

Focus on the reporter. You don't want to lose what she's saying.

". . . again, I want to remind you that what we are seeing is live video from atop the Morgan Stanley Tower at Forty-fifth Street and Broadway. I'm being told the ABC television network, which had been broadcasting from that location, is permitting it to be used as a pool camera by the rest of the news media until other transmissions can be restored in the area. There are no pictures coming out of Times Square at street level . . . whatever happened has caused extensive equipment damage . . . and while there are unconfirmed reports that the explosion was caused by a bomb, we want to caution you that there is no, I repeat, *no* evidence at all that it was a nuclear device, as stated by a commentator on one of the other networks. Word from the White House is that the President is expected to make a televised statement within the hour . . .''

Gordian felt an icy finger touch his spine as he suddenly recalled a phrase he hadn't used, or heard anyone else use, in many years: *Spooky's working.* It was yet another special delivery coming to him from the Vietnam of thirty years ago. The Spookies had been AC-47s mounted with 7.62mm machine guns that would stalk enemy positions in the black of night, unleashing sustained curtains of fire at a rate of six thousand rounds a minute, every third or fourth round a tracer. While American ground troops at a distance would find reassurance in the solid red wall of illumination that had poured down from the unseen aircraft, Charlie, huddled in his trenches, had been terrified by those firing missions. For him, it must have felt as if Heaven itself were venting its wrath. As if there were no safety anywhere.

''. . . Wait, just a moment,'' the anchor was blurting, her hand held to her earpiece. ''I hear now that the governor of New York has issued a general curfew in the city and that it will be strictly enforced by police as well as National Guard units. Repeating what I just said, a curfew has gone into effect throughout the five boroughs of New York . . .''

Ah God, Gordian thought. *Ah, God.*

Tonight, in America, Spooky was working.

SEVENTEEN

POLICE COMMISSIONER BILL HARRISON NEVER HEARD the blast that killed his wife.

There were, however, many other memories of that terrible event—far too many—that would haunt him as long as he lived.

He would remember sitting beside Rosetta on the VIP platform, holding her hand, one bemused eye on the folk-singing duo that had joined the mayor center stage, the other having been snagged by a couple of FAA bomb-sniffing dogs making a commotion some yards to his right. He would remember spotting a vender's stand over there, and thinking wryly that the dogs had caught a whiff of something far less lethal than an explosive, unless they happened to be on diets that prohibited vanilla custard donuts and such. But then he'd noticed the serious look on the K-9 officer's face, noticed his body language as he spoke to the man in the vender's smock, and become more concerned. He had been doing police work for a quarter century, and started out his career as a foot patrolman in upper Manhattan, and he knew the cautious, attentive habits cops observed when approaching suspicious persons.

He's staying about eight, ten feet in front of the guy so he can watch his movements, watch his hands, making sure they stay in sight, Harrison had thought. *And he's keeping his own hand near his sidearm.*

Harrison would always remember feeling his stomach slip toward the ground when he saw the vender reach into his pocket, then saw the cop reaching for his weapon. Always remember his sudden fear, and the sense that time was accelerating, running much too fast, like a movie video that had been fast-forwarded in the middle of a critical scene. And then his gaze had swung to the Panasonic screen above him, and he'd noted the time display read 11:56, and thought, *Four minutes, midnight on the head, that's when they'd want to do it all right, unless something happens that makes them get to it faster.*

He would always remember whipping his head around toward Rosetta and his daughter, Tasheya, thinking he had to get them off the stage, get them away from there, and then his fingers had tightened around his wife's hand and he'd risen off his chair, pulling at her arm with wild urgency, and she had given him a surprised, questioning look, she had mouthed the words "What's wrong?"—but before he could give her an answer everything had dissolved into a blinding flash of nova brilliance, and he'd felt a blast of superheated air smack his body, felt the ground rattle and tremble, felt himself being hurled off his feet, tumbling helplessly in that hellish, searing bright light, and he'd held onto Rosie's hand, held onto Rosie's hand, held onto Rosie's hand—

Then suddenly the enveloping brightness peeled apart, and the heat, though high, was no longer a solid thing. Harrison became aware that he was still on the stand, sprawled on his side, his left cheek mashed into a rough, splintery nest of debris. His face felt wet, sticky, and the world seemed to have gone into a sickening tilt. Somehow his feet were higher up than his head.

There was fire and smoke all around him. Broken glass

was hailing down from above. Sirens shrilled into the night and there were people everywhere, many of them bloody and motionless, others running, crawling, screaming, wailing, crying out to one another. Everywhere.

Harrison heard loud crashes from somewhere, heard the groan of buckling metal above him. He realized dimly that the platform had collapsed near the middle, its ends pitching downward and inward, accounting for his weird, dizzy angle. It was as if he were lying on a slantboard. Flames were crackling and spitting up through the planks, and the once-neat rows of folding chairs had been thrown about and upended, scattered like the pieces in a game of jacks. Huge blocks of concrete stretched endlessly across a zone of devastation that looked more like a moonscape than Times Square.

Harrison saw a gigantic toadstool of fire throbbing and churning somewhere off to his right, realized it was swelling out of a huge crater, an actual *crater*, and instantly decided that must have been where the vender's booth had been, where that cop and his dogs had been standing, where the detonation had occurred . . .

Somehow that thought jerked his mind out of the hazy suspension of shock in which it had drifted for the first seconds after the blast, and an incredible realization descended upon him with anvil force—he had not yet checked on Rosie or Tasheya.

Until now only half-conscious of the position in which he'd landed, Harrison realized that his left hand was stretched out behind him, and that it was still gripping his wife's smaller, far softer hand.

"Rosie?" he groaned weakly.

There was no answer.

"*Rosie . . . ?*"

Still no answer.

Harrison forced himself to move. The grate of complaining metal overhead had become louder and more ominous, jolting him with a fresh sense of fear and dismay. He rolled over stiffly toward his wife, groaning her name again, afraid to ask himself why she had not yet answered.

"Rosie, are you—"

His sentence broke off as he saw her lying on her back, one eye closed, the other one staring blankly upward from a face that was covered with blood and cement dust, giving it the appearance of a ghastly Kabuki mask. Her hair was in disarray and there was a dark, murky puddle of wetness around the back of her head. Except for the arm he was clinging to, she was buried under a dune of jumbled wreckage from her neck to her waist.

He couldn't see her breathing.

"Honey, please, *please*, we've got to get out of here, find Tasheya. You have to get up . . ."

She didn't move. The dead expression on her face didn't change.

Frantic, knowing in his heart that she was gone, that any human being would have to be crushed under a pile of rubble that huge, Harrison climbed up on one knee and tugged at her arm, tugged at it almost savagely, tugged at it with sobs choking his throat and tears streaming down his cheeks.

It came away from her body on the fifth tug, severed above the elbow, leaving a jagged shoot of bone protruding from her buried shoulder.

Harrison stared down at her, his eyes feverishly wide in their sockets.

It took a moment for his unwilling mind to fully absorb what had happened.

And then he began to scream.

• • •

In every explosion, there is a violent outward rush of air, followed by a rapid compression as the hungry vacuum draws the displaced air back toward its center. This is the principle by which demolition experts will set off charges of HMX, TNT, and ammonium nitrate inside buildings to make them collapse upon themselves. The larger the initial release of energy, the more significant this effect can be, and the suction after the Times Square blast was enormous—blowing out windows, tearing doors off their hinges, bringing down steel scaffoldings, toppling walls, lifting motor vehicles off the ground, and pulling human beings into its monstrous throat as if they weighed nothing at all. Eyewitnesses to the catastrophe would later compare the sound of the inrushing air to that of a train moving toward them at top speed.

Above the VIP platform on Forty-second Street, the tortured groan of metal grew louder with each passing moment as the Astrovision display's structural supports, badly damaged from the force of the detonation, and further weakened by the subsequent vacuum effect, continued to bend and twist past their tolerance.

Within seconds of the bombing, the giant television had tilted sideways on the uptown face of One Times Square, where it hung like a crooked picture frame, hundreds of pounds of glass spilling from its shattered screen and fluorescent discharge tubes. The broken glass poured down onto the street in a mangling torrent, lacerating flesh, severing veins and arteries, amputating limbs, slicing people open as if with daggers even as they ran to escape it, claiming dozens of victims before the echoes of the blast had died down. In mere minutes the pavement below had become covered with a grisly slick of blood that overspilled the curb and ran tendrils down to the sewers, backing up at the debris-clogged gratings.

The blizzard of shards came on in waves as more of the screen's fastenings bent and snapped, shifting it farther to one side, then a little farther, and still farther, tilting it nearly ninety degrees from its original position.

At last, with a final protesting groan, it succumbed to gravity and crashed to the earth.

In the bright glare of the fires sweeping the streets, the shadow of the descending screen spread over the crowd like a huge mantle of darkness. Trapped by their own numbers, the men, women, and children below could only scream as it came plunging down on their heads, crushing many to death under the sheer weight of its thirty-foot-long metal frame and shattered electronic guts, maiming others with a shrapnel storm of steel, wire, and glass.

It was eight minutes into the year 2000 when this happened.

Two minutes later, the first of the satchel charges planted around the square detonated.

"This is the 911 operator, what is the emergency?"

"Thank God, thank God, the line's been busy, I'm here at a pay phone and I didn't think I'd ever get through—"

"Ma'am, what is the emergency?"

"My daughter, she's . . . her eyes, oh Jesus almighty, her *eyes* . . ."

"Is this a child you're talking about?"

"Yes, yes, she's only twelve. My husband and I, we wanted her to be here tonight . . . we thought . . . oh, shit, never mind that, please, you've got to help her—"

"Ma'am, listen to me, you need to calm down. Am I

correct that you're on Forty-third Street and Seventh Avenue?''

"Yes, yes, how did you . . . ?''

"Your location automatically shows on our computers—''

"Then get somebody over here, damn it! Get somebody over here *now*!''

"Ma'am, it's very important that you listen to my instructions. We are aware of the situation in Times Square. There are rescue teams arriving as we speak, but it will take them some time to reach everyone, and they are going to have to prioritize. I need to know what condition your daughter is in—''

"*Prioritize?* What are you saying?''

"Ma'am, please try and cooperate with me. A lot of people need assistance—''

"Don't you think I know that? Don't you think I *fucking* well know? I'm talking about my little girl's eyes, her eyes, her *eyes* . . .''

Sirens lashed the air, shrieky and urgent, throwing an ear-piercing lattice of sound over the city. On the streets and highways, fleets of emergency vehicles rushed toward Times Square with their tires screeching and flashers throbbing on their rooftops.

Escorted by two police cruisers, the first EMS crew reached the scene at 12:04 A.M. and hastily established a triage on Forty-fourth Street off Broadway. Victims were evaluated according to the seriousness of their injuries and the ability of the paramedics to treat them with the limited resources at their disposal. Ambulatory patients with minor cuts and burns were steered toward an ad hoc first-aid station near the parked medical van. Those in the worst condition were laid out on stretchers, and when no more stretchers were available, on whatever space could be cleared along the pavement. Scores of individuals were intubated with glucose-and-saline IVs. Oxygen was given to many more. Broken bones were splinted. Hemorrhaging wounds were stanched. Painkillers were administered to burn victims with blackened skin and charred clothing. There were nine cardiac cases in the immediate area requiring CPR and electronic defibrillation, two of whom expired before the overwhelmed emergency teams were able to get to them.

The dead were tagged and lined up on the street in double rows. Workers ran out of body bags within minutes and were forced to leave the corpses uncovered.

Around the corner on Broadway, a teenage boy and girl lay pinned under a heavy steel beam and scattered debris that had fallen from a construction site in the percussive shock wave of the blast. The young couple had been embracing when the bomb exploded and their bodies were trapped together and still partially entangled. The girl was dead, her chest horribly crushed. The boy had been spared because the beam had landed at a diagonal and come down across his legs rather than his body. Though semiconscious, he was slipping into shock and losing a tremendous amount of blood from his ruptured femoral artery.

Ignoring the threat to their own lives from raging flames and falling, burning debris, TAC-team cops from One-Truck had been laboring to extricate him even before the EMS ambulances arrived, carrying off broken masonry by the armload, and hurrying to deploy Jaws of Life hydraulic spreaders and multi-chamber rescue bags from their vehicle. Only two inches thick when deflated, the neoprene airbags had been easily inserted between the pavement and the beam, then connected by an inlet hose to a compressed air tank and joystick controller. The officer operating the joystick carefully expanded the bag to its maximum height of four feet, keeping a close eye on the pressure gauge centered in his command console. To prevent further injury to the boy, it was vital that the lift be gradual, with no more than fourteen to sixteen inches of inflation at a time.

By 12:08 the boy had been freed from underneath the beam and wheeled away on a gurney to exultant cheers from rescue workers. But neither they nor their lifesaving equipment were about to gain a respite: someone had been heard screaming for help underneath yet another pile of rubble across the street.

With the police, medical teams, and firefighters on Forty-fourth Street struggling to their job under these hazardous, chaotic conditions, it was simplicity itself for Nick Roma's man Bakach to slip past their attention, drop his satchel charge on the ground near the EMS vehicle, and then nudge it under the vehicle's chassis with the toe of his shoe.

Minutes after the sidewalk triage was set up outside her window, the barmaid on shift at Jason's Ring, a tavern on Forty-fourth Street, began passing out bottled drinking water to grateful rescue workers and victims. There was a large stock in the basement and her boss had been hauling it up himself by the carton, totally unconcerned with what it was costing him in future profits.

The barmaid had just gone to the rear of the tavern for a fresh supply when she heard a loud boom behind her on the street, snapped her head around in terror, and saw the EMS vehicle blow apart in a dazzling orange-blue fireball. A millisecond later, smoking hunks of wreckage came streaking through the window of the tavern, smashing it to countless pieces, slamming into walls, breaking bottles, crashing onto the bartop like some bizarre meteor shower. The blast of heat that came scorching through the broken window at the same time rocked her back on her heels as the ambulance and everyone around it—rescue workers, police, patients, *everyone*—was incinerated.

Behind her, staring out the shattered window of the bar, her boss stood with his box opener in his hand, scarcely able to credit his eyes, telling himself that what he was seeing, or thought he was seeing, had to be some kind of horrible dream.

Tragically, this wasn't the case—although it would be a long, long time before either of them was able to sleep without having the explosion replay itself in their darkest nightmares.

His face smudged with soot and tears, Bill Harrison was digging madly through the remains of the platform, screaming his daughter's name, *bellowing* her name over and over, trying to find her, half-crazed with grief, shock, and desperation. His glassy, darting eyes were those of a man who had experienced what he'd thought would be the worst, only to be overtaken by the fear that it was but a prelude to even deeper horror.

He crawled through the wreckage on his hands and knees, scooping up chunks of concrete, sharp pieces of glass, splintered wooden boards—anything that might be concealing some trace of his youngest child. The tips of his fingers were skinned and blistered from the burning planks and red-hot bits of metal that he had grabbed and then tossed aside in his frantic search.

Exhausted and winded, he shouted her name again, his voice cracking this time, fresh tears blearing his vision. He felt an unmanageable tide of grief rise in his chest and smashed the piece of debris he was holding against the planks, smashed it down once and then again, smashed it in hopeless rage and loss, and was about to sledge it down a third time when a hand fell on his shoulder.

He looked up at the face above him.

Blinked.

"Baby?" he said, sounding as if he'd been jolted out of a trance. He covered her hand with his own. Needing to touch it, to feel her, before he would let himself believe she was really standing there. "*Tasheya?* My God, I thought you . . . your mother . . ."

His daughter nodded wordlessly, crying, tightening her grip on his shoulder. Her cheek and forehead were gashed, and the sleeve of her tattered coat was soaked in blood, but she was alive. Sweet mercy, *alive.* That singer, Zyman, was with her, helping to support her with one arm, though he was also bleeding and nearly as unsteady as she was.

"C'mon, man. We gotta get down off this stage while we can," he said, reaching out to Harrison. "Ain't gonna be much longer before it collapses altogether."

Harrison grabbed hold of his hand, let himself be helped to his feet, and then was crushing Tasheya to him, feeling her chin press into the hollow of his neck, feeling the warm flood of her tears against his face. And for a brief moment, standing there amid the destruction, he understood that, while things might never be okay for him

Tom Clancy's Power Plays

again—no, not even close to okay—there was reason to
hope they would eventually get better.

"Our friend's right," he said finally, nodding toward
Zyman. "We'd better go."

EIGHTEEN

IN HIS OFFICE AT THE PLATINUM CLUB, NICK ROMA sat in pensive silence, his lights out, the dance hall on the floor below him silent. It was two o'clock in the morning. All but a handful of the people who had begun the night shaking their asses off down there had left hours ago, their partying having come to a finish after news of the Times Square explosion infiltrated the room like a plague virus. The few who remained were mostly core members of his crew, men who wouldn't give a damn about anything except getting drunk at the bar.

Of course, he had known what was going to happen, known that the New Year's celebration would become a national death rite before it was all over. But somehow, it wasn't until he had seen the reports on television that he grasped the enormity of the destruction he'd helped bring about.

Nick sat in the darkness, not making a sound, thinking. He'd noticed there was very little sound out on the street, either. Every now and then the lights of a passing car would sweep across the windows overlooking the avenue, throwing a crazy quilt of shadows over his features, but otherwise the people down there had disappeared. They had seen lightning strike suddenly from the sky and burrowed down into their holes like frightened animals.

Could anyone really get away with what he'd been part

of? If he was linked to it, the worst terrorist attack ever on American soil, on this particular night, in the heart of its largest city . . . The country had never taken a hit like this before, and the pressure on law-enforcement agencies to find those behind it would be tremendous.

Roma pondered that for a moment. Could it be they would wind up tripping over each other's feet? He supposed there was that danger for them. In the horse race to see which agency could make the first arrests, they might conceal leads, refuse to share information. Such things had happened before in investigations that threatened to become trouble for him, and he'd turned the situation to good advantage every time.

Still, he'd always been someone who dealt with expedients. His concerns were with running his business interests, not radical politics. He neither knew nor cared why Vostov had become involved in this affair, and had made it clear to his messengers that, while preferring to avoid a rift with the *organizatsiya,* he would not be controlled by anyone in Moscow. If Vostov wanted to reach out for assistance in smuggling the C-4 into the U.S., it was going to cost him. And if he wanted him to provide a broader range of support to Gilea and her group, it would cost even more. In money, and in favors owed.

A million-dollar payment from the Russians had settled his misgivings enough to win his participation, but Roma still wondered if he had gotten in over his head. He supposed he would feel less vulnerable when the strike team was out of the country . . .

The sound of his doorknob quietly turning pulled him from his thoughts with a start. He leaned forward, his hand dropping into his desk drawer and closing around the grip of his MP5K.

He continued to hold it even after Gilea entered the room, her slender silhouette gliding forward through the dimness.

"You could have knocked," he said.

"Yes." She pushed the door shut and he heard the deadbolt click behind her. "I could have."

Roma regarded her in the scant illumination coming in from the streetlights outside his window.

"There's a light switch on the wall beside you," he said.

She nodded but made no move toward the switch.

"We were successful," she said, coming farther into the room. "But I suppose you already know."

"I had the television on earlier," he said, nodding. His hand still on the gun.

She took a step forward, then another, stopping in front of the desk, her fingers going to the collar of her black leather coat, unbuttoning the top button, then the button underneath it.

"Why are you here?" he said. "You know Zachary won't have your papers ready until tomorrow. And I don't suppose it's just to say good night."

"No, not really," she said. She put both hands flat on the desktop and leaned forward, her face coming very close to his in the semidarkness.

Gilea finished opening her coat, shrugged out of it, tossed it onto the chair beside her. She was wearing a dark sweater underneath.

He waited.

"I've been enjoying this night too much to have it end, Nick," she said. Leaning closer, her voice almost a whisper. "You don't have to be holding that gun."

Roma swallowed. *Enjoying this night?* What kind of

woman was she? Two hours earlier she had been responsible for untold carnage, yet now, out of the blue . . . ?

He felt something akin to horror, and yet . . .

And yet . . .

The thing that horrified him the most was his own unbidden physical response to her nearness.

The attraction she held for him was incredible.

She leaned closer still, putting her face next to his, her lips brushing against his ear.

"You know what I came here for," she said. "You know what I want."

Roma's throat felt dry. His heart was pounding.

He breathed. Breathed again.

He took his hand off his gun and reached out to pull her against him. And as her soft flesh touched him, warm against his skin, he glanced at the mirror and smiled a small, private smile.

NINETEEN

6:30 A.M.

THE CITY WAS IN SHOCK.

There was no other word for the malaise that gripped New York. Not even the World Trade Center bombing had so tested the people and resources of Manhattan and the surrounding boroughs.

Of course, the World Trade Center bombing hadn't taken out the heart of the city.

Times Square was nearly as packed with people at this moment as it had been when the explosion occurred. The red and blue strobes from the emergency vehicles that ringed the blast site and the arc lights that the rescue workers had brought in were fading, giving way to the slanting rays of dawn.

The day promised to be clear and cold, and the early morning light threw everything into stark relief. Ten-foot-tall temporary chimneys, hastily put in place by city workers to cover broken steam pipes in the streets, spouted clouds of vapor, shielding workers from the hot blasts and directing the flow upward. Wisps of fog from the chimneys flowed around and through the site, wreathing it in clouds and backlit rainbows, giving it an otherworldly appearance. People with acronyms—FBI, NYCFD, ATF,

NYPD—silk-screened onto their nylon coats crawled though the wreckage, sifting the debris for the smallest fragments that might lead them to those responsible for the atrocity. Members of the National Guard, hastily mobilized, kept gawkers at bay so that the site would remain undisturbed—if that was a word that could be applied to what was essentially a bomb crater—except by the rescue workers. Everybody, no matter how intent they were on their search, gave way to emergency workers and the teams combing the wreckage with dogs. The dogs were looking for victims. Their handlers were praying for survivors.

The long night had been punctuated by this search. A dog would whine and scratch at the crumpled remains of a massive neon sign, the tangled web of a broken bleacher, the tortured fragments of a skyscraper. An ants' nest of activity would erupt around the excited dog. Rescue workers would bring an amazing array of instruments to bear on the spot—infrared heat sensors, supersensitive microphones, tiny video cameras on flexible probes, ultrasound machines, metal detectors, motion detectors, X-rays.

If there was even the slightest indication that the person trapped inside was still breathing, no effort was spared to shift the wreckage and get him or her out. Cranes, bags that could be inserted into the smallest crevices and then inflated to lift the obstructions slowly and gently, levers, braces, and plain old manpower were used to get to the people who needed help. But as time dragged on, the desperate effort to extract survivors was giving way to the heartbreaking act of marking remains. Fluorescent orange flags on slender wire stakes fluttered in the breeze, each representing a life lost. Eventually, when it was clear that there were no more survivors, the grim task of retrieving the corpses would begin.

And through it all, the men and women in the nylon coats continued their search for evidence.

Half a mile away, the morning light slanted through the stained glass windows of St. Patrick's Cathedral. The air of the church, heavy with incense and smoke from thousands of candles lining the walls and altars, took on a rainbow hue. But the people who filled the pews were immune to its beauty. Many of them had been in Times Square when it happened. More had seen it on CNN or the local news. Some had lost friends and family. The deadly blast and the screams of the dying echoed in their memories. Nothing, not even the solace they'd sought here in an all-night mass for the victims, would ever silence them.

The meeting took place a little past noon in a sub-basement conference room at UpLink's corporate headquarters on Rosita Avenue, in San Jose. With its clean lines, direct overhead lights, beige carpeting, and coffee machine, it looked very much like the upstairs conference rooms minus the windows. But being sealed away from a view of the Mount Hamilton foothills was only its most superficial difference.

Access was restricted to those in Gordian's inner circle, all of whom were provided with digital key codes that unlocked the door. Two-foot-thick concrete walls and acoustical paneling soundproofed the room from the keenest human ears. Steel reinforcements within the walls had been implanted with noise generators and other state-of-the-art masking systems to thwart monitoring of electronic communications. Sweep teams went through the room on a regular basis, and telephones, computers, and videoconferencing equipment going in or out of it were checked for bugs using spectrum and X-ray analysis.

While Gordian felt the term ''secure'' was a relative one, and supposed that someone who was crafty enough, determined enough, and had enough sophisticated hardware at his disposal could still find a way to listen in on his top-level discussions, he was confident that this part of his operational center was as resistant to eavesdropping as caution and countersurveillance technology allowed. In the comint game, the most you could ever do was stay one step ahead of the droops—a word of Vince Scull's creation meaning ''dirty rotten snoops.''

Now Gordian looked at the faces around the conference table, considering how best to start a meeting that was light-years from business-as-usual. Present in the flesh were his Foreign Affairs Consultant Alex Nordstrum, Vice President of Special Projects Megan Breen, and Security Chief Peter Nimec. On a video docking station across the table, Vince's puffy-eyed, basset-hound face was scowling at him over a high-band satellite link from Kaliningrad.

Gordian took a deep breath. He had observed that, to a person, their features reflected his own low, grim mood.

''I want to thank all of you for coming in virtually without advance notice,'' he said. ''I don't know how many of you lost friends or loved ones in Times Square last night. For those who might have, my profound condolences.'' He paused and turned his gaze toward Megan. ''Have you gotten any word from your brother and sister-in-law?''

A trim brunette in her late thirties, Megan looked at him with alert, sapphire-blue eyes.

"Not yet," she said, "but that isn't any reason to assume they were hurt. The long-distance phone lines to and from New York are choked."

Megan's unworried tone didn't fool Gordian. He had once—long ago—made the mistake of thinking she was just another starched and stuffy executive clone cranked out by the Harvard Business School—in her case, one with an added sheepskin in psychology from Columbia. An executive clone who was apt to play mind games, then. That had been pure bias, a last prickly vestige of the blue-collar resentments that were the bulk of his familial inheritance. It had taken him years to discard his unfair, limiting preconceptions about those with upper-class backgrounds. Dan Parker had been the first to make him see things differently. Meg had taken him the rest of the way down the road.

In a sense, though, those stereotypical notions had worked in Meg's favor when he'd originally employed her as a human resource executive/headhunter for the R&D divisions. He'd wanted someone who could make hiring and firing decisions in a detached, intelligent manner, and that she had done. But he'd also gotten an inspired thinker, and a trusted confidant, in the bargain. And that was something he hadn't expected of her.

"Pete, you have people out east. You think they can do anything to help Megan find out about her relatives?" he said.

Nimec tipped his narrow jaw downward slightly, his tightly wound version of a nod.

"I'm sure they can," he said.

"Good." Gordian was quiet a second, his eyes moving

around the table again. "I think we'd better do some talking about what happened last night. Ask ourselves why in God's name anybody would want to do something like that. And who would be capable of it."

"Turn on the tube, and you'll hear the talking heads blathering about domestic terrorism," Nimec said. "Present company excepted, Alex."

Nordstrum was looking down at his eyeglasses, wiping their lenses with a cleaning cloth he'd pulled from a pocket of his herringbone blazer.

"I'm a part-time consultant for CNN and several other news-gathering agencies. They pay well and give me an opportunity to air my views. Not all, uh, talking heads warrant immediate disregard."

Scull's voice came from the video setup. "Watch your ass, Nimec."

He shrugged. "My point was just that their general opinion is kind of ironic, when you recall that the knee-jerk reaction once would've been to pin any terrorist act on the Arabs. Oklahoma City changed all that."

"I take it you disagree with the media consensus," Gordian said.

"Even from what little we know about the bombing, I very much doubt it could have been pulled off by some borderline retardates from Ephraim City."

"Reasons?"

"Several," Nimec said. "For openers, their justification for homegrown violence is a paranoid hatred and suspicion of the feds, and a sense of themselves as latter-day minutemen fighting for their constitutional liberties. Their targets have always had some connection, whether real or symbolic, to government agencies. The killing of ordinary citizens is something they view as collateral to the struggle.'' He paused a moment, sipped his coffee. ''Remember, the real intent in bombing the Alfred P. Murrah Building was to take out FBI and ATF employees with offices on the upper floors. The damage to the lower stories was unavoidable given that the drums of fertilizer and fuel oil McVeigh detonated weighed over four thousand pounds, couldn't have been smuggled into the building, and therefore had to be left in front of it. What I'm saying is that he couldn't pinpoint his target, so he convinced himself all those kids in the day-care center were necessary casualties of war. Acceptable losses.''

''What about the bombing in Olympic Park?'' Megan asked. ''That was a public space.''

''The verdict on who was behind that one's still out,'' Nimec said. ''But even there, I can see the message they might have been sending. A hard-core belief among the superpatriots is that all three branches of government have been infiltrated by an international Zionist conspiracy . . . a secret cabal bent on absorbing the United States into a New World Order. And the Olympics has been a symbol of globalism since its origin. You can see where I'm heading.''

''If you follow that warped thinking, though, you can imagine how they might have seen the Times Square event as something comparable,'' Gordian said. ''A kind of worldwide jubilee bringing people of every nation together.''

Nimec wobbled his hand in front of him. ''That's a little tenuous. At best, we're dealing with prosaic minds when we talk about the movement's leadership. And once you come down to the foot soldiers, you're really dredging the bottom of the IQ curve. These are men who get confused if it takes more than a single stroke of the pencil to connect the dots.''

"If you don't mind, Pete, I'd like to get back to what you said a minute ago. About not believing they could have pulled it off . . .''

"Let's use Oklahoma City as an example again,'' Nimec said, nodding. "The bomb that was detonated was big and crude because the perpetrators couldn't get their hands on more sophisticated, more tightly controlled demolitions . . . not in sufficient quantities to achieve their goal, at any rate. So instead they follow a recipe that's been disseminated in cheap kitchen explosives handbooks, Internet message boards, you name it. A scene in the *Turner Diaries* becomes their mission blueprint, and the rest is history. The whole episode's characterized by a lack of imagination, and a reliance on materials that can be obtained easily and legally.''

"The eyewitness accounts I've been hearing all agree that the initial blast emanated from a vender's booth on Forty-second Street,'' Nordstrum said. "There's also supposed to have been an incident involving a K-9 cop and the vender just minutes earlier.''

"That's been confirmed by the visual record,'' Nimec said. "I've already had our experts do computer magnifications of the televised footage. And we're trying to dig up amateur videos. There must have been thousands of people with minicams at the scene. But even in the absence of other evidence, I think we can assume the bomb was inserted into the area by means of the booth. Whether it was with or without the knowing complicity of the donut man is still anybody's guess.''

"One thing's for sure,'' Scull said, "whoever planted the charge got plenty of bang for his buck.''

Nimec looked stiffly at the eyehole camera lens atop the video monitor.

"The charge was very compact in proportion to its effectiveness, yes," he said, his frown making it clear that he disliked Scull's particular shorthand. "I'm guessing it was something like C-4 or HBX."

"And the secondary explosions?" Gordian asked.

Nimec shrugged. "Hard to tell at this stage," he said.

The room was quiet for a moment. Gordian drank some coffee.

"Okay, Pete, supposing we go along with your assessment for now, and put aside homegrown terrorists as the culprits," he said. "What about militant Islamic fundamentalists?"

"All of them, you mean?"

Gordian looked at him. "I wasn't trying to be funny."

"Neither was I. It's just that things aren't always very straightforward when it comes to our enemies in the Arab world. On the one hand, they're more likely to be interested in causing mass destruction for its own sake. Their hatred of America makes no distinction between its government and its citizens," Nimec said. "On the other hand, we in this room really *must* draw a distinction between state-sponsored terrorism and acts committed by extremist fringe groups, or by lone wolves with nebulous ties to both. The line between them isn't always clear, but it exists. And it may be very relevant in this instance."

"As I'm sure you'll explain," Gordian said, still regarding him steadily.

"In my opinion, the World Trade Center bombing fits more or less into the third category," he said. "There's never been any conclusive proof that would link the conspirators to a foreign government. Ramzi Yousef, the so-called mastermind of the plot, was an incredible bungler. His bomb was supposed to cause the largest of the Twin Towers to crack up and fall into the other, which didn't happen. It was also supposed to release a poisonous cloud of cyanide gas. Obviously that didn't happen either, since the sodium cyanide he'd impregnated it with vaporized in the heat of the blast . . . something any high school chemistry student with a B grade average would have foreseen. Two years later, Yousef sets his Manila hotel room on fire while making liquid explosives and takes off for Pakistan to avoid arrest, leaving behind a computer whose hard drive is full of incriminating data files. If this fool was an agent of a hostile Middle Eastern nation, his superiors must have been quite desperate for a henchman.''

"Okay, so he was a regular Shemp. I've got no problem with what you're saying," Scull said. "But while we're doing Terrorism 101, I think we ought to mention the guys that knocked Pan Am 103 out of the air.''

"Scull's right, we should," Nimec said. "Even at this early stage, it seems to me there are at least superficial comparisons to be made. Both were efficient, well-financed, and bloodthirsty operations. And, God help humanity, the men who did the work were slick professionals.''

"We know that the Pan Am 103 disaster was underwritten by Libya," Gordian said. "What you're suggesting, then, is that last night's attack has the earmarks of state-supported terrorism.''

"I'm not at all ready to go that far. But it certainly meets several of the criteria," Nimec said. He smoothed a hand over his bristle of close-cropped hair. "The question is, who'd want to do the deed?''

"I think I see what Pete means," Nordstrum said. "All

the usual suspects have been quiescent for some time now, though for different reasons. The Khatami government in Iran's trying to impress the European Union with a more moderate posture than its predecessors. Ditto for Iraq, where Saddam's been hoping to achieve an easing of Gulf War sanctions by acting like the boy next door. We know the Syrians are engaged in back channel peace talks with Israel . . . offhand, I can't see that any Moslem regime would want to rock the apple cart right now.''

''I didn't hear you mention Khadafy in that list of the born again,'' Scull said.

Nimec was shaking his head. ''He'll always have fangs, but there's no benefit to him in stirring up trouble at a time when the rest of his Arab brothers are reaching out across the water. He's not going to risk isolating himself.''

The five of them were silent awhile. Gordian rose from the table, went to the credenza, topped off his coffee, and sat back down. He stared into his cup without drinking for several more seconds, then looked up at the others.

''I may as well be the first to say what's on everybody's mind,'' he said at last. ''It's conceivable that it could be Russia. Or factions within the Russian government, anyway. Starinov has any number of political opponents who would like to see him get egg on his face . . . and who'd have access to money, materials, and highly proficient operatives.''

He noticed that Megan's eyes had narrowed in thought. ''Meg?'' he said.

''It's just that the whole thing isn't coming together for me. Nobody's claimed responsibility for the bombing—''

''And it could be nobody ever will, if I may interject,''

Nimec said. "The trend for the past decade has been for terrorist groups to *avoid* drawing attention to themselves, the idea being to keep their enemies guessing, and jumping at shadows."

"I'm aware of that," Megan said. "But in this instance the act would have been committed with very specific aims in mind—namely a chilling of relations between our two countries, and the weakening of Starinov's prestige and authority within his own government. Seems to me, there'd be no sense in it unless the finger of blame very clearly pointed in his direction. Furthermore, why would Starinov have engineered the strike, unless he wanted to bring about his own downfall? Like I said, it doesn't gel. There's no damn *logic* to it."

"Not apparently, and not yet," Nimec said. "But our players might have a subtle strategy that we just aren't grasping at this juncture."

"I agree," Nordstrum said. "It may feel like forever since the bombing, but the fact is it's barely been twelve hours. We have to wait for more information, see how everything develops—"

"And do what in the meantime? Sit on our hands?" Scull said. "Gord, listen to me. Can you imagine the negative impact on our plans for the ground station if the blast *is* pinned on Starinov? I'm the one in Russia. I've got a close-up view of what's going on politically. And I can tell you, there are a lot of people in high positions who'd love for our Yankee asses to ride on out of here on horseback."

"Jesus, Scull," Megan said. "Hundreds of innocent people were killed last night, we've been discussing a situation that could destabilize an entire region, and you're—"

"What? Being up front about why I'm talking to my videophone at midnight Kaliningrad time and trying to figure out the big picture? If *we* aren't concerned about our interests in Russia, who's gonna be? And how come Gord called this coffee klatch in the first place?"

Nordstrum sighed and rubbed his eyelids. "Obviously we all know why we're here, Scull. But I think Megan was trying to add some perspective to the—"

"Wait," Gordian said, holding up his hand. "I'm sure that none of us have had much sleep, and everybody's frazzled. But some extremely important issues have been raised, and I'm glad we didn't postpone this discussion. Somebody, I think it was Julius Caesar, once said that the art of life is more like the wrestler's art than the dancer's, and what I've always thought he meant was that you've got to meet the unexpected head-on, grapple with it, rather than try to tiptoe around it. That's the reason we developed the Sword project." He paused for comment, received none, and turned toward Nimec. "Pete, I want Max Blackburn to assemble a team that will gather information about who may have been responsible for the bombing. He's to spare no expense."

Nimec nodded. There was a look Gordian occasionally got in his eyes, a tight, hard focus, that always evoked a mental image of someone holding a magnifying glass into the sunlight to set a leaf on fire. A look that made whoever it was turned upon feel as if he were being bathed in combustible heat. It was a look that he was giving Nimec right now.

"I think it'll be best if Max flies to Russia as soon as possible. He can coordinate things from there, use the ground station as our primary base of operations," Gordian continued. "At the same time, Pete, you track down whatever leads you can here in the U.S. I'm hoping for fast progress.''

Nimec nodded again.

"We keep a low profile, okay?" Gordian said. "If the intelligence community gets the slightest hint we're conducting an independent investigation, they'll shut us down.''

Gordian swung his gaze around the table.

"Any comments?"

"Only one," Nordstrum said.

Gordian looked at him, waiting.

"You know that quote about the wrestler and the dancer?''

"Right.''

"It comes from Marcus Aurelius, not the emperor Julius.''

Gordian looked at him another moment. Then he slowly lifted his coffee to his lips, drained the cup, and nodded.

"Appreciate that, my friend," he said.

The Blue Room at New York's City Hall, where official press briefings normally took place, was too small to hold the crowd of print and film journalists who wanted to attend the city's first press conference since the explosion. Figuring out where to hold this briefing had been only one of a hundred decisions that had to be made by the mayor's office.

But the mayor was gone. Dead. Killed in the blast like a thousand others.

The deputy mayor was in the hospital and expected to be there for at least a week. Internal injuries. He'd taken a chunk of the bleachers in the gut and was considered to be lucky to be alive. Nobody knew when he'd be back on the job.

Half of the borough presidents were too battered to attend, and the police commissioner was both too shattered by his personal tragedy and too focused on the actual investigation to, as he put it, waste his time on PR bullshit.

But the news media was clamoring for anything. For crumbs. So Press Secretary Andrea DeLillo had spent the last fifteen hours pushing her coping skills to world-class levels. She'd fended off politicians determined to make political hay in the glare of the spotlight focused on Times Square. She'd gotten numbers from the crews at the site, from all of the hospitals, and from the EMS sites that had survived. She'd pushed the pain of her own losses into the background, not to mention the fear that she'd probably lose her job as soon as a new mayor took office. If anything she could do would shake loose the killers who had brought the angel of death down on her city, she would do it. She would feed the media the facts as she knew them, and turn them loose to find the perps. It was all she could manage right now. She could only pray it was enough.

The mikes were set up at a podium at the top of the City Hall steps. A huge crowd of reporters of all kinds, all bundled up against the cold, flowed down the stairway and into the street, which had been blocked off and barricaded by the police department. Flanked by representatives from the police, the fire department, the city council, and the FBI, Andrea surveyed the crowd.

Finally she stepped up to the mike and began her presentation. As the grim statistics rolled off her lips, she made a silent vow: Somebody would pay for this if she had to see to it herself.

TWENTY

WASHINGTON, D.C.
JANUARY 2, 2000

FROM THE *WASHINGTON POST*:

FBI Official Leaves Questions of Fifth Bomb Unanswered

Fuels Conjecture With Statements About Evidence at FBI Explosives Lab

WASHINGTON—During a news conference today at the J. Edgar Hoover Building on Pennsylvania Avenue, Assistant Director Robert Lang remained vague about whether the FBI is in possession of physical clues to the identity of the bomber or bombers responsible for the bloody New Year's Eve attack that left an estimated 700 persons dead and injured thousands more in Times Square.

In a prepared statement to the media, Lang officially confirmed for the first time that the powerful explosion that occurred at 11:56 P.M. was followed by three secondary blasts of "a deliberate nature," ruling out the possibility that they may have stemmed from violent damage to underground gas mains in the bombing, as had been reported by some news organizations. He went on to term eyewitness accounts "extraordinarily helpful to the investigation," and expressed confidence that photographs and video tapes taken at the scene will provide law enforcement agents with a clear picture of "matters of relevant interest that occurred before and after the event."

Lang was considerably more guarded, however, when asked about an item found by investigators rumored to be a fifth explosive device that failed to detonate. "I can only tell you that we do possess substantial evidence believed to have been left behind by the perpetrator or perpetrators, and presently under analysis in our Laboratory Division's Explosive Unit–Bomb Data Center," Lang said in a brief Q&A session following his prepared statement. "We are unable to be more specific right now for investigative reasons, but want to reassure the public, and especially the relatives of those indiscriminately killed or injured in the blast, that we are as sickened by what happened as anyone else, and have committed all our resources to solving this case."

Rather than quell speculation that another bomb may have been discovered by members of the New York Police Department Emergency Services Unit within minutes of the fatal explosions, Lang's comments drew attention for having mentioned the EU-BDC—

which serves as the FBI's primary laboratory for the examination of bombing devices—as the unit where the mysterious evidence is being processed. Also, while noting that tests of explosive residue and other trace materials are among the functions normally performed by the EU-BDC, Lang refused to "limit the categorization of evidence to one particular type or another" when responding to follow-up questions by reporters.

The implications of this may be significant, say many forensics experts. Even partial remains of an explosive device are likely to reveal "signature" characteristics that can be matched against those of devices used in other bombing incidents and potentially link it to a suspect or terrorist organization . . .

The reports about the mysterious fifth bomb were almost on the money.

The undetonated satchel charge was, in fact, found outside a storefront on Fifty-second Street and Seventh Avenue, although by firemen rather than police officers. In response to a request for operational support from the NYPD, technicians wearing bomb protective suits from the FBI's New York field office were quickly dispatched to collect the evidence. When it was determined that the device's fusing system was inoperative, and that it was therefore safe for transport, the specialized unit—in a procedure okayed by the local assistant director—arranged for the satchel charge to be delivered to FBI HQ in Washington, D.C., where it was given over to the EU-BDC for scientific examination. A further discovery at the bomb scene by agents equipped with ultraviolet lights had caused the laboratory to buzz with anticipation well in advance of the package's arrival: fluorescence had been detected in both the unexploded charge and debris samples collected near the site of the initial blast, strongly indicating the explosives had been tagged with chemical markers by their manufacturer. Their reaction was strongly warranted—while not yet legally mandated in the United States, tagging had been required by the Swiss government for years and was a voluntary practice among an increasing number of international explosives suppliers. If indeed present, the expectation was that the markers would lead investigators back to the point of sale, and produce valuable information about the purchaser of the bomb-making material.

Soon after the C-4 satchel charge reached the lab, a microthin sliver was taken from it, placed on a specimen slide, and then exposed to a Tesla coil magnet for the purpose of orienting the tags of melamine plastic—each chemically inert particle about the size of a speck of pollen and striated with color—that it might contain. Typically taggants were mixed with explosive ingredients at concentrations of 250 parts per million, a ratio that allows the explosive to retain its full stability and performance, while showing up for easy viewing under microscopic examination. In this instance, an Olympus binocular light microscope equipped with 35mm Polaroid video was used by a forensics specialist who immediately verified the presence of markers and, working with feverish excitement, read and photographed the taggants for their color-coded information about the manufacturer, production date, and batch number of the plastique.

From there it became a fairly routine computer search. The information was checked against the main charge identification database for commercial explosives which had recently been added to the Explosives Reference and Search System—dubbed EXPRESS by government techies with a fondness for acronyms—and drew a hit on the first shot.

The manufacturer was ID'd as Lian International, a chemical firm that was part of a larger Malaysian conglomerate based in Kuala Lumpur, and headed by an ethnic Chinese businessman named Teng Chou. Though this was an important and satisfying investigatory link, it paled in comparison to what was uncovered next: when a trace was run on the plastique's batch number, it turned out to match that of a shipment recently sold to a Russian munitions distributor with strong government ties.

With that piece of info under their belts, the investigators in the EU-BDC knew they had come onto something big.

From beginning to end, it was a textbook example of how careful and diligent analysis of evidence throughout the entire chain of custody could yield phenomenally successful results.

It was also the first step down the garden path for the entire American intelligence community.

TWENTY-ONE

SNOW FELL GENTLY ON THE TREES AND MONUMENTS that surrounded him. Under any other circumstance, he'd have thought the scene was beautiful. Rosetta would have liked it, too, if she could have seen it from inside a room with a good heating system. She got cold too easily to appreciate winter landscapes under any other conditions. He'd had them put blankets with her, in her coffin. He hated the thought that she would never be warm again. But then, he hated everything about this.

Police Commissioner Bill Harrison stood on the edge of an open grave. He knew he wasn't alone. This scene would be enacted hundreds of times as New York buried her dead. But that was no comfort. It just made it worse somehow.

How was he supposed to go on, without Rosetta? She was his heart, his center, his reason for existence. When the job got to be too much for him, when the things he saw every day overwhelmed him, he would go home to this woman and she would make it all right again. She couldn't change what he saw. But every moment he was with her, he knew what he was fighting to protect. She represented all that was good in the world.

And now he was putting her in a hole in the ground. They'd be bringing the coffin here any minute.

The pain was devastating.

For the millionth time, he asked himself why he'd let her go with him to Times Square. He could have said no, claimed that there weren't enough seats to spare for real working people after the politicians took their cut. He'd had that option, in his infinite wisdom but he had decided Rosie's certain pleasure outweighed the risks.

It was something he found hard to forgive.

His daughter stood next to him. Her tears were acid in his wounds. She could have died, too, all because he hadn't seen it coming, hadn't stopped it before it started. As it was, her nightmares were as haunted by that moment as his were. She'd been scarred, this child he cherished— on his watch, at his side, when he should have been able to prevent it.

Why hadn't he?

It was no good blaming it on the mayor. The man was dead. He'd paid the ultimate price, if his relentless politicking had made the target too good to pass up.

It was no good blaming his men. The vender's cart had looked fine to him in the split second he'd seen it. How could they have found anything? The earliest reports from the blast site indicated that this was a slick, professional job, invisible to even the most careful inspection.

The pallbearers, most of them police officers in full dress uniform, brought the coffin, slowly placed it onto the straps that would lower Rosie into the ground, gone from him until the next life claimed him, too.

His heart nearly burst from the pain of it.

He reached out and took his daughter's hand, squeezed it.

The news cameras hummed and clicked.

Even their grief was a public matter.

The coffin was slowly lowered. When it reached its final resting place, the thud of the wood hitting the dirt was the loneliest, most final sound he had ever heard in his life.

Like the noise of the blast, it would haunt him, too.

The preacher intoned words of comfort. The sounds washed over him, useless now, but perhaps later, alone, as he sifted through his memories of this day, he would find a small measure of the peace they were intended to impart.

Now he dropped the bouquet of roses he'd brought with him onto the casket. Bright splashes of scarlet against the polished wood surface, they were slowly, slowly covered by the white flecks of snow, still falling gently. Like his heart, the blossoms were soon sheathed in ice.

Tasheya's forget-me-nots joined his offering. As the service wound to a close, he watched them, too, fade under the onslaught from heaven.

He had lost his Rosie. The emptiness inside him was so vast he wasn't sure how his body could contain it. But he had something to do that kept the grief that threatened to swamp him at bay.

He was the police commissioner of the city of New York. It was his job to find out who had done this. The day he brought those people to justice, his healing could begin.

TWENTY-TWO

THE BATHHOUSE ON *ULITSA PETROVKA* WAS A FAVORite recreational spot for gangsters, government officials, and those for whom the distinction was negligible, and Yuri Vostov came there two and often three times a week to relax in the hot tub or sauna, always at noon on the dot, and never without at least two women on his arms.

Vostov considered his visits to be therapeutic as well as sources of profound physical pleasure—and pleasure was something he would not let himself take for granted. This was because of a scare he'd had some years back, when he was approaching his fiftieth birthday. Right around that time, he had found his sexual vigor to be on the wane, and even begun to fear he was becoming impotent after several horrid and ignoble embarrassments between the sheets. Though he had a large roster of young, beautiful women available as bedroom partners, and though each was talented and imaginative in her own way, nothing they did seemed to stimulate him. His encounters with these lovers continued in a rather lackluster, almost perfunctory fashion until one night, under advice from a friend in government, he engaged in a ménage à trois—something he'd inexplicably never done before—with a pair of sisters known for their willingness to perform as a team, and gained salvation between their sweating bodies.

He supposed the secret had been in admitting that he was a man who valued quantity above quality. As with food, drink, and possessions, the key to his greatest fulfillment turned out to be getting what he liked all at once.

Today his companions in the sauna were Nadia and Svieta, not the sisters who had originally shown him the path to middle-aged carnal enlightenment—not relatives at all, to his knowledge—but a willing and enthusiastic pair in their own right. An auburn brunette, Nadia was wearing a pair of gold hoop earrings and nothing else. Svieta, a cinnamon redhead, had chosen to accent her nudity with a gold anklet. Both were on their knees in front of Vostov, who had also shed his towel, and was seated on a wooden bench watching their heads bob up and down below his ample stomach, their breasts swimming freely in a pearlescent haze of steam.

That was when a rap on the door suddenly tore Vostov and his companions from their rapture. Nadia's gold hoop stopped banging against his inner thigh, Svieta's spread of red hair rose off his lap, and both looked up at him with somewhat baffled expressions on their faces, as if unsure how to proceed.

He frowned, thinking foul thoughts about whoever had ruined the moment.

"What is it?" he barked.

"*Prasteeyeh*, Mr. Vostov," the attendant said from the hallway. "There's a call on your cellular phone—"

"A *call*? I told you we weren't to be disturbed!"

"I know, sir, but it's been beeping constantly and—"

"Shit! Enough!" Vostov stood up, snapped his towel off its hook, and wrapped it around his waist. Then he opened the door a crack and reached an arm out, steam curling around his fleshy elbows. "Hand it to me, will you?"

The attendant passed the phone to him and backed away. Pushing the door shut, Vostov fingered a button on the keypad to accept an incoming call.

"Yes?" he said, lifting the phone to his ear.

"Ah, Yuri. I sincerely hope I'm not disturbing you."

Vostov recognized Teng Chou's voice and frowned again.

"You are," he said.

"Forgive me, then. But I had been trying to reach you at your office for some time."

Vostov glanced over at Nadia and Svieta, who had taken places on the bench and were speaking to each other in whispers punctuated by low giggles. Was there something funny here that he was missing?

"Never mind," he said, growing more sharply annoyed. "What is it?"

"I've had trouble getting calls through to a certain party of our mutual acquaintance. Indeed, I'm sure that I transferred some of my impatience with him onto you."

"I told you to forget it," Vostov said. "Why get me involved, anyway?"

"My friend," Teng said in a mild tone, enunciating his words carefully in Russian, "you are already quite deeply involved."

Vostov blanched.

"You know what I mean. I'm not some permanent go-between between the two of you."

"Of course not. But you did broker the deal." Teng paused. "Probably the deficient line of communication, shall we say, means nothing. These are hectic days for us all. Still, my backers need some reassurance that they will receive full satisfaction. That matters will proceed as had been discussed.''

Vostov turned away from the two women and dropped his voice a notch.

"Look, I don't give a damn about them," he said. "Regardless of what you're trying to imply, my part in this is done. You want me to call our friend, see what's going on with him, I'll do it. But as a favor, not an obligation, you understand?''

Teng paused.

"Yes," he said finally, his tone still soft. "Although you should remember the search for truth can be steered back on course as easily as it was diverted.''

Vostov's gut pulled in. These Asians made him edgy with their elliptical ways. "Meaning what, exactly?''

"You need to reexamine your interests, my friend. It would be unfortunate if they suddenly came into collision with my own. The backers you so casually dismiss have a long reach, and an even longer memory for holding grudges.''

Vostov felt his stomach tighten a little more. There was a sharp burning sensation in the center of it. Damn, he thought. His ulcers hadn't acted up like this for ages.

He tossed a glance over his shoulder at Svieta and Nadia. They were still whispering and tittering and seemed to be paying him no attention.

Desire was a precarious and fickle sort of thing, he reflected. It could pull a man from the filthiest gutter to the top of the world, then push him right over into the abyss.

"I'll call our friend right now," he said, and pushed the Disconnect button on the phone.

Nadia moved closer to him then, hoping to distract him

from the business of business, and refocus his attention on the business of pleasure. "Soon," he said as he pushed her roughly away. "As soon as I finish dealing with this lamentable mess." Then he turned his attention back to the phone. It rang—on the minister's private line, so no secretary would remember the call. Five rings, and then he heard an irritated greeting. He responded in kind.

"Hello, Mr. Minister," he said.

"Vostov? Are you insane, calling me at my office?"

"I'll make it brief."

"That isn't the point. This connection isn't secure—"

"Listen to me, Minister. I don't like politics, and I'm beginning to regret having gotten tangled up in this business. But men have to live with their choices."

"Would you quit sounding philosophical, and come to the point? And remember, we're possibly not alone here."

"Fine, then. I'm going to give you some advice," Vostov said. "Do whatever you want with it, but I suggest you at least pay attention."

"All right, all right. What is it?"

"Our associate abroad feels he's being neglected at your end. He says—"

"The man is no associate of mine. Merely a mover of goods, who is in turn moved by others."

"Whatever. You've been dodging his calls, or so he claims. And I think it's important that you talk to him."

"Vostov, can't you see I'm trying to lay some groundwork here? I don't have to jump at his whim. If he thinks he can have carte blanche with my time now, I can only imagine his future impositions. And those of his shadow masters."

"Talk to him, Minister. Pacify him. I don't want the man on my back."

"And I don't like the idea of him playing us against each other. He'll wait until I'm ready to speak to him, and he can fuck himself in the meantime."

"Look, you must understand that he's capable of turning this whole damn thing on its head—"

"We have enough to occupy our minds without being concerned with him. I have intelligence about that American operation in Kaliningrad. Something may be going on there that could spell trouble, although I don't know precisely what it is. We must be prepared to take quick action should the need arise. I think, under these circumstances, it's time for you to make yourself useful."

"That's not my business. I've already done—"

"You'll do more. I'll require supplies. Equipment. Perhaps even manpower. Don't make the error of thinking you can wash your hands of this now."

"Fucking politics. As I said before, I never should have let myself become involved in it."

"One can't help but be, Vostov. Life is politics. From the time we're children competing with our siblings for our parents' attention, trying to outgrab one another for what we desire. I'm convinced that's when the betrayals begin. The family is a Judas circle, the brother we love is our enemy, eh?"

"I don't know. You're losing me."

"Am I? Well, just don't forget you were on that boat in Khabarovsk."

"Is that everything?" Vostov inquired with some sarcasm.

"No. I need you to utilize your many contacts, as much as I may despise them. It seems that it's time to cloud the landscape a bit. There are factions out there that might very well share our common goal. I think it would be wise to turn the bright light of public scrutiny on them.''

"What do you mean?'' Vostov asked.

"The nationalists, the separatists, the Communists, and the reformers all have an interest in blocking foreign aid. I believe it's time that someone pointed this out to them, hmm'? And the military and the KGB, unfairly squeezed out from distributing the largesse of our enemies—and so prevented from raking off their percentage from the top. Don't you think someone should ask them how they feel about this and what they plan to do about it? Even the church and organized crime have something at stake here. My dear Vostov, the more pressure Starinov and the West are under, the sooner we'll achieve our ultimate goals. Your tentacles reach everywhere. I think that you should use them.''

"What you're asking—'' Vostov spluttered, "it's hardly the work of a few moments.''

"Then I'd suggest you get started immediately. Remember, Vostov, a man who won't make himself useful is a man who is expendable. Now is there anything else you'd like to discuss?''

"You haven't given me an answer on the matter I called you about. The mover of goods, as you called him—''

"I said he can go *fuck* himself! From here on in, I will deal only with his superiors, and only when it suits me. And if you don't come through for me, Vostov, the same will apply to you. If you're around at all. Now good-bye, Vostov. See that you're ready when I need you.''

"Wait, don't hang up. Hello? Are you still there? Goddamn it, are you still there? Hello, hello, *hello* . . . ?'' A dial tone emerged clearly from the phone in his hand. He threw it across the room.

"Damn."

A slight sound drew his attention back to the women, now huddled in the corner and looking slightly fearful.

"Well, what are you two staring at? Get over here and make yourselves useful." That was the phrase the man on the phone had used. *Useful!* He sat down and waited. As they approached him hesitantly, he shut his eyes. Politics. It was a dirty business. There were other activities he much preferred.

TWENTY-THREE

WEARING A GRAY SWEATSUIT, A BALTIMORE ORIOLES
baseball cap, and Nikes, Alex Nordstrum jogged west
through the Mall, a look of quiet concentration on his
features as his long legs carried him over the path with
unbroken rhythm. He was past the midway point of his
run and his blood felt pumped with oxygen and the muscles of his thighs and calves were pleasantly loose.

Arms moving in smooth coordination with his feet, he
ran on toward Constitution Gardens and the conspicuous
marble shaft of the Washington Monument, where he
would ordinarily swing back east to complete his regular
two-mile circuit. Today he might have to wait around a
bit, depending on whether Blake was on time ... which
Nordstrum doubted would be his good fortune, considering the assistant secretary of state, Foreign Affairs Bu-
reau, was someone whose internal clock had seemed to
have its workings irreparably gummed up even when he
was Alex's top poli-sci student at Georgetown.

Nordstrum trotted along at an easy pace, seeing no reason to hurry. North of the park, the massive cluster of
Federal Triangle buildings extended continuously to Fifteenth Street, their red rooftops visible through the winter-
bare treetops. To the south, Nordstrum could see the white
colonnades and porticoes of the Department of Agriculture Building. Vapor puffed from his mouth with each

measured breath but his metabolism was up and he was hardly aware of the cold Potomac gusts snapping moisture off his cheeks and forehead. The back of his sweatshirt was dark with perspiration between his shoulder blades, a good, healthy sweat, the kind that always seemed to wash the tension from his pores.

To his right, well-dressed men and women swept past in expensive cars, most turning north or south on Seventeenth Street for the downtown museums and government buildings, a smaller percentage of the traffic continuing past the Reflecting Pool to where Constitution Avenue became Route 66 and spooled on out across the bridge to Arlington. Maybe a mile behind Nordstrum, morning sunlight fanned over the Capitol dome in golden spokes that had already begun to glance off the red brick turrets of Smithsonian Castle. In the broad stretch of landscaping he'd covered on his way down the Hill, walkers and joggers were strung out along the paths at various stages of their exercise routines, squirrels and pigeons were squabbling over sparse winter pickings, and vacationing college kids dressed in goose-down jackets and long elf-like knit caps were strolling toward the small round skating rink next to the Museum of Natural History, carrying their ice skates over their shoulders by the laces. The kids seemed about as traumatized as the squirrels and birds by what had happened in Times Square just one week before, which was not at all.

The resilience of youth? Nordstrum wondered. Or perhaps the inurement of a generation that had been born in an era when terrorism was an ever-present threat, something on a par with environmental calamities like earthquakes and hurricanes? He wasn't sure he wanted to know, and could only hope it was the former. For him, anyway, the grandeur of the Capitol was always enough to fill his head with refrains of "Stars and Stripes" and rouse a tremendous sense of obligation to his adopted country.

He reached Fourteenth Street, jogged in place while waiting for a break in the flow of traffic, then crossed out of the Mall proper onto the monument grounds, where the lawn began its gentle rise to the base of the towering obelisk.

He had started up the knoll when he heard the slapping of feet against the pavement behind him, and looked back to see Neil Blake following only a few yards downhill. An athletic man of thirty-five with handsome features and longish—for Washington—brown hair, he was wearing a black Speedo running suit with an electric blue stripe down the side, looking exactly like what he was, a member of the smart and spirited power elite.

"Neil," Nordstrom said, slowing a little, "how long have you been stalking me?"

Blake nodded his head back toward Fourteenth Street. "I came in from over by the Ellipse, saw you crossing the road," he said. "I'd've caught up to you sooner, but there was a nice young lady on the path who needed directions, and I sort of had to stop. Besides, I thought I'd let you get in a few extra minutes of peaceful exercise."

"Such a considerate fellow," Nordstrum said. "Did you take her phone number? In case she needs more help getting around."

Blake patted his pocket.

"It's already tucked away in a safe place," he said.

Nordstrum smiled. They ran side by side awhile in silence, cresting the knoll and then heading down toward the Reflecting Pool. The water sparkled in the morning light.

"I've got something for you," Blake said. "It wasn't easy. Anyone finds out I leaked it, I can open up that bagel joint my cousin Steve in Chicago always wanted me to go in on."

Nordstrum nodded but said nothing.

"You know the Lian Group?" Blake said.

"Of course."

"They made the goods," Blake said.

Nordstrum nodded again. His face was serious and thoughtful.

"What about the end purchaser?" he asked.

"The trail leads to a Russian distributor. After that, it's an open question."

There was a long pause.

"Crap," Nordstrum said finally, shaking his head.

"I didn't figure you'd like my news much," Blake said.

Nordstrum was quiet another moment.

"Is that all of it?" he said.

"So far, yeah," Blake said. "I'll let you know if I dig up anything more."

"Thanks," Nordstrum said. "I'm glad I gave you an A in class."

"I earned it," Blake said.

Nordstrum looked over at him.

"Insolent pup," he said.

"It's looking more and more as if you were right the other day, Gord," Nordstrum said into his telephone.

Freshly showered and wrapped in a bathrobe, he was back in his Pennsylvania Avenue townhouse after his jog, and had just gotten through telling Gordian what he'd learned from Blake.

"I'm almost wishing I'd been wrong," Gordian said. "This Lian Group . . . I've heard of it before. Didn't the name come up in the Thompson campaign finance hearings a few years ago?"

"Right again," Nordstrum said. "The evidence that it was involved in funneling Chinese government funds into our election wasn't as conclusive as it was for Lippo, among other foreign contributors . . . but it was strong nonetheless. In my opinion, Lian money gave at least two senators a considerable edge against their opponents, and may very likely have won them their seats."

"I'm still pretty much with Megan insofar as being confused. What's the connection between Lian and the Russians? And specifically *which* Russians?"

Nordstrum sat forward on his living room sofa, absently winding the telephone wire around his fingers.

"The best I can do is speculate," he said. "I mean, I'd need to look into my files, do some research, before I could expect you to bank on this information."

"Go ahead, I understand."

"There are circumstances that would point toward Russia's Agricultural Minister, Yeni Bashkir, being knee-deep in this affair. He and Lian have a long relationship. As do members of the Chinese regime and Bashkir. Also, Bashkir's family held commercial interests throughout Asia until after the Bolshevik Revolution."

"And his motive?"

"Bashkir's hardly an Americanophile . . . is that the proper term?"

"I'm not sure," Gordian said, "but the meaning's clear enough."

"Be that as it may, he distrusts capitalism and democracy, and like many in his generation would have preferred to save the old Communist system by fiddling with it, rather than see it dismantled. Also, while not an extreme nationalist in the Pedachenko vein, he's unquestionably something of a cultural chauvinist."

"So you're saying he might have wanted to disrupt Starinov's pro–U.S. initiatives, make him look ineffectual."

"In essence, agreeing with what you suggested at our meeting," Nordstum said. He realized he'd gotten his phone cord hopelessly tangled and worked to extract his fingers.

Gordian sighed at the other end of the line.

"Doesn't the fact that Bashkir helped *negotiate* the assistance package undermine our hypothesis?" he said. "Look at any photo of Starinov when he was at the White House back in October, you'll see the minister at his side."

Nordstrum made a sound in his throat that was the verbal equivalent of a shrug.

"Gord, I know you're a glass half-full sort of person. But you're as aware as I am that Russian politics hasn't come very far from the imperial courts of Catherine or Nicholas II. There's a long, cherished tradition of back-stabbing intrigue in the capital, whether you're talking about modern-day Moscow or St. Petersburg in the nineteenth century."

There was a brief silence. Nordstrum struggled to untangle the knotted up wire, letting his friend think.

"Okay," Gordian said finally. "Can you put together a brief for Nimec, get it to him via e-mail by tonight?"

"Might be a bit thin on detail . . . but yes, I can do it."

"Send copies to Blackburn and Megan in Kaliningrad. And to Vince Scull, for that matter. Let's see what our combined brain trust can accomplish."

"Right," Nordstrum said. He was getting hungry for breakfast. "Anything else?"

"Only one small favor."

"Shoot."

"You ought to work on that habit of playing with the telephone wire while you're talking, or at least get a cordless," Gordian said. "I'm hearing all kinds of static here at my end."

Nordstrum frowned.

"For you, boss, I'll certainly do my best," he said.

TWENTY-FOUR

SAN JOSE, CALIFORNIA
JANUARY 7, 2000

A FEW MOMENTS PAST ELEVEN O'CLOCK AT NIGHT,
Pete Nimec sat at his laptop computer in his home office,
his face a study in concentration as he read the e-mail that
had just appeared on its display regarding Gordian's ongoing investigation into the events in Russia, code-named
''Politika'':

Status: Reply 1 of 1, 3 attachments (PEM Sign
and Encrypt)

Re: "Politika"
>Pete,
>It's 2 A.M. here in D.C., but I wanted to
>complete and upload the data files you
>requested before hitting the sack.
>Knowing you as well as I do, you're
>probably online looking for them right now,
>and won't be able to tear yourself away from
>the damn machine until they've popped into
>your mailbox. So here they are—a bit on the
>sketchy side, but the best I could do on short
>notice. I suggest you give the material a
>quick review and relax. It's already much too
>late for me to get a decent night's sleep, but
>there's no sense in both of us staying up to

>greet the Wolf.
>Best, Alex

Nimec moved his cursor to the menu bar, clicked on the Download option, then rocked backward in his chair and waited, smiling a little. Alex was so often correct it was uncanny. And he never disappointed.

When the transfer was done, Nimec logged off the Internet server, opened the first of the three files, and began scrolling through it:

Profile: Bashkir, Yeni

HISTORY

PERSONAL:
Born 2/12/46 in Vladivostok, Primorsky Kray.
Paternal grandfather operated pre-Bolshevik
import/export firm with offices throughout China
and Korea. Father (deceased) among the first
generation of naval officers in Soviet Pacific
Fleet. Mother (deceased) of Manchurian Chinese
ancestry. Bashkir is married and presently lives
in Moscow. The eldest of his two adult sons is a
concert violinist who has toured with . . .

Nimec let his eyes go down to the following section; what Alex meant by "sketchy" might have constituted a full academic treatise for other researchers.

MILITARY/POLITICAL:
Followed his father into distinguished naval
career; served with Soviet Pacific Fleet during
Cold War; captained November-class and Echo II-

class nuclear submarines berthed in Kamchatka
Peninsula. Promoted to rear admiralty in 1981,
eventually achieved command of entire nuclear
sub fleet. Former Communist Party member;
joined Yeltsin's party approx. 1991. Close
associations with Beijing regime, esp.
government trade officials, extended through
period of strained Sino-Soviet relations.
Handpicked by President Mikhail Gorbachev to
be special consul to China, 1992; instrumental in
strengthening political and economic links
between the two nations. Primary author of
Chinese-Russian cooperation agreements in
1996 and 1997 . . .

The next few paragraphs were devoted to a summary
of the agreements, which were more declarations of principle and intent than formal pacts. Something he read farther down in that same section, however, made Nimec sit
up straight with interest:

In August 1999 Bashkir attended trade summit
in Beijing and was chief negotiator of bilateral
arms/technology exchange agreement.
Delegation of Russian arms merchants included
representatives of *Zavtra Group* (see
accompanying file), of which Bashkir is said to
be a major shareholder. Also among business
executives present were *Teng Chou*, Chairman
of the Malaysian *Lian Chemicals* (see file),
reputed to be Chinese-controlled.

Nimec read those lines twice before continuing, his eyes riveted to the screen, a low, thoughtful sound issuing from his throat. It seemed to contain the answers to a lot of questions—and that was what bothered him. He mistrusted the obvious.

He sipped the lukewarm coffee on his desk and scanned the rest of the document.

Bashkir was appointed minister of the interior by President Boris Yeltsin 1999, retains post to present. Friendship with Vladimir Starinov said to have begun while Starinov was commanding general of elite Air Assault Force (VDV) division stationed in Petropavlovsk, Kamchatka region. While still professing personal and political loyalty to Starinov, he has been a vehement critic of his accelerated economic decontrols and Western-style democratic reforms . . .

Ten minutes later Nimec reached the end of the dossier. He printed it out, closed the file, and opened the next one on his download queue, a detailed rundown of the Lian Group's various international holdings.

It was midnight before he'd finished looking over Nordstrum's reports, and the feeling he had after having skimmed the last of the three was a more intense version of how he'd felt midway into the Bashkir file—a sense that things were just too damn easy. Somehow, he was reminded of a trip he'd taken to the Great Adventure Theme Park in New Jersey many years before. You drove along automobile paths that led through simulated wildlife habitats, but the truly dangerous animals were restrained behind not very well camouflaged fences. The idea being for visitors to have the illusion of traveling down a safari trail while in fact remaining on a safe, contrived, and carefully overseen route.

Rubbing his eyes, Nimec again made hard copies of the reports, then abandoned the program, switched off his computer, and closed its cover. He pushed back his chair, stood, and stretched, rotating his neck and shoulders to work the kinks out of his muscles. He was simultaneously exhausted and wired, and knew himself well enough to realize he would be unable to sleep. There was something else here, something he wasn't getting, a layer of understanding that seemed just out of reach.

Nimec shook his head. He needed desperately to unwind.

Leaving the office, he went across the wide, unpartitioned space of his living room, dining room, and kitchen to his private elevator. He thumbed the Call button, and when the car arrived rode it to the upper level of his triplex condominium apartment.

The elevator opened into a rec/training complex that spanned the entire floor and was divided into four large areas, all enclosed by a circular indoor jogging track: the dojo where he conducted his daily martial arts exercises, a fully equipped boxing gym, a soundproof target range, and the room he was headed into now, a faithful recreation of the dingy Philadelphia pool hall he'd haunted as a teenager, learning the game from some of the best players, not to mention the most seriously degenerate gamblers, ever to work magic with a cue stick . . . his own father unrivaled among them.

He pushed through the door and went inside. The room held two rows of antique championship tables with scarred frames and green baize playing surfaces that had been restored to their original appearance and leveled for optimum performance. There was a Coca-Cola soda bar with a Formica snack counter and rotating vinyl stools. There was a Wurlitzer jukebox that was wrapped in neon tubing and stocked with vintage rock and roll 45s. There were cheap plastic light fixtures from which a bilious glow seeped through conscientiously preserved layers of grime. The wall-to-wall memorabilia Nimec had scavenged from innumerable secondhand shops and flea markets included outdated nude pinup calendars, as well as signs stipulating ancient game rates and prohibitions against betting by minors.

The only thing missing was the pervasive bouquet of sweat, brilliantine, and cigarette smoke, and while Nimec supposed he was better off without that final touch of authenticity, he often had a perverse longing for it all the same.

Flicking on the lights, he pulled one of his custom twenty-ounce cues down off the wall and went to a table. He took six of the balls out of the built-in storage shelf at its foot and arranged them in a semicircle around a side pocket, having decided to work on his drills instead of racking up for continuous shooting. It had been over a week since he'd gotten in any practice.

Nimec chalked his stick, bent over the table rail, then laid the cue tip in the bridge he formed with his fingers and methodically sawed it back and forth.

Out of habit, he had placed the eight ball in the lead spot, his way of discharging any bad luck at the onset. He always took luck very seriously into consideration, had since his days in the Army Rangers, when he'd developed a host of elaborate—some had called them superstitious—rituals for courting good fortune in battle. Though his propitiations to Fate had assumed different outward forms in civilian life, the general practice had stuck.

Now, as he visualized the intended path of the cue ball, his gray eyes showed the quiet, steady focus of a sharpshooter. The trick here was to pocket the balls in sequence from right to left, using draw English to gain position each time for the following shot.

Keeping his wrist loose and his arm close to his side, he brought the stick straight back and then came through with a fluid, precise stroke, striking the cue ball below center to apply reverse spin. It sank the eight ball and came rolling back toward him, stopping right behind the next ball in line.

Exactly where he wanted it.

He pocketed three more balls in rapid succession, but on his fifth shot inadvertently tightened his hand around the butt of the cue stick, causing it to jerk upward at the last instant. To his annoyance, the cue ball went clattering down along with his fifth object ball.

A scowl creased Nimec's angular face. He had scratched like a rank amateur.

He took a deep breath. A lot more than just his game was off tonight. A whole damn lot. Nordstrum's reports seemed to indicate that the FBI was, as the press had been claiming for days, in possession of an intact explosive package; he doubted the Lian-Zavtra connection would have been made so quickly without a scientific check of taggants or traceable components within the instrument of destruction. Of course the chemical residue of tagged, *detonated* charges also would have yielded that information, but the bottom line remained the same either way. Bashkir's handprints were everywhere. There was good reason to suspect he was at the innermost level of the bombing conspiracy, if not its principal architect. But what would his motive have been? To fire up isolationist sentiments in the U.S., provoke a reassessment of the food relief effort that was drawing Russia closer to the West? That was the only explanation that made the slightest bit of sense, and there were too many problems with it. Bashkir was a military man. Someone who had held one of the highest posts in the Russian Navy, commanding the world's second largest fleet of ballistic-missile subs. He was also a dealmaker, used to carefully weighing his decisions. Would he really be able to justify the wholesale murder of civilians for such indirect and uncertain gains? Moreover, he recently had been involved in negotiating major arms transactions between his country and China, and perhaps even had a financial interest in a Russian firm that listed weapons distribution among its diverse shipping enterprises. He would know how easy it would be to follow the trail of the explosive from manufacturer to purchaser, and that the search would eventually lead to questions about his role in the bombing. Where was the sense in the thing?

Frowning, Nimec crouched down, reached into the pool table's innards again, and set the balls up at one end of the table for a point-of-aim drill. The more he thought about Bashkir's possible complicity, the greater his misgivings. It wasn't just that the puzzle was incomplete; he felt as if he'd been given pieces that didn't fit at all, and had been slipped into the box to confound him.

He supposed there was nothing to do except take it one step at a time . . . and the logical way to proceed was to follow the explosives from their point of origin to the final point of sale.

He put some more chalk on the tip of his stick, leaned

over the table, and began firing balls into the corner pocket opposite him. First thing in the morning he would give Gordian a call. As an exporter of American technology, Roger had constant dealings with people in Customs, and one or two of them might be good for a tip. If Lian was the producer of the explosives, and Zavtra had acted as the middleman outfit, who had received them in the United States? And how exactly had they been moved?

Somebody had completed the transfer, and Nimec intended to find out who it was.

TWENTY-FIVE

THE MOMENT HE GOT OFF THE HORN WITH NIMEC,
Gordian rang up Lenny Reisenberg, who headed his regional shipping office in New York.

"To what do I owe a call from the *gantse knahker*?"
Lenny said, taking the call from his secretary.

"I thought I was the *groyss makher*."

"There's a subtle difference," Lenny said. "The first
means 'big shot.' The second's somebody who makes
things happen. Generally speaking, though, the terms are
interchangeable, since most *makhers* are also *knahkers*,
and vice versa." He paused. "Now, on the other hand, if
I were to call you an *ahlte kakhker*, you'd have reason to
be peeved."

Gordian smiled tolerantly, shaking his head. He had no
idea why, but Lenny seemed convinced it was vital that
he learn Yiddish, and had been giving him these lessons
in regular installments for over a decade. Were the best
employees always so full of idiosyncrasies, or was it just
that he knew how to pick them?

"Len, I need a favor," he said.

"And because it's only nine in the morning in your
neck of the woods, and you're still on your first cup of
coffee, I'm assuming it's urgent."

"Very," Gordian said. "There's a Russian exporter,
the Zavtra Group—"

"Hold it a sec, let me jot this down." Gordian heard Lenny shuffling things around on his desk. "Okay, that's spelled Z-A-V-T-R-A?"

"Right."

"Don't think we've ever done business with them. Off the top of my head, of course."

"That's not important, Len. What I want are chronological records of everything Zavtra's shipped into the New York area over the past, say, six to eight months. We may eventually have to go back further, but let's start with that. I'll need to know the ultimate purchaser, too."

"May I ask *why* I'm getting hold of this information?"

"On this one, it's better you don't."

Reisenberg huffed out a breath. "Okay, I'll see what I can do. There's a guy I know in the customs office over at the World Trade Center. If we end this conversation in the next ten seconds I might be able to get hold of him, take him out for a bite. I've got just the thing to make him feel kindly toward us, come to think of it."

"Whatever it takes, as long as you don't get yourself in hot water."

"Right, right. I'll call you back soon as I find out anything."

"Thanks, Len."

"No problem. This is why I'm known far and wide as a stud among prizewinning thoroughbreds."

"And a genuine *mensch*," Gordian said.

"Sorry, don't speak French," Reisenberg said.

And hung up the phone.

"You ask me, it's a crying shame those antismoking Nazis made it against the law to light up anywhere in the city, including your own fucking toilet." This out of Steve

Bailey, the customs supervisor Lenny Reisenberg had mentioned to Gordian. He was sitting across from Lenny in a leather booth at Quentin's, a British-style pub across the street from the twin towers, with a lot of dark wood wall paneling, an enormous horseshoe bar, and middle-aged waiters who had been working there long enough to recite the menu backward and forward by heart.

Lenny gave him a noncommittal shrug.

"There are pros and cons," he said.

"You going to tell me something's wrong with restaurants having smoking sections? The way they used to before the world got taken over by prudes and sissies?"

"Truth is," Lenny said, "I feel sorry for the poor waiter who's put at risk of lung cancer because of the secondary smoke he's got to inhale on the job."

"Spoken like the reformed three-pack-a-day man that you are." Bailey snorted. "I mean, the owner feels compunctions about his staff, he can go ahead and hire smokers to *serve* the smoking sections."

"Even so, Steve," Lenny said, "what they'd do in the old days was calculate the *size* of the sections according to seating capacity, which made it kind of hard for the Board of Health to enforce the regulations. The inspectors would have to come in and count heads to make sure there were no violations, you know what I'm saying." He shrugged again. "Meanwhile, the people that ran the places would cram the tables so close together, the guy at the next table practically would be sitting on your lap . . ."

"Or *gal* at the next table, to look at the positive side . . ."

"Whatever." Lenny snorted. "The point is—"

"That I just finished eating a delicious lamb stew, and

191

have a fresh Macanudo tucked away in my pocket, and want to smoke it to round out my dining experience,'' Bailey said, brushing a hand through his frazzle of white hair. ''At fifty years old, with a prostate that's bigger than a basketball, I don't have many ways left of having fun. A guy deserves some slack, Lenny.''

Lenny looked at him. He figured that was about as perfect an opening as he could have asked for in a million years.

''That reminds me.'' He reached into a pocket of his sport coat, pulled out a slim envelope with the Madison Square Garden logo on it, and slid it across the table.

Bailey stared down at it, keeping his hands under the table.

''Jesus,'' he said. ''What the hell's that?''

''A little gift, Steve. From the New York Knickerbockers to me, and me to you.''

''The Knicks?''

''Uh-huh.''

''Jesus.'' Bailey swallowed, one hand appearing and reaching for the envelope. He picked it up gingerly, almost as if it were hot to the touch, then lifted the flap with his fingertip and peeked inside.

His eyes widened.

''Jesus,'' he repeated for the third time, his head wagging from side to side. ''This is a goddamned *season pass*.''

''Well, partial season, technically, being as it's already January,'' Lenny said. He glanced at Bailey. ''Why're you shaking your head?''

''I'm not shaking my head.''

''You are,'' Lenny said. ''If you don't like my gift . . .''

''Of course I like it, you know I do, how the fuck could

I *not*? But being that Christmas is over, and you don't know my birthday, there's got to be some other reason you're giving this to me, and I'm not sure I want to know what it is.''

"You wound me, Steve." Lenny used his fork to slice off a wedge of the blueberry cheesecake he was having for dessert. "The pass is yours free and easy, just because we're friends." He grinned. "Of course, now that you mention it, there *is* something you . . .''

"I didn't know I'd done that.''

"Done what?''

"Mentioned it.'' Bailey stared ruminatively at the envelope, seeming to weigh it in his open palm. A few seconds later he grunted and stuffed it into his pocket. "But now that *you've* gone and raised the subject of how I can reciprocate, please feel free to give your suggestions. Bearing in mind I try to be a law-abiding fellow. Whenever possible, that is.''

Lenny nodded, ate the slice of cheesecake, and wiped his lips with his napkin. Then he leaned forward and told Bailey what he wanted.

"I'll take anything you can get me," he concluded in a hushed voice. "Cargo manifests, bills of lading, authorization documents—you name it. The more, the better.''

Bailey looked at him. "This Zavtra outfit in Russia . . . is it an air or sea carrier?''

"Could be both for all I know. Does it matter?''

"Only insofar as it'd make my life easier. I mean, ninety percent of import and export transactions are filed electronically these days, which makes the info I pull out of my computer practically up-to-the-minute. But there

193

are different systems depending on the method of transport."

"Don't they interface?"

"Sure they do. Like I said, it's no big problem to run a global search. I'm just trying to cut down on the time involved." Bailey scratched behind his ear. "How soon you need this stuff, by the way?"

"Five minutes ago," Lenny said. "And that was pushing things to the wire."

Bailey ballooned his cheeks, slowly let the air whistle out.

"Do you always lay this kind of fucking bullshit on your wife and kids when you give *them* presents?"

Lenny shook his head.

"The love I've got for my family is unconditional," he said. "I only associate with foul-mouthed sports fans like you out of necessity."

Bailey grinned.

"Hurry up and ask for the check, asshole," he said.

"Michael Caine!"

"No, it's Tom Jones."

"Tom Jones is a singer. The question was what British *actor* worked in a coal mine before he was famous."

"I seen him act in that movie about the Martians attacking, Boch—"

"That was what they call a cameo, which ain't the same thing. And besides, Tom Jones was a fucking grave digger—"

"No, no, I'm telling you *Rod Stewart* was a grave digger, Tom Jones . . ."

"Look, *stunade,* I don't wanna hear no more about

Tom Jones, okay? If it wasn't Michael Caine it's gotta be Richard Harris . . ."

"Who the hell's Richard Harris?"

"Jesus Christ, what planet you from, anyway? He's the guy who—"

"Hey, Boch, how you doing?" Lenny Reisenberg interrupted from the entrance to the Quonset.

He had been freezing his rear end off for the past five minutes, listening to Tommy Boccigualupo, the dockyard foreman, argue with his pal about a question that had been posed on the quiz show they were watching on Tommy's small color TV. Behind him on the Twelfth Avenue wharf, hydraulic winches hissed and forklifts clanked as cargo was shuttled between ship holds and wide-load semis. There were a couple of pigeons squabbling with a dirty seagull over a pizza crust near the piles to Lenny's right. Beyond them, the sky and the river merged in a smear of gray.

Lenny heard a jubilant commotion of bells, whistles, and contestant screeches from the television. They seemed to jangle off the corrugated walls of the hut. Somebody on the program had apparently won something.

"Aw crap, Len," Boch said. "You made us miss the answer."

"Sorry." Lenny gave the coil heater beside Tommy's chair a longing glance. "It all right if I come in?"

"Sure, *mi* shithole *es su* shithole," Boch said. He motioned to a sofa with sunken Herculon cushions. Lenny remembered having dumped one just like it around 1974.

He sat. Springs creaked, groaned, and poked into his bottom. The armrest felt as if it had absorbed a large quantity of used motor oil at some point in its long life. Still, the warmth from the heater had quickly taken the chill out of his bones, and he couldn't help but be appreciative.

"How's the son?" Boch said, rotating his swivel chair toward Lenny.

"He took the purple streaks out of his hair last week, started wearing what they call dreadlocks instead. Like those guys in Jamaica." Lenny spread his hands haplessly. "Gets straight As in school, though, so what can I say?"

Boch grunted his commiseration, smoothed his palm over his brilliantined hair. "My oldest daughter, Theresa, she's pregnant with her second. Husband's a slacker, *capisce*? I don't know whether to congratulate him or break his fucking kneecaps."

Lenny leaned down and wriggled his fingers in front of the heater.

"Kids," he said, shaking his head.

"Kids," Boch repeated. He sighed. "What can I do for you, Len? 'Cause if this is about another rush job for UpLink, you're outta luck. The Port Authority's been wrapping the red tape around my balls since the bombing . . . ''

"Nothing like that." Lenny gave him a significant glance and tipped his head toward the other man in the Quonset, who was still watching the game show.

Boch nodded.

"Joe," he said.

The guy wrenched his eyes from the tube. "Yeah?"

"Get out there and check on that shipment from Korea," Boch said, pointing out his window at the dock. "Remind the boys I want it at the warehouse before they knock off for the day."

"Sure," Joe said.

"And Joe?"

"Yeah?"

"Then go get us some coffees."

"Sure."

Joe buttoned his mackinaw and left.

Boch waited until he was out of earshot and turned back to Lenny.

"So," he said. "Talk."

"Friend of mine in Customs tells me an outfit called Mercury Distribution has a lot of merchandise come in at this yard. Received a shipment from Russia maybe a month, month and half back."

He paused. Boch made an indeterminate sound, gestured for him to continue.

"I need the skinny on Mercury," Lenny said. "It legit, or what?"

Boch looked at him. "Why you asking?"

"Because my boss asked me to ask," Lenny said.

A moment passed.

Boch kept looking at him.

"They been saying on the news it might be Russkies did that number in Times Square," he said.

"Yeah."

"And now you come in with your questions about Mercury."

"Yeah."

"I don't believe in coincidence," Boch said.

"Me neither, but I swear I don't know any more than I'm telling you," Lenny said. "I'm doing this on faith, Boch."

There was another silence. Boch meshed his knuckles on his lap, glanced down at them, cracked them.

"Mercury's run by a hood name of Nick Roma," he said, finally. "Don't let the handle fool you, he's no *goombah.* Can call himself anything he wants, still stinks like fucking borscht to me.''

Lenny nodded. ''What kind of stuff he import?''

''Ain't my lookout,'' Boch said. ''I got to stay healthy for the wife's sake, you know?''

Lenny nodded again, rose from the couch, moved toward the entryway, turned to face Boccigualupo. Though he was still inside, he could feel the cold seeping back into him as he moved farther from the emission of the heater.

''I owe you one,'' he said. ''And FYI, the answer to that question on the game show was 'Richard Burton.' ''

''Thanks, I'll make sure Joe finds out,'' Boch said. He chewed his upper lip. ''And you tell your boss to be careful, Len. These are dangerous people he's messing with.''

Lenny took a step closer to the door, then paused half in and half out of it. On the dock, the seagull had won its competition with the tag team of pigeons and was triumphantly shaking the pizza crust in its beak. The sky seemed a little grayer than it did before.

''I'll tell him,'' he said.

Gordian buzzed Nimec in his office at three P.M.

''Good news,'' he said. ''I just heard from our man Reisenberg.''

Nimec's fingers tightened around the receiver.

''He's got the material?''

''Scads of it. Or so he says,'' Gordian said. ''You want me to have him FedEx it to us?''

Nimec considered that a moment. FedEx was normally reliable, but even they had been known to misplace the occasional package—and this was one shipment that couldn't afford to go awry. Nimec didn't know where

Lenny had gotten the information from, but he knew someone would be in trouble if word got out that he or she was leaking information like this. Besides, he thought, if he was going to have another sleepless night, he might as well spend it packing his travel bag.

"No," he said. "I think I'd better fly into New York tomorrow morning."

There was a brief silence before Gordian commented.

"Something tells me you've been wearing out your carpet again, Pete," he said.

Nimec stopped pacing.

"Goes to show how little you know about your employees," he said.

Gordian grinned, but sobered quickly. "Is your team ready to go, Pete?"

"Always," Nimec said. "On a moment's notice."

"Good," Gordian said. "Because a moment may be all we get."

Nimec nodded. "I'll put 'em on alert," he said. "And then I think I'll go pack."

Pressing the button on his phone, he disconnected from Gordian and then punched in the first phone number.

TWENTY-SIX

AS LEGEND GOES, WHEN ALEXANDER THE GREAT WAS presented with the riddle of undoing the Gordian knot, he simply severed it with a blow of his sword rather than ponder its intricate twists and turns. Problem solved, according to Alexander, who was always pragmatic and direct.

When Roger Gordian, Megan Breen, and Peter Nimec had conceived of a troubleshooting and crisis-control team within UpLink, the idea to name it Sword had flashed into Megan's mind as naturally as a beam of sunshine piercing the clouds on a midsummer morning. The play on Roger's last name seemed exceedingly appropriate, given how his own realistic, determined approach to tackling obstacles paralleled that of Alexander.

Sword was, in effect, his answer to modern Gordian knots: a global special intelligence network that relied on a combination of risk management and scenario planning to anticipate most outbreaks of trouble, defusing them before they threatened international peace and stability, his country's interests, or the interests of his firm—all three of which generally coincided.

This did not, however, mean Sword was without physical resources in the event things got rough. Comprised of hundreds of men and women who had been carefully screened by Nimec, and hired away from police and intelligence agencies around the world, its security arm could aggressively do whatever it took to handle dangerous, and even violent, situations. The organizational and operational framework upon which Nimec had built this force was clear, consistent, and almost elegant in its simplicity: for maximum secrecy and effectiveness, regional offices were to be established separately from UpLink's corporate locations; members of the group were to be based in areas with which they had close personal or professional familiarity; and field teams were to abide by the laws of the nations to which they were assigned, employing non-lethal weapons whenever possible.

Right now, Nimec was thinking that his local section chief, Tony Barnhart, had followed every one of those guidelines to the letter, giving him high confidence that their operation would go off according to plan in spite of the wicked nor'easter that was slamming the area.

The turn-of-the century meat packing factory that had been converted into Sword's New York headquarters was inconspicuously tucked away between Hudson and Dowar streets in Soho, a part of downtown Manhattan whose name not only reflected its position on the city map—which was *so*uth of *Ho*uston Street—but was also a nod to the renowned London theatrical district from the neighborhood's large artsy population. In the old days, before the onslaught of the high-rises, someone looking out the French doors that gave onto the building's third-story terrace could have seen the Washington Square Arch amid the twisting streets of Greenwich Village, and Gramercy Park to the north, and farther uptown the Empire State Building towering resolutely above an agglomeration of more modern—and less graceful—basalt-and-glass skyscrapers. These days, however, the old landmarks were invisible, all but buried in a sea of newer, taller buildings.

Tonight even this skyline had been blotted out by the storm, and Nimec saw nothing but thick curtains of mixed rain and snow charged with pyrotechnic lightning.

Turning from the balcony, he let his eyes tour the room where Barnhart and his teammate, Noriko Cousins, were quietly engaged in last-minute preparations, with fitted black tactical hoods pulled back behind their necks. The room had been done up in shades of gray and white, the fireplace surrounded by marble tiles, no mantel or hearth, very sleek and spare. The crackling flame threw a soft orange glow across the pile carpet, the plump white sofa, and the wall panel that had fulcrumed open at the touch of a hidden button, revealing the equipment cache from which Nimec had extracted the tools and weapons they would be using on their break-in.

Laid out across Barnhart's lap was a Benelli semiautomatic combat shotgun with a rubber-coated pistol grip, nonreflecting synthetic black finish, and barrel-mounted target light. The tubular magazine he had slapped into its stock contained six 12-gauge sabots, each of which would peel away upon firing to release a fin-stabilized CS teargas bomblet. In pouches on the nylon utility harness worn over his chest were a half-dozen additional magazines filled with rubber stingball cartridges, blunt-impact foam rounds, incendiary rounds, and other types of disabling and distraction projectiles. Also attached to the crisscrossing straps of his rig were pen-shaped aerosol canisters of dimethyl sulfoxide, or DMSO, a chemical sedative which human skin would rapidly absorb like a sponge. There was a high-voltage taser baton in the scabbard clipped to his belt.

Cross-legged on the floor, Noriko was carefully arranging her lockpicking tools on the tabletop, her black hair in a tight ponytail, her dark Asian eyes narrowed in concentration. Holstered at her hip was a Foster-Miller suppression weapon she called her webshooter, after the device used by the Spiderman comic book character. About the size of a flare gun, it discharged filament-thin netting coated with a polymer superglue. On the carpet to her right was a lightweight jamb spreader that looked something like a car jack, which she would strap over her shoulder and use only if doorway entry became more a matter of speed than stealth.

Beside her on the floor, within easy reach, was the hard plastic capsule of a Saber laser-dazzler. Before they moved out, the last thing she would do was to insert the Saber into a 40mm grenade launcher, itself fitted beneath the barrel of an M16 rifle. A targeting control box for the optical weapon was snapped to the underside of the grenade tube. The ammunition she had fed into the gun's banana clip consisted of 5.56mm bullets encased within .50-caliber plastic sabots. Fired at a low muzzle speed from the specially designed VVRS upper receiver, the sabots would remain in place as blunt, less-than-lethal cushions. At a higher velocity they would split apart to release the deadly metal rounds within them.

Nimec smiled a little. It was all so very high-tech, wasn't it? A far cry from some of the improvised SpecOp gear he'd carried way back when. But old habits died hard and he was still something of a traditionalist. He would go in carrying smoke and flash-bang grenades, OC spray canisters, and his 9mm Beretta—loaded with standard ammo in case lethal force was needed despite his intentions to the contrary.

He checked his watch.

It was seven-forty-five, almost time to roll.

"You think Roma's going to stick to his routine even in that mess?" he said to Barnhart, nodding his head back to indicate the sheets of wintry precipitation outside the sliding doors.

Barnhart glanced over at him.

"Unless Nicky's snowed in to his ears, he'll stay true to form," he said.

"Let's just hope there's something in his office we can use," Noriko said without looking up from her tools.

Nimec nodded. He slipped his hand into his trouser pocket, crossed his fingers out of sight.

"Let's," he said.

TWENTY-SEVEN

THE SKY OUTSIDE THE WINDOW WAS A BLUR OF FALL-
ing snow. It blew in rippling cataracts, tinged eerily pink
by the vapor light across the street.

Putting his cordless phone back on its base, Nick Roma
cursed inwardly. He could hear the wind keening outside,
hurling flakes against the pane like fistfuls of sand. Although the rain that had soaked the pavement earlier had
delayed any accumulation, he knew the city would be buried under mountains of white by morning.

Well, Nick thought, he had enough to worry about
without letting the weather get to him. Better to look
ahead toward what was in store. A moment ago on the
phone, Marissa had said that she missed him. Why hadn't
he been in touch?

It was good to keep them wondering. She would be
generous with her affection tonight, would want to make
sure he hadn't tired of her. And if expenses, not sex, were
on her mind as she arched against him, so what? The
maintenance on the Shore Road co-op in which he kept
her was nearly two thousand dollars a month. And then
there was the small fortune she spent on clothes and trin-
kets. Money was what moved her to passion—although
she gave as well as she got. As in any fair deal, each party
came away satisfied.

Rising from behind his desk, he went to the coatrack,

took his Armani sport coat off the hanger, and slipped it on. Then he stood in front of the mirror, smoothing and combing. Let the snow come down. Let the city choke on it. He would spend tomorrow luxuriating in soft, warm flesh.

Satisfied with his appearance, he returned to his desk. In a plastic bag beside it were two bottles of Pinot Noir. A French label—the American vintages didn't even belong in the same class.

He glanced at the dial of his watch. Ten minutes to eleven. It was Sunday and the nightclub downstairs was closed. And as usual on Sunday nights, Nick had been at the office to meet with his captains, receive his skim, give them instructions, mediate their disputes, and so forth. Most had grumbled about having to come out in the storm, but they didn't have any idea what it was like to stand in his shoes. He believed in keeping tight control of all his projects. Anybody who didn't was asking for chaos.

That, of course, was the problem with his participation in what had been done New Year's Eve. So much of it had been out of his hands from the beginning. And then there was the business of the satchel charge, the one that hadn't gone off. He had suspected even before the press leaks that something like that had happened. The earliest stories on the news had mentioned only three explosions following the initial blast, and at the time he had optimistically hoped they were wrong. But he'd had his lingering doubts, and day by day the hard evidence had mounted, eventually becoming conclusive. Three explosions. Not four. This according to every eyewitness, every inch of video footage, every photograph taken at the scene. When the story surfaced that an undetonated bomb had been discovered and given over to the FBI for testing, he'd known it was all true. And had gotten to thinking. Could that possibly have been what Gilea and her people wanted? And if so, why? He'd been aware that they meant to throw a wrench into certain political developments between the United States and Russia . . . but his biggest mistake had been to distance himself from the intricacies of their plan, and therefore remain half-blind to its intended outcome. Had he been caught up in a scheme that was more devious than he'd guessed? And if so, might it be that he was to be sacrificed as part of it?

It seemed like a lot of wild imagination . . . but before the first of the year, the same might have been said about a bombing on the scale of what had occurred in Times Square. Suppose he'd been set up to take the heat? He had to wonder about that, in spite of how Gilea had acted toward him the night of the attack, and what they had done together afterward, done right here in his office . . . or maybe because of it. She had been all over him that night. It had been as though she were on fire. As though the flames that had killed those hundreds of people had brought about an unquenchable heat of a different sort inside her body. He didn't know how else to describe it. Gilea, Gilea. Here and then disappeared. What was he to make of her? A woman like that was capable of anything. Anything in the world.

And say he was getting carried away with his suspicions? Admittedly, he'd been on edge for the past couple of weeks. Say he *was* getting carried away, and he hadn't been used as a pawn in some treacherous game, and the failure of the bomb to detonate was strictly an accident. Would the fact that it had nothing to do with Gilea's planning make the position he was in right now any better?

It didn't have to be that he'd been double-crossed. Things went wrong, and people went down as a consequence. What had been worrying him was the possibility that analysis of the explosives would lead to a connection between the distributor and his import company. He was no expert when it came to the science, but he knew that might be done with certain kinds of testing. The authorities would want badly to make an arrest. How might the evidence be stacking up against him? He wasn't sure yet, couldn't be sure. But he wasn't going to just stand around and wait for a gigantic fist to come crashing through his wall.

The wind thumped against his window, pelted it with sharp crystals of snow. The sound was loud enough to give Nick a start. Frowning, he cast off his thoughts with a visible shake of his head and returned to his desk.

He had done all that he could—for now, at any rate. He had his own men out, trying to discover what the Feds had learned—and throwing up smoke screens wherever they could. And if that wasn't enough . . . well, he had his insurance, his films of Gilea fondling the plastique. He was sure he'd be able to cut a deal if he had to.

He picked up the phone again, called downstairs, told his men to get his car warmed up. He wanted to forget his concerns for a while, wanted to sink himself deep into Marissa, wanted to relax.

Otherwise he might go crazy thinking about what might lie ahead.

TWENTY-EIGHT

"THERE'S NICKY AND HIS ZOO CREW," BARNHART said.

Nimec sat beside him in the front passenger seat of the station wagon, looking out the windshield in silence.

"Like clockwork," Noriko said from the vehicle's rear section.

Nimec gave her a small nod but remained silent. They were in a parking space a half block down from the Platinum Club. Their engine and headlights were off. There was no heat issuing from the vents. A film of snow had formed on the glass, making it difficult to see through, but for the past few minutes they had refrained from clearing it with even intermittent swishes of the wipers.

They were being careful to do nothing that might draw attention.

His face intent, Nimec watched Roma walk toward the curb in front of the Platinum Club, the folds of an outback coat whipping around his ankles, a pair of hulking body-guards on either side of him. Two more men were waiting on the street. The guards hung there until Roma got into the first of two large sedans that had pulled in front of the entrance, and then went back to the second car and crammed themselves into it.

Nimec and his team watched and waited. Snowflakes blew around them in tight little clots that burst apart like milkweed pods as they struck the hood of the wagon.

"He always surround himself with that much man-power?" Nimec said, breaking his silence at last.

Barnhart shrugged.

"The muscle's a little thicker than usual," he said. "Could be Nicky's feeling a little paranoid these days. He likes to be prepared."

Nimec thought about that. Barnhart, a former member of the FBI's Organized Crime Task Force, had assembled an extensive file on Roma that went back years. In the past week Nimec had read every word of it, and learned nearly everything there was to know about Roma and his criminal network . . . very significantly including information about his behind-the-scenes control of Mercury Distribution, an all-purpose clearinghouse for transport cargo, both legal and illegal, that he was moving into, out of, and around the country.

On November 28, Mercury had obtained delivery of a shipment of combined articles, marked generally as "theatrical effects," the ultimate purchaser of which was Partners Inc., yet another of Roma's multitude of shell companies, and the nominal owner of the Platinum Club.

The merchandise had arrived at the Red Hook shipyards aboard a freighter that belonged to the Zavtra Group.

Click-click-click.

"Rain, snow, sleet or hail, Nicky heads on over to his girlfriend's crib every Monday night," Barnhart said now, watching the automobiles carrying Roma and his crew swing away from the curb, make U-turns on Fifteenth Avenue, and then glide off in the opposite direction along the two-way street.

"Either he's a creature of habit or she's something else," Noriko said.

"Probably a little of both," Barnhart said. A smile touched his lips. "You jealous, Nori?"

"I'd rather mess around with an electric eel," she said.

Nimec had been watching the taillights of the vehicles recede into the snow-clogged night. He waited for ten minutes after they were gone, listening to the snow rasp and rattle across the roof of the car. Then he glanced over at Barnhart, met Noriko's eyes in the rearview, and nodded so both of his companions could see him.

The three of them pulled their Nomex hoods up over their heads.

"Here we go," he said, and reached for the door handle.

TWENTY-NINE

NIMEC WAITED IN THE MOUTH OF THE ALLEY, STAND-
ing lookout as Noriko and Barnhart moved through the
shadows in back of the Platinum Club. Barnhart had a
pair of cable cutters in one hand, a MagLite in the other.
His Benelli pump gun was slung over his shoulder. They
were leaving footprints in the snow, but there wasn't
much they could do about that. Besides, if Nick stayed
true to form and didn't come back until the next day, the
footprints would have filled in before they were spotted.

The telephone connection box was mounted at eye level
on a wall outside the building; on a surveillance run two
nights earlier, Nori had found it by tracking the lines coming from a telephone pole on the adjacent side street.

She stopped now and examined the rectangular metal
box, moisture steaming from her nose and mouth, snow
rustling between her ankles. After a moment, she reached
out to Barnhart and he handed off the cable cutters, directing the flash beam onto the box. The phone wires entered the bottom of the box through a PVC plastic conduit.
The same line, she knew, would be used to transmit signals from the alarm system to its monitoring station. Although it was possible Roma had installed a dedicated line
for his system, or even a cellular-link backup, she doubted
it. As a member of Barnhart's undercover strike force during his years with the FBI, she had broken into many

mob-controlled premises, and almost to a one had found them protected with crude, easily circumvented systems. Big Paul Castellano's mansion on the hill had been the singular exception, but the Gambino family don had always held lordly pretensions. Not so Roma. He was a gangster of the old school and would undoubtedly rely on his heavies for security.

Noriko brushed some snow off the PVC conduit and opened the cable cutters around it. The air trembled with lightning. A food wrapper broke away from a trash spill up the alley, skittered past her foot. Her lips compressed with effort, she clipped the pipe halfway through, then rotated the cutters and clipped the other half of the pipe, exposing the insulated wires inside it. She severed them with a single quick cut.

Barring some unlikely fail-safe, the phones and external alarms were out of commission.

She passed the tool back to Barnhart and gestured to her left. Several yards farther along the wall, he could see a back door that opened into the alley. He nodded and they hastened over to it, Nori in the lead.

She crouched at the door as Barnhart turned his flash onto the lock plate below the knob. Then she produced a flat leather case from a patch pocket on her coveralls. Zipping open the case, she selected two needle-like steel shims from the large set inside it, clamped one between her teeth, and inserted the working end of the other into the keyhole. She raked it deftly across the bottom cylinder pins, felt one, then two, of them activate. Seconds later she extracted the pick from the keyway, switched it with the one in her mouth, and used the second to jiggle open the remaining tumblers.

The latch slid back with a metallic *snick*.

Noriko glanced over her shoulder at Barnhart and he nodded again. She reached for the doorknob. If there were a fire bar or something of that nature across the inside of the door, they would have to try to gain access from the street, where they would be in a much more visible—and risky—position.

She twisted the knob, applied slight pressure to the door with her shoulder.

It eased inward a crack.

"Abracadabra," Barnhart muttered, squeezing her shoulder.

A relieved breath hissing out between her teeth, the tension draining from her muscles, Noriko carefully replaced the shims in their case and returned it to her pocket. Barnhart swung the MagLite toward the mouth of the alley and thumbed it on and off twice. Nimec returned the all-clear signal and sprinted out of the shadows to his companions, a nylon duffel bag in his hand.

Suddenly they heard the rumble of an engine, saw the yellow sweep of headlights on the snow-covered blacktop, and froze outside the door, waiting. A second ticked by. Another. Then a Sanitation Department snowplow went clattering past the alley, turned left at the corner, and moved off down the avenue.

Nimec motioned for them to enter the building.

Barnhart went in first, his tools in his pockets now, both hands around the pump gun. Its underbarrel light threw a tight conical beam into the gloom beyond the door. They could see a narrow back stairwell leading upward to the left, a hallway straight ahead of them.

Barnhart glanced at the others, angled his chin toward the steps, and started to climb them.

They followed him up without hesitation.

• • •

Lightning ripped into the street lamp on the corner of Eighty-sixth Street and Narrows Avenue just as Nick Roma's car turned off Shore Road in that direction. His face registered surprise as the sodium bulb flared brightly and then blew in terminal overload, sprinkling the road with its jagged, smoking remains. On the Lincoln's radio the voice of Michael Bolton dissolved into snaps, crackles, and pops.

"Son of a bitch," the driver muttered.

In the backseat, Roma stared out his window. All along the avenue, spindly winter-bare trees swayed in the wind roaring off Gravesend Bay.

He shot a glance at the dash clock.

"It's almost eleven-thirty," Nick said edgily. "What the hell's taking you so long to get where we're going?"

"It's this fucking weather," the driver said. "I take it any faster, our wheels'll be all over the road."

Roma responded with an indeterminate grunt. He wondered if Marissa would be wearing that short, white lacy thing he'd given her last week. Wondered how fast he would peel her out of it once he stepped through her door. God, God, he was so coiled with tension, so wound up with *need,* he didn't think he'd be able to wait until they got into bed. Maybe later they would take a bath together, bring one of his bottles of wine with them . . .

"Shit!" he said abruptly, slapping his leg in frustration. What was wrong with him? The wine. He'd forgotten the goddamn wine at the club.

He glanced over his shoulder at the sedan following behind them, glad he'd instructed his bodyguards to stick close until he reached Marissa's. At least now they'd have a chance to make themselves useful.

"Val, listen to me," he said, leaning forward over the seat rest. "Call the others. There's a plastic bag in my office, near the desk. It has two bottles of wine in it. Tell them to head back and get it, bring it over to the girl's place, and ring her bell. I'll come to the door and take it from them."

Val nodded, took one hand off the steering wheel, reached for the flip phone in his pocket.

"And Val . . . ?"

The driver briefly met his eyes in the rearview.

"Tell them to be quick about it," Roma said.

"Our boy Nicky's been living the high life," Barnhart said quietly, angling his underbarrel flash into the plastic bag beside Roma's desk. The light glinted off two bottles of red wine. "He's got a couple bottles of Chambertin just sitting around in here."

"And expensive cologne," Noriko whispered. She was at the desk opening drawers, her hand feeling around inside them. "Seems to be it, though. There's zip in these drawers. No papers, no pens, not even a stick of chewing gum."

Barnhart stepped over to her, pulled one of the drawers completely off its tracks, and set it on the floor. Then he reached back into its empty slot, searching for hidden compartments.

Meanwhile, Nimec was moving along the walls, sliding his gloved hands over them, probing for a recessed safe or cabinet. The only hidden devices they'd found so far were Nick's giant television, theater-quality sound system, and a VCR/DVD reader that fed both systems. Predictably, the disk in the hopper was the first *Godfather* movie. But there were no other tapes, no disks, nothing else in any way unusual. The office was a blank slate. They had been inside the room for five minutes, and Nimec wanted to be out within ten. So far they'd been lucky, having located the office almost as soon as they reached the upstairs landing—aside from the entrance to a stockroom, there weren't any other doors along the short, dead-end corridor—and its lock had presented no more of an obstacle to Nori than the one downstairs. Still, there wasn't a moment to waste.

Finding nothing immediately, Nimec paused, looking around. Even in the darkness, he could see that the place was fastidiously neat and clean. If there were squirrel holes, Roma would be careful to keep them well camouflaged.

His gaze fell on the mirrored wall opposite the door and he turned quickly to Barnhart, tapping his arm.

"Shine the light at the mirror," he said, pointing. "Start over toward the middle."

Barnhart nodded and swung the Benelli around.

As Nimec moved closer to the wall, Barnhart's flash shone on the floor-to-ceiling panels, throwing starry winks of brightness into the room.

Nimec's eyes slid up and down the wall. Gesturing with his hand, he silently directed Barnhart to shift the flash to the left, signaled him to bring it down a little, then sliced his palm through the air in a halting gesture.

"You see that?" he said in an excited whisper. "Hold it steady. Right there."

Barnhart nodded again. With the beam hitting the panel straight on, he could see a tiny area, no more than a half inch in diameter, in which its surface seemed to be transparent, as if there were a chipped or bald patch on the reflective layer behind it. Then he realized the spot was a perfect circle—much too perfect to be any kind of defect.

Nimec was practically standing flat against the mirror now, pressing down on it with the heel of his hand.

At the same moment that Barnhart realized he was looking at a two-way mirror, the panel opened out into the room, almost like the door of a medicine cabinet.

"My, my," he said, training his light into the cubby behind it. "What have we here?"

Nimec knew there was no need for him to answer. What they very obviously had was a covert video-recording system—a surveillance camera and portable duplicating unit for creating automatic backup tapes. The blank round eye of the camera was lined up with the transparent part of the wall mirror and pointed directly into the room. Roma might not keep written records of his various dealings, Nimec thought, but that clearly did not mean he was without any records at all.

He stood there looking into the hollow space. On a shelf below the electronic components were three or four scattered videotapes and a sheet of color-coded adhesive labels. The cassettes themselves were unlabeled.

"Looks like he hasn't gotten around to cataloging his latest epics yet," Nori whispered. She came up behind Nimec, her laser-dazzler against her leg. "Wonder what's on them."

"I think that's something we need to find out," Barnhart said.

Nimec hastily snatched the tapes off the shelf, put them into his duffel, then ejected the tape that was in the camera and dropped it in with them.

"Come on." He snapped the panel shut and turned toward the others. "We'd better get out of—"

The sound of an approaching vehicle clipped off the

end of the sentence. The three of them exchanged quick, anxious looks. They could hear the sound of tires crunching on fresh snowpack. It was close, very close, maybe right outside the building. Then the engine shivered into silence, doors slammed, and there were voices. Coarse male voices out in the street.

Nimec crossed the room, stood to one side of the window, and peered cautiously around the frame. There were two men downstairs near the club's main entrance, the dark outlines of at least two more in the car's front seat. One of the men on the sidewalk wore a brown military-surplus bomber jacket with a fleece collar. The other had on a long tweed overcoat. Both were huge. He recognized them instantly, just as he did the vehicle in which they'd arrived. They were Roma's thugs, the bunch who had been flanking him when he left the building half an hour earlier.

As Nimec stood watching them, the pair that had gotten out of the car turned toward the entrance, then strode under the awning and were blocked from sight.

Nimec snapped his head around to Barnhart and Nori. "We've got a problem," he said.

"Hey, come here," the man in the Air Force bomber jacket said.

"What is it, Vasily?"

"Just come over here and take a fucking look, will you?"

The man in the gray overcoat stamped snow off his shoes and then trudged heavily up beside him.

Vasily had paused inside the entrance and was facing the wall, scrutinizing the status window on the security system's master control box. The alarm was set on a thirty-second entry delay, so that anyone with the deactivation code would have enough time to punch it into the keypad—and turn off the system—after passing through the door. He'd been about to do exactly that when he noticed the reading on the LCD.

The second man looked at the backlit display. Its pale blue digital characters said:

CODE29: SYSTEM FAILURE

Vasily glanced at him. "I don't get it."

"Could be it's the storm. Wind might've knocked out the power awhile. Or the phone lines."

"I dunno, Pavel." Vasily was shaking his head. "You want to check out the back door?"

Pavel was still for a second, his broad brow crunched in thought, balancing the minor hassle of having to walk out back against what his boss would do if it turned out that something really was wrong, and he and Vasily didn't go investigate.

"Yeah," he said, drawing a pistol from under his coat. "Better we don't take chances."

In Roma's office, Nimec, Barnhart, and Nori heard the two bodyguards speak agitatedly to each other as they discovered the unlocked back door. Instants later they heard them racing up the stairs, saw lights blink on in the outer corridor, heard more rapid footsteps.

They were hustling toward the office.

The footsteps stopped outside the door.

Then extended silence.

The silence pressed.

The doorknob rattled, turned.

Nimec touched Nori's arm above the elbow and he saw her glide into position, a dark silhouette against the deeper darkness of the room.

The door flung open, both thugs framed inside it, Uzi carbines held out in front of them.

Nori fingered a button on the control box of her laser and a blinding beam of high-intensity light streaked from the M203's muzzle, hitting Vasily full in the face. He released a high-pitched, whooping scream, the subgun seeming to leap from his grip, hands clawing at his eyes. Nori held the weapon on him another second, its laser beam pulsing in the air like a bright white strip of the sun. He went jigging back into the hallway, slammed into Pavel's shoulder, then went reeling into the corridor, his contortions throwing a delirious crop of shadows across the walls.

"*My eyes!*" he shrieked, sinking to his knees. His hands stayed over his face. "*God, God, my fucking eyes!*"

Ignoring him, Pavel threw himself back against the door wall, reached around the jamb with the Uzi, squeezed out a burst. Rounds crackled from the snubby barrel. Nori sprang out of the way as the deadly stream of 9mm bullets came rippling into the office, shattering the window, blasting chunks out of the walls, punching holes into the side of Roma's desk, knocking over his chair amid flying wads of its chewed-up cushions. Spent casings swirled around the Uzi in a glittery blizzard.

Launching himself out of the darkness, Barnhart swung the Benelli toward the door, a flash-bang round already jacked into its chamber, and fired. There was a loud *whump* in the corridor, a sudden flare of brilliance, a swirling bubble of smoke. Pavel's gun stopped chattering and withdrew from the entry. Almost simultaneously Nori took her finger off the laser control, hooked it around the trigger of the modified M16, and unleashed a sustained burst of VVRS sabots, laying a band of covering fire for her teammates.

"Now!" Nimec shouted.

The three of them plunged out of the office, Nori's gun spewing a torrent of non-lethal rounds. When they reached the corridor, she pivoted to the right, spotted Pavel crouching near the door with the Uzi in both hands, and aimed for his chest. He flopped back in a graceless heap, his finger spasmodically squeezing the trigger of his carbine, the weapon discharging rounds in a crazy up-turned fountain.

Gobs of plaster rained from the ceiling. Ricochets whined through the corridor in wild trajectories.

"Ah, *shit!*" Barnhart said through gritted teeth behind Nori.

She jerked her head around, saw him clutching his side, his face a twist of pain, blood slicking his fingers. A dark wet stain was already spreading over his coveralls. He started to wobble forward, his legs folding beneath him, but Nimec rushed over and got an arm around him an instant before he would have fallen to the floor.

The thug's gun, meanwhile, continued to jolt and rattle. Nori whipped her head back around, leveled her rifle downward, and hit him dead-center in the chest with another gust of fire. A scream ripped from his throat and he thrashed on the floor as though suffused with voltage. After a moment he passed out, the Uzi dropping from his fingers with a metallic clatter.

"How bad is it?" Nimec said, helping Barnhart to his feet. He nodded his chin at the blood-saturated middle of his coveralls.

"Don't know exactly." Barnhart winced. "Hurts like all hell, though."

Nimec regarded him steadily, his lips clamped together.

"We'll try and get out of here the way we came in," he said after a moment. "With any luck the rest of those guys will still be out front."

Barnhart shook his head vehemently. "I'm not sure I can make the stairs. Head on down without me . . . I can hold my own if any more come up here . . . I'll use that mope's Uzi—"

"Do us a favor, Tony, okay?"

Barnhart looked at him.

"Shut up and cooperate," Nimec said.

Barnhart shook his head again, but this time didn't voice any protest.

Noriko hustled over to Barnhart's left side, lifted his arm, and slung it around her shoulders. At the same time, Nimec continued bracing him on the right. He had drawn his Beretta from its holster with his left hand.

He swapped glances with Noriko, then nodded.

Half-carrying Barnhart between them, they started toward the entrance to the stairwell.

They had no sooner reached the steps than a third thug appeared on the landing below. He had a Glock nine in both hands and was raising it in a shooter's stance.

His eyes slitted with concentration, Nimec got off two shots with his own pistol before the bodyguard managed to fire a single round. The first caught him in the right kneecap, the second in the left. He crumpled to the base of the stairs and rolled around there in spastic agony, howling at the top of his lungs.

"Shut him up," Barnhart rasped. He unclipped a

DMSO canister from his utility harness, passed it to Noriko. She noticed that its tubular surface was slick with blood, but said nothing.

Slipping out from under Barnhart's arm, she sprinted down the stairs, held the canister over the screaming man's pain-knotted face, and depressed the nozzle. A fine, nearly invisible mist hissed out of it. The thug raised his hands in front of his face in a warding-off gesture, his eyes wide, white, and bulging. Then his arms dropped like deflated balloons and his features went slack and he fell off into sedated unconsciousness.

Nori turned back toward her companions. They had almost reached the bottom landing, Nimec gripping the rail with one hand, supporting Barnhart with the other. Barnhart's face was blanched of color and she could see a greasy patina of sweat on his cheeks. He was biting his lower lip, gasping a little with each descending step.

She hurried over to help him the rest of the way down, got his arm back around her neck. Together the three of them pressed through the rear door to the alley.

Cold air and snow blasted them the moment they got outside. Thunder was still skipping across the sky. They moved awkwardly toward the mouth of the alleyway, Barnhart stagger-stepping forward, a tortured grimace on his face, blood dripping from his midsection to the snow.

A fourth bodyguard appeared in the alley entrance, directly in front of them, sweeping an outthrust carbine back and forth like a divining rod. Slugs churned from the gun and whapped into the snowpack at their feet, kicking up powdery spurts of whiteness. Nimec hauled Barnhart sideways out of the line of fire, then jostled him against the diamond-mesh fence dividing the alley from the adjacent property. More rounds shivered from the bodyguard's weapon, pecking at the brick outer wall of the building, striking a shower of sparks off a fire escape somewhere overhead.

Nimec extended his gun toward their attacker, triggered two rounds. But he was off balance, unable to take decent aim, and they went sheering ineffectually into the darkness.

The killer prepared to fire again. He seemed to have realized that one of his prey was wounded and swung his gun in their direction with a kind of slow, deliberate confidence, like someone about to take out a crippled fowl.

Nimec huddled against the fence, shielding Barnhart with his own body.

Nori fired her webgun a beat before Roma's thug would have pulled the trigger. A hollow *pop!* issued from its barrel, and then the sticky webbing bloomed over him, ensnaring him from head to foot in a cocoon of microthin filaments. Stunned, he tried to tear free, but only became more tangled up in the cottony shroud, skidded on the snow, and took a pratfall that might have been comical under far different circumstances.

Nori dashed over to him as he lay there thrashing, and sprayed him full in the face with the DMSO. An instant later he ceased to move.

The webgun still in her hand, Nori ran past him to the alley mouth, peered up and down the sidewalk through blowing sheets of snow. Lights were flickering on in the apartment buildings along the street—obviously the sounds of the firefight had drawn some attention—but there was no one in sight.

She turned and padded back down the alley to her companions.

"You all right?" she asked Nimec.

"Yeah," he said.

She looked at Barnhart. The perspiration was streaming down his face now, and the glazed, somewhat abstracted cast of his eyes gave her cause to fear he might be slipping into shock.

"Coast's clear, as far as I can see," she said, gripping Barnhart's arm. "We have to get back to the wagon before somebody calls the cops, though. Think you can make it?"

He looked at her a moment and somehow managed a wan, grim smile.

"Race you," he said.

THIRTY

THE SEX WAS QUICK AND DIRTY. SO WAS THE CON-versation that preceded it—"dirty," in this instance, meaning distorted and semiaudible on playback.

It wasn't the fault of the recording equipment. Nick Roma had simply been speaking in a low voice when the woman in the black leather coat entered his office.

"Let's see that part again," Barnhart said.

"You mean when he's behind her, or on top?"

"Don't get smart."

"I'll cue it up from where it's still rated PG, and just about to segue into triple-X," the thin, long-haired man at the audio-video processor said with a mock frown. He pushed a button on his console, and Barnhart heard the faint whir of the hard disk spinning in the silence.

They were in a sound studio in the basement of the Sword headquarters in downtown Manhattan, Barnhart and the techie seated shoulder-to-shoulder at the workstation, Pete Nimec and Noriko Cousins standing behind them.

Barnhart leaned stiffly forward in his chair, feeling his stitches pull under the bandages around his midsection. His wound still gave him a lot of discomfort, but the bleeding had made it look more critical than it actually turned out to be. Though a long, shallow furrow had been plowed into his right side, the slug had been deflected from his internal organs by a ridge of hard muscle before exiting. According to the emergency room physician his superb physical condition was what saved him.

"You think you can get us to what he's saying?" Nimec asked.

"If I hadn't been reasonably certain the audio streams could be cleaned up to your exacting demands, I wouldn't have bothered committing this blue romp into digital form," the man at the workstation said. "After all, the moans of ecstasy were already loud and clear enough to get *my* motor running."

Nimec and Noriko exchanged looks of pained commiseration. Jeff Grolin was one of the most skilled forensic A/V specialists in the country—Megan wouldn't have snagged him for their organization if he wasn't—but he was also a vexingly juvenile pain in the buttocks. Was social maladjustment something that people in his field acquired, a sort of professional hazard, Nimec wondered, or some intrinsic characteristic of those with a high degree of technical aptitude?

"Okay, guys and gal, hold onto your cookies," Grolin said, fiddling with a dial. "It's Nick Roma's Big Adventure, alternately titled Badguy Lust. Scene one, take two."

Their eyes turned toward the workstation's twenty-one-inch monitor.

On the screen, a door opened into Roma's office and the woman came in, then stepped toward the lens of the stationary surveillance camera. Her dark hair was pulled back, her lips were parted, and she moved with an apparent awareness of her body and the reaction it elicited from the man she was approaching.

The date/time stamp on the lower left-hand corner of the image read: "01.01.2000 1:00 A.M."

Nimec studied the woman intently. Though the room's fluorescents were dimmed, there was sufficient ambient light coming in from the windows to reveal her features without any sort of computer enhancements. In fact, a still image had already been extracted from the video footage and was being cross-indexed with Sword's file of known and suspected international terrorists.

"You could have knocked," Roma said through compact Audix speakers. At this point only the back of his head was visible.

"Yes. I could have." Shutting the door.

"There's a light switch on the wall . . ."

"Bounce it to where it's been giving us trouble," Barnhart said, watching.

"Sure," Jeff said. His finger stabbed a button with the double-arrow fast-forward symbol on it. "Though I personally get a charge out of the suggestive dialogue during the buildup—clichéd as it may be."

The video zipped ahead.

Grolin hit Play again.

Now the woman was much closer to the desk, her coat partially unbuttoned, unmistakable desire in her expression.

"Why are you here?" Roma said, and then paused. His voice had become husky, dropping to a near whisper.

"Right. Like he's really that clueless," Grolin commented. "The guy's choking on his own drool—"

"*Shhh,* this is it," Noriko said.

"*Yno . . . zrrywn't . . . hvyrrpstl . . . mrrow . . . pssed . . . syight.*"

"It's still nothing but gobbledygook," Barnhart said.

"That's because I haven't worked my electronic wizardry yet." Grolin froze the image, then shifted his hands to a smaller console which consisted of more dials and pitch slides, as well as a dozen or so keys the size of the Tab button on a standard computer keyboard.

As his fingers clicked over the keys, a tool bar appeared across the top of the screen and the video image shrank into a window, with graphical level meters and editing controls appearing to its right.

"Now, let's try it again, giving it a little mid-range gain, eliminating some audio dither."

Grolin hit Rewind, Pause, then Play.

"Why are you here?" Roma said from the speakers. Paused.

Grolin quickly tweaked a dial, and then another, his eyes narrow behind the intentionally nerdish horn-rimmed glasses.

Roma said, "You know . . . *zarry* . . . *wnnt* have your *parrrrrsrdy* until tomorrow—"

Grolin stopped the progress of the virtual image, ran it backward to the point just before Roma's voice dropped off in volume, started it going forward again.

His fingers clattered over the buttons of his console. Graph lines and status bars rose and fell in the edit window.

"Why are you here?" Roma husked. "You know *zakrry* won't have your papers *rdy* until tomorrow. And I don't suppose you've just come to *syngnnnight*."

"You hear that?" Barnhart jerked his head around toward Nimec, wincing in pain from the abrupt movement. "He's talking about providing her with papers. Presumably travel documents."

"I'll bet," Nimec said. "That son of a bitch facilitated the attack from beginning to end."

"Speaking of which," Grolin said, "one more run-through, and I'll have every last word on this tape popping out at us like braille.''

Noriko's fingertips rapped an impatient quintuplet against the back of Barnhart's chair.

"Come on," she said. Thinking: *Aggravating twerp.*

Grolin rewound, paused, played, tinkered with his MIDI controls.

"Why are you here?" Nick Roma said to the woman unbuttoning in front of him. "You know Zachary won't have your papers ready until tomorrow. And I don't suppose you've just come to say good night."

"By Jove, and fucking-A, I think we've got it," Grolin said. "Who's Zachary, by the way?"

Nimic was looking at Barnhart. "You think that's a first or last name?"

Barnhart shook his head. "Could be either, but I'll ask around. My guess is he'd be one of Roma's forgers. Or somebody who works for one of his forgers. Roma's steadiest, ugliest source of income is the flesh trade. Smuggling desperately poor women from Russia to America as prostitutes . . . essentially sex slaves . . . with fraudulent visas and identification. That's also how the *organizatsiya* imports its soldiers and hit men."

"The bunch that did the job in Times Square would have wanted out of the country pronto," Noriko said. "We find this Zachary, seems logical he'd be able to lead us to them."

"Or steer us in their direction, anyway," Barnhart said. "And that's providing we can get him . . . or her, now that I think about it . . . to talk."

"Leave the second part to me," Nimec said, his eyes still on Barnhart. "How soon can you dig up the information we need?"

"Won't take long, assuming we're right about this person's specialty and connection to Roma. I know G-men, detectives on the NYPD, even people in the Attorney General's Office, who keep tabs on every player of importance in Roma's outfit. And who'll talk to me no questions asked."

"Make sure that's the way it is," Nimec said. "I've been pulling strings for two days to see that the record of your ER treatment gets erased before it's released to the police. I don't want anybody tumbling to our investigation."

Barnhart nodded, started to push himself up off the chair, but then sank back into it, obviously hurting.

"If one of you'd give me a hand, I'll head upstairs to my office and start making some calls," he said.

"And miss the climax to the flick?" Grolin said. "I plan on repeating it in its prurient entirety."

Noriko looked at him with sharp irritation.

"Jeff, trust me," she said. "You'll have a much better time watching it alone."

Roger Gordian sat alone, with his cell phone in his hand. With all the chaos at work, with all the emergencies he had to react to, plan for, juggle, and worry about, his home situation was threatening to overwhelm him.

He loved his wife.

His wife had left him.

It had been nearly three weeks, and she hadn't come home, and she hadn't called.

Sometimes he felt like marriage was a game in which women made the rules and the poor slobs who married them had to figure those rules out blindfolded.

He still didn't understand what he'd done wrong.

The things he felt for the woman he married had never faltered from the moment he saw her. They'd changed, but only to become richer and deeper.

The better he came to know her, the more he loved her.

And the more he realized he would never solve the mystery of her.

In all the years since they'd been together, he'd never once felt more than a fleeting tug of attraction to the beautiful women who moved through the corridors of power. Like any man, he'd see a pretty woman and his basic reaction was immediate. But acting on those feelings was out of the question. No matter how beautiful they were, they weren't Ashley.

She was as beautiful to him for who she was as for what she looked like.

He'd had more than enough sex, especially during his fighter jock days, to learn the difference between that momentary tug of attraction and the real thing.

Love. Commitment. Marriage.

He'd been scared to death of all of them, terrified he'd miss out on the fabulous smorgasbord of women in the world, until the day he met Ashley.

He learned the difference the first time they touched.

What he couldn't understand was that she didn't believe that he loved her still. Even more than he had when they first married. Why didn't she understand that?

That wasn't fair. Deep down, he knew what the problem was.

Time.

He'd had it to spend with her back when they were first starting out. The business was smaller then, the problems manageable.

Nowadays, it felt like the fate of the free world was

impacted every time he made a decision. It was kind of hard to justify chucking it all and going home at the end of a business day when kids in Russia wouldn't eat if he left things undone.

But had he ever taken the time to explain that to her?

It was time that he did.

He picked up his cell phone and dialed Ashley's sister in San Francisco.

Even before her sister Ann handed her the telephone, Ashley Gordian knew by the look on her face that it was Roger. Nobody but her husband could bring that tight look of disapproval to her sister's face with a simple greeting.

It had been like that ever since the beginning. Back then, Roger had been young, driven, and—by Ann's standards—poor as a church mouse. Not nearly good enough for her baby sister. She'd been opposed to the marriage before she'd even met the man. All the respect, the acclaim, the financial success Roger had accumulated had never changed Ann's mind. In her posh world, it was all too new to count.

But Ashley had taken one look at the burning intensity in Roger's eyes and known she'd found her soulmate. And she'd been right. She'd married the man, not the pedigree, and she'd never regretted it. She loved Roger. In every way that a woman could love a man. And for the past twenty years she'd built her life around him. It wasn't a sacrifice, despite what her sister said. He was such a good man, so caring about the world, and so fiercely determined to make it a better place. But that world had been stealing him from her, bit by bit, moment by moment.

In the last few years, she'd seen less of Roger than she'd seen of her hairdresser. And, unlike many of the society women she knew, she didn't spend that much time with her hairdresser. Though she'd given up her own career to more easily accommodate her schedule to that of her husband, she had a life, a good mind. But when Roger was free, she didn't want her own activities to fill that precious time and keep them apart. She wanted to be able to be with him, talk to him, enjoy his presence. She wanted to be able to drop everything and accompany him on his frequent business trips, if he wanted her along.

But lately, he'd been so busy that, no matter how flexible she was, she still rarely saw him. She'd tried to fill her time with volunteer activities and subsist on the moments they spent together, but those moments were now often in the middle of the night, as she watched him sleep after he'd come in so exhausted he could barely manage to say hello before he crashed. Her life was hollow, empty, lacking in purpose.

Roger had his work.

She had nothing, not even Roger.

It was too much. She'd used this time at her sister's house to do some hard thinking. For her own survival, she had to change things. One of them had to give. Roger had to make more time for her, for them, or she'd have to make a life on her own.

As she took the phone from her sister, she took a deep breath. "Roger?"

"How are you, Ashley? I've missed you."

Trite words, perhaps, but Ashley could tell he meant them. As she rejoiced in the sound of his voice, she wondered how long it had been since he'd spoken to her like this, since he had really listened to her. Too long. It hurt to think about exactly how long. "I'm surprised you even noticed I was gone," she said.

"Believe me, I noticed," he said. "You're not at the breakfast table. I start every day missing you, and it gets worse from there." Roger sounded so tired.

"Since when do you eat breakfast at home?" Ashley asked quietly. "Usually, you're out of the house before seven, grabbing something on the way to the office."

There was a silence on the other end of the line as Roger digested that. Knowing him, he'd want to deny it; then, because he was a fair man, he'd start counting back in his head. Roger's memory was legendary, photographic. At this moment, he'd probably gotten to the hundredth muffin he'd consumed at his desk, and he was now starting to count back through fruit plates and toasted bagels. The silence stretched on, a little strained.

"You're right." The admission undoubtedly hurt him like fire.

"I know I am."

"It was never because I didn't love you." Roger swallowed. The sound carried clearly over the line. "No matter what I'm doing, I'd always rather be spending time with you."

"Then why don't you? How many meals have we shared in the past six months?"

Again, silence. Finally, the answer. "Thirty-eight?"

"Subtract banquets, political functions, work-related functions, and parties." Ashley knew this wasn't fair, but she was fighting for time and life with the man she loved. "By my reckoning, the answer comes to eighteen—three meals a month."

"I know it's hard for you, but it's been tough for me, too." Roger stopped for a moment, clearly picking his words with care. "I don't always have the freedom to make my own choices."

"Why not? You own the company."

"Lately, with the ground stations going in, I've been so embroiled with politics worldwide that my time isn't my own. Once this stage is over, things should get better."

"And how many times have you told yourself—and me—that before? Will they really get better, or will you just launch into the next big project once you get some breathing room?" Ashley wanted to cry, could hear in her voice the sound of tears too close to the surface. She could only hope that Roger was too preoccupied with his own pain to notice.

"I know I've said it before, but this time I mean it."

"Roger," Ashley said, "you mean it every time. I probably don't tell you this enough, but I am so proud of you—of who you are and what you've done. I know that everything you've accomplished out in the world makes a huge difference to people everywhere. I know that it's your calling, something you have to do. What I don't know is if I'm strong enough to wait until you're done."

"Ashley, all the success in the world doesn't matter to me if you're not by my side to share it."

"Do you mean that?" Ashley felt that faint, terrible thread of hope. Maybe, just maybe, they could work this out. "Can you come up here, spend some time with me, maybe go to a therapist with me until we find some common ground?"

There was a long pause. Again she could hear Roger swallow, take a deep breath. "Honey, work is in a real uproar right now. There are global consequences if I leave at this exact moment . . . maybe in a week or two?"

"And in a week or two some new hot spot will erupt, and you'll be called in to deal with it—because you're the best." The tears she'd kept at bay through the whole conversation finally overflowed. "You're the best," she sobbed, "and I don't know what I can do about it. I love you. Good-bye." Before she could change her mind, she pushed the Disconnect button on the phone. Then she put her head in her hands and sobbed as though there were no tomorrow. Because for her and Roger, that might just be the case.

THIRTY-ONE

ANTON ZACHARY WAS A SOLID BELIEVER IN ROUTINE. In structure and regimentation. Without it, he felt, the minutes and hours of the day turned to sludge, the significance of actions paled, diligence turned to sloth, nothing meant anything, and everything fell apart. For him, life without margins was a valueless blur of inconsequential events.

He hadn't always held this outlook; it had grown and developed over many years, and more or less in tandem with his professional responsibilities. Zachary was a busy man, a man Nick Roma frequently called upon to perform impossible tasks within unimaginable deadlines. This was not done out of disrespect, not really, but, as with most overlords, Roma's mind lacked the fine appreciation, so to speak, that would allow him to understand the hard work, the painstaking discipline and attention to detail, that went into the creation of a convincing fake, a successful lie, a counterfeit passport, visa, marriage license, or birth certificate that would deceive even the most careful and discerning eye. To Roma, Zachary was little more than a forger of papers, a duplicator of documents, a living stamp pad, a photocopy machine that happened to be made of flesh and blood, a tinkerer who did what anyone else could do if only he had the spare time. By Roma, craftsmanship was appreciated only insofar as it translated into instant results; fail to meet his demands just once and you were labeled incompetent, inept, a fool who could not perform a task that could have been assigned to any dilettante, perhaps even some drunk who had been dragged out of the gutter by his collar.

Zachary knew and accepted this as the lot of the artist. What incomprehensible pressures must Michelangelo have faced under the demands of his patrons? Or Shakespeare? Paint that ceiling now! Finish that play by tonight and give us some damn good lines! Make us laugh, cry, gasp with awe and excitement, and hurry, hurry, hurry! Ah, how they must have despaired. Yet where would they have been without those financial supporters? What would they have done for a livelihood? The tension between art and commerce was a vital if maddening constant. The fuel of productivity. The yin and yang—yes, yes!—the *yin and yang* of the creative process.

If only it didn't result in insomnia, heart palpitations, ulcers, and premature hair loss.

Now, as he walked across the boardwalk on Brighton Twelfth Street, the weathered wooden planks under his feet bare of snow due to some vagary of the ocean gusts, gulls wheeling and scissoring above his head, the roiling gray sea to his left, Brighton Beach Avenue to his right, his apartment building behind him, the newsstand where he bought his Russian-language newspaper two blocks ahead, the bakery where he would pick up his breakfast rolls two blocks farther on, his travel agency a block beyond that across from the elevated D train tracks . . . as he walked to work this morning along the route he took every morning at six o'clock on the dot, never a second shaved—never, never a second—Zachary told himself it was time to push these useless, egocentric musings, these petulant blips of dissatisfaction, out of his mind and get down to thinking about the important business of the day.

Roma had placed an order for a half dozen student entry visas that were to go to some women a local pimp and strip club manager was bringing over from Moscow. For whatever reason, Roma needed to have these forgeries completed and delivered to the flesh peddler by one o'clock in the afternoon. Roma had placed the order late the previous night and had been in no mood to be negotiated with. In fact, Roma had been unusually excitable for weeks now, and he'd gotten worse in the past several days. Rumor had it that he'd been badly affected by something that had happened at his club some nights ago, though none of his closest men would say what the event was, or even confirm *that* it was.

Well, Zachary told himself as he stepped off the boardwalk, Roma had his worries and responsibilities, and he had his own. He did not pretend to be interested in the nuts-and-bolts mechanics of Roma's operation, had no time to be interested, no time to think, no time to do anything but what was required of him. Six entry visas, six hours to complete the order. That was all he—

"Excuse me."

Zachary stopped short on the pavement, looking at the man who had stepped in front of him, actually bumped into him seemingly out of nowhere. Where had he come from?

"Yes?" he said, startled. The man was thin, sinewy, with hair cut almost to the scalp. He wore a long trench coat and had his right hand in its pocket.

"I want to talk to you, Mr. Zachary," the man said. And dipped his head slightly to his left. "In there."

Zachary glanced over in that direction, saw a car sitting

at the curb with its rear door ajar. There was someone huddled behind the wheel.

"I don't understand," he said.

Shifting his gaze back to the man. To the bulge made by his right hand pressing against the inner lining of his pocket. Could he be holding a gun?

"What do you want from—"

"Get in the car," the man said. He noticed where Zachary's eyes had landed and jabbed whatever was in his pocket against his stomach. It felt hard. "This won't take long. And nobody's going to hurt you if you cooperate and answer some questions."

"But I have a *schedule*—"

"In the car, now!" the man snapped, shoving the hard object against his belly again. "You go first."

Suddenly trembling all over, Zachary nodded and turned toward the partly open rear door of the vehicle, the trench-coated man falling in behind him, the thing in the man's hand jabbing against his back.

Climbing in the backseat after him, Nimec nodded for Noriko to drive off.

He kept his hand on the roll of Certs in his pocket, kept pressing it against Zachary, wondering if he'd just given new definition to the term "non-lethal weapon."

Sadov had made them as law enforcement agents moments after passing through the security check. FBI, he suspected, though it was just as easily possible they belonged to one of the other covert organizations. He was accustomed to keeping a wary eye out for stalkers and had recognized their colors and markings immediately.

What first alerted him was the way they had positioned themselves. One by the magazine stand in the corridor, another beside the entry to the waiting area, a third near the gate. It was where they stood and how they stood: the lift of their chins, their straight postures, their discreetly observant eyes, taking everything in without seeming to move. It was their dark suits and overcoats, their pastel ties, the slight catches in the fabric of their pants several inches above the hemline, giveaway signs of ankle holsters. It was their scrubbed, clipped, efficient appearance.

He lowered himself into a contoured plastic chair and glanced up at the bank of monitors displaying estimated arrival and departure schedules. His flight to Stockholm was to take off in half an hour, and he expected to hear the boarding announcement very shortly.

Normally the surveillance wouldn't have ruffled his calm. He had spent many years masking his trail across scores of countries, and was wise to the ways of eluding pursuit. And while the cast of the net was wider now than in the past, the spaces one could slip through remained as large as ever. Larger, in fact, than it had been in some previous instances. The national origin of the bombing suspects was unknown. What was more, their sponsor had not been identified, and even the connection to Russia remained uncertain. He should have felt secure in being a faceless, invisible presence, camouflaged like the mantis. And would have, had it not been for the photograph.

It had appeared in the *New York Daily News* the very day after the explosion, and then had been splashed all over the media, a grainy image taken off an amateur videotape, made by someone who'd been high above the square on Seventh Avenue and Fifty-third Street. A circle had been drawn around the man that the headline declared was responsible for having left behind one of the secondary charges. In the picture, he was setting a nylon athletic bag on the sidewalk near an unmanned police barricade. While it was clear he had dark hair and wore a leather jacket, his features were shadowed and indistinct. Still, Sadov had recognized himself. He had feared the people who were looking for him would be able to sharpen the image with computer enhancements, and hesitated to enter a busy airport at a time when his photograph was being exhibited on every newsstand. It had meant staying in New York nearly a full week longer than Gilea and the others, laying low in Roma's safehouses. During that week he had lightened and cut his hair, obtained a pair of stage eyeglasses, and traded his clothing for an expensive business suit. The disguise was satisfying, and he was confident he could make it through the airport despite the heightened state of alert. Nevertheless, he would be glad once he was up and walking through the jetway.

Yes, he'd relax once he was on the plane. The undercover surveillance of key transit points had been expected, and well considered by Roma's people when they plotted out his return to Russia. The route they had arranged would take him from Sweden into Finland by rail, then through the border crossing at Nuijaama to the outskirts of St. Petersburg. Though circuitous, and requiring some extra paperwork, this had been deemed the best way to go. The Finnish and Russian border guards were known for their laxity, and gave automobiles only perfunctory inspections. There would be a quick customs check afterward—an X-ray scan of his luggage, two steps through a metal detector, and that was all. He would be safe on familiar ground.

Now Sadov sat flipping through a magazine without giving any attention to its contents, looking over the tops of the pages, carefully watching the agents who were watching the departure area. Had the red-haired man by the gate had his eye on him, glancing away just as he, Sadov, glanced up? Sadov turned another page. Almost certainly he was letting his nerves run away with him. It was the photograph, the extended period in New York.

He waited.

The announcement came over the speakers ten minutes later: flight 206 to Stockholm was now boarding, handicapped passengers and those with seating in rows A through L could enter the gate, please have your tickets ready.

Sadov slowly closed his magazine and zipped it into a side compartment of his carry-on bag. Around him, other fliers rose off their chairs and got in line at the gate. He let his gaze skim over the redheaded agent. The man had his arms crossed over his chest and seemed focused on the waiting area. As Sadov stood to join the line the man bounced up and down on his toes. Once. Was that an indication of boredom and restlessness, a reflexive little stretch? Or an indication he might be preparing to make a move? For one small second, Sadov had thought he'd felt eyes on his face.

He slung his travel bag over his shoulder and moved to the back of the line. He noticed the agent who had been posted at the entrance to the waiting area start walking in his approximate direction. The man had bristle-cut hair and a pointed, vigilant face. Like a fox.

Sadov ground his teeth. He remembered the close call he'd had after the job in London. That had been a little over a year ago. A pair of bobbies had identified him, followed him for several blocks. He'd left both in an alley with bullets in their skulls. But now, here, he was unarmed. And with all these people around, he would be trapped.

The line moved forward. He moved with it, his ticket in hand. The redhaired agent was now almost directly in front of him, to the right of the gate, scrutinizing the passengers as they stepped through. Sadov wondered to what extent the image of him could have been refined. There was a great deal of technology available to the authorities. And wasn't it also possible they had been tipped off? There was a reward. New York City alone had offered fifty thousand dollars. And he did not fully trust Roma or his men. They might have been tempted. Think of the things he himself had done for money.

Sadov continued toward the gate. There were only three passengers ahead of him. An elderly couple, and a well-dressed woman in her forties. The couple exchanged brief pleasantries with a flight attendant as she took their tickets, then disappeared into the jetway. The woman was next. The redheaded man gave her a cursory glance, looked past her at the shrinking line.

Sadov squeezed his tension into a tight ball and pushed it somewhere deep inside him. He had no choice but to continue ahead toward the gate and hope he got through.

He held out his ticket. The attendant's mouth was smiling. He nodded, peeled his own lips back over his teeth to mimic the expression. The redhead was almost beside him now.

"Excuse me, sir," he said, "would you please step off the line a moment?"

Sadov kept his eyes on the stewardess's teeth, peripherally glimpsed the fox-faced agent approaching from the right, joining the redheaded man. He did not yet see the third agent, the one he'd spotted at the magazine stand, but felt sure he would be closing in as well.

"Sir, did you hear me? We'd like to ask you a few questions."

Sadov's blood surged into his ears. He would have to comply, there was really nothing else to do.

He looked over at the redhead.

And realized the agent wasn't speaking to him at all. Was in fact addressing someone in line behind him.

He expelled a breath, spared a moment to glance over his shoulder.

Three places down the line was a man about the same age and height as Sadov himself, wearing jeans and a short ski jacket. His hair was dark brown, the same color that Sadov's had been before he dyed it. The agents had gently taken hold of his elbow, steered him aside, and asked to see his identification. He looked confused, agitated, and embarrassed as he reached into his shoulder bag.

Sadov turned back to the flight attendant. He felt his smile transform into something authentic, like a stone sculpture that had suddenly become imbued with life.

The agents had come close, but they were off by three. Pulling a sheep in wolf's clothing, he thought with amusement.

"Have a nice flight, sir," the attendant said.

His grin expanded.

"Thank you," he said, entering the gate. "I'm sure that I will."

THIRTY-TWO

WASHINGTON, D.C.
JANUARY 26, 2000

"BALLS," THE PRESIDENT SAID TO HIS GATHERING OF
the National Security Council. "Colossal fucking balls."

He slammed his hand down on the classified CIA/FBI
intelligence report on his desk, drawing looks from the
men at the table in the conference room down the hall
from the Oval Office. In an unprecedented show of inter-
organizational cooperation, the two agencies had gotten
together, combined their investigative researches into the
Times Square bombing, and reached certain mutual assessments that likely spelled disaster for his Russian foreign policy agenda—shooting his self-image all to the
moon in the process. What accounted for his multileveled
chagrin and dismay was the understanding that, if those
assessments were right, he would have to reexamine his
commitment to prop up Starinov and his closest government associates. He'd always been quick to read popular
currents of opinion, always recognized when they threatened to capsize him, and was nearly always willing and
able to jump ship when his political survival was at stake.
Criticism tended to roll off his hide unless there were
polling numbers to make it stick, and he was especially
unaccustomed to having that thick and famously lubri-
cious epidermal layer pierced by straightforward jabs of
morality.

But it had happened when he'd read the intelligence

reports. Happened in a big way. The presidential hide had been weakened, compromised from within. And the implications this presented about his own deepest nature were unexpected and jarring.

If the conclusions laid out in those documents were correct, *if,* he would be outraged, horrified, and soul-sick. And the hell of it was, he had realized he would have to act on those feelings or be unable to live with himself. What kind of national leader would that make him? A President whose major policy decisions were prompted by heart and conscience? Jesus Almighty, he'd be great white Washington shark food!

"The way I see it, we've still got some wriggle room here," Vice President Humes said. "The Bashkir connection is based on inference. Implication. Circumstantial evidence. As far as I can see, it's going to be impossible for anyone to conclusively establish his guilt—"

The President propped his right elbow on the table, formed a wide V with his thumb and forefinger, and leaned the bridge of his nose down into it. He simultaneously pushed his right palm out in the air like a traffic cop signaling Humes to a full stop.

"Listen to me, Steve. Listen carefully," he said. "This isn't about what we can prove. It's about what we believe or do not believe to be true. And these reports make a convincing case that the Russian minister of the interior brought about the deaths of a thousand American citizens, on American soil, the mayor of America's largest city among them." He paused a moment, his head still lowered into his hand, looking almost penitent. "This puts the attack nearly on a scale with Pearl Harbor . . . and it occurred during my goddamned watch."

"I agree," said Kenneth Taylor, the national security

advisor. "And it's probably worth mentioning that the Japanese were going after a military target, not civilians."

"There's a more important distinction to bear in mind, though," said Secretary of Defense Roger Farrand, stroking his scrupulously trimmed Mellvillian beard. "Should Bashkir be responsible, he would have been acting as a member of a renegade cell, not a representative of the government in power. In fact, it goes beyond that. What he did, if he did it, was a deliberate attempt at bringing down one of his own country's leaders."

"Qualifying him as a subversive and traitor within Russia, as well as an international criminal," Secretary of State Bowman said, nodding. "I think I see Roger's point, and tend to go along with him on this."

Which, given the two men's usual contentious relationship, was yet another source of inner upheaval for the President. What next? Would the world tilt on its axis, the sun go dark at noon, the sky itself turn upside down? He had been launched into uncharted waters, and there were dragons beneath his keel.

"I'd appreciate it if one of you would explain what you're getting at," he said. "Maybe I'm overtired, but I need it served up nice and plain."

Bowman nodded again. "Starinov could very publicly expose Bashkir. I can't see any reason why he wouldn't want to, considering Bashkir's disloyalty. Should he oust him from his cabinet post immediately, it would be a start at salvaging Starinov's reputation *and* our relationship with him. After that, we can talk about bringing him to trial, maybe establish a U.N. tribunal that could charge him with crimes against humanity." He paused. "I know I'm broad-jumping here, but it's a direction in which we really ought to move."

"Everything you've said sounds fine, but there are a couple of aspects to the situation you may be overlooking," President Ballard said. "The evidence we've obtained is highly subject to interpretation, and Starinov is liable to draw less certain conclusions from it than we have . . . if and when we present it to him. These two men have been friends and allies for decades."

"He could be pressured," the Veep said. "Starinov needs our support to continue sharing power with Korsikov and Pedachenko, and probably to win election once the state of emergency in Russia is lifted. We can make it clear that backing will be withdrawn unless he gives up Bashkir."

President Ballard looked at him with mild wonder. A few minutes ago Humes had been talking about giving their administration wriggle room, a way to avoid holding Bashkir accountable for mass murder in pursuit of political goals. By what shortcut of reasoning had he gone from there to his latest suggestion? Had he always been this cynical? Ballard suddenly felt like someone who'd found religion, or gone from being a three-pack-a-day smoker to being an anti-tobacco activist. But what place was there for a born-again idealist in office? He needed to get a grip.

"I'm not averse to maneuvering Starinov if it comes to that," he said. "But I think I know the man a little and, believe me, his personal allegiance isn't to be underestimated."

"*Et tu, Bruté,*" Taylor said.

"Exactly." The President straightened in his chair. "Right now, I'm wondering if we ought to be less concerned with reaction in Moscow than in Washington. We've got Delacroix sitting on the Senate Foreign Affairs Committee and the Intelligence Committee. He's objected to our foreign aid package to Russia from the beginning, and these reports will finally give him something to hang his hat on.''

''You can bet on it being a circus ringmaster's hat, too,'' Humes said. ''The only question is what sort of dog-and-pony show he's going to put on.''

President Ballard looked at him.

''This report's going to be in his hands by tomorrow afternoon,'' he said. ''Something tells me you'll have your answer soon enough. I suggest that you have a response formulated and ready to go before the good senator takes the stage.''

They met near midnight, in the square outside Saint Basil's Cathedral. Just the two of them, as arranged, although each arrived with an assignment of bodyguards, who hung a short and inconspicuous distance back in the shadows. Whatever trust there was between them was bought and maintained with power.

''Arkady,'' Starinov said with a nod of greeting.

His hands in the pockets of his trench coat, Pedachenko gave him an agreeable, artificial smile.

''I'm glad you agreed to meet tonight, Vladimir,'' he said.

Starinov said nothing in response. It was bitterly cold and he was bundled in a heavy wool coat, scarf, and fur hat. Pedachenko, however, stood with his thick hair whipping in the wind, and the top buttons of his coat open, as if in brash challenge to the elements.

The man was steeped in his own arrogance, Starinov thought.

Pedachenko turned, craning back his head to look up at the unlikely group of turban domes above them. The floodlights that illuminated the cathedral for tourists were switched off at this hour; in the darkness, its fanciful architecture took on the strange, alien nature of a half-forgotten myth.

"I've been thinking a little about St. Basil tonight," he said. "The Holy Fool who shunned all creature comforts, walking naked in the snow, eating and drinking only what he needed to survive. Yet known for always speaking the truth. For being the living conscience of the Russian people. A man so good and pious that even Ivan the Terrible tolerated his barbs."

Starinov looked at him.

"I hope," he said, "you aren't going to profess to that sort of self-denial."

Pedachenko chuckled.

"Nor anything like St. Basil's virtue," he said, turning back toward Starinov. "We are politicians, Vladimir. That in itself damns us, don't you think?"

Starinov shrugged and looked directly into the other man's pale blue eyes. He wanted to get down to business.

"If we are to discuss matters of state, as I assume is the case, then shouldn't Korsikov be with us?"

"He is the reason we've come here rather than to a pleasant old government chamber. One where we could clink snifters of brandy and stare meditatively at crackling logs as we speak," Pedachenko said. His smile, though unmoving, had somehow become derisive. "If you will pardon the term, Korsikov is the weak sister in our troika, Vladimir. And he is also a prying one. There's no point in having him meddle. We will make our decisions tonight, and he will go along with them."

Starinov kept looking at him.

"Whatever your opinion of Korsikov, he is still in place within the Kremlin."

"But perhaps not for much longer," Pedachenko said.

Starinov was quiet for several seconds. His breath puffed from his nose in little jets of vapor.

"Hours after Yeltsin died, the three of us formed our interim government, and mutually decided that it would last until there is an election," he said. "I will not engage in conspiratorial back-stabbing—"

Pedachenko held up his hand.

"Please, Vladimir, you misunderstand me," he said. "What I am about to propose is strictly aboveboard. There will be no garrotes in the night, either literally or figuratively."

Starinov regarded Pedachenko appraisingly.

"Let's hear it, then," he said. "I want to get home before dawn."

Pedachenko nodded.

"What seemed a good idea when Yeltsin sank into a tub of vodka has obviously proven unworkable," he said. "Have you noticed the GUM department store across this very plaza?"

A mordant smile touched Starinov's lips. "I've not had much time for shopping lately."

"Ah, but even from your high perch, it must be clear that the lines at the shops and food stands have vanished. Merchandise gathers dust on the shelves. The hollow prosperity your deceased president once trumpeted has crashed down into a black hole." Pedachenko spread his hands. "Our nation is in deepening turmoil, Vladimir. The international food relief effort has stalled, crime barons rape the people at every turn, a moral degeneration has—"

"My God, Pedachenko, look around you! There are no television cameras here. So, please, save the sanctimony for your viewers. I've already asked you once to get to the point."

Pedachenko's face showed its rigid, superficial smile again. Starinov felt as if he were looking at a cardboard mask.

"The country needs one leader to guide it, not three," Pedachenko said. "The troika's fractured vision has made our people stagger in descending circles." He gazed at Starinov with unblinking eyes. "I've come to propose that you step down. Cede power to me for the good of our motherland."

Starinov looked at him.

"I wish I could say you've surprised me, Arkady," he said. "But this is just the sort of thing I expected."

"And?"

"And what alternative do you offer? This third Great Patriotic War I've been hearing about?" Starinov laughed. "It is nothing but an admittedly stirring diversion. Icons and fanfare and ethnic superiority holding it together. I can't help but be reminded of the rallies at Nuremburg."

Pedachenko's smile drew in at the edges until it was gone. "You should choose your words more carefully," he said.

Starinov gave him a look of mock surprise. "Ah, you take umbrage. I'm reminded of Milosevic in the Balkans."

"Whom you embraced."

"Out of political necessity, as I do in your case," Starinov said. "How sensitive men like you become when we evoke comparisons with the Nazis. Why is that, Pedachenko? Do you fear the demon in the mirror?"

"I fear the loss of our national honor and dignity. I fear the humiliation of going to the United States for handouts. I fear having Russia sold out to its enemies. *Zgranista nam pamoshit*, foreign countries will help us. That is your solution to every problem."

The wind flapped Starinov's collar. He felt cold fingers of air slip under his scarf and fended off a shiver

"Listen to me, please," he said quietly. "The world is not as either of us would wish it to be, yet we are in an age when no nation can be a fortress." He paused. "Do you know the American satellite station in Kaliningrad? The one being built by Roger Gordian? When it is completed, it will be technically possible to place a telephone booth on an upper slope of Mount Everest, and communicate with someone tens of thousands of miles away. Without wires, and with only solar batteries for power. Think of it, Arkady. Is that not miracle and wonder? You must recognize that mankind will be linked in the future, not divided."

"And if your miracle means the mountain reaches will echo with American popular songs?"

"Then we will pray that what we have gained is worth what was lost," Starinov said. He waited a moment, then shrugged. "To be plain, Arkady, I reject your proposal. There will be no retreat into the glorified past."

Pedachenko stood there in silence. His eyes were a wall of ice.

"You can't prevail," he said finally. "The people will not stand by while the country goes to ruin. They will assemble behind me."

"You speak so confidently, I might indeed think you had the power of prediction," Starinov said. "Like Saint Basil."

Pedachenko remained motionless for another long moment, fixing Starinov with his cold, blue stare. Then his shoulders stiffened, and he whipped around and strode across the cobbled plaza to his guards.

Starinov watched him move away until he'd faded into the darkness, then walked off in the opposite direction.

THIRTY-THREE

THE LIGHT WAS LIT ATOP THE ORNATE CAPITOL
dome. A red bulb glowed above the north doors. A bell
tolled out a single extended note in the chamber. The majority and minority leaders greeted each other with courtly
decorum and then repaired to their front-row desks at either side of the center aisle. The parliamentarian, clerks,
and secretaries were seated, the president pro tempore
took his gavel in hand, unobtrusive C-SPAN cameras
winked to life, and the day's session of the august legis-
lative body came to order.

Up in the gallery, Roger Gordian watched the opening
speaker, Senator Bob Delacroix of Louisiana, take the
floor, striding toward the rostrum with starch, dark-suited
dignity, a pair of well groomed young aides respectfully
following at his rear.

The stuffed black bear the aides were carrying between
them stood six feet tall and had on red satin wrestling
trunks embroidered with the hammer and sickle emblem
of the long gone U.S.S.R.

"Friends and colleagues, today I'm going to introduce
you to Boris the Wrestling Bear!" Delacroix boomed.
"By the way, the reason he dragged his old shorts out of
the closet is that they fit a whole lot better than the new
ones!"

Chuckles and applause on his side of the aisle.

Sidewise glances and enduring sighs on the other.

"Boris might look like a nice bear, but don't let him fool you. No matter how much he eats, he's always hungry. That's because he's growing bigger and stronger every day . . . and you better believe he'll bite the hand that feeds him!"

Gordian stifled a disgusted groan.

Ladeez and gents, he thought, *welcome to the main attraction.*

"Let me tell you a little story about Boris. It's not pretty, and it won't be for the fainthearted. But, hey, there's a lesson to be learned from it," Delacroix went on. "Once upon a time, Boris had an appetite so big he thought he could eat the whole world. Nothing would satisfy him! He ate and he ate and he ate until he got so heavy he collapsed from his own weight. That was when his kindly Uncle Sam stepped along, put him on the Dr. Freemarket diet, taught him manners, taught him how to be *civilized,* and tried convincing him to give up his gluttonous ways."

Again there were snorts of laughter from slightly more than half the senators in the hall. The remainder looked embarrassed.

"Well, folks, for a few years the diet seemed to work, and Boris even squeezed himself into a pair of trunks that were the same red, white, and blue colors as Uncle Sam's clothes—with the stripes in a different pattern, of course, just so nobody'd call him a copycat!" Delacroix's voice projected to the chamber's vaulted ceiling.

Gordian was suddenly reminded of Burt Lancaster in *The Rainmaker.* Or was he thinking of that other movie, the one in which Lancaster played a tent-show evangelical? And the amazing thing was that it seemed to be working. Even if he was only preaching to the converted and semiconverted, they were becoming visibly roused.

"But then Boris fell back on his old, bad habits," Delacroix continued. "Boris got hungry again. Only this time he'd become used to begging for handouts from Uncle Sam, sort of like those grizzlies in Yosemite that'll come right up to your tent for food. And Uncle Sam, decent, generous soul that he was—overly generous, if you ask me—couldn't bring himself to say no. See, Sam had convinced himself that by keeping Boris close to his tent, by letting him watch Uncle Sam conduct his daily business through the flaps, Boris would learn how to stand on his own two feet. Believe it or not, Uncle Sam gave him hundreds of thousands of tons of food. Tens of millions of dollars. You heard me, *tens of millions,* just to keep him sticking around! And you know what happened? Can any of you guess? Boris turned on him! Boris sneaked into the tent and did something so horrendous, so unthinkable I can hardly bring myself to tell you about it. But I have to, you see, I *have to.* Because some of you still haven't realized that you can take the bear out of the hammer and sickle, but you can never take the hammer and sickle out of the bear!"

Rapt silence in the hall. By now every one of the senators had read or heard about the intelligence reports linking Bashkir to the Times Square bloodbath, and they pretty well knew where Delacroix was heading.

Gordian realized that even he was leaning forward, riveted by the performance. He had wondered earlier if Delacroix would step out of his Boris spiel when he got to this point, perhaps curb the histrionics, but that surely wasn't going to happen. The senator with the Cajun roots was a showman to the end.

". . . crept into Sam's tent one night when he let down his guard, a night when he was celebrating, a night that was supposed to be about hope and peace and prayers for a glowing new century, and sank his teeth deep into his flesh," Delacroix was saying. "He ripped at him, tore a chunk out of him, wounded him so badly, scarred him so grievously, that the pain will last forever. *Forever!* And you know what? Hold onto your seats with both hands, my dear friends, hold on tight as you can, because what I'm going to tell you next is really incredible." Delacroix strode from behind the podium, his head craned exaggeratedly forward, his gaze ranging back and forth across the large room. "Are you listening? Are you holding on? Okay, here it is: The bear had the audacity to come back the next day and pretend nothing had ever happened. To actually beg for more food! And some people, some misguided, foolish people—I won't mention any names, but we all know who they are—wanted Uncle Sam to close his eyes and do it!"

Delacroix stalked over to the bear now, grabbed it by the shoulders.

"Well, I'm not going to let that happen. Decide who to root for, everyone, make up your minds, because I'm getting in the ring with Boris. I'm taking a piece of him. I'm going to show him that his days of feeding off Uncle Sam are through, and that he'd better get on his way once and for all!"

Gordian had thought he was prepared for anything, anything at all, but what he saw next made his eyes open wide.

"Come on, Boris, wrestle me, *take me if you can!*" Delacroix frothed.

Then, the tails of his suit jacket flying out behind him,

the tongue of his necktie whipping back over his shoulder, Delacroix took a running leap at the bear, knocking it down, locking his arms around it, tumbling around there before the eyes of the assembled senators, and the astonished observers in the public galleries, and the television cameras, until he'd rolled on top of the stuffed animal and pinned it to the floor.

"It's over, Boris!" he shouted. "It's over!"

And watching from the gallery, looking at the rapt faces of the senators, thinking about how Delacroix's antics would play with public opinion once they made it to the nightly news, Gordian had the sinking feeling that it very well might be.

THIRTY-FOUR

COME ON, BORIS. WRESTLE ME. TAKE ME IF YOU CAN!

Almost twenty-four hours after he had watched Delacroix's antics on the floor of the Capitol building, Gordian could not get the scene out of his head. This was in part because it had been precisely the sort of sensational media lure he had expected it would be. Every network nightly news broadcast had led off with the story. CNN had done the same, and also made it their topic of discussion on *Inside Politics, Crossfire,* and *Larry King Live,* as well as their regular ten P.M. update on the Times Square bombing investigation. And this morning it was the lead story above the fold in the *Washington Post* and the *New York Times.*

He had to hand it to Delacroix, who had served two terms as mayor of New Orleans before making a successful bid for the Senate—he had brought a big, glittery suitcase full of Mardi Gras pizzazz to Washington with him, combined it with a sharp instinct for public relations, and turned it into a unique, and perhaps unmatchable, political asset.

Now Gordian tried to make himself comfortable in a commercial airline seat that even in first class wasn't as comfortable as his own desk chair, and tried to take his mind off the possible ramifications of yesterday's congressional session. But there was no retreat from his difficulties. What was the line in that poem? *Things fall apart; the center cannot hold.* He thought about the conversation he'd had with Ashley before leaving for Washington. She had been staying in their San Francisco apartment for the past month and wanted to take steps to "fix" their marriage. Until she left him on New Year's Eve, he hadn't realized it was broken. In need of a minor tune-up, maybe, but that was about it. And then she had gone away. And now he faced the prospect of sharing their deepest intimacies with a third party whose profession he mistrusted. Of laying himself open to a perfect stranger.

It all seemed to Gordian a painful and distracting waste of time. He and his wife had been married for nearly twenty years. They had raised a wonderful daughter. If they couldn't make sense of their own lives, how could they expect someone else to do it for them? He recalled the therapists he'd seen after being freed from the Hanoi Hilton, the endless, unendurable decompression program he'd been required to undergo by the Air Force. It wasn't a memory that gave him confidence. He supposed it had done a lot of good for some men, had little doubt it had, but he'd gotten nothing out of it. Zero.

Still, he needed to make a decision. And knew that the wrong one could result in Ashley leaving him forever.

The voice of the stewardess intruded on his reverie. "Ten minutes until takeoff, make sure your carry-on baggage is stored in the overhead compartment or under the seat in front of you." Where the hell was Nimec? After receiving Pete's late-night phone call in his hotel room, Gordian had exchanged his ticket for a nonstop return flight from D.C. to San Francisco, and gotten booked aboard a connecting red-eye at Kennedy Airport, in New

York City. The same plane Nimec was flying on. Or was supposed to be, anyway. Pete had said he had something important for him, and wanted to present it in person. And as soon as possible. Had he always been this damned cryptic? Or, Gordian wondered, could it be that he himself had never felt so jangled and impatient? He knew Pete had been making tremendous progress in New York, and could hardly—

A plain manila envelope dropped onto Gordian's lap and he once again lost his train of thought. He looked up and saw Nimec standing there in the aisle.

"Sorry I'm late," he said. "Airport traffic."

"I wasn't concerned," Gordian replied, poker-faced. He lifted the envelope. "This what you said you had for me?"

Nimec nodded, pushed his bag into the overhead compartment.

"Can I open it now, or do I wait for next Christmas?" Gordian asked.

Nimec sat down. He had a local tabloid in his hand. There was a photo of Delacroix under the front-page headline.

"Not that long," he said. "But I'd hold off till you're back in your office."

Gordian tapped the envelope against his knees. Took a deep breath.

"Okay, enough suspense, tell me what's in it."

Nimec smiled.

"Very good news about very bad people," he said.

THIRTY-FIVE

MAX BLACKBURN'S AFFAIR WITH MEGAN BREEN HAD caught him totally by surprise; it wasn't quite as though he'd opened his eyes one night and found himself between the sheets with her, but it wasn't really so different from that either. If he'd been told a month ago, hell, even a *week* ago, that he'd be lying naked in bed right now, watching her stride across his room in nothing but a short kimono-style robe, admiring her long, coltish legs, thinking about the things they'd done the night before, thinking about how much he wanted to feel her body pressing against him that very minute, he'd surely have laughed. There couldn't have been a more unlikely pairing—the battle-scarred former Special Air Service officer and the Ivy League intellectual.

They had never been friends in the past, and the damnedest thing was that he wasn't sure they were now. Wasn't even sure they had much in common besides a die-hard loyalty to Roger Gordian, jobs that had required them to be sent thousands of miles from home to a country neither particularly wanted to be in, and a physical attraction that had seized them both fiercely from the moment they had realized it was there. They hardly knew each other, hardly knew what to say to each other when they weren't discussing professional matters, and yet they were passionate, almost insatiable, lovers. No ambiguity on that account.

"I have to get going, Max," she said, sitting down at the edge of the bed. "Scully wanted to meet me over at the communications center this morning."

He sat up against his headboard. "It's only seven o'clock."

"*Early* this morning," she said. "What can I tell you? Scull's got a way of making people humor him."

"What's the fire?"

"Depends on when you're asking." She shrugged. His eye caught how the material pulled slightly over the curve of her breast. "A couple days ago he was concerned that we had too many of the technicians involved in reconfiguring the mainframe software for the Politika databases. Feels the operation's draining manpower and technical resources away from completion of the satellite facilities . . . which, in his opinion, ought to be our foremost priority here."

"And his latest worry?"

"It builds on the first. He says that the security detail's stretched thin, given that we've shifted our emphasis toward intelligence gathering, and inserted ourselves into a volatile international situation. My guess is he's going to give me a grand tour to prove his point, then push for me to expand the force."

"I didn't know that sort of thing fell within his bailiwick." Max smiled. "Actually, it occurs to me that it ought to be in mine. Last anyone told me, I was assistant director of Sword."

She put a hand on his chest. It felt cool where it touched his skin, yet oddly made him warm at the same time. He supposed that was a rough but adequate metaphor for their relationship.

No, he thought. Not relationship. *Involvement.* That was a much better word.

"Scull has problems recognizing that his authority has limits. And because he's been giving orders to people for so long, so does everybody else," she said.

"I wonder if he's gotten wind that we're sleeping together," Max said. "That's just the sort of thing that would piss him off."

She looked amused. "You really think so?"

"Scull hasn't been having a good time of it being stuck in the middle of nowhere. And when he's miserable, he doesn't want to know about anyone else enjoying himself."

"Or herself."

"Glad to know it's mutual."

"Exceedingly, and perhaps even multiply on occasion." She glanced down at the sheet over his waist, saw the response her touch had elicited in him, and gave him a look of mild but unblushing surprise.

"Dear me," she said. "I didn't mean to distract you from our conversation."

He looked down at himself.

"*Semper fi*," he said.

"Spoken like a true ex-marine." She was still smiling like that cat that ate the canary. "Uh, if I may get back to the previous subject a moment, how do you think I should address Scull's concerns? His *stated* ones, that is."

Blackburn was thinking he didn't want to talk about that now. Didn't want to talk, period. As she obviously was well aware.

He traced a finger lightly up her thigh, reached the hem of her robe, considered venturing higher.

"I think I'd like to persuade you to give him a buzz and advise him you'll be a half hour late."

"I think I'd like that, too, which is why I'm not going to let you get any further." Her hand clamped his wrist. "Seriously, how *do* you feel?"

He sighed, frustrated but trying not to show it.

"I couldn't tell you whether the timetable for getting the station fully operational's been thrown off. Unlike Scull, I stick with what I know. But he's right about security needing to be cranked. There's no way we can kid ourselves that Sword's mission is strictly business."

"Which, I assume, means you agree that we need additional personnel," she said.

"Not necessarily. I'd prefer to keep it lean and mean for the present, concentrate on reorganizing and tightening up procedures. Plenty can be accomplished by—"

The chirping of the bedside phone caused him to abort his sentence.

Megan looked at him.

"You don't suppose that's Scull, do you? I mean, would he have the nerve to call *your* place trying to get hold of me?"

"I wouldn't put it past him." Blackburn shrugged, reached for the phone, then let his hand rest on the receiver a moment. "If it *is* Scull, you want me to curse him out?"

"If it's him, I'll be the one to do the cursing," she said.

He smiled a little and picked up the receiver.

"Hello?"

"Max, sorry to disturb you, I know it's early in Kaliningrad. But this is very important,'' a voice said at the other end of the line.

"No, no, it's okay.'' Blackburn turned to Megan, covered the receiver, mouthed the word "Gordian.''

An odd expression came onto her face. Was it his imagination, or did the unflappable Megan Breen look flustered? He suddenly recalled water-cooler rumors that she'd been pining for Roger since she joined the firm. Could they have been true? And if so, what business was it of his? And why should he feel bruised?

"Max, you know the crew Pete's been tracking down?'' Gordian said guardedly. "The ones who crashed the New Year's Eve party?''

"Uh-huh.''

"We've got descriptions, points of exit, and points of entry for them,'' Gordian said.

Blackburn straightened.

"I should really take this in my office, it's got a more secure line,'' he said. "I'll hang up and get right back to you.''

"I'll be waiting,'' Gordian said, and hung up

Blackburn tore off his sheets, threw his legs over the side of the bed, and hurried to his clothing closet.

"Now what's *your* fire?'' Megan said, perplexed.

"Better get dressed,'' he said, slipping on his pants. "I'll tell you on the way out.''

THIRTY-SIX

HIS BACK TO THE DOOR, HANDS CLASPED BEHIND HIM, Starinov was standing by the window, watching the sun leap at severe angles off the golden helmet domes of the Assumption Cathedral, when Yeni Bashkir entered his office.

On Starinov's large mahogany pedestal desk was a bound report. Printed on its first page in Cyrillic were the words "CLASSIFIED MATERIAL."

Letting the door close softly behind him, Bashkir grunted to himself and took two steps forward over the medallion-patterned Caucasian rug. He was reminded, as always, of the rich history of his surroundings. Going back through the centuries, how many tsars and ministers must have stood just as he and Starinov were now?

"Yeni," Starinov said without turning to face him. "Right on time, as always. You're the only man I know whose obsession with punctuality equals my own."

"Old military habits die hard," Bashkir said.

Starinov nodded. He was wringing his hands.

"The report," he said in a heavy tone. "Have you read the copy I had delivered to you?"

"I have."

"There is more besides. A bill has been introduced in the American legislature. It would force the President to discontinue all agricultural aid to our country and result in a complete economic embargo. Business enterprises between our nations would be suspended.''

"I know.''

"These sanctions can be avoided, I am told, if I prosecute a man the Americans have implicated as the originator of a heinous conspiracy and act of destruction. A man who would surely deserve the harshest of punishments should the accusations against him be proven.''

There was silence in the room for perhaps two full minutes. Bashkir didn't move. Starinov's eyes didn't leave the great crownlike cathedral domes.

"Just once," he resumed finally, lowering his head, "I would like to feel as sure of myself as I remember being in my younger days. Does everything sooner or later cloud with uncertainty, so that we go to our graves knowing less than we did as children?''

Bashkir waited a moment, staring at Starinov's back. Then he said, "Let's get this over with. If you need to ask me, then do it.''

Starinov shook his bowed head. "Yeni—''

"Ask me.''

Starinov expelled his breath in a massive sigh. Then he turned and looked sadly at Bashkir.

"I want to know if the report the Americans have given me is true. If you are responsible for the bombing in New York," he said. "I need to hear it from your lips, on your honor.''

"The truth," Bashkir echoed.

Starinov nodded again.

Something turned in Bashkir's eyes. "If I were the sort of man who would slaughter thousands of human beings in a cowardly terrorist attack, the sort who believed that a political agenda would be worth spilling the blood of helpless women and children—be they Americans, Russians, or innocent citizens of any nation—then what trust could you place in my word of honor? And what value would our friendship have? Would a man behind such a deceitful coup against you, a man capable of betraying you so completely, have trouble answering you with a lie?''

Starinov smiled ruefully. ''I thought I was the one with questions here,'' he said.

Bashkir had remained rigid and motionless. His cheek quivered a little, but that was all. After a moment he spoke again.

''Here is truth for you, Vladimir. I have been clear about my mistrust of the American government. I have dissented with your open-door policies to American investors. I still subscribe to the basic ideals of Communism and am convinced we must build closer ties to China, a nation with which we share a four-thousand-mile frontier. I am open about all these things. But I also openly abhor terrorism. And as a sworn member of your cabinet, I have always acted in what I believe to be your best interests. Dissect me if you will, discard the parts that conflict with those that have cast my loyalty and integrity in doubt. That is the easy way out for you, I think. But I would have expected you to look at the whole of who I am. Who I have been for as long as we have known each other.'' He paused. His eyes bored into Starinov from under his shaggy eyebrows. ''I did not have anything to do with the bombing. I would *never* become involved in creating such horror. You speak of my honor? I will never again be *dis*honored by responding to such a question as you have asked me. Lock me away in prison, execute me . . . or better yet, have the Americans do it. I have spoken my piece.''

Silence.

Starinov regarded him steadily from across the room, his outline framed in the hard winter sunlight flooding in the window.

''I will be leaving for my *dacha* on the coast next week,'' he said. ''I need to be alone and think. The pressure from the United States will be intense, and will be joined by those here at home who want us to cave in to them, but we will find a way to stand against it all. No matter what they do, we will stand.''

Bashkir gave him a stiff, almost imperceptible little nod.

''There is a great deal of work ahead of us, then,'' he said.

THIRTY-SEVEN

THE SUN FROM THE OFFICE WINDOW WARM AGAINST his face, Namik Ghazi sat relaxing with his hands linked behind his head, his feet crossed under his desk, and a shiny silver tray on the blotter in front of him. On the tray was his morning glass of spiced wine, a glazed ceramic bowl filled with mixed olives, and an elaborately folded cloth napkin. The olives were cured in oil and imported from Greece. Better than the Spanish varieties, and far superior to those grown here in his own country. They had been delivered just yesterday, and though the shipping had cost him an arm and a leg, he had no regrets. Had not the ancients believed the olive to be a gift of the gods, a preventor of disease, a preserver of youth and virility? Was it not the fruit that grew from the branches of peace? Give him a constant supply, and the occasional tender attentions of his wife and mistress, and he could live out the final third of his life a happy man. Members of his American and European complement at Uplink's Near Eastern ground station often chided him for his breakfast preferences, but what did they know? It was his belief that their colonial heritage got in the way of their maturation as human beings. Nothing really against them, of course. He was a benevolent manager. He tolerated most of them, liked a few, and called a small handful close friends. Arthur and Elaine Steiner, for instance, had been invited over to his home quite often before Gordian snatched them away for the Russian enterprise. But even that dear couple . . . well, gourmands they weren't.

Aya, but the Westerners loved to judge. As if their tastes in eating, drinking, and loving were based on some empirical standard. Did he ever comment on their ungodly consumption of sizzled pork flesh with their morning eggs? Their relish of bloody, ground-up cows for lunch and dinner? The vulgar fashions of their women . . . What perverse mind had conceived of *pants* on the female form? Aya, aya, Westerners. How presumptuous for them to think they could write the encompassing definition of worldly pleasure. His day began and ended with olives and wine, and nearly everything else in between was toil and struggle!

Releasing a wistful sigh, Ghazi unmeshed his fingers, leaned forward, and gingerly plucked an olive from the bowl. He slipped it into his mouth and chewed, closing his eyes with delight as its flavor poured over his tongue.

That was when his intercom beeped.

He ignored it.

It beeped again, refusing to leave him be.

He frowned, pressed the flashing button.

"Yes, what is it?" he said grumpily, spitting the olive pit into his napkin.

"Ibrahim Bayar is on the line, sir," his secretary said. As always her voice was pleasant and even. How could he have been so brusque with her?

"I'll take it, Riza, thank you." He lifted the receiver, suddenly curious. The head of Sword's regional security force had been assigned to the Politika affair by Blackburn himself. What could be up? "*Gün aydin,* Ibrahim. Have you made any progress finding the black sheep?"

"Better than mere progress," Ibrahim said. "We have found the hiding place of at least one of the terrorists. Perhaps even the woman."

Ghazi's heart galloped. "Where?"

"A Kurdish sanctuary outside Derinkuyu. I'm in a village inn right now. The Hanedan. I'll give you the rest of the details later."

"Will you need additional men?"

"That's why I'm calling. Send me three teams, and be sure Tokat's is among them. This may be difficult."

"I'll get on it right away," Ghazi said. "And Ibrahim?"

"Yes?"

Ghazi moistened his lips.

"Have great care, my friend and brother."

THIRTY-EIGHT

EVEN BEFORE THE HITTITES SETTLED THE REGION four thousand years ago, Bronze-age troglodytes were tunneling into the strange volcanic domes, knobs, cones, spires, and furrowed massif ridges of Cappadocia, digging a network of subterranean communities whose rooms and passages extended for miles beneath the chalky tufa, providing separate housing for hundreds of people at a time. Living quarters were equipped with bedrooms, living rooms, and kitchens, as well as shrines, water cisterns, stables, storage areas, workshops, and wine cellars. There were public hospitals, churches, and internment grounds. Entries, ledges, balconies, staircases and pillars; frescoes and sculptures; even furnishings such as tables, chairs, benches, and sleeping platforms were carved whole out of the firm yet malleable stone. Tiny slots in the walls between individual dwellings allowed communication throughout daily routines, and provided an efficient civil alarm system in periods of emergency.

Over the centuries of Roman occupation, diverse groups of ethnic tribesmen, and then early Christians—including, it is believed, Paul the Apostle—found refuge from persecution in this hive-like underground megalopolis. Later it sheltered reclusive monastic orders from the brutalities of Mongol, Arab, and Ottoman invaders. In recent decades, isolated portions of it—the equivalent of

contemporary neighborhoods, towns, and belt cities—
have been excavated by archaeologists and in a few cases
opened to tourists. Some parts of the complex remain either undiscovered or known only to local peasant popu-
lations. A few were occupied by Kurds streaming
northward from Iraq in the wake of the Gulf War, and to
this day function as hidden strongholds for Kurdish militia
bands at violent odds with the governments of Turkey and
its international allies . . . including, for a variety of reasons, the United States.

For that, Ibrahim thought as he spurred his horse forward over the rugged slopes, if for no other reason, the
man-made caves south of Derinkuyu would have been an
ideal hideaway for Gilea Nastik and her cousin Korut
Zelva after the Times Square bombing. There were many
Kurdish sympathizers in these isolated regions, hillmen
who tended to be suspicious of anyone they didn't know,
and who would resent intrusions into local affairs by outsiders. Even those who were politically neutral would
have nothing to do with the group that had come hunting
for the terrorists.

And since he was Roger Gordian's man on the spot in
this isolated territory, Ibrahim worried that if any local
tribesmen spotted his riding party, the butchers were almost certain to be alerted.

He rode at a steady gallop, the muscular, sweat-slick
sides of his steed rippling like oil beneath his stirrups.
The sun was plunging solidly down on his shoulders, giving a bleached-out shimmer to the terrain . . . a wasteland
so stark and craggy that nothing on wheels—not ATVs,
not even Sword's small fleet of fast-attack vehicles—
could have traversed it.

There were stretches here that seemed to exist in a still

pocket of eternity, Ibrahim mused. Stretches where change was resisted at an elemental level, where roads and telephone lines came to the end of their reach, and large distances were traveled on horseback or not at all. The land did not compromise; you adapted or you were defeated.

Ibrahim rode on, his hands loosely gripping the reins. The neck of his horse rose and fell, rose and fell, with an easy, swaying sort of rhythm. To his left and right, the hooves of his teammates' mounts slapped the ground, beating up little clods of pebbles and ashy soil. The men wore lightweight dun-colored fatigues and carried VVRS M16 rifles fitted with M234 RAG kinetic-energy projectile launchers. They had gas masks and protective goggles strapped around their necks.

Perhaps a kilometer distant, Ibrahim could see a huge arch-backed formation pushing up from the surrounding terrain. The honeycomb tiers of openings on its high rock walls had once led to the lodgings of a caravansary. There traveling merchants would come to a temporary halt in their routes, bringing supplies to the cities beneath the ground, descending from the upper chambers through long stepped passages.

Now, Ibrahim knew, the passages would be filled with scorpions—human scorpions as well as the traditional ones. And the mission of his team was to flush out their hiding place, and capture the deadliest of the creatures, without killing any of them. The quarry, however, would show no such compunction. Given a chance, they would slaughter him and every one of his men, leave them to rot on the barren earth.

Well, no struggle was ever fair to all sides. Ibrahim and his brothers-in-arms knew the job they had to do, and would try as well as they could to get it done. The rest was up to Allah.

The lair of the scorpion ahead of them, they clipped along through the desert silence.

The porter at the Hanedan hotel had left the village at dawn, barely ahead of the strangers who had arrived over the past two days. He took little-known shortcuts between the slopes of the forbidding moonscape, driving his animal relentlessly toward the humped shelf of land that served as the main access to the underground hideout. Other rabbit holes existed through which men could enter and leave the chambers, but most led to passages that had become blocked, or collapsed, over hundreds of years.

Korut would have positioned the bulk of his sentries at the shelf, and they needed to be warned. Aya, they did, and fast.

The young hotel worker shot a glance back over his shoulder, saw the armed riders and their horses as small advancing dots at his rear, corkscrews of desert dust winding into the air above them. He did not know who had sent them on their manhunt; in truth, it was of no matter to him or his fellow villagers. Some weeks ago Gilea and Korut had returned to Derinkuyu, needing shelter and protection, and they had gotten it. Gilea and Korut were linked to his people through blood and clan lines, and had their allegiance to a soul.

He would not fail. He would get to them before the interlopers, tell them of the advancing threat, even if it meant running his horse to the ground.

Nothing his relatives could have done—nothing— would prevent him from aiding in their escape.

• • •

Korut snapped a full 30-round magazine into his Kalashnikov AKMS, slung the assault rifle over his shoulder, and ran down the corridor, his footsteps thudding flatly off its pocked and pitted stone floor. Minutes ago, an anxious voice had shouted to him through the slot in his wall, alerting him to a raid. Strangers were coming across the waste. Less than a klick to the south, and getting closer by the second. They had ridden out of the village that morning, a mixed group consisting of Turks, Americans, and Europeans.

It was a stroke of good fortune that Gilea had already departed, leaving him behind to train and recruit new operatives. By now, she would have made her rendezvous with the minisubmarine in Amasra, on the northern coast, and be halfway across the Black Sea to her destination.

He did not think his pursuers were CIA or Interpol. They would have come with helicopters, even planes, but not on horseback. Whatever its multinational composition, this force was commanded by men who knew the land, using inbred native tactics. Could it be the mysterious organization he'd had been informed about, the same one that had sent a team into Roma's office in New York?

There was no way to be sure, and ultimately what was the difference? They had sought him out, they had located him, they were coming for him.

Korut only prayed he could make them live to regret it.

Ibrahim saw the sun heliographing off the automatic weapons on the bluff even before they released their first volleys. He glanced up at the shooters poised in the cave openings, their rifles kicking against their arms, rattling out bursts of fire.

He jerked back on the reins of his horse, rearing it to a halt, simultaneously bringing his hand up and down in a slicing gesture. The other men pulled alongside him, their mounts snorting and whinnying, jets of dirt fanning over their hooves as Parabellums sprinkled the ground up ahead. At the distance from which they were being fired, the guns would be inaccurate, barely within range of their targets. Still, the terrorists held the high ground. And they had been ready, clearly informed of the Sword team's approach.

It wasn't the best thing that could have happened. Nor was it the worst, in Ibrahim's estimate. He'd hoped to have surprise on his side, but had considered the eventuality that it might turn against him. And had familiarized himself with the lay of the land, making sure he had a few tricks of his own up his sleeve.

He turned to the American at his right.

"Take your men around the front, Mark," he said. "I'll bring my team to where our man is sure to try wriggling from his nest."

Mark's blue eyes regarded him from under his sunburned brow. Then he nodded, signaled to the dozen men behind him.

As their horses thundered toward the rock shelf in an arrow-straight line, Ibrahim broke to his left with the other half of the team, leading them there as quickly as his mare could carry him.

Racing up to the foot of the bluff, the American-led Sword team instantly lifted the RAG launchers—weapons with a range of forty to sixty yards—to their shoulders and took aim through their built-in sights. Rounds snapped down at them from the defenders on the ledges, close enough now to present a deadly threat. Mark saw one of his men go tumbling off his saddle, clutching at his throat, blood spraying between his fingers. Another man fell to the dust, crimson petals blossoming on his desert tunic. Beside him, one of the horses was raked across the chest and collapsed in a writhing heap, its legs giving out all at once, throwing its stunned rider several yards through the air. The screech of pain that issued from the dying animal sounded horribly, sickeningly human.

"Fire!" Mark shouted. "Hit the bastards hard!"

In a tightly coordinated fusillade, his remaining teammates released the ring-shaped energy grenades from their tubes, sent them spinning toward the cave entrances at five thousand revolutions per minute, spirals of propellant trailing behind. The gyro-stabilized airfoil projectiles flew upward with flat, dead-on trajectories, slamming into the men on the rock ledges, hurling them off their feet with yelps of agony and confusion. Soft rubber O rings fitted around the grenades gave way on impact, pouring CS1 tear gas into the cave entrances.

Satisfied that the opening wave of his strike had had its desired effect, Mark barked out another command. In response, his men pulled their gas masks down over their faces, dismounted their horses, and began scrambling up the slope, their boot heels scuffing over the arid soil, triggering off a near-continuous volley of VVRS rounds as they ascended.

The tear gas–blinded men above them thrashed atop the overhanging ledges, screaming, seized by convulsive, wracking coughs. Some stumbled blindly for several seconds, arms pinwheeling for balance, and then tripped off their feet and dropped earthward. Others tried to retreat, groping, crawling on hands and knees, helpless, unable to use their weapons, barely able to find the cave openings in their pain and disorientation.

Reaching the ledges, the Sword team hastily reloaded their airfoil launchers and fired another salvo of RAG/CS grenades into the cave mouths.

Then, clouds of gas swirling in the dimness ahead of them, they went storming into the tunnels to mop up what was left of the resistance.

Korut dashed toward the stairs rising toward the fallback exit, the dim electric lights on the walls throwing tiger stripes of shadow across his features. He could hear the screams and stricken gasps of his fellows echoing in the shaft behind him, but there was nothing he could do for them now. He had thought that even with half their number in Russia, they would be able to fend off attackers unfamiliar with the terrain. But the men that had come after him were hardly performing like outsiders. Who were they? How had they discovered the underground complex?

He would have to figure it out. Have to send word to Gilea about what had happened here today. But all that was for later. Unless he made off right away, he wouldn't be able to do anything at all. For her, or for himself.

He slipped into the narrow stairwell and bounded toward the surface, taking the steps two at a time, his gun held out at the ready. He could see daylight splashing into the chamber from above, could hear the frightened whinnying of his horse in its stable.

He reached the top of the stairs, turned a jutting corner, plunged into the stable. Though cross-tied in its stall, the horse pawed the ground with its hooves in a jittery little dance, obviously rattled by the sounds of combat down below.

Korut pulled the saddle blanket off its steel wall peg, then the saddle, and tossed both of them over the beast. He tightened the girth quickly, praying that he'd gotten it secure. Then he shoved his foot into the stirrup, hefted himself onto the horse's back, yanked the reins so the animal turned toward the stable exit, and dug his heels deep into its sides.

The horse bridled for only a moment. Then, with a shrill, startled neigh, it left the stable, bolting into the glare of the undiluted desert sun.

Ibrahim's team had been told about the stable, had had its precise location mapped out for them by a local merchant who had valued their U.S. currency above tribal loyalty. And after splitting off from Mark's group, he and his men had gone to wait outside the rim of rock that formed its entrance, knowing Korut would try using it as an escape route if he eluded the frontal assault.

He caught sight of them as soon as he emerged from the cave, sitting astride their horses in a loose semicircle, their weapons trained in his direction.

"Pigs," he rasped, realizing he'd been trapped. "Fucking pigs."

He raised his weapon to fire it, thinking he would take down as many of his enemies as he possibly could, but a RAG projectile smashed into his midsection before his finger had even curled around the trigger, bouncing him from the saddle, sending him crashing to the ground in an agonized ball, his knees drawn up, his hands wrapped around his stomach.

"Let's scrape him up and get him out of here," Ibrahim said, and climbed off his horse.

THIRTY-NINE

GREGOR SADOV WAS AT THE FIRING RANGE, WORKING
with Nikita, when the phone call came in. He had a cell
phone clipped to his belt, its ringer set to Silent, but he
felt the vibration in the small of his back.

Slamming home a fresh magazine in the AKMS, he
pulled back the cocking lever, handed it to Nikita, spun
away without a word, unclipped the phone from his belt,
and took the call. "Yes?" he said into the cell phone.

"It's time." The voice on the other end of the line was
masculine, but that didn't mean anything. It had obviously
been altered electronically, and could have belonged to
his own grandmother for all Gregor could tell. He did
know, however, even with all the electronic modifications,
that it was the same voice that had originally hired Gregor
for this series of missions, and that relayed Gregor's orders to him. He had no idea whom he was speaking to,
but that wasn't unusual. In Gregor's line of work, he was
used to several layers of insulation between himself and
his employer. What wasn't usual was the fact that this
time Gregor didn't actually know whom he was working
for. He knew it was someone high up in the government,
and he could make a good guess who was selecting his
targets, but with this job he knew he was better off not
knowing.

"Do you have the target selected?" Gregor asked.

"Yes. A satellite ground station in the Kaliningrad region."

Gregor nodded to himself. He didn't ask why this particular site had been targeted. He didn't need to know. "Any special requests?" Gregor didn't need to explain what he meant. He needed to know if there were any individuals in particular who needed to be killed—or who needed to survive.

"None. Just make sure you're thorough."

Sadov nodded again. "Understood," he said.

"There's one more thing," the electronically altered voice said.

Gregor's hand tightened around the tiny phone. That little "one more thing" would invariably turn out to be something he didn't like.

"The mission needs to be carried out as quickly as possible."

Gregor smiled, but there was no amusement in the quick, tight quirking of his lips. "How quickly?" he asked. "We'll need time to plan, to reconnoiter, to—"

"Tonight," the voice said, its tone harsh and unyielding. "Tomorrow night at the latest."

"Impossible—"

"We'll double your fee."

That stopped Sadov in mid-protest. "Triple," he said.

The man—if man he was—with the altered voice didn't hesitate. "Agreed," he said immediately, making Gregor wonder how much higher he *could* have gone. "As long as it's done by tomorrow night."

"It will be," Gregor said. Hanging up, he turned around again, grabbed the weapon from Nikita, and started peppering the target. "Come on," he said when the clip was empty. "We've got work to do."

FORTY

"**POWER'S OUT AGAIN, ELAINE.**"

Elaine Steiner looked up from the junction box she was working on. Her husband had just come into the room, bearing bad news once again. "What is it this time? Don't tell me they ran the back hoe into the generator again."

As part of Gordian's agreement with the Russian government, the ground station purchased electricity from the surrounding grid—but Gordian was no fool. He knew how unreliable the service could be in the remote areas he picked for his ground stations, and so each site was provided with a generator large enough to keep the facility on-line. The problem was that many of the spare parts required for the generator were purchased locally, as was the fuel it ran on, and none of these were ever up to the Steiners' usual standards.

"Nope," Arthur said. "The generator came on-line smoothly and automatically, just like it was supposed to. But we can't figure out why the power from the grid stopped. We put in a call to the local substation, and no one else is without power."

Elaine frowned and started putting her tools away. She and Arthur had been doing this for long enough, and had worked in enough violent places, for her to have sharpened her sense of caution to a fine edge. "How long has the power been out?" she asked.

"Ten minutes or so. The substation's sending out a crew to check the lines, so we'll know more shortly."

Elaine blew out her lips in silent frustration at her husband's perpetual optimism. "A local crew?" she asked. "We'll be lucky if they can even *find* the lines. No, dear, if we want this repaired quickly, we'd better do it ourselves."

Gregor Sadov looked at the downed power lines and allowed himself a small smile of satisfaction. Three utility poles in a row had been knocked down, victims of a little bit of C4 plastique planted just above ground level.

Their target was an American satellite ground station, so Gregor knew the loss of electricity would not knock out all their defenses. But he also knew that most of their generator's output would be directed toward maintaining the most vital systems, including the satellite uplink and the communication channels.

Gregor wanted to take out that generator. He wasn't too worried about the phones inside the compound. This compound was so far from any real civilization that there simply wasn't anyone the people inside could call—no one, that is, who could get there in time to do any good. But Gregor hadn't survived this long by taking unnecessary chances. He couldn't cut off all the communications from the compound, not without finding some way to knock their satellite out of orbit, but he could try and take out their generator.

He signaled his team members to mount up. He had seven people with him, the three survivors of his current team and four new people Gilea had sent to help him. Gregor hadn't had much chance to work with the newcomers. That didn't matter, though. They were Gilea's people, not his, and even if they'd been with him for a year he still wouldn't have been able to trust them.

He'd split his team evenly among four BTR-40s. Gilea's men were together in two of them, he and Nikita were in one, and the last of his own men were in the remaining armored personnel carrier. Each vehicle had a KPV 14.5mm machine gun mounted on the roof of the driver's compartment and an impressive array of extremely lethal weaponry stored ready to hand. His orders were to be thorough, and he intended to carry those orders out.

They started their engines and, with Gregor and Nikita in the lead, headed toward the compound some three miles away. He'd wanted to make sure that no one at the ground station heard the explosions when they took the power lines down.

As they approached the compound, Gregor saw an American Jeep heading their way, a corporate logo painted on the side. He couldn't see who was in it, but it didn't matter. He knew it had to be a repair crew sent out to investigate the loss of power.

Under other circumstances he would have let them go. A small crew of technicians was meaningless in the larger scheme of things. But his orders were to be thorough.

Braking to a stop, he turned to Nikita. "Take them out," he said.

Nikita nodded once. Breaking out one of the RPGs in the back, she climbed out of the carrier, took careful aim, and fired.

The road was bumpy enough that Arthur had put his seat belt on. Elaine refused to. She said she had had enough of that back in the States, where the law required you to wear seat belts and motorcycle helmets and to put your kids in car seats—not to protect you but to protect the state from additional medical payments in the event of an accident.

Arthur was driving. He always drove. Truth was, Elaine was the better driver, but whenever the two went anywhere together, Arthur always drove. Because of this, and because he had his attention focused on the goat trail they called a road in this part of Russia, it was Elaine who first saw the enemy.

That's how she thought of them, from the moment they crested the small rise a couple hundred yards ahead. *The enemy.* Her suspicions had been raised as soon as Arthur told her about the power outage, and how the local substation had said no one else had been affected. It was too coincidental, especially given what had happened back in Times Square only a little while earlier. She would have given a month's pay to have a gun with them—any sort of gun—but the few small arms the compound had were kept locked up in times of peace . . . and no matter what her suspicions were, this was still officially a time of peace.

Now, seeing four unmarked armored personnel carriers heading toward the compound, Elaine knew what she was seeing: the enemy.

''Arthur—'' she said, but it was already too late. The four BTR-40s slowed to a stop, and Elaine saw a woman step out of the lead vehicle, pull something out of the back, and point it in their direction. ''Turn around, Arthur,'' she said. ''Turn around *now*.''

Her husband looked up, his hands starting to shift on the wheel, but at that moment the woman fired.

• • •

Nikita's shot fell short, burrowing into the ground directly in front of the oncoming Jeep and opening up a crater before it. But that was all right, Gregor thought. The effect was the same. The Jeep slammed into the sudden hole in the ground, driving its grill into the far wall of the crater and throwing someone out of the passenger's side.

Putting his own vehicle in gear, he motioned for Nikki to get back in. "Come on," he said. "Let's finish this and get going."

At first, Elaine couldn't feel anything, couldn't even remember what it was that had happened. All she knew was she was lying down, looking up at a sky that seemed too blue, too peaceful, to belong to anywhere on earth. And then it all came rushing back to her—the enemy carriers, the woman, the rocket exploding in front of them, Arthur . . .

"Arthur," she said. She moved, then, rolling onto her side, and that's when the pain hit her, a great, white wall of agony that started somewhere down around her toes and ended just past her hairline. She knew then that something was terribly wrong with her, that either the blast itself or her landing on the hard, frozen ground had damaged her beyond any repair, but none of that mattered anymore. All that mattered was Arthur.

Ignoring the pain, she forced herself onto her hands and knees and began crawling back toward the crumpled wreck.

Arthur was there. His seat belt had kept him from being thrown from the Jeep, but it hadn't done him any favors. As she got closer she could see that the steering column had been driven backward into his chest. He was pinned against his seat, and he was not moving.

"Arthur," she said, her voice somewhere between a cry and a prayer. "Arthur . . ."

She made it to his side, crawling through the open doorway and curling up against his motionless body. She knew he was dead. He wasn't breathing, his wounds had stopped pumping blood, and she knew there was no hope for either of them.

"Oh, Arthur," she said. Reaching out, she closed his eyes gently and then, fighting the pain that threatened to overwhelm her, she leaned forward and kissed him gently on the lips. "Sleep well, my darling," she whispered, and let her head fall against his shoulder one last time.

Gregor approached the broken American Jeep slowly, his Beretta in his hand. He was sure there was no one still alive within it, or at least no one who could be a serious threat, but still it paid to be cautious—especially since it was so difficult to see through the starred and bloody glass remaining in the windshield.

Coming around the side, he looked through the passenger door and took in the scene before him. The man was dead, that much was obvious. The woman, though. She'd been thrown from the Jeep, and had made her way back. She could still be alive.

He raised his Beretta, but before he could fire she turned her head, slowly, obviously in great pain, and looked him in the eye.

"Why?" she said, her voice shattered as badly as the Jeep. "We're here to help, not to harm. Why kill us?"

Gregor shrugged. "Orders," he said, in English. And then he fired. The bullet caught her high up in the forehead, snapping her head back against her husband's shoulder. She slumped forward, falling away from the man she obviously loved so much.

Gregor paused for a moment, then reached out and pushed her back into position, laying her head gently against her husband's shoulder. Then he turned, got back into his BTR-40, and headed for the American compound.

FORTY-ONE

AS HE WALKED UP TO THE DESK SERGEANT AT ONE
Police Plaza, Roger Gordian was on edge, uncomfortable.

Part of it, he knew, was the tour of Times Square he'd
just taken. The site of the bombing was haunting, filled
with reminders of the tragic cost it had exacted. As awful
as it had looked on CNN, nothing had prepared him for
the emotional impact of being there and seeing it in person.

It wasn't really the scope of the destruction that caught
him off guard. It was the small details that brought the
tragedy down to a personal level. A bloodied teddy bear
with a bedraggled pink ribbon, much the worse for a
month's exposure to New York's dirt and weather, had
been trapped beneath the wreckage of a sign. He could
only hope that the bear's owner was alive somewhere, free
enough of pain and worry to be able to mourn the loss of
her toy.

Yes, Times Square had shaken him. And he'd already
made plans to help rebuild it. But that wasn't, he knew,
the only reason he felt uneasy. He was all too aware of
the risks he was about to take, and the explosive nature
of what he was carrying in the pocket of his overcoat.

He walked up to the desk sergeant.

"Commissioner Harrison, please. I have an appoint-
ment."

• • •

When his secretary buzzed to tell him Gordian had arrived, Bill Harrison put down the pile of reports he'd been combing for details, pulled off his reading glasses, and rubbed his eyes.

"Give me a minute, then bring him in," he told her.

He hadn't slept well since his wife's death. The department shrink had told him that it was to be expected, but knowing that his emotions were predictable didn't make them any less painful. Nor did it help him deal with the nightmares. Or the loneliness.

He'd given up sleeping in his bed. The memories of Rosie were overpowering there. He was unable to function when he walked into their room. All her clothes, the smell of her perfume—he'd just grabbed what he needed and put it in the guest room. But even that didn't help much. Every time he closed his eyes to sleep, he'd dream. In those dreams, he'd replay that night over and over again. And wake up screaming in terror.

Worst of all were the dreams where he saved her, where he got them all out, only to wake up and have to face that terrible truth all over again.

Rosie was gone.

He'd taken to sleeping in an easy chair in the living room. It was so uncomfortable that he never really went completely under. It helped with the dreams, but it wasn't doing his concentration any good.

And he needed every scrap of concentration he could muster if he planned to solve this thing.

He ran his hands over his face, across his hair, and straightened his tie. Distraction, he told himself. That's the key to surviving this. Think about something else.

He wondered what the big man wanted with him.

It was a long way from the mean streets of Manhattan to California. Especially the California somebody like Gordian lived in.

Hell, his co-op apartment would probably fit in Gordian's garage with room left over to park an RV.

So why had Gordian's secretary called and arranged a private meeting? Police business? It seemed unlikely.

Well, he'd find out soon enough. His curiosity—that endless nosiness that had driven him into police work in the first place—was the only emotion he had that was unaffected by the tragedy.

As the door opened and a man he'd seen on countless magazines and news broadcasts walked in, Harrison stood to greet him. If the grim look on Gordian's face was anything to go by, this wasn't a rich man's idle whim. Gordian walked in quietly and set his coat on the couch, then turned to the police commissioner.

The two men shook hands and introduced themselves.

Formalities completed, the men sat down facing each other and exchanged small talk. Bars of morning light slanted in through the minimalist venetian blinds, giving a strange cast to a stranger meeting. Gordian was no more at ease than he was. Apparently they both felt the awkwardness—Harrison finally decided to cut through the chitchat and go straight to the heart of the matter.

"You flew six hours to see a man you've never met. Me. Your secretary tells me that you're planning to fly back to San Francisco tonight. I think we can assume you didn't come here to discuss the weather. Why don't you tell me why you're here?"

The moment of truth. Harrison could see it in Gordian's face.

"It is," Gordian said, "a very long story." He paused.

"And it may not have a happy ending." He pulled a thick, rather lumpy envelope from the pocket of his overcoat, which he'd chosen to bring in with him rather than give to the secretary to hang in the coat closet. Odd behavior for a man like Gordian, Harrison had thought. Gordian probably had servants underfoot around the clock at his home. Gordian balanced the envelope in his hands and looked down at it as if he expected it to explode. Then he seemed to recall where he was, and looked up at Harrison. Harrison sat quietly, ready to listen.

"I don't know if you are aware of this," Gordian said, "but I spent time as a prisoner of war. I was shot down over 'Nam, and became a guest of the Hanoi Hilton."

"It's common knowledge," Harrison confirmed, totally at a loss to guess where this was leading. What in the world was going on here?

"I came back from that experience a changed man. I wanted to challenge the world, open it up, make sure that nothing like that ever happened again if it was in my power to prevent it." He paused, looked at the police commissioner. "I have people in my employ all over the globe. They're working for the greater good of all of us, far from home and vulnerable to the political tides of their host countries. I put them there. I'm responsible for them."

"I can understand that," Harrison said. "I send thousands of men in blue uniforms out into harm's way every day."

"Then you can understand that there is very little that I won't do to protect my people."

"Exactly where do you draw the line? Where do you stop when it's important to you?" Harrison was beginning to get an inkling, finally, of what this was about.

"It depends—certainly, where law-abiding citizens are concerned, we follow the letter and spirit of the law of the land. Always. I'm proud of my company. But where criminals and terrorists are concerned, shall we just say there are gray areas in my corporate security measures, and leave it at that?" Gordian tapped the envelope against his leg. It rasped a little across the fine British wool of his suit. The tiny noise was loud in the quiet office.

"I'll make it a point not to inquire too closely into your methods unless I have to." Harrison, like Gordian, stared at the envelope.

"The Times Square incident was a terrible tragedy," Gordian said. "I was watching on television when it happened. It reminded me far too much of my days in Vietnam. If I haven't mentioned it, you have my deepest sympathies."

Harrison took a deep breath. He could tell Gordian knew what he was feeling now, knew it all the way to the gut from hard experience. Gordian had been there. He'd survived it. Harrison swallowed hard. "Thanks. That means a lot, coming from you."

"I don't like terrorists." Gordian tightened his jaw. "And when they threaten my people, I refuse to sit still, wring my hands, and watch. Some of my employees had family in that crowd."

"So did I," Harrison said softly. "So did I . . ."

"I'm sorry—I wasn't thinking . . ." Gordian looked appalled, clearly realizing what he'd just said.

"It's okay. I spend every day going through pictures of the crime scene, looking at the evidence from my men, from the FBI and the ATF, trying to see a pattern, see who did this. Believe me, the reminders are everywhere I turn. I'm going to find out who did this to my wife and my city. I've got 400 guys working on nothing but this twenty-four hours a day. We'll get to the bottom of it if I have to dig the pit myself. We have to. For the city. For the mayor. And for my wife. It's what's keeping me going.'' Harrison gave Gordian a long, level look. ''I'd be willing to deal with the devil himself for a shot at the evidence to break this case.''

Gordian held out the envelope. Hands trembling, Harrison took it. He didn't open it.

''I'd be lying if I told you I didn't know what was in there,'' Gordian said. ''Nor will I say that we went through strictly legal channels to get it. We took some shortcuts.''

Harrison didn't ask. There were some things a man preferred not to know. ''I'll assume you covered your tracks.''

''Maybe not—I'll deal with that problem if we get to it. Everything that we've been able to find out is in that envelope, along with the supporting evidence, if we've got it. If you'd like me to keep you updated from our end, I will. If you find it in your heart to do it, I'd like you, as far as you're able under the law, to return the favor.''

''Thank you.'' Harrison looked down at the envelope, now in his hands. ''I'll keep your name out of it if I can.'' He looked back at Gordian, clearly gathering his things to leave now that his mission was accomplished. ''I have one question. Why me? You don't even know me.''

''It seemed to me that you had the greatest right to it. Use it well.'' With that, Gordian shook Harrison's hand, a warm, firm grip that somehow conveyed sympathy, confidence, and comfort without saying a word. Then he left, as quietly as he had come in. It seemed, Harrison thought, he was so bowled over by the encounter with this man he was unable to move, that Gordian's reputation, considerable though it was, didn't do him justice. It had taken balls to do what he had just done; balls, and a finely developed conscience, whatever the man said about gray areas.

He shook his head a little to clear it.

Tearing the envelope open, he poured the contents across his desk.

"Jesus!"

Names, photos, times, points of entry and exit, transcripts of conversations, audio cassettes, video cassettes—they were all there.

He shuffled them around, read snatches. He popped the VCR tape into his machine and watched for a second. His jaw dropped. Then he realized what the two people making out in that tape were saying.

Jesus!

He ran to his office door.

"Jackie," he yelled, "get me the heads of the Times Square special squad, and get them in here right now. Call the D.A.—we're gonna need some subpoenas. And call the FBI."

He turned his attention back to the TV, now officially X-rated.

He was looking at the faces of his wife's murderers.

It was time to take action.

Security had tightened at the Platinum Club. The number of guards had tripled, and new video cameras hung down from the ceiling beneath understated black plastic bubbles.

Boris smiled to himself as he surveyed the arrangements. Boris wasn't his real name, but it was the name he was using for this assignment. He couldn't help thinking that Nick's effort to increase his security after the break-in was too much like that old American saying— what was it again? Ah, yes: locking the barn doors after the cows had gone.

Too little, too late. That was another American saying, and one that was just as true.

Feeling the weight of the silenced SIG Sauer P229 riding comfortably beneath the jacket of his stolen UPS uniform, he shifted the oversized bubblepak envelope resting on his electronic clipboard and started up the stairs leading to Nick's private offices.

Two big, burly bodyguards, one with a close-trimmed beard, the other clean shaven, met him at the top of the stairs, cutting him off before he could do more than look around. *Right on time,* Boris thought.

"I'll sign for that," one of them said.

Boris glanced up. There was one of those opaque plastic bubbles up here, too, hanging down from the ceiling at the far end of the plush, carpeted hallway. He wasn't surprised, though. From what he'd heard about the man, he knew that Nick Roma liked to record everything.

"No problem," he said, handing the oversized envelope to the bodyguard on his left, the one without the beard, and holding the clipboard out to the one on his right. As that bodyguard reached for the clipboard, Boris pressed a button built into its bottom, triggering its concealed taser and also setting off the small flash unit buried in the envelope.

The taser hit the bodyguard with the beard, burying its tiny dart lead into the soft flesh directly beneath the neatly trimmed black beard. Beside him, the other bodyguard had started to scream as the flames from the suddenly burning package ate at his hands.

Boris was already moving. Drawing his 9mm, he put two quick, subsonic bullets into each bodyguard, and then raced forward toward the door that led into Nick's private office.

He knew his target was inside. He also knew that the door would be unlocked—Nick relied too much on fallible humans for his personal safety—and that the warning from his security force would come too late.

Nick Roma looked up as the door of his office swung softly open to reveal a man in a familiar brown uniform.

"A package? Who's it from?" he asked, even as it dawned on him that his personal bodyguards weren't flanking the UPS man as they should have been. He started to reach for the gun he kept in a drawer in his desk, but his hand didn't make it that far.

"Our mutual friend, Yuri Vostov, sends his regards," said the man in the brown UPS outfit.

Nick Roma's eyes widened in surprise and sudden understanding—an understanding that came too late.

"Wait—"

But Boris didn't wait. He put two shots directly into Nick's head, the first right between the eyes, the second— a difficult shot with the head still moving from the first impact—slightly higher. Unscrewing the hot, spent silencer from the barrel of his pistol, he screwed a new one in place, slipped in a new clip, and turned toward the fire exit. He paused only once on his way out, to toss a quick smile and a jaunty wave at the mirror, and then he fled the office.

FORTY-TWO

THE AMERICAN COMPOUND ROSE UP OUT OF THE darkness like a silent fortress, but its air of solidity and protection was a mere illusion. There were ten buildings, none of them more than two stories tall, and a concrete wall running around the perimeter. Gregor knew there were infrared beams and sensors running along the top of the wall that would sound an alarm if anyone breached their security. He also knew those infrared beams and sensors were going to do those inside no good at all.

There was one gate in the wall nearest them. Wide enough to permit two trucks to pass through at the same time, the reinforced metal gates swung open past small guard booths mounted on either side.

A typical American setup, Gregor thought. Within, there would be only a handful of poorly armed security guards, and maybe a score or two of technicians. None of them would be a match for him and his team.

As planned, the four BTR-40s came to a halt fifty yards from the metal gates, well beyond the perimeter of light cast by the spots set along the wall. Their headlights were already off, and all the team members had their night vision goggles in place.

Gregor looked over at Nikita. "Get ready, Nikki," he said.

She looked at him silently for a moment and then nodded. Climbing onto the back of the armored personnel carrier, she went to the M-38 82mm mortar bolted to the floor and made her final sighting adjustments.

She waited a moment longer, giving the passengers of the other three BTR-40s time to get ready, and then fired off the first of her rounds. An instant later, three rocket-propelled grenades arced through the night, streaking toward the metal gate.

Nikki didn't stay around to watch. As soon as she fired, she dove back into the already moving vehicle, plucking an RPG for herself from the back as she did so.

The peace and stillness of the quiet night erupted in sudden death and destruction. One grenade impacted directly on the metal gates, blasting them off their hinges and flinging them farther into the compound. Two other grenades hit the two guard shacks, cutting off any communication and killing the guards within. Nikita, however, hadn't aimed at the gate or the guard shacks. She'd had a trickier shot, lifting her mortar shell high above the wall and dropping it directly onto the roof of the building that housed the generator. It was their only shot at taking out the Americans' communications completely—and even though Gregor knew the Americans had no one to call, still he believed in taking no unnecessary chances.

Nikki's shot was perfect. Gregor smiled to himself and, closing the fifty yards quickly, he plunged through the debris left behind by the grenades, ignoring whatever damage he might be doing to his tires and the underside of his carrier. His team had already identified the motor pool inside the compound. They planned to leave that untouched, except for any personnel who might be working or hiding in there, and if their own vehicles were damaged they would simply ride out on stolen Jeeps once their mission was accomplished.

The personnel carriers went through the gates single file, Gregor in the lead, then Gilea's four men in the next two, and the last members of his personal team in the final vehicle. Once inside, each of the four veered off, heading to their preplanned corners of the compound. When they were all in position, they turned and started heading toward the building in the center—the low, concrete building with the satellite uplink equipment mounted on the roof—firing as they went.

There was no resistance. Gregor hadn't expected much, but he'd expected more than the Americans managed. A couple of security guards were cut down early, caught out in the open with confusion on their faces and fear in their eyes, but beyond those two it appeared that all the remaining personnel were holed up in their prefab apartment buildings, keeping their heads down and hoping to just survive this onslaught.

Unfortunately for them, Gregor's orders were to the contrary.

As they passed each building, Gregor's team sent a grenade into the doorway, causing additional destruction and sealing the survivors within. His mission priority was the satellite uplink building. Once that was destroyed, he would be able to devote his full attention to the rest of the compound.

The only building that slowed Gregor down at all was the one where the Americans kept their small supply of firearms. Two of his BTR-40s converged on that building and paused long enough to level it with grenades. Then, turning down the sensitivity on his night vision goggles,

Gregor Sadov resumed his methodical advance toward the command and control section of the compound.

Max Blackburn was on the phone with Alan Jacobs, the head of security at the compound, when the link went dead. Max and his team had been out following leads and were on their way back to the compound. Alan had called him the moment the power went out. No one really suspected there was anything devious or deliberate about the power outage, but standard protocol was to maintain an open line until the problem was identified and solved. Blackburn and his security detail were on their way back to the compound already—except for Vince Scull who had stayed behind to check on a few loose ends—but when the call came in he'd told his driver to speed up a bit.

Max did not hang up when the phone went dead against his ear. Instead, he kept the line open and turned to Meg. They were in the back of a covered truck, the kind used to haul produce from small local farms into the nearby towns for sale, bouncing along on the local equivalent of a road.

"Call in," he said to her, giving her Jacob's direct dial.

"Trouble?" she asked, already punching in the number. Standard protocol was to not record any numbers in speed dial, and to always clear the last number in redial memory after completing a call.

"I don't know," he said. "Maybe."

Meg pressed Send and then lifted the phone to her ear. "It's ringing," she said after a moment.

Max leaned forward. "Step on it," he said to the driver.

Meg looked at him, a quizzical expression on her face.

Blackburn hadn't even waited for anyone to answer before reacting.

"There's trouble," Max said. "You should have gotten a busy signal. The fact that you didn't means that the primary phone lines are down." Turning his head, he called back to Lee "Seal" Johnson, the team's radio expert. "Use the TAC-Sat," he said. "I want satellite communication established with the compound, and I want it now. Something's happening there, and I need to know what it is."

"It's no good, sir," Johnson said after a moment. "The satellite's responding, but the ground station isn't."

Blackburn nodded, his lips pressed into a grim line. "How long until we get back there?"

"Ten minutes, sir," the driver said.

Blackburn shook his head. He knew all too well just how long ten minutes could be in a firefight. "Make it five," he said.

"But, sir. The axles won't take—"

"I don't give a damn about the axles," he snapped, "or the ruts in the road. I care about the people who are being attacked back at that compound, and who are relying on us to protect them—which we can't do from here. Get us back there in five minutes. That's an order."

"Yes, sir," the driver said. "Five minutes."

Blackburn nodded, then turned away and began issuing orders to his team. They had five minutes to get ready, five minutes to prepare for a battle against an unknown adversary, against unknown numbers and unknown firepower.

Five minutes—an eternity for those back at the compound, but not nearly as long as Blackburn would have liked for his team.

• • •

Gregor's men had run into some trouble. Nothing they couldn't handle, but it had slowed them down more than he liked.

He had expected the guards to be unarmed, but as Gregor's team approached the pillbox building in the heart of the compound, their armored vehicles illuminated by the fires burning around them, they ran into some small arms fire coming from gun ports in all four sides. From the sounds, the guards didn't have anything bigger than .38-caliber, but that wasn't what worried him. If the personnel in any of the apartment buildings also had weapons, Gregor and his men could be caught in a deadly crossfire before they accomplished their mission.

This was the point where the battle plan went to hell. Up until now, everything had gone like clockwork—which was especially pleasing considering how little time they'd had to prepare. But now it was time to improvise.

Reaching down, he grabbed the headlight knob and gave it a quick yank. At the same moment, he stomped on the switch on the floor, flipping the lights to bright.

"Get ready, Nikki," he said, pulling hard on the hand brake.

Diving out of the still moving BTR-40, he rolled a couple of feet, being careful to stay in the zone of darkness created behind the bright headlights. Coming up to one knee, he sharpened the focus on his goggles, raised his rifle, rested his elbow on his left knee, and sighted carefully on the nearest gun port.

He could see the face of a frightened guard staring down over the barrel of what looked like a 9mm Beretta. A nice weapon, but pretty much useless under these conditions.

Gregor took a deep breath, let some of it out, and then, holding the rest of it to calm the slight shake of his rifle, he gently squeezed off a single shot.

Even with his goggles, he couldn't see the bullet hit home. He was still riding the recoil of his shot when it struck, but a moment later he could see that the gun port was empty, and there were no more shots coming from this side.

A moment later he saw Nikki fire off another round from the BTR-40's mortar, dropping it squarely on the roof of the pillbox. The remaining gunfire fell silent, and the rest of Gregor's team opened up with their own grenade launchers. Within minutes the little white building was little more than a burning ruin.

Gregor turned to his team and gave the order to fan out. With their primary objective accomplished, their orders were to search for any survivors and to neutralize them.

Using hand signals, he motioned the three members of his personal team to hang back slightly. This part of their job wasn't war. It was simple murder, and he'd be happy to let Gilea's men do most of it.

Max Blackburn could see the flames as they drew near the compound. He was leaning forward in the back of the truck, trying to will the driver to go faster. Beside him, Megan had gone still and silent as the impact of what they were seeing hit home.

"My God," she said, her voice little more than a whisper.

Max didn't say anything. He merely clenched his fists tighter.

His team was ready. They had all seen the flames leaping into the night sky, and they all knew what those flames meant. All of them, even the driver, had their Kevlar on and their night vision goggles adjusted. They had their weapons prepared and their lines of fire planned out. They had received their orders and made all the plans they could. Now all they needed was a target and a chance for revenge.

Fifty yards out, their headlights off, Max ordered the driver to slow down and head around toward the back. This close to the compound, the road was finally smoothing out, and every part of him wanted to take that command back, wanted to tell the driver to drive even faster, but he knew he couldn't. The personnel in that compound were counting on him—if any of them were still alive—and waltzing in there like an idiot and getting himself and his team killed wouldn't do any of them any good.

No, as much as he would have liked to ride in like the cavalry, Blackburn knew he had to play this one by the book.

Slowing near the first corner, Blackburn motioned for four of his twelve-man team to jump off the truck. It would be up to them to get over the wall and take up positions with two men at each of the front corners. Four more would take up similar positions at the rear corner, and Blackburn, Megan, and the other three would come over the back wall, directly opposite the gate. The driver would stay with the truck.

Please, God, Blackburn thought, watching as the driver went around the first corner. He'd intended to pray for survivors, for God to let at least some of the Americans survive this night. But that's not what formed in his head. *Please, God, let them be there. Help me to make them pay for what they've done.*

Beside him, Megan reached out and touched his hand, offering silent support, but he didn't notice. He was too intent on the sounds of stray gunfire coming over the wall, and the visions of vengeance playing in his head.

Gregor heard the gunfire taper off and he smiled. A few more minutes and he'd recall the team.

"Good work tonight," he said to Nikki. And he meant it, too. She had performed flawlessly, making all her shots clean and keeping her cool when things got hot. She was a good fighter, a good soldier, and he was pleased that she'd made it through this far.

To his right, he heard a single AKMS snap off two shots and then fall silent.

That was it, he thought. The last one. Reaching for the transmitter on his belt, he pressed the squawk button three times—short, long, short—giving the signal to join up at the motor pool, with the only undamaged building in the compound. Once his team joined up again, they would take the building, clean out any survivors, and then take whatever vehicles Gregor thought he could resell.

That was the plan. Gregor's first clue that the plan had gone wrong was when a hand fell on his arm and the blade of a knife pressed against his throat.

Max was proud of his team. Like true professionals, they had turned off their emotions and were going about their jobs in complete silence and with utter proficiency. With tactics learned from the Army Rangers, the Special Forces, the Navy SEALs, and other SpecOps groups, they identified the enemy and took them out by ones and twos, all without firing a shot. What was even more surprising was that, ignoring the rage that had to be burning within them as brightly as the compound, they neutralized the attackers without firing a shot and, as far as Blackburn could tell, without killing a single one of the enemy. This was one band of terrorists that *would* live to see a trial.

Seeing the last two enemies in front of them, Max raised his hand, signaling for extra caution, and then moved forward. Megan was on his left, and the two of them were flanked by two other members of his team.

Under other circumstances, Blackburn might have played it more cautiously and let one of the others take the point. Then again, he might not have. He and Gordian had argued about this countless times, but the simple fact was that Max refused to consider that any member of his team, no matter how new or how young or how inexperienced, was less indispensable than he was himself. And he absolutely refused to send men in where he himself would not go.

Slipping forward on silent feet, he waited for the man's hand to come off the radio at his belt, and then he acted, reaching forward and seizing the man's arm with his right hand and laying a knife along his throat with his left hand. He didn't say anything. He was more than half hoping the man would react, would start to fight, would do anything to give him a reason to use that knife.

Beside him, Megan wasn't so nice. Stepping forward in tandem with him, her own short-bladed knife in her hand, she closed on the woman who was her target. Reversing her blade, she brought the hilt down hard on the base of the woman's neck. The woman tumbled to the ground, unconscious, long, dark hair spilling out from beneath her helmet as she fell.

Too easy, Blackburn thought. He wanted blood. He wanted to pull the knife hard across the neck of the man he'd captured. But he couldn't. He was a soldier, first and foremost, and though he worked for a company rather than a country, still he had a code to uphold.

Besides, someday this pain and rage would fade, and on that day he wanted to be able to live with himself.

He maintained control of the man he had captured until his men had secured him. Then he sheathed his blade and said, "Get them the hell out of here."

Spinning away from them, he started the process of searching for survivors. It had been a long night already, and he knew that it was only going to get longer.

FORTY-THREE

"YURI VOSTOV," GORDIAN SAID TO HIS DESKTOP videophone. His voice was dull, inflectionless, almost mechanical. It somehow reminded Nimec of the way robotic voices had sounded in science fiction movies that were made in the 1950s. He'd never heard Gordian speak in that sort of tone before, and it disquieted him perhaps more than anything that had happened over the past twenty-four hours. What was going on inside the man?

Gordian sat there in his office and continued looking at Max Blackburn's image in the small LCD monitor. Across the desk from him, Nimec sipped his third coffee of the morning. None of the men had gotten any sleep, and it showed in the dark crescents under all their eyes.

"According to everything Pete's got on him, Vostov's a black marketeer. A drug dealer. A cheap John Gotti knockoff," Gordian said. "Are we really expected to believe he'd be behind a plot of this complexity?"

Blackburn's voice came through the speaker. "What Korut Zelva would like us to swallow isn't important. He probably decided that by flushing Vostov he could throw us off the trail awhile."

"Whose trail? And long enough for what?" Nimec said. "I don't care if this guy's some kind of dimwit, he has to know we're going to look into his information." *Especially after what was done to our people at the ground station,* he almost added, stopping himself at the last moment.

"That's just it, Pete," Blackburn said. "I tend to believe there's a very large grain of truth in the things he's told us about Vostov. I mean, it makes perfect sense that he's the next link up in the chain from Nick Roma's outfit."

Gordian shook his head. "That still doesn't address Pete's essential point. How far does knowing about Vostov really get us? I don't care how deeply the Russian mafia are involved, they wouldn't have brought Zelva and the woman . . ." He glanced down at the notes in front of him, searching for her name. ". . . Gilea Nastik into this. Those two are professional terrorists. Freelancers."

"With a grudge against the United States that goes back to the days after the Gulf War," Nimec said. "From what Ibrahim's told Max, they blame our government for having reneged on a promise to support the Kurdish rebellion against Saddam Hussein. And God help us, there may be truth in that."

"Their grievance doesn't concern me, not after they've butchered thousands of innocents," Gordian said. "And it has nothing to do with the fact that Vostov could have used his own people and kept it simple."

"Roger—"

"It doesn't sit right," Gordian interrupted. "It doesn't goddamned *sit right.*"

Nimec saw Roger's hand clench and unclench in the air, and again wondered what the deaths of the Steiners, and all the others, were doing to him inside.

"Gord, listen, it seems to me we're all saying the same thing here," Nimec said. "If we're agreed Vostov's in it, then our next step is to go after him. Squeeze him hard. See what he'll give up."

"I don't think we can assume he'd give up anything." Gordian looked at Nimec, then turned back to the screen, a set expression on his face. "Don't you see? According to the reasoning I've heard from both of you, this Korut gave us Vostov as a diversion. But why bother if he thought Vostov would crack and send us in the right direction?"

Nimec pursed his lips, thinking.

"Maybe he underestimated the sort of pressure we'd be willing to apply," Blackburn said in a low, meaningful voice.

"Somebody left a dead body for us to find in a Milan hotel room, and another corpse on a beach in Andalucía. The first man was hanging from a noose. The second man's throat had been slashed almost to his spine. And both were members of the bombing team. Whoever killed them is obviously convinced we intend to get to the bottom of this affair."

"Roger," Blackburn said, "I'm only saying . . ."

Gordian went on as if he hadn't spoken. "They slaughtered Art and Elaine Steiner in cold blood—two of the kindest, most decent human beings I've ever met, married forty years, both looking toward retirement. They killed dozens of our technicians, administrators, and construction workers, people who'd never lifted a weapon in their lives. People who were just out there doing their jobs, making an honest wage, and perhaps doing a little good for this world in the process. They killed my friends and my employees and tried burning my ground station to the ground, Max. They know we're in it up to our necks. They know, and they've been trying to scare us off, and yesterday they took it as far as they could. But they made a mistake. Because I swear to God, I'm going to bring those bastards down for what they've done.''

He closed his eyes then, and sat there in silence, his lips trembling, hands balled into fists. Nimec looked at him a moment and then shifted his eyes to the wall, feeling somehow like a trespasser.

The pain he's in must be indescribable, he thought.

''Roger, I want to go after Vostov, see where that takes us,'' Blackburn said after what seemed a very long time. ''But I need your permission to do it fast and dirty. And if it means putting a real hurt on the sonovabitch . . .''

He let the sentence hang in space somewhere between Russia and the west coast of America.

Gordian didn't make a sound for another full minute. Then he nodded, more to himself than to anyone else.

''There's to be no killing on our part unless it's in self-defense,'' he said. ''I won't sink to the level of these scum. And I want this done so the entire world can learn the truth.''

''I understand.''

''I know you do, Max. And I'm sorry for jumping down your throat.''

''No problem,'' Blackburn said. ''These are rough times for all of us.''

Gordian nodded again.

''I want to make sense of this,'' Roger said, swallowing thickly. ''I need for it to make sense.''

Neither of the other men said anything to that. Neither of them knew what to say.

Make sense?

Sitting there with his eyes fastened to the wall, still

reluctant to look at Gordian, Nimec found himself wondering if it ever possibly could.

They came prepared for a siege.

They had a warrant, but nobody was expecting Nick Roma to open the door and stand quietly and calmly while they cuffed him and read him his rights.

They figured they were going to have to work for this one.

So they brought out all the good stuff—high-tech surveillance equipment and low-tech battering rams, full-body armor and tear gas grenades. Everything they could think of, and more.

They even had the SWAT team on standby.

They never expected to find the Platinum Club as silent as a tomb.

Or the door wide open.

But that's exactly what they found.

"Dammit, the guy has snitches everywhere. He knew we were coming for him. He's probably halfway to Russia by now." The officer in charge, police lieutenant Manny deAngelo, flipped off his radio and pulled his gloves back on. He'd have cussed a blue streak, but it was too cold to waste the energy.

"Think it's a trap?" one of the cops asked.

"Nah." Manny sighed. "Nick's smart, but nobody's ever accused him of being subtle. But it wouldn't hurt to be careful going in." He signaled his men to move forward.

So they did. Cautiously. Two by two, in covering formation.

The warehouse was deserted, and it had been looted. Whoever had done it had left a mess behind, but not a single thing of value. They'd pulled the phones from the walls and busted open the canned drink machines to get at the change. They'd tagged the walls with graffiti—more than one gang had been here. Some of the spray paint was still wet.

Penny-ante stuff. And very recent.

It seemed Mr. Roma had enemies in low places.

"These guys better hope Roma's outa here—he's likely to cut their balls off if he's still around." Manny surveyed the wreckage with a jaundiced eye. "I wonder what they knew?"

"Yeah."

They kept moving. The deeper into the building they got, the worse the damage was, probably because the street resale value of the missing contents rose as they got farther in. When they reached Nick's office, it looked like it had been stripped clean by hungry locusts. But the hoods had left something behind.

"The chief isn't gonna like this." Manny looked down at Nick's body, tumbled to the floor so somebody could steal the chair the man had clearly died in.

"I don't know—seems to me Nick got what he deserved." The cop gave a tight grin. "But I'm glad it's your job to call it in."

Manny had it right.

Bill Harrison was still in his office. It was close to midnight, and his desk was stacked so high with reports and associated materials that he'd need an archaeologist to get to the bottom of it.

The photos of Nick Roma at the crime scene occupied a prominent position on the top of the pile.

Harrison didn't like it.

He'd wanted to put this man who had caused so much unbearable grief on trial. He'd wanted to confront him, along with all the other victims, and tell him what he'd done. Tell him about the nightmares and the pain and the loneliness.

He'd wanted to lock him away and watch the system slowly eat Nick Roma alive.

And then, only after he'd been through decades of it, Bill Harrison wanted to watch Nick Roma strapped down and killed.

But now it was too late for that.

Unlike most of his victims, Nick had died fast and easy. He'd probably barely had time to know it was coming.

Harrison was cheated of his revenge.

He didn't like it at all.

He looked at the eight-by-ten glossies of the man who'd gotten away—permanently.

That's when he heard Rosie's voice, as clearly as if she were standing there beside him. "It's better like this. Now you can get on with living."

He turned to look around him. He was alone, not a soul in sight. Downstairs, the usual business of the city at midnight went on at a feverish pace. But here, there was nobody but him, and a voice that he couldn't possibly have heard.

"Rosie?" Nothing. *"Rosie!"* Silence. The pain came crashing down again. But through it, he felt, for the very first time, a sense of peace. Rosie—*had that really been Rosie?*—was right on target. As usual.

His thirst for revenge was as destructive as the man in those pictures. It would tear him up, slowly eat his soul if he let it.

Instead, he needed to look for justice.

The people who did this needed to be stopped. They had to be caught and caged so that they couldn't do it again.

Nick Roma wasn't going to cause any more trouble in this life. Once the paperwork was filed, his case was over.

He'd not acted alone, of course. Bill Harrison wouldn't rest until he'd gotten them all, one way or another.

But not for revenge. For justice. And to preserve the peace for all of the good people he'd sworn to protect.

That was his job, and he was going to do it.

He stood up, turned his back on his desk, and went to get his suit jacket and overcoat.

He had a daughter to go home to, and a life to put back together. He had a future. He owed it to his wife to make it a good one, to live the very best life he could without her.

He turned off the light and left, closing the door behind him.

Tasheya was waiting for him.

FORTY-FOUR

MINUTES AFTER LEAVING THE TELEVISION STUDIO from which he conducted his nightly talk show broadcast, Arkady Pedachenko stepped into the backseat of his Mercedes and had his chauffeur take him to the exclusive Hotel National opposite the onion domes of St. Basil's Cathedral. He was dropped off outside the front doors, strode through the chandeliered lobby with a familiar nod to the concierge and desk staff, and then took the elevator up to the luxury suite he had been reserving on a long-term lease for several years.

This was very much a matter of routine for Pedachenko, who would arrive once or twice a week, most often alone, to be joined by a *dostupniey dyevochkia,* or "easy woman," in his rooms shortly afterward. The driver and hotel staff knew this well enough, but it was hardly regarded as scandalous behavior, even for a prominent politician. Pedachenko, after all, was unmarried, and his reputation as a playboy only enhanced his charismatic appeal to a public seeking Western-style youth and glamor, as well as a slight flavor of eroticism, in their leaders. Besides, Russians—particularly the upscale Muscovites who formed the core of Pedachenko's following—valued the good life, and found it difficult to understand the sexual prudishness that seemed to have overtaken the United States. Let the man have his little adventures.

Tonight Pedachenko had no sooner gotten to his room than he heard a soft knock at his door, opened it, and stepped back to admit a beautiful woman in a short black skirt, black stockings, black leather jacket, and black beret. The concierge had seen her enter the lobby in her spike heels, guessed immediately that she was going to Pedachenko's room, and admired her long-legged figure with a kind of wishful envy aimed at the politician, whom he was sure would be enjoying his tryst even more than usual this evening. The woman was like a pantheress, he observed. One who was no doubt in heat.

Now she sat down on a plush Queen Anne wing chair, pulled off her beret, and shook her head so her hair spilled loosely over her jacket collar.

"The money before anything," she said coolly.

He stood in front of her, still dressed in his sport coat and slacks, and shook his head ever so slightly.

"It makes me sad to know our relationship is based so exclusively on payment for services rendered," he said with a pained look. "After everything we've done together, one would think some kind of deeper bond would have formed."

"Save your cleverness for the viewers of your program," she said. "I want what you owe me."

Pedachenko made a slight tsking sound, reached into his inner jacket pocket, and brought out a thick white envelope. She took it from him, opened the flap, and glanced inside. Then she dropped it into her purse.

"At least you didn't feel it necessary to count it in front of me, Gilea," Pedachenko said. "Perhaps we have the beginnings of a closer, more trusting relationship here, after all."

"I told you to play the raconteur with someone else,"

she said. "We have urgent business to discuss." Her cheekbones suddenly appeared to sharpen. "I haven't heard from Korut. He was supposed to contact me two nights ago."

"Can you try to get in touch with him?"

"The members of my band don't spend their nights in the comfort of expensive hotels, with telephones at their bedsides and fax service at the push of a button," she said, with a single quick shake of her head. "The surroundings in which they sleep are far more Spartan."

He gave her a hard look. "How concerned should we be?"

"Not too, yet. He could be on the move and feel it's unsafe to communicate. That's happened before. But we'll have to wait and see." She paused. "He'll get a message through to me if he's able."

Pedachenko kept his eyes on her face.

"Well, I don't like it," he said. "In view of the failure at the satellite station—"

"It wouldn't have happened if I'd been in charge of the operation instead of Sadov. You should have waited for me."

"You may be right. Certainly I'm not inclined to argue. The important thing now, though, is for us to rectify our mistakes."

"Your mistakes," she said. "Don't try that psychological ploy with me."

He sighed and moved closer to her. "Look, let's dispense with the antagonism and talk straight. I have another job, Gilea."

"No," she said. "We've gone far enough. The minister, Bashkir, has been set up for a fall and Starinov will follow him into the pit. Just as you planned."

"But there's the possibility someone's stumbled onto us. You know it as well as I do. That incident at the headquarters of the New York gangster, the rumors that it was somehow connected to UpLink. And then the resistance at the ground station . . ."

"All the more reason to keep a low profile," she said.

He expelled another sigh. "Listen to me. Starinov has notified the Ministry that he's going to be at his cottage outside Dagomys for the next several days. I've been there before and can tell you it's particularly vulnerable to assault."

"You can't be serious about what you're suggesting," she said. But her eyes had suddenly brightened, become razor sharp, and her lips had parted a little, showing the upper edges of her front teeth.

"I'll pay anything you ask, make any arrangements you wish for your safe haven afterward," he said.

She stared into Pedachenko's eyes, her tongue moving over her lip, her breath coming in short, rapid snatches.

A second crawled past.

Two.

She stared into his eyes.

Finally she nodded.

"I'll take him," she said.

FORTY-FIVE

**MOSCOW
FEBRUARY 12, 2000**

THERE WERE THREE MEN IN DARK SUITS, WIDE-brimmed fedoras, and long gray overcoats hanging around outside the bathhouse when the Rover pulled up in front of it.

"Will you take a look at them?" Scull said from the backseat. "It's like they're fucking play-acting at being gangsters."

"They are and they aren't," Blackburn said, glancing out the front passenger's window. "In some ways, I really don't think these monkeys can distinguish reality from what they've seen in old-time American gangster flicks. But you have to remember that every one of them is packing a weapon under his coat."

"You guys want me to come in with you?"

This from Neil Perry, who was behind the steering wheel.

Blackburn shook his head.

"It'd be better if you wait here, in case we need to take off in a hurry," he said, and halfway unzipped his leather jacket. Scull could see the butt of his Smith & Wesson nine in a shoulder holster underneath it. "I don't think they'll give us much trouble, though."

Perry gave him a small nod.

Blackburn looked over the seat rest at Scull.

"Okay," he said. "You ready?"

"Been ready for days," Scull said.

The two men exited the car and strode across the sidewalk. It was a sunny day and a few degrees above freezing, warm for Moscow in winter, but despite the relatively moderate weather the street was nearly empty, and business was slow in the trendy shops along *Ulitsa Petrovka*. It was the uncertainty about worsened food shortages, and the withdrawal of NATO assistance, and a potential economic embargo, Scull thought. People were holding onto their money in anticipation of the worst.

The hoods closed ranks as Blackburn and Scull approached the bathhouse entrance, blocking their path to it. One of them, a tall man with dark hair and a large shovel chin, said something to Blackburn in Russian.

"*Ya nye gavaryu pa russkiy,*" Blackburn replied.

Shovel Chin repeated what he'd said, motioning the two Americans off. Out the corner of his eye, Blackburn noticed another of the men edging forward, opening the middle button of his coat. He was shorter than the first one and had a mustache that looked as if it had been traced over his upper lip with an eye pencil.

"I just told you I don't speak Russian," Blackburn said, and started forward.

Shovel Chin bumped him back with his shoulder.

"I tell you again in fucking *Engleeski,* then," he said, shoving out his chest. "You get the fuck out of this place right now, you motherfucking American asshole."

Blackburn looked at him a moment and then punched him hard in the sternum, pivoting toward him as he connected, putting his full weight into the blow. Shovel Chin sagged to his knees, grimacing. He heaved twice and then threw up all over his coat.

Still watching him peripherally, Blackburn saw the thug

with the mustache stick a hand into his coat. He whirled and drew his Glock, shoving its barrel into the thug's throat, cocking its trigger. Mustache's hand froze under his lapel.

"Get your hand out where I can see it," Blackburn said. "You understand?"

The guy nodded, a fearful, bolting look in his eyes. His hand appeared from inside his coat. Scull hurried over and patted him down, reached under his lapel, extracted a Glock pistol, and shoved it into the right hip pocket of his jacket.

Blackburn glanced at the third man. The guy hadn't budged from where he'd been standing when they got out of the car. He shook his head quickly back and forth as Blackburn's gaze fell on him, then put his hands up in the air.

"No trouble," he said. "No trouble."

Scull frisked him, found his gun, and pocketed it, shoving it somewhere inside his jacket.

Blackburn screwed the bore of his gun deeper into Pencil Mustache's throat.

"Help your *komerade* to his feet."

The gangster did as Blackburn asked. The three of them stood there, trembling.

Blackburn gestured again with the gun. "All three of you, I want you to walk slowly and quietly into that bathhouse. If you make a sound that I don't like, you won't live long enough to regret it. We'll be right behind you. Now move!"

A moment later, all of them were headed down the sidewalk. Shovel Chin was still unsteady, and had vomit dripping from his chin.

They pushed through the door of the bathhouse and a

kind of stewy, humid warmth spilled over them. An attendant peeked his head out of a doorway. A moment later he pulled his head back and quietly closed the door.

Scull looked around and started opening likely-looking doors. Halfway down the corridor he found what he was searching for. A closet, stacked high with towels and cleaning supplies. He pushed the gangsters inside, whispering a chilling promise of what he'd do to them if he should hear a sound from this closet in the next hour or so. Then he closed the door, shutting them in, and propped a chair against the knob. They'd be able to break out eventually, of course, but not without making lots of noise—and they'd be too scared to do that for a while.

"Come on," Blackburn said to Scull.

The sauna was on their left toward the back. They could hear groans coming from inside it. A man, at least two women. Blackburn nodded to Scull and reached for the door handle, pulling open the door to release some of the steam. The Smith & Wesson was in his free hand.

Yuri Vostov was naked. So was the woman on his lap, her back against his rolling middle, his hands on her belly. And so was the second woman with her head between both their thighs. The three of them looked up from the bench in shock and bewilderment, jumping apart as they saw the armed man in the doorway.

Scull pulled a couple of towels off hooks on the wall, tossed them to the women.

"Good-bye," he said, cocking his thumb over his shoulder at the steamroom door. "*Da svidaniya!*"

They got out in a hurry, the towels draped haphazardly around their bodies.

Vostov started pushing up from the bench.

"Hold it." Blackburn raised his palm, training his gun on Vostov. "You sit right where you are."

Vostov's small, flat eyes skipped between Blackburn and Scull like stones off the surface of a pond.

"Who are you?" he said in English. "What is it you want from me?"

Blackburn moved closer to him, his gun still aimed steadily in his direction.

"You're going to tell us who ordered the bombing in New York," he said. "Right now."

"Are you mad? How would I have any idea—"

Blackburn shoved the gun between Vostov's legs.

Hard.

Vostov flinched in pain. His back seemed to slide up the tile wall behind him.

"Tell us," Blackburn said, and cocked the hammer of his nine.

Click.

Vostov looked down at himself, wattles forming under his meaty chin, and drew a ragged breath. His eyes bulged.

"Are you CIA?" he said. "My God, this is *criminal*!"

Blackburn rammed in the gun. Vostov mewled and cringed, tiny rosettes of color forming on his cheeks.

"CIA won't blow your balls off," Blackburn said. "I'm about to. Unless you talk."

"Please . . ."

"You've got three seconds," Blackburn said. "One. Two . . ."

"Pedachenko," Vostov said, and swallowed. "It was Arkady Pedachenko. And others from outside this country." He swallowed. "Look, take the gun away from there, I've told you what you want to know.''

Blackburn shook his head, his mouth a tight seam.

''No, no you haven't,'' he said. ''In fact, you've only gotten started.''

FORTY-SIX

VLADIMIR STARINOV STROLLED ALONG THE SHORE
dressed in a light windbreaker, sweatpants, and sneakers,
staying just above the tide line, salt-tinged semitropical
breezes slipping over his cheeks like a warm caress. His
cocker spaniel trotted along behind him, bounding over
the talc-white sand, chasing incoming and retreating
wavelets, occasionally snatching straggles of seaweed
from the surf, shaking them in its jaws in an antic flop of
ears and fur, and then tossing them back where he'd gotten them. It was a clear, gorgeous night, coppery partial
moon over the water, stars glimmering in the sky like
diamonds scattered randomly over a black satin jeweler's
cloth.

Starinov felt at peace. For the first time in much too
long. At peace. Many miles to the north, he knew, the
cruel deceits of winter still prevailed, and the threat of
national hunger threatened to sweep over the Russian population like a whirlwind. Here, though, there was a respite,
a caesura, from the unrelenting martial rhythms of leadership and political survival.

Sometimes, he mused, life in the Kremlin was like being caught in some colossal machine, one that was running down and down beyond control.

Now he paused, hands in his pockets, looking out over
the water. Perhaps a third of a kilometer off, he could see

the running lights of a small boat moving slowly across its surface, almost like a snail on smooth, dark glass.

"So, Ome," he said, leaning to scratch his dog's head. "There's more to my existence than trouble, you see? Here we can think, and remember that there's a purpose to our struggles." He looked at the grinning expression on his dog's face and had to chuckle. "Or do you neither know nor care what I'm prattling about, baby angel?"

The dog swiped at his hand with his tongue.

Still smiling, Starinov turned and looked back across the dunes at his cottage. Pale yellow lights glowed in its beachfront windows. Barely visible in the darkness, he could see two members of his guard detail standing watch outside, their outlines still and straight. Ah, how they fretted over his insistence on these solitary walks. But there were times when a man needed to be alone.

He stood there at the water's edge a few more minutes, watching the boat ply its lazy track to some unknown port of call, and then decided to head back inside for some tea. Perhaps he would read a little before going to bed. At any rate, it was getting late, and he was feeling pleasantly tired.

"Come," he said, clapping his hands to get the spaniel's attention. "We don't want to make our guards any more unhappy with us than they already are!"

He started back toward shore, the dog playfully following along at his heels.

Perfect, Gilea thought, peering at the beach through the double circles of her NVD goggles.

"How's our friend doing?" a male voice said behind her.

"He's apparently broken from his rapture and turned

back to the *dacha*." She lowered the binoculars, blinking away spots of green as normal darkness flooded around her. "Perhaps he's sensed that the cold black sea waits for him tonight. Do you think, Adil?"

The tall, rawboned man grunted neutrally. Like Gilea and the others on the trawler, he wore a black spandex wet suit and swim fins, and had a diving mask pushed up over his forehead. There were depth gauges on all their wrists and waterproof weapon and equipment cases over their shoulders. Once they were underwater, the closed-circuit breathing apparatuses on their chests would recycle their own breaths, absorbing exhaled carbon dioxide, mixing the cleansed air with oxygen supplied by pressurized tanks.

"We've got the Subskimmers ready," Adil said.

She looked at him. Nodded. In her pupils, the reflected light of the moon looked like slivers of broken glass.

"Then it's time," she said.

Light and quiet, the ATVs tooled across the strand, hopping rises and troughs with nimble ease, sound-baffled engines humming as they powered the vehicles forward. Specially designed for Sword by an UpLink subsidiary, they were equipped with fully automatic trannies, accommodated two-man driver-gunner teams, and had pintle-mounted VVRS weapons aft of the cockpit. There were blackout shields over their off-road lights. The riders wore black Nomex stealthsuits, shock vests, and protective goggles, with microfilament radio headsets under their impact helmets. Their faces were daubed with camo paint.

There were a dozen vehicles in total, Blackburn and Perry's out front, the rest following behind in single file.

Gripping his handlebars with confidence, Blackburn

peered anxiously through his goggles at a procession of low dunes, wishing Starinov's cottage would come into view, wishing he'd had more than a few hours to organize this mission, wishing he'd known when and how the hit team intended to strike so he could have picked up a phone and given Starinov and his guards some warning. But he had been concerned that the cottage might be bugged, and that any attempt at contact might provoke Gilea Nastik to accelerate her plans. In the end, he'd had to balance one evil against another and resign himself to living with his choice—just as he'd done earlier that morning when striking a devil's bargain with Vostov.

Now he jockeyed the ATV over a big wave-shaped dune, cresting it easily, sand whipping his cheeks, thoughts of their agreement clipping through his head. It had been a simple trade-off: The Russian mobster's role in the bombing plot would be swept under the rug, and his *cojones* would remain intact, in exchange for complete disclosure and cooperation. He had spilled everything, not only about Times Square and the Bashkir setup, but also what he knew about tonight's planned takeout of Starinov . . . which was plenty. He had provided Gilea with manpower, weapons, and transport in exchange for a million dollars American currency. The assault would have an aquatic element, and perhaps additional land-based support. And its aim was to be decisive and final—Starinov would die. No more Machiavellian games, no more subtleties, no more waiting for governments to grind and groan through their weighty processes.

A good man would die, and that would be the end of it, the coup de grâce against democratic reform in Russia.

Unless he and his ad hoc counterstrike team, cobbled together from survivors of the ground station raid and a

handful of reinforcements from Sword's Prague headquarters, headed the bad guys off at the goddamned pass.

Blackburn goosed his ATV to full speed, issued a command to the riders behind him on his radio's proprietary
frequency, and heard their engines revving to keep pace.

He remembered resisting the temptation to make a cavalry charge the night the ground station was burned, and
realized grimly that circumstances had forced him to do
something very much of that nature this time around.

It went against instinct and training, went against his
every fiber.

Because the worst fucking thing about cavalry charges
was that they could turn into headlong suicides if the enemy happened to be waiting for you.

Their flotation bladders deflated, the air vented from their
buoyancy boxes for underwater action, the Subskimmers
glided beneath the chop like manta rays.

The sleek rubber submersibles had been easily transported aboard Gilea's trawler and offloaded with coordinated precision. Each was powered by compact but
muscular twin outboards and carried a trio of divers, shadows on the shadowcraft, toward the beach. Silent running
and undetectable, they could travel seventy nautical miles
on their electric motors. The divers themselves could have
stayed under for over four hours without having to worry
about the telltale bubbles produced by standard scuba
tanks. If they went any farther down than forty-five feet,
however, the greater water pressure would have caused
the pure filtered oxygen produced by the apparatus to have
a toxic effect on their systems. Neither time nor distance
was a concern tonight; the shore was in short range, and

their method of approach called for a rapid and shallow dive.

Within minutes of their deployment the skimmers resurfaced and gunned to top speed, streaking at better than eighty knots, moving like hot oil on Teflon. As they leaped from the surf, narrow wakes of foam kicking up in their slipstream, the divers rapidly abandoned the craft, extracted their rifles and nightscopes from their watertight cases, and began stealing inland on foot.

Several hundred yards downbeach, Vladimir Starinov's cottage perched on its low, isolated bluff, its guards unaware of the approaching killers, its windows still throwing their fragile light into the darkness.

Lifting the teapot from the stove, Starinov moved to his table nook and poured boiling water into his cup.

Before sitting down, he took a dog biscuit from the box on his counter and called Ome through the kitchen archway, holding out the treat, hoping it might settle the animal. The dog glanced at him but didn't budge. Moments earlier, he had padded out of the room and flattened onto his belly near the front entrance, whining and sniffing, his tail switching back and forth.

At first Starinov had thought the shrill whistling of the teapot was the cause of his pet's skittishness, but now, despite repeated goading, Ome continued lying by the door, ignoring his master.

Starinov shrugged, dropped the spurned biscuit into a pocket of his robe, and blew on the tea to cool it off. Although the dog's behavior was perhaps a little unusual, he didn't think too much about it; Ome sometimes became agitated by the guards making their rounds, and this was probably the case tonight.

Well, fine, let the dog stay where he was, Starinov thought. The minister was feeling rested and relaxed after his walk on the beach, and wanted to savor that rare state of affairs.

The little nuisance was certain to be underfoot soon enough.

Outside the *dacha,* the guard in the Russian army uniform had thought he heard a sound at the foot of the bluff and had gone to investigate, aware it was most likely nothing—the wind rustling up sand or a twig, some sort of foraging rodent.

Now, glancing over toward his teammate at the far side of the cottage, he wondered if he ought to beckon him over, but then he saw the orange glow of a cigarette in his hand, and figured it wouldn't hurt to leave him be.

He climbed down to the foot of the embankment, stopped, looking and listening. Moved a little farther out onto the beach and paused again. His brow furrowed. While he'd seen no sign of movement in the sand, he thought he heard a different noise now, a drone, like that of an approaching engine. No—*many* engines. Still a distance away, but getting nearer. It sounded like wasps to him. A whole nest of wasps. But what did it have to do with the whispery rustling he'd heard? And might it signal a threat to the minister?

Suddenly uneasy, he made up his mind to alert the others after all, and was turning back toward the cottage when a hand clapped over his mouth and a bony arm locked around his neck, snapping it with a quick, brutal twist.

• • •

"You hear that sound?" Gilea hissed to Adil. "Like motors."

He stood with her below the bank, head craned into the night, a vulpine expression on his features. The rest of the men were moving up the beach behind them and the dead guard lay in the sand at his feet.

"I don't—" He broke off abruptly, gesturing up the ribbon of beach.

Gilea's eyes followed the course of his finger, widened.

"*Shit!*" she exclaimed, bringing up her rifle.

The bluff with the solitary cottage atop it rising to his left, Blackburn rounded the curve of the beach, the cones of his headlamps immediately revealing the wet-suited figures in the sand, the abandoned watercraft at the surfline, the uniformed guard lying with his neck at a crooked, broken angle.

"This is it!" he shouted into his mike. His eyes scoured the beach, taking in everything at a glance. "Full offense, *let's go!*"

He maxed his throttle as the hit team dispersed across the strand, the pair that had been standing over the body breaking toward the bluff. In the rear of the ATV, Perry hauled his VVRS machine gun around in wide arcs, triggering short, rapid bursts. Fire had erupted all around the beach, flash-suppressed Kalashnikovs swinging up at the swarm of vehicles and stuttering out sound.

One of the divers instantly fell before Perry's stream of fire, plastic sabot rounds slamming into his chest, his weapon twirling out of his grasp like a relinquished baton. Another dropped down after him in a gush of sand.

Blackburn saw the vehicle Vince Scull was piloting slew off to his right, harrying a pair of wet-suited men, driving them back toward the water. They waded out as deep as their thighs but Scull remained in close pursuit, his vehicle splashing into the surf, ramming into them like a charging bull. Then a bullet pecked into the side of Blackburn's ATV and he veered off sharply in a zigzagging evasive maneuver.

The air quivered with incoming, and though surprise had given the Sword team an edge, their opposition was determined and murderous. A rippling onslaught of 7.62mm bullets scored a direct hit on one of the ATVs and its driver went sailing over the handlebars like a rag doll, blood showering from his chest. The vehicle flipped over twice in midair, spilling the man in the gunseat. He rose, disoriented, blood ribboning down from under his helmet, and was shot dead before he could regain his bearings.

A second ATV was tagged off to Blackburn's right, its tire rupturing with an explosive outrush of air, peeling away from its rim like a shed snakeskin. It overbalanced and went skidding onto its side in a spray of sand, dislodging its stealthsuited riders. Blackburn saw one of them dash over to his partner, saw him help the man to his feet, saw a member of the hit team take aim at both of them, and knew he had to act fast.

They were pinned.

He wrenched his vehicle in their direction, zooming in close, taking a hand off the handlebars long enough to motion to Perry. Perry nodded, leveled his gun, clouted the diver with a tight, controlled volley before he could pick off the unseated pair.

Angling away, Blackburn suddenly heard gunfire from up on the embankment and swore under his breath.

Starinov, he thought, and urged his ATV toward the slope.

The assassins were up there.

Up there with Starinov.

Gilea and Adil sprinted across the crest of the bluff, toward the cottage, now less than ten feet up ahead. Behind them a dead guard lay spilling his blood into the sand, his uniform tunic spotted with bullet holes. They reached the door and halted, Gilea stepping back out of Adil's way, giving him room to move in front of her and kick it open.

She pivoted away from him, watching his rear, her eyes flicking warily left and right. A guard came racing around the side of the house and she cut him down before he even spotted them, stitching bullets across his middle. Two more Russian soldiers appeared from around back just as she heard the door crash inward amid spears of broken wood, one of them falling instantly to a burst from her weapon, the other managing to squirt off a volley before she took him out. He staggered in a wide circle, made a moist coughing sound, and keeled over sideways, the gun slipping from his grasp.

She turned back to the cottage. Adil was sprawled in front of the open door, half his head blown away. The second man had gotten him with his salvo, she thought, registering his death without emotion.

Her mind was on her job, and her job was making sure Starinov joined Adil in his fate.

Blackburn crested the rise in just enough time to see the Nastik woman leap through the door over her companion's body.

He braked the ATV to a sand-spitting halt, leaped off the vehicle, and tore after her, drawing his Smith & Wesson from beneath his shock vest as he ran. Perry was at his heels.

Blackburn plunged through the entryway, snapped a bullet into the gun's chamber, glanced left and right. He wanted Nastik alive, but if it came down to a choice between her and Starinov, he would do whatever he had to.

The foyer was empty. Which direction should he look in? Where the hell *was* she?

He heard Perry behind him, motioned crisply for him to search the left side of the house, and was turning toward the right, toward what looked like the bedroom, when he heard the dog growling, heard the gunshot, and then heard the loud crash of someone falling back against the wall.

Starinov had been in the kitchen when the shooting started and, realizing what was happening, realizing that his home was under attack, he had plunged into his bedroom to get his personal firearm from his dresser drawer. It was just a small .22 caliber handgun, and he knew it would do little good against the kind of automatic weapons he heard out there in the night, but it was all he had.

He pulled open the drawer and was fumbling under his clothes for the pistol when the woman burst into the room and raised her AK at him, holding it at point-blank range. The grin stretching across her face seemed barely human.

That was when Ome came springing from under the bed, his teeth bared, growling and snarling as he lunged at the woman, clamping his jaws around her ankle.

Caught off guard, she stumbled backward, triggering a wild burst as she smashed against the wall. She tried to recover her balance, kicking at the dog, but only managing to get it off her after its teeth had sunk deep into her flesh.

"Don't *move*!" Blackburn shouted at the top of his voice, training his Smith & Wesson on her with both hands. "Drop the rifle, you hear me? *Drop it!*"

She looked at him across the room, clinging to the gun, the dog barking in front of her. The leg of her dive suit was soaked with blood. Behind Blackburn, the men he had radioed on his com-link were pouring into the room, led by Scull, shuffling the minister out of harm's way in a protective phalanx.

"Don't be suicidal," Blackburn said. "It's over."

She looked at him. Shook her head. Grinned. Still holding the machine gun, her hands clenched tightly around it, trembling.

And then, before Blackburn could react, she swung the AK upward so that its bore was fixed directly upon his heart.

"Over for me," she said. "Over for both of us."

His mouth dry of spit, the blood thundering in his ears, Blackburn kept his gun trained on the woman even as she kept her weapon on him, watching her hand for the slightest twitch, hoping to God he'd be fast enough to anticipate her next move. His concentration shrank to a narrow tunnel that encompassed his hand, Gilea, and nothing else.

A moment of slow time passed. Another. Neither of them budged. Neither weapon was lowered. The air around Blackburn felt like gelatin infused with current.

He was unaware of the sudden movement behind him until it was too late. It all seemed to happen with lightning rapidity—the oiled click of a firing mechanism near his ear, the loud crack of the gun discharging behind him, the surprised, almost quizzical expression on Gilea's face just before the bullet struck her forehead, producing a perfectly round dot of red above the ridge of her nose. Blackburn saw the machine gun jerk in her hand, and for a heartstopping instant was sure her finger would spasmodically lock around the trigger, sure he would be blown off his feet.

But the weapon slipped from her grasp without firing a round, and then her eyes rolled up in their sockets and her legs gave out and she slid loosely to the floor, trailing blood, brains, and skull fragments down the wall as she crumpled.

Blackburn lowered his pistol, turned his head on muscles that felt much too tight.

Starinov was standing directly behind him, having shoved through the Sword operatives that had converged around him. Smoke curled from the barrel of his outthrust .22.

His eyes met Blackburn's. Held them.

"It is better like this," he said.

Blackburn swallowed dryly but said nothing. The smell of cordite stung his nostrils.

"Your people saved my life, I saved yours." Starinov brought down his gun. "Now perhaps you will be kind enough to tell me where you have come from."

Blackburn was silent another moment. He looked past Starinov at the members of his team, men who had assembled from every corner of the globe to do a job that was both thankless and immeasurably dangerous. Thought about Ibrahim and his desert riders in Turkey, and Nimec's operatives in New York, and the diverse, ordinary people who had done what they could to help along the way.

How was he to answer?

He considered it another few seconds, and finally just shrugged.

"We're kind of from everywhere, sir," he said.

FORTY-SEVEN

THE SETTING SUN HAD TINTED THE SCATTERED CLOUDS in the sky over Jamaica Bay glorious shades of scarlet and gold. The skyline of Manhattan was silhouetted in the distance against the sunset. Lights were going on all over in the city that never sleeps, and New York was beginning to take on its nighttime fairy-tale glow. But Roger Gordian stood alone at the end of a runway, oblivious to the beauty spread out before him.

He was about to bring his people home.

The pain, and the sense of terrible responsibility he felt, threatened to bring him to his knees.

As he stood there waiting, he cast his mind back over the events of the last few months. Was there anything, he wondered, that he could have done differently, that would have forestalled this moment? Anything that he or his people could have changed that would have brought these people home alive instead of in boxes? That would have brought their families together to celebrate instead of to mourn?

If there was, he couldn't think of it now. Hindsight was usually all it was cracked up to be, but even in retrospect, he couldn't think of a moment he'd wasted, a shred of information he hadn't acted upon as soon as it had been verified.

Tragedy had come upon them all as silently as a mist

in the night. It had drifted into their midst, burst upon them completely without warning. Set into motion half a world away by a handful of opportunists driven by greed and ambition and completely unrestrained by conscience or morality, it was too late to stop it, any of it, from the moment it had been conceived.

And the costs, God, the costs . . .

Gordian ran a hand over his eyes.

Times Square had only been the beginning. Over a thousand people dead, many thousands more injured. All the families and friends who would never again share the simple pleasures of life with people they loved. The survivors who would never again be able to enjoy a day without pain, who were left broken in mind and body to pick up the pieces of their lives and go on as best they could. All because they had wanted to celebrate the glorious beginning of a new millennium.

Roger Gordian knew from hard personal experience just how high that price was.

But those people, as much as he mourned their passing and grieved for their losses, hadn't been his. He had been diminished by their loss, but not directly responsible for their deaths. He had not personally sent them into harm's way.

More than twenty people, working at his behest in places he had sent them to, were coming home in coffins. From his ground station in Russia. From Cappadocia in Turkey.

He knew most of them by name, some of them well. A few were among the small circle of people he counted as his dearest friends.

He'd sent them out to die.

He would never take a waking breath again without thinking of them.

He would never forgive himself.

And what had it all been about?

Politics.

Miserable, stinking, corrupt politics.

His people had died because some power-crazed demagogue had wanted to throw an election.

It made him physically ill, nauseous.

Every single one of his employees had been, each in his own way, a good person. Pedachenko wasn't worthy to be in the same room with them. But with his grandiose plans of conquest, he had killed them all.

Oh, God, the pain . . .

Stop, it, Gordian, he told himself. *Take a deep breath. Take a step back from that endless cycle of guilt and recrimination. It doesn't change the past, and you know where it leads you.*

Right.

So where did that leave him?

With the present . . .

Russia was stable for the moment. Starinov had used the furor over Pedachenko's actions to consolidate his government. Aid was flowing into Russia from the U.S.A. and Europe. The threat of a famine which would kill millions of innocent men, women, and children had been averted for now.

Was it worth Arthur and Elaine Steiner's deaths?

No. Nothing was worth that.

But nothing could change what had happened, either.

Roger Gordian, mover and shaker among the world's power elite, was powerless to alter the past, even a single second of it. He was just a lonely man with a guilty conscience, standing and waiting for a chartered plane to land, a plane full of the dead he would never be able to expunge from his conscience.

It hurt. God, it hurt.

What could he do about it?

How could he go on from here?

He searched the heavens for an answer.

For the first time he noticed the beauty of the sunset, now in its fullest glory. It was stunning. For a second he just emptied his mind and let himself bask in the beauty of it. It was, he realized, the first time he'd really looked at something and allowed himself to open his emotions to the experience since the Times Square bombing.

The world was still out there in all its imperfect beauty. It was still turning on its axis, and it would continue to do so, no matter what the humans—good, evil, or indifferent—who crawled on its surface did.

The future was his to make what he could of it.

It was a gift that Arthur or Elaine Steiner would have grabbed with both hands. He wished they were here with him, alive and happy, to do it. But they weren't, so it was up to him.

And maybe that was the answer he was seeking.

He couldn't change the past.

He could only embrace the future and give it his best.

It was time to begin again.

The plane he'd been waiting for, a gray-skinned IL-76, now bathed in the slanting golden light of the setting sun, taxied down the runway in front of him. Men waving fluorescent orange lights guided it to a halt, and more men rushed forward to chock the wheels. Someone driving a motorized staircase revved the engine and drove it forward, bringing it to a gentle halt inches from the door of the plane. The stairway driver turned the engine off, put on the brakes, and scrambled out to make the last few adjustments manually.

The door of the plane opened and people began exiting. These were the survivors, some of them swathed in bandages from their recent ordeal. Some of the more serious burn victims were still in Europe, too critical to be moved. Roger Gordian's eyesight blurred as the tears he refused to shed gathered. At least his people hadn't all died. Thanks to Max and his crew, many of those who would have certainly died without help were walking down the runway under their own power. He blinked to clear his eyes.

At the rear of the plane, a hatch opened. Musicians he'd engaged for this occasion began playing in the background—the solemn strains of Bach filled the evening. And a coffin was handed down. It was the first of many, Roger knew. Again guilt threatened to swamp him. He turned it aside, and concentrated instead on the memories. Flashes of the days he'd spent with Arthur and Elaine at ground stations all over the world. The surroundings had changed often, but one thing was constant, as immutable as time. The Steiners' love for each other had been a beacon and an example to anyone who knew them. Death hadn't changed that. A love like that was too enduring for an assassin's bullet to kill. Gordian knew they were together, wherever they were, and that that's the way they would have wanted it.

More coffins were gently laid on the tarmac. More memories surged through Gordian's mind. He owed these people. He owed them more than he could ever repay.

It was time to build monuments in their memory.

He would rebuild that Russian ground station and others like it, and use them to make sure that information would flow freely across the steppes and all the world. If anything could keep this from happening again, could stop the violence before it started, it would be that. He was in a position to make it happen.

He would keep pressing on.

But somehow, it wasn't enough.

Again, the picture of Elaine and Arthur as he'd last seen them flashed across his mind. No longer young, they had the memories of a long, rich, shared past to bind them together; they'd been holding hands like teenagers, walking through a field scattered with the first bounty of spring flowers. Their love had been palpable.

That, too, was a monument.

He knew what they'd have wished for him.

It was time to call Ashley and work things out.

He loved her. She loved him. That was too beautiful a gift to waste. Like Arthur with Elaine, he needed to learn to cherish his wife. He owed it to himself and the Steiners to give his marriage a real chance.

Tonight, he thought. I'll call her tonight.

And I'll make it so.

As the last coffin was placed on the runway, as the last light of day faded from the scene and the white splash of arc lights replaced it, Roger Gordian signaled the beginning of the ceremony he'd arranged. The world, he thought, would never forget what had happened to them all.

Neither would he.

It was time to forge the new beginnings his people had died to bring about.

He owed it to them all to see it through.

A drumroll sounded as the ceremony for his people began.

Roger Gordian took a step forward to take responsibility for the precious cargo.

And as he took the step, he realized his journey was just beginning.

Roger Gordian opened his heart to embrace the future.

RED STORM ENTERTAINMENT, INC.

Red Storm Entertainment, Inc., was founded in November 1996 by bestselling author Tom Clancy and Virtus Corporation, the leader in 3-D multimedia authoring tools, to create and market a new generation of interactive computer games focused on the exploding online and CD-ROM based multiplayer gaming market.

At Red Storm Entertainment, our vision is to lead the market in the development of massively multiplayer online games. To that end, we are developing products which will answer key design questions about multiplayer gaming, which Tom Clancy has called ''a new art form.'' More than an entertainment software company, Red Storm Entertainment is a multiple media company—all its products are designed from the start for delivery via a variety of media, including print, television, motion pictures, and more.

Tom Clancy's Politika is both Red Storm Entertainment's first product and the author's first political game, and is unique for its relevance to current geopolitical events. Special features include videos of breaking news reports and interviews with Mr. Clancy. *Tom Clancy's Politika* is the first major Java-based game ever produced.

Red Storm also has numerous products in development and will launch new games in 1998 and beyond. We will market and distribute our products through our partnership with Pearson plc and via the Internet.

TOM CLANCY'S POLITIKA
THE COLLABORATIVE ONLINE GAME OF
POLITICAL INTRIGUE IN RUSSIA

Free game demonstration on enclosed mini-CD!

Whether you've never played a computer game before or you're an experienced gamer, you'll find *Tom Clancy's Politika* intriguing and fun. The game's simple yet elegant design makes it easy for beginners to learn the basics while accomplished players will be challenged by the more subtle aspects of the game.

The combination of *Tom Clancy's Politika* book and game gives you the opportunity as a reader to enter the gripping realism of the novel, and as a game-player to enjoy a new art form in storytelling as you develop your own plotlines and outcomes.

While the *Politika* book and game share a common theme revolving around Russia after the death of President Yeltsin, the game was developed as a separate entertain-

370

ment vehicle that can be enjoyed entirely on its own or in conjunction with the book.

Game Overview

You're in Russia. President Boris Yeltsin has died suddenly with no obvious successor, leaving a power vacuum. The nation has fallen into chaos. The military, mafia, church, KGB and several other factions are all vying for power. You command one of these political factions. Your goal: to take control of the Motherland. With everything negotiable, cunning, diplomacy, and backstabbing become just a few means to accumulate more money and influence than your opponents.

Welcome to *Tom Clancy's Politika*—the first game designed for free-form interactive play among groups of players. *Tom Clancy's Politika* introduces a category called "conversational gaming," which raises collaborative game-playing to a level never possible before. People anywhere can play *Tom Clancy's Politika* together and build their own stories and outcomes.

In developing *Tom Clancy's Politika*, Red Storm Entertainment is the first entertainment software company to leverage IBM's new Java™-based software technology, code-named InVerse, to develop collaborative games for the Internet. This technology allows players with different forms of hardware and software to play together over the Internet.

Playing the Game

Tom Clancy's Politika combines two major forces in the online market—multiplayer gaming and online chat—into a single notion: *conversational gaming*, in which you and other players decide the outcome. As a conversational game, *Tom Clancy's Politika* catches the flavor of this social interaction in an online setting:

- **Gaming clubs.** Create private or public gaming clubs.
- **Waiting area.** While waiting for a game to begin, chat, meet, and determine whether you are compatible with other players in the area and then decide when to start a game.
- **Conversing.** Write messages to other players throughout the game. You can broadcast messages to everyone, or just chat privately with a single player.
- **Eavesdropping.** During the game, you can attempt to eavesdrop on private conversations.

Tom Clancy's Politika is played on a map of the current Russian Federation, which extends from the Baltic Sea to the Pacific Ocean, and which is divided into twenty-three distinct regions. When you enter a game, you'll automatically be assigned to one of the following eight factions:

- **Russian Orthodox Church.** Strong politically, but most of their work is behind the scenes.
- **Communists.** Represents the old guard, complete with political machine.
- **KGB.** They officially disappeared with the Soviet Union, but many are still there.
- **Mafia.** Just like our own, their goals are money and profit, no matter what.
- **Military.** Like most generals, they want a stronger military force.

POLITIKA

- **Nationalists.** They want to return to a unified Soviet Union under a strong fist, and are riding a wave of discontent.
- **Reformers.** Represent the party of President Yeltsin, and want to maintain control and continue the capitalization of Russia.
- **Separatists.** This movement wants to allow ethnic regions within Russia more political autonomy.

Each region of the country displays three "influence tokens," which show how political power in that region is distributed among the players.

Tokens represent uprisings and areas of political unrest which you can try to control. There are three kinds of uprisings you'll have to contend with—bourgeois, labor, and student.

At the beginning of each turn, the current player "turns over" the top production card. Each production card displays three regions indicating those which generate income for that turn. Mixed in with the production cards are event cards, which can signal good or bad news and which take effect immediately.

At the end of each turn, players have the option to buy action cards. These allow limited duration advantages in challenging, defending, and production. They cost $20,000 each—and may be traded freely among players.

Tom Clancy's Politika board game available exclusively at

TOYS'Я'US

EarthLink Network TotalAccess software is included on enclosed CD-ROM so you can play today.

$25
SET UP FEE
WAIVED

&

5
DAYS
FREE

We started it!

$19⁹⁵

All the Internet you can eat." The feast continues.

EarthLink Network® was the first to offer you all the Internet you can eat for $19.95 per month. The price stays the same and the service keeps getting better. EarthLink Network offers you reliable, high-speed nationwide Internet access with all the goodies you expect, and more.